# ATKINSON FOR ENGLAND

## A COMIC NOVEL BY MARK BROWN & GARY JAMES

EMPIRE Publications Ltd

First published in 2001

EMPIRE PUBLICATIONS LTD
1 Newton Street, Manchester M1 1HW


© Mark Brown and Gary James 2001


Illustrations by Ray Allen
Cover: Ashley Shaw

**ISBN** 1-901-746-178

Designed and Typeset by
Ashley Shaw and Stuart Fish
and printed in Great Britain
by Cox and Wyman, Cardiff Road,
Reading, Berkshire RG1 8EX

To Elaine, Alex, and Natalie Brown, and to Heidi, Michael, and Anna James. Thanks for all your support and for putting up with night after night of silly conversations about ballcocks and undersoil heating.

Also to all those plumbers, electricians, builders, mechanics and systems analysts who have often wanted to pick the national side, but have never had the chance. This book is for you.

# ACKNOWLEDGEMENTS

The authors would like to thank the following for their help:
Ron Atkinson, for his support, enthusiasm and for being
the celebrity he is. Whatever your involvement with football
– whether professional or avid armchair supporter - Ron's
touched your life at some point over the years, with his
positive views and sheer love of the game.

Ashley, Stuart and all the staff at Empire Publications for
their support, faith and belief in this project. Also, special
thanks go to John Maddocks who sadly passed away shortly
before this book was published.

Elaine for the brilliant idea that became the Three
Spanners logo, and Heidi for various ideas, contributions,
and sanity checks along the way.

From a publicity point of view thanks to Ross and all his
colleagues at Waterstones, Deansgate.  Jimmy Wagg and
Mike Sadler at GMR.  Carl Morris at Granada.  Richard
Whitehead at the Times.  Denis Campbell at The Observer.
Noel Bayley, Ashley Birch, Simon Clegg, Julia Byrne, Geoff
Donkin, Michael Quarry and all the usual crew.  Sorry if
we've missed your name but rest assured that we do value
your contribution.

.A big thank you to all the real people mentioned in the
book.  We hope we've done you justice, and hope that you
enjoy the book.  Please understand that we wouldn't have
mentioned you unless we appreciated you in some way.

Finally, special thanks to all those who have bought this
book.  We hope you find it as enjoyable to read as we did
to write. Thanks.

# ABOUT THE AUTHORS

**Mark Brown** was born in the same hospital as Mike Atherton. Surprisingly, Mike never mentions this. Mark was raised and educated in Manchester and helps dispel the myth of United supporters being from down south by supporting them regularly from the comfort of his armchair. He now lives in Oldham with his wife Elaine and two children – Alex and Natalie. Although the author of numerous short stories including *The Boot*, *Touch* and *Reckless Streak*, this is his first novel.

**Gary James** is a big fan of British comedy and for years has been inspired by the comedy talents of Will Hay, Leonard Rossiter, and Manchester City FC. As a supporter of the Blues since birth, he has realised never to take life too seriously. Prior to this book, he has written articles for publications as diverse as *The Times* and *Bert Trautmann's Helmet*. He has also had four books published, including the highly acclaimed *Football With A Smile*, the biography of former England manager Joe Mercer, OBE and the encyclopaedic *Manchester – The Greatest City*. Gary now lives in West Yorkshire with his wife Heidi, and children Michael and Anna.

# CONTENTS

# BIG DECISIONS

There comes a time in a man's life when he makes a decision that will be the beginning or the end of him. On a warm September Tuesday evening, Reginald Stanley Atkinson was about to make that decision.

At 42 years of age, Reginald Stanley Atkinson had been a plumber for two thirds of his adult life. Until now he had never aspired to greatness – content with servicing the plumbing needs of Nottingham. Was it the hand of fate that guided him now as he stood before the bright red Post Box on the corner of Venus Street and Maple Drive with an envelope in his hand? Wondering…

Born in Preston, schooled in Manchester, he had never been one of life's achievers. His father had high hopes at the time of his birth – the name Stanley had originated from Stanley Matthews, match-winner for Blackpool in the 1953 FA Cup Final: his father's hero – his father's God.

"If yer 'alf as bloody good as Matthews, you'll be bloody fantastic," his father used to tell him. "Forget cricket – that's a bloody poncey game. Football's a man's game – get crackin' at it kid."

Football had always been a part of his life, his father had ensured that. But even after his father's death 19 years ago, despite the fact that he'd always been nothing more than mediocre, Reginald Stanley Atkinson loved the game. That was why, after he'd posted this letter – if he posted this letter – he was off to the Forest Inn to give a team talk.

The letter dallied in his hand. How long had he been stood there? Five minutes? More? Someone would be calling the police soon. This was a good neighbourhood. Very good in fact. Twitching curtains would soon identify anyone loitering with intent to do harm to post boxes. Especially at teatime.

"Knackers," he said out loud and thrust the white envelope straight into the jaws of the red box. His hand returned from the maw empty – the envelope had been posted.

"Right then," he added under his breath and walked away.


The bar at the Forest Inn was quite crowded. Usually at this time of the early evening there would be one or two people sat minding a half of lager and reading the Evening Post. Tonight, the football crowd was in.

"All right, Reg?" murmured a few voices from the bar as he entered. Reg smiled. He had asked his players to assemble tonight to discuss tactics for the Sunday morning Cup-tie against the Dog and Duck, and they had not disappointed him.

Reg had lived in Nottingham for the past fifteen years having married Shirley Dunstan, a local girl who he had met on holiday in Magaluf. He set up his own plumbing business and had done well in that fifteen years – not well enough for Shirley, who had left him for an aerobics instructor after ten years of marriage – but well enough to keep him comfortable.

"What y'aving Reg?" It was Norman. Norman Whaddon had been Reg's right hand man for the past twelve years, both in the business and with the football team. Indeed, it was Norman that had convinced Reg to become manager of his pub team. Norman had been a fine footballer in his day, playing inside-right for Barnsley, Sheffield United and finally moving back to his home town to play for Notts County, where he finished his career. He had never won anything, but looked upon his career with fondness. At seventy-two he couldn't stop playing, although his appearances these days were limited to the last ten minutes as substitute as he just didn't have the stamina any more. Still a great big heart beat within his wiry frame.

"Pint please Norman," said Reg.

"Do you want lime in that Reggie?" Carol, the barmaid, had a soft spot for Reg and flirted often. Reg liked her but had never dared go any further than banter... not that he hadn't thought about it.

"I thought you said I was sweet enough already!" said Reg.

"Just normal straight up and down then?" Carol responded.

"Jeesus," croaked Norman, "she'll be sucking you up with a straw in a minute. "'Ee y'are luv," he added and handed her a ten pound note.

While Carol moved to the till, Reg whispered in Norman's ear.

"I've sent off that tender."

"Yer what? The Wembley thing?"

# BIG DECISIONS

"Aye. I nearly bottled it though. I can't imagine I'll get a sniff, but like you said, 'You can't win the raffle if you don't buy a ticket'."

"Blimey," said Norman. "If it comes off, it'll open up a whole New World. Bloody 'ell, just think – 'undersoil heating at the new Wembley stadium, installed by Reg Atkinson'. That'd go down well on your CV."

"Aye," was all Reg could say. Carol was on her way back with the change.

"Oy, that's my hand the change should be goin' in, not 'is!" shouted Norman, as Carol reached towards the taller man.

"Oh sorry luv," smiled Carol, looking at Reg but talking to Norman. "Can't help it if I'm drawn to the bugger, can I?"

Reg smiled to himself. Maybe if he got this contract he'd ask Carol out on a date. Forty-two years old and thinking of asking a girl on a date... Christ, a girl. Carol was about thirty-five he reckoned... Good looking, nice figure...no spring chicken, but then again neither was he.

"So what did yer put down in the end?" interrupted Norman. He had helped Reg with the tender but had not seen the final version.

"All the bits we talked about... oh and the fact that I worked as apprentice under Tom Finney... and my middle name was Stanley after Stanley Matthews..." He paused. Norman waited patiently "...and I'd fitted the showers at Buxton United; central heating in the lounges and dressing rooms at Burton Albion... and ...that I had so many footballing connections, they'd be daft not to give it me."

"Yer what? Why the bloody 'ell did yer do that?"

"Well it's like sense of humour isn't it. I thought they

might appreciate it – it's more interesting don't you think?"

Norman didn't, but contented himself with swilling half his pint. Reg thought about a further explanation but remained silent. He excused himself – best to get comfortable before he started on the team talk. A saying of his Dad's always came to mind at these times – "a wise man pees when he can, a fool pees when he has to." Unconsciously, it was the sort of advice that sinks in. Reg always emptied his bladder before taking any action likely to last longer than half an hour.

Reg did what was required and as he washed his hands, he checked himself in the mirror. His hair was more grey than brown now – people were saying how distinguished he looked. Reg thought he looked old. The tan helped, although that was fading now. Two weeks in the Spanish sunshine soon lost its magic when followed by a few weeks back in Britain. He was still fairly fit but had the beginnings of a spare tyre that just wasn't shifting. That's age, he thought. Brown eyes – no need for glasses yet. Maybe he could do with an eye test; he was getting headaches if he read for a long time. Might make him more distinguished. Nah, he was Mr Average – average height, average weight, average everything: didn't stand out from the crowd. He wondered if Carol would see him differently and shrugged. He stood up straight and puffed out his chest. Fancies me rotten, he thought, and went back to the bar.

He motioned for the lads to gather round. He had team matters to discuss.

Sunday morning saw the Forest Inn take on the Dog and Duck from neighbouring Leicester in the Midlands' pub equivalent of the Premier League. A couple of days' rain had made the pitch wet with a few boggy patches, but Reg thought this would make no difference to the Forest Inn. A typical match day for the pub leagues, he thought. He then watched his players produce a poor first-half display that saw them 2-0 down at half-time. Reg tore into his players at the interval.

"What the bloody hell are you playing at?" No one looked up – they were all very intent on their boots.

"Johnny Mullen – why are you not running that full back into the ground? You're yards faster than he is and you've not gone past him once."

"But some bugger's let his dog crap on that wing boss... it's still steamin'," replied a crestfallen Mullen. Reg looked skywards and Johnny saw this as confirmation he could expound.

"Watch out for it Joe, it's about ten yards before you get to the box. Great big dollop o'..."

"Jesus God," said Reg – as full back Joe Allison was nodding his thanks and scanning the pitch to see if he could see it – "now he wants to describe it. For God's sake, get a bloody shovel and shift it if it upsets you. Now all of you just get out there and play some football. I want to see some commitment and a bit of skill. Go on." Reg hoped his words would rally his troops as he watched them jog back on to the pitch.

Forty-five minutes later and, following a scintillating second half performance, the Forest Inn had defied the odds to win 5-3. Johnny Mullen had overcome his reluctance to hurdle mounds of dog deposits to set up three goals and score another. Geordie Best, after scoring one goal, ran towards the touchline in celebration and dived theatrically, skidding along the surface. Fortunately for him, this wasn't on the dog's dumping ground, but he did manage to take in a large puddle. As Geordie 'belly-surfed' through it, he seemed to pick up speed and catapulted himself into three spectators on the touchline, spraying a dozen more. As Geordie picked himself up, he ran foul of Joe Allison's Mum's handbag. Joe still lived at home with his Mum and she rewarded her son by coming to watch every game. She was one of the most vociferous supporters and was known to attack opposing players who tackled her son. Today she had been hit by a tsunami of mud, grass and water for her trouble and wanted revenge – she followed Geordie back on to the pitch to vent her spleen and walloped him with her handbag. Geordie looked suitably sheepish – and soaked – when he returned to the centre circle.

Reg was thrilled with the result. This saw them clear at the top of the league and at such an early stage of the season, all was looking well for another assault on the title. Reg loved these amateur football days – they brought something completely original to football. Spectators and players were a breed apart from the normal football crowd. Players tried to emulate their heroes on the pitch, both with goal celebrations and attempts at skill, and this often brought laughter from the crowds rather than cheers.

As the players trudged from the pitch, weary but smiling, Reg patted them all on the back for a job well done. He turned to Norman, whose services had not been required for this game.

"Spanner of the Day award, Norm?" Reg said.

"'S gotta be Geordie," said Norman with a chuckle.

"Aye, bloody funny that," tittered Reg and with his arm around Norman's shoulders, he guided his friend back to the car.

# BIG DECISIONS

That afternoon in the Forest Inn, the usual post game chat had taken place and everyone was relaxing waiting for the big game on the pub's Sky TV. Atkinson allowed the lads to let their hair down a bit – they had deserved it. Geordie Best, after showering and changing, sat with a green toilet seat around his neck. Reg had instigated the 'Spanner of the Day' award as a way of building team morale. There was a recipient after each game and the winner had to sit in the pub for the remainder of the afternoon with a toilet seat over his head, supplied by Atkinson Plumbers.

"Green loo seat goes well with Geordie's cream jacket," Norman laughed.

"I've told you before Norm, it's Wild Sage, not green," said Reg with feigned indignance.

Most of the lads were in high spirits – they had enjoyed the game and were celebrating in the only way they knew: drinking and singing the Forest Inn anthem, to the tune of "I'm H-A-P-P-Y".

"We're Forest and we drink,
We're Forest and we drink,
We know we are
We're sure we are
We're Forest and we drink!"

Reg smiled, how could such a ragbag of players gel so well? They'd been playing together for three years and were used to each other's style of play. The best player he had by far was Baldy Charlton, the pub's top scorer for the last three years. Baldy, dear God! He was the hairiest man he had ever known. He had been christened Jeremy, but he'd not been called that since school. Baldy was how everyone knew him and that was how it was going to stay.

If there was one player he would dearly like to get rid of

it was Malcolm Mercer, son of Ken, the pub landlord. Malcolm played left wing in an area of least damage. He played and the team got the kit and match fees paid for by Ken. If Malcolm didn't play, Reg would have had to foot the bills. As a result Malcolm was always the first name on the team sheet. Roy 'Cropper' Brooks was a giant – six feet seven of pure baby. Reg had known him to burst into tears on the pitch if anyone got hurt, but that didn't affect the way he played – very hard.

Reg had honed the Forest Inn side into a unit in the past three years. Most of the players had been there when he started and had tendencies to run about chasing the ball without actually knowing why.. Now he had instilled some discipline and told them what to do when they didn't have possession, they were much better players. Michael 'Rocky' Quarry had a reputation for bookings and sendings off when Reg arrived, but the young man had learned to overcome his temper under Reg's tuition and was now the engine room of midfield... Reg likened him to a young Roy Keane.

If there was one thing he'd never been able to cure, it was Andy Tate's libido. Reg laughed to himself at the attraction 'Randy' Andy had for women. Bees round a honeypot, Reg thought constantly – Norman had a different expression, but it didn't affect the way Andy played so Reg wasn't too bothered.

Reg glanced back at the TV – he liked the coverage on Sky. He reckoned he learnt more about the game because of the analysis of Andy Gray and other former players and managers. He'd like to have his twopenn'orth one day...

On this particular occasion, most of the pre-match reports concerned the shock departure of the England manager after some sort of row.

"Ken, turn the telly up will yer," Reg bawled at the landlord, who was still pulling pints. Ken reached for the remote and increased the volume.

"…at probably the worst possible time only ten days before the Germany game. We look at the background to Glenn Gould's decision to quit and what the FA now intend to do to ensure a smooth transition before the most important game in the last ten years."

Reg was enthralled. Everyone in the pub had quietened down. The coverage had moved to what looked like a press conference at Lancaster Gate with the Chief Executive of the FA, Brendan Fendon and his assistant, the taller Sir Richard Scratcher. Questions were flying at them.

"….only ten days before the game against Germany, Brendan. Have you anyone in mind for the job?"

"It's too early to say yet, but we are aware of the timescales and the need for a quick decision…"

"….how do you feel about Glenn Gould – does he have a point?"

"…well obviously he's entitled to an opinion – it hasn't helped the situation, but we need to move on and put somebody in the job quickly…."

"…anyone in particular? Reid? Robson? Atkinson?"

"Eh, is that you Reg?" barked Lance Lovejoy, midfielder and wit. Roars of laughter from the boys. Reg smiled. Lance was always the first in with a witty retort. Reg always wondered why he hadn't chosen a more lucrative career as a comedian or television presenter. He seemed wasted at the printers where he toiled daily.

"I'd do it if I could," he said.

Brendan Fendon was carrying on manfully.

"…but we are not at liberty to confirm any names at present. Now if you'll excuse me gentlemen…" His assistant stood from the table and left quickly while still being assaulted by questions and flashbulbs.

"Well this ain't too good, is it Reg?" muttered Norman. "That's the World Cup buggered up. Who do you reckon'll get it?"

"Dunno Norm, I reckon a caretaker might get it for the one game and then they'll appoint somebody permanent afterwards. But you can't tell with the FA – I'm not sure they know what they're doing from one day to the next."

"…it's been common knowledge that Glenn Gould has been at loggerheads with the FA following what he calls 'an above average desire to become involved in team affairs'," the report continued.

"I'd put my money on Peter Reid," shouted Baldy Charlton, "he's done a good job at Sunderland."

"…the England squad which Gould selected for this game have been advised and are awaiting news of Gould's successor…" continued the reporter.

"Yeah, but he's had no European experience, has he?" replied Norman. "We need somebody who's done a bit."

"Back to you again Reg!" barked Lance Lovejoy, bringing titters and drunken guffaws from the players.

"…the row continues…" The report went on "…Glenn Gould has resigned from the England manager's position less than two weeks before the most important game in years. The FA have accepted his decision but are not yet in a position to confirm his successor. This is Sean Winters, Sky Sports, Lancaster Gate."

As the commercial break began, more discussions broke out amongst the players.

# BIG DECISIONS

"I just hope my tender doesn't get lost in all this fuss," Reg said, downing the rest of his pint. "Same again Norm?"

"Why not. Nowt else to do."

The following day at Lancaster Gate, Brendan Fendon held his head in his hands. He had already decided upon the next England manager but due to the current climate of Equal Opportunities, he had to open up the position for other applicants.

Brendan had got his position through pure cleverness and had no intention of losing it just because some idiot had decided to think for himself for the first time. Bloody managers, he thought, just who the hell do they think they are?

Under his jet black hair, Brendan scowled. Many had wondered whether he died his hair black but none had dared ask. It was made blacker by the addition of Brylcream to slick it into place. Despite his sinister exterior, Brendan was a slight figure. It was his expression of distaste and his voice which made him appear larger. Behind his back, his colleagues and rivals called him Hannibal – he saw this as a mark of respect rather than an insult. Brendan had reached his early fifties and had the power he'd always craved through hard work and determination. He'd begun life as a journalist, realised his talents were wasted and moved into public affairs. He had wanted to make the move to television, but had been considered too 'unsympathetic' to the camera. He now ran the FA with autocratic ease.

While Brendan pondered over his situation, his secretary was opening the mail. June Whitless had worked at the FA for two years as Brendan's secretary and for eighteen months as his bit on the side. Unfortunately she showed no apparent knowledge of football, as she was proving right now, but had proven herself useful to Brendan in other ways, not least showing him a thing or two which he had not previously enjoyed during the forty-odd years since puberty.

The Monday morning post had brought a mass of mail. June was attempting to divide it up into three piles – two for applications: Manager and Undersoil heating, and one for general dross. Her lack of knowledge was holding up progress.

"Dynarod. Is that a Russian football team?" she asked, looking at an application from Eric Trump, plumber of distinction. "Oh it's okay – it has plumber on the letterheader."

Brendan shook his head. "June, just sort them out as best you can – remember, look for Ron Atkinson's application and make sure that one gets put into the right pile. He'll probably mention Forest and United and perhaps West Bromwich Albion if that's any help."

"Yes Bre...er Mr Fendon." June always tried to keep her professional head on at work.

June picked up Reg's application and opened it. As she was reading it, the phone rang.

"It's all right June – I'll get it," said Brendan, "you just get through those."

"Brendan Fendon, can I help you..."

June read the tender. She recognised the name Atkinson and sat up straight. Reg, she thought? Didn't Brendan say Ron? She thought about asking him, but he was heavily involved on the telephone. Oh hang on, must have heard wrong – Forest, Buxton United, Burton Albion all mentioned and Tom Finney, yes, heard of him, oh and Stanley Matthews too. June heaved a sigh of relief and put the application onto the managers' pile.

As she continued through the pile of post, Brendan came off the phone. June opened her mouth to speak, but Brendan beat her to it.

"You found the Atkinson one yet?" he asked.

June nodded and beamed.

"Great. Chuck the other manager applications you come across and concentrate on the undersoil heating. I'll go through them when I get back."

"Oh, where are you off to, I thought we were going out tonight…."

"Brazil. Urgent FIFA business – corner flag convention. I tried to cancel, what with this manager business, but apparently the President of FIFA sees it as a personal favour if I attend. Can't refuse that sort of blackmail can I? I'll be back before weekend – I'll make it up to you then."

With that Brendan shot out of the office to locate his second in command.

June simmered for a moment. She'd had big plans for that night but at least she'd found the Atkinson application – Brendan was pleased about that. As she opened the next envelope she noticed the name – Ron Atkinson. Coincidence, she thought, and skimmed through it. This letter was headed: 'Let me sort out the leaks, and I'll do it early doors.' It seemed to be a slogan of some description. References to 'leaky defences' and 'going down the pan' swung it for her – definitely plumber. She put it into the pile for undersoil heating.

Brendan found Sir Richard Scratcher in the bar. He usually had no time for the man and certainly would not leave him in charge of anything important unless it was cut and dried.

In Brendan's mind, Sir Richard was six feet two inches worth of upper class twit who had no footballing instincts whatsoever. At seventy-three Sir Richard could easily pass for sixty. Nevertheless, he was greying but his shiny silver-white hair bore the mark of aristocracy, rather than the dull metallic grey of the impoverished. Sir Richard had worn well, thought Brendan, despite his passion for alcohol.

Lucky bugger had been in just the right place at the right time to win the knighthood – he had provided an important alibi for Bobby Moore during the bracelet allegations before the 1970 World Cup. His mere presence in the same shop as the England Captain had been enough to earn recognition from the Queen. Prior to that day, he had merely been a government attaché on the strength of his Harrow education. Since then, he had sat on the board of numerous football clubs without actually knowing the first thing about them.

"Morning Sir Richard, early start?" quipped Brendan, motioning toward the gin and tonic which was never far from Sir Richard's hand.

"Morning Brendan, everything shipshape?"

"Listen Dickie, something important has come up and I need you to be in charge." Sir Richard coloured slightly. It wasn't often that Brendan trusted him with something.

"FIFA have been on the phone. Remember that conference in Brazil regarding the elasticity of corner flags? Some chaps down there have been injured while colliding with them – bit stiff, no bend, you understand? Well, I tried to cancel but FIFA were having none of it. It's imperative that I attend, personal favour to President of FIFA – can't not go or our next World Cup bid may suffer."

"I see," said Sir Richard, although he didn't. He had lost

concentration after the word 'Brazil', remembering an encounter with a certain energetic young lady called Ramona during the Mexico World Cup in 1970. Very athletic, young Ramona.

"Anyway, it's up to you to interview the candidates for the England manager job," Brendan continued, interrupting Sir Richard's memory.

"Pardon," croaked Sir Richard, suddenly paying attention again.

"Shouldn't be too difficult. June and I have already weeded out the best candidates so you shouldn't have too much to get worried about. Just make sure Atkinson gets the job," said Brendan.

"Atkinson…do I know him? Watford wasn't it?" blurted Sir Richard.

"Nottingham Forest was the last one. Look Dickie, Atkinson has had more clubs than Jack Nicklaus, but he has experience, he's the people's choice, and he knows how to get the best out of the players. Best of all, he's between clubs at the moment so it won't cost us a penny in compensation. Just make sure Ron Atkinson has been installed as England manager by the time I get back okay? That's all there is to it. We'll get him in to cover us on this game and then we'll take our time to review the situation afterwards."

"Yes, I understand. Atkinson."

"Interview a couple of others, just to satisfy the media, but the job is Atkinson's, okay?"

"Okay, I've got it. Interview some others, but Atkinson gets it. Can't go wrong there – leave it to me Brendan, you can trust me," beamed Sir Richard.

Brendan looked doubtful, but then again, what could go

wrong? It was so simple; nothing could go wrong, even with this drunk in charge. He left Sir Richard and walked jauntily out of the building smiling to himself – Rio here I come.

Sir Richard ordered another drink from the bar. He still couldn't remember what Ron Atkinson looked like. Ah well, it would come back to him at some point. The good thing was he was now in charge and Hannibal was out of the way.

June Whitless had almost finished sorting out the post when Sir Richard Scratcher sauntered in to Brendan's office.

"Good afternoon Sir Richard," she said politely.

"Please Jane, call me Dickie," he offered.

"Only if you call me June," she smiled back.

"Ok, June," he replied, now slightly confused. Why she wanted him to call her June he had no idea, but if it made her like him, he would do it.

Sir Richard had lusted after June Whitless for the length of her employment with the FA. He had no idea that she was seeing Brendan but thought with the main man out of the way, he could make his move. She had to be impressed – after all he was a knight.

June was less than impressed. She had an inkling that Sir Richard would like nothing better than to pounce on her and make an old man happy, but she was not that sort of girl. She loved Brendan and knew that as soon as he found the opportunity to tell his wife about the pair of them, he would divorce and marry June. So what if there was a twenty-year age gap, so what if he had two grown-up children and a wife he'd been married to for thirty years. She made him happy, June Whitless, not some old crone who didn't understand him.

"Brendan has asked me to take charge while he's away," said Sir Richard, forcing June out of her reverie. "Firstly, do you have the manager's applications for me to review?"

June handed three envelopes to him. He read the names on each one – Robson, Reid, and Atkinson. This was going to be easier than he thought.

"Jane, I mean June, I'm going to ring each of these people and ask them to come down for an interview. I'd like you to make the arrangements for the visits though – I have a tight schedule you know.

June knew about Sir Richard's 'tight' schedule, but just nodded. She might just arrange the Atkinson interview for a mid-afternoon slot, just to see how 'tight' Sir Richard could get. In fact, the more she thought about it, the better that seemed. At least Atkinson would be able to say nothing wrong.

"Ah Jane…"

"June," she reminded him.

"Oh yes, June. You are a remarkably attractive young woman," simpered the rosy-cheeked knight.

"Thank you Dickie"

"I'm at somewhat of a loose end this evening and was wondering if you'd do me the honour of coming to dinner. What do you say?" asked Sir Richard.

"Well I was planning to go out with some friends," June responded, having already prepared the lie.

"Bring them along," said Sir Richard undaunted, "more the merrier. I'll send a car to pick you up at eight. Just tell the driver where your friends need picking up."

With that, he left the room. Sir Richard was not totally dim when it came to women's wiles. Friends indeed.

June was dumbstruck. That hadn't quite worked as planned. Then again she might be able to turn the evening to her advantage. She could definitely find out what plans Sir Richard had for the manager's position – she couldn't let Brendan down – Atkinson had to get the job.

Later that day Reg Atkinson was at a park with the Forest Inn players. They were doing their customary Monday night training with Reg trying to coach them. He didn't have any real footballing experience, but he felt he had a great deal of knowledge of how the game should be played. Often he would confuse his players with silly formations and banal tactics, but despite this his players maintained a respect for him, and usually followed his wishes as best they could. He had spent a great deal of time reading about the great formations and tactics of the past – Arsenal's third back game of the 20s; Manchester City's Revie Plan; the Italian Catenaccio 'sweeper' system; Alf Ramsey's 'wingless wonders' etc. – and had devised a number of his own formations. His current favourite was the 'Rambling Rose', which required one of his strikers to start the game in defence and then 'ramble' all over the field to confuse the opposition. Ultimately the striker would be able to make a move into a true centre-forward position unmarked and hopefully score.

Reg had split the Forest Inn players into two 6-a-side teams and was busy shouting instructions as his mobile phone rang. "Hello... Shoot 'Baldy'... shoot," he shouted as he concentrated on the match rather than the call.

"Err, hello. Is that Mr Atkinson?" asked the elderly male caller.

Reg, still a little distracted replied: "Yeah, Atkinson here.

What can I do you for? Give it to Norman… Don't muck about…"

"Sorry, I'll give you the facts straight away. My name is Sir Richard Scratcher and I'd like you to come and see me about…"

Reg interrupted: "You want a job doing, don't you? Well, I can't come now, or at least if I do I'll have to charge you a call-out rate."

Sir Richard: "Oh, I didn't realise. Well, it's not necessary for you to come tonight and in any case I need the rest of the Committee around me."

"The Committee? Look, I'm not a con man! I can tell you're an old boy, but I'm not gonna fiddle you. You can trust me!" Reg was convinced Sir Richard had phoned him to perform a plumbing job.

"I should hope I can trust you. We've had problems here before. You've probably heard about Venables and Graham."

"Can't say I have. Which is unusual because I know all the tradespeople round here… Stick it in Baldy…"

Sir Richard: "Are you all right?"

"Yeah, sorry, I'm at a football training session. For God's sake hit it when you've got the chance. Jeez…"

"I didn't realise you were still involved. Which team is it?" asked Sir Richard.

"The Forest Inn."

In where, thought Sir Richard, and then realised Reg meant Nottingham (thank you Brendan) – blast these mobile phones, always cutting out. He continued: "I was told you weren't involved with them any more. Ah well, never mind. It won't stop you doing a job for me will it?"

Reg: "I doubt it, although I'll have to see if I can fit you in. Are your waterworks playing up then?"

"That's a bit personal. I know I'm not as young as I was, but it's all still in working order!"

Reg: "I'm getting a bit confused here. You've got to tell me what you want, otherwise I can't help you. I've got plenty of work you know, I can pick and choose. Now, speak clearly and tell me exactly what you want doing!"

Sir Richard was surprised that Atkinson had other work, and in his current state of anticipation for the evening ahead with the lovely June, just wanted to get things over with.

"Right, I'm from the FA and I want you to come to Lancaster Gate for a formal interview. Your application is being considered and, I think it's fair to say, you are the favourite for the appointment. I'd like you to come to our offices on Thursday for an interview. Can you make it?"

Realisation dawned and Reg nearly choked.

"Really," was all he could say.

"Well that's super, look forward to seeing you. My secretary will fax you the details," said Sir Richard.

Reg was stunned. From seemingly nothing, he was convinced he was close to achieving his dream of obtaining a lucrative, high profile plumbing contract.

"Yes, I'll be there. I'm sorry about earlier, but I do get quite a few time-wasting calls. Lots of people phone me up with piddling little jobs. I've done them before and I don't intend doing them again."

Sir Richard, remembering Brendan's 'more clubs than Jack Nicklaus' remark, said "I quite understand. You need a contract like ours to prove you're still the best in the business, don't you?"

Both men said their goodbyes and the call ended. Reg gazed into the distance – the training in front of him carried on haphazardly, but he was now too preoccupied to notice.

"Reg? Reg?" Norman called out. "You all right?" Malcolm Mercer had made an unsightly challenge on Baldy Charlton and Reg, under these circumstances, would have torn a few strips off the less than talented Mercer. Instead, Reg just stared into the distance absolutely nonplussed over the conversation he'd just had. He could not believe it. It was so quick – he'd only posted the tender last week. He had thought that the manager's job would have taken preference.

Who was that on the phone Reg? old Norm asked

"Bloody FA. I've got an interview on Thursday."

"You're jokin' man. Well done." Norman got up and slapped Reg heartily on the back. "You must have put some good stuff in that application," he said.

"Like I told you, I listed my experience and the fact that I'd been plumbing apprentice under Tom Finney, my middle name was Stanley after Stanley Matthews and with my footballing connections, they'd be daft not to let me do it. I said that I'd fitted the shower at Buxton United…" Reg was rambling – his mind was whirling. Part of him knew he'd told Norman all this before but…wow!

"'Eh Reg. Look at this – d'yer think it means owt? Like an omen or summat?" asked Larry 'Fat' Jennings, team goalkeeper. He had a copy of the Evening Post in his huge hand. The headline proclaimed 'ATKINSON FAVOURITE' with a large picture of Big Ron and the three lions of England.

Reg looked at it dreamily.

"Dunno lad. I hope so". He looked at the faces of his team. By the look of them, they were delighted for him, even though it may mean the end of his involvement with them for a while. He couldn't think straight — obviously, he'd be one of many applicants but his eyes kept drifting down to the headline 'ATKINSON FAVOURITE' and he decided he needed a pint.

# TUESDAY

At nine o'clock on Tuesday morning, June Whitless stood by the fax machine in her office at the FA headquarters in Lancaster Gate. Sir Richard had given her the details of the interview dates for the applicants for the England manager's job. The previous evening had gone better than expected – Sir Richard had been charm personified. If she hadn't been so much in love with Brendan, the old gentleman's efforts might have paid off.

She had been expecting a lecherous old man – Sir Richard had been anything but. In fact, most of the flirting – granted the champagne helped – was done by June herself. The meal was fantastic – Sir Richard had really splashed out. He had even arranged for her to be picked up in a limousine. Dickie certainly had style, she thought, much more than Brendan. Put those thoughts out of your head young lady, she reminded herself. As Sir Richard had kissed her hand as he said goodbye, she had momentarily cast herself in the position of Lady June Scratcher. Maybe that was the drink, she thought. Whatever, he had asked her out to the theatre tonight – no harm in that, she thought. She liked the theatre but Brendan thought it too public.

She fed the first fax into the machine. Better get this right, she thought. Atkinson's interview was at two o'clock in the afternoon on the Thursday. Sir Richard had just given her the dates; it was up to her to allocate the times. She had given both Bryan Robson and Peter Reid morning slots, but she wanted Sir Richard as amiable as possible for Reg Atkinson. Amiability was Sir Richard's middle name after his lunchtime tipple.

June had arranged hotels for each man as well. She had booked rooms at the Kippax Hotel for Reg as that was closest. She wanted him to look his best for the interview – create a good impression. It wasn't just Sir Richard she had to worry about; there were the other committee members too. Hopefully, the golf course would beckon some of them in the afternoon, leaving Atkinson with an easier interview than the morning slots. The FA committee members were infamous for their short tempers in the mornings as they counted down the minutes to lunch.

She had booked rooms for Reid and Robson some way across the city, purposely giving them no option but to take a minimum of two tube trips. With any luck, their moods would be slightly off during the high-pressure interviews in the morning. She smiled to herself – Brendan would be so happy. She couldn't wait to see him again to tell him how she had thought through all the possibilities.

Later that morning, Reg stood in the kitchen of one Mrs Butterman of Fairfax Street, Nottingham, watching Norman work. He found it difficult to concentrate – his mind was in one place while he was in another and that was bad. What if he didn't get it? What if he did? Which was worse – jobbing along as usual or hitting the plumbing jackpot? Too many things to consider – what will they ask at the interview? What will he wear? He had received the fax this morning and that was the only thing on which his mind could settle.

"Oy. Are you gonna help out here or what?" Old Norman was on his hands and knees with his head under the sink. He had stopped momentarily to see that Reg was undergoing some mental trauma.

"I'm sorry Norm. Bit distracted you know," Reg said.

"Well don't let that get in the way of the bread and butter things. You've got a business to run 'ere you know."

"Yeah, I know, but..."

"But nowt. Get upstairs and turn the taps on while I sort this sink out."

Reg sighed. Norman was right of course. Mrs Butterman was having a new kitchen installed. As part of the design, she wanted plumbing for a dishwasher and washing machine. This was Reg's job. He'd been contracted by the kitchen fitters to perform the plumbing tasks. Although mundane, this was the work that paid his bills every month. If he didn't get it, he'd be up the creek.

Reg made his way upstairs. Nice house this, he thought. Mrs Butterman was obviously not short of a few bob. On the landing, he had a thought.

"Cheeky bugger. Whose bloody firm is this anyhow?" he said to himself. It was usually him sending Norm running about the house doing this sort of work. Ah well, he thought, I'm here now I suppose. He went into the bathroom and turned on the taps. Norman had already turned off the water at the stopcock so Reg saw the bath and sink taps slow to a trickle and then nothing.

He walked through the master bedroom to the en suite, where he turned on the sink taps. The effect of all this was to drain the pipes of water, so Norman could carry on downstairs in a 'squirt-free' environment. Mission accomplished – Reg headed back downstairs to join Norman in the kitchen.

"Look," said Norman with a mouthful of cheese and pickle sandwich, "just put it out of yer 'ead until tonight. I'll help yer prepare for the interview."

"Easier said than done Norm," Reg replied, looking down at his turkey salad bap – it was oozing mayonnaise. He wished he had gone for ham now.

The two men had stopped for lunch while the kitchen fitters were out of the way. They sat around a makeshift table comprised of a Black and Decker Workmate and a length of worktop. After Reg and Norm had finished the plumbing, this worktop was to be replaced around the sink area.

"D'you not want that," said Norm, gesturing to Reg's lunch.

"Nah. Do you?"

"Aye, go on then. Consider it payment for me doing all the work," chuckled Norm. Reg made a face.

"Go and turn them taps back off then, there's a good lad, while I finish off this buttie," said Norm, just before ramming a good third of the sandwich into his mouth. Reg considered a clip round Norman's ear, but laughed it off. He rose and headed towards the stairs.

He smiled to himself as he climbed. Norman was a

scamp. Reg had known him ever since he'd arrived in Nottingham fifteen years before. Reg had set up the business and placed advertisements for an assistant. What he actually wanted was an apprentice, what he got was Norman Whaddon – the only applicant. Norman had been made redundant at the age of 57 and did not care how little he earned as long as he pulled in a wage. Reg admired that – the man had pride. Reg's initial doubts during the interview had soon given way to a remarkable fondness for the older man. Over the intervening years they had become firm friends and although Norman was well past retirement age, Reg could not imagine a day's work without him.

Reg turned off the bathroom taps and returned downstairs.

"Okay?" asked Norman.

"Aye," said Reg.

Norman turned the stopcock back on.

"There y'are. Jobs a good 'un," said Norman, looking intently at his handiwork. Leak free, he thought.

"Be nice when it's finished, eh Reg?"

"Should be. Looks good upstairs too. They've got an en suite as w... oh shit!" Reg sprinted out of the kitchen and leapt up the stairs three at a time. He swung into the master bedroom and noticed water spray before he got into the en suite.

"Oh knackers," he said when he saw the full extent of his mistake. When he had turned off the taps in the bathroom, he had completely forgotten about the en suite and left the taps in a full on position. As a consequence, the pressure of the water had forced most of it out of the small sink and it was currently rebounding out on to the lavatory, shower cubicle and carpet.

Reg hurriedly turned off the taps and surveyed the damage. The toilet and shower cubicle would easily wipe down, but the carpet was sodden.

"Y'all right up there Reg?" shouted a concerned Norman from the bottom of the stairs.

"Yer'd best come up and give us hand," Reg shouted back. As Norman came up, Reg grabbed all the available towels and used them on the carpet in an effort to mop up some of the flood.

"Bloody 'ell," said Norman as he popped his head around the door, "we had a tidal wave or summat?"

"As good as. I forgot these bloody taps when I came to turn off the bathroom ones," said Reg.

Norman tutted. "Schoolboy error that."

"Just have a look in the wardrobes for more towels. There's got to be more," Reg barked.

He looked down at the towels he had already laid on the floor. Typical, he thought – they were the sort of fluffy towels that Shirley, his ex-wife, used to buy: nice to look at, expensive, but with a tendency to stroke the water all over your body rather than absorb any of it. The towels on the floor were not doing the intended job – they just lay there, expensively.

"Here you go," said Norman, handing Reg some more towels. These looked better: older, used, absorbent – the sort he used at home. Reg set about laying them on the floor of the en suite and stamping them down.

After about half an hour of towel laying and stamping, the result of Reg's endeavours was a pile of soaked towels in the bottom of the shower cubicle and a still damp carpet.

"That'll 'ave to do," he said informedly.

"Turn the central heating on, open the window and leave

the door open. That'll do the trick," offered Norman, who was nothing if not resourceful.

"What about them?" asked Reg, nodding towards the pastel heap of sodden towels in the shower cubicle.

Norman considered their options.

"Best get 'em round to our Jackie's and slap 'em in the tumbler."

Reg nodded his agreement. He blew a breath of resignation and began collecting up the towels.

Jackie Aveyard was Norman's daughter. She was surprised to see the white van with 'Atkinson Plumbing' emblazoned down its side pull up outside her house and her father get out. Normally it would be her visiting him – he only came to see her when he'd had a formal invitation. It was because, he said, he didn't want to put her out – she had a house to run and a family to consider.

Norman's wife Ann – Jackie's mother – had died six years previously. She sometimes worried about her father and his ability to cope on his own, but her fears were usually unfounded – he had his mates, his football and his work. She looked upon Reg as a saviour. By rights, her Dad should have retired around the time Ann died, but Reg had kept him working. This had probably saved her Dad's life.

She met Norman and Reg at the door, before they had a chance to knock.

"Hiya Dad, Reg. Come on in. What's up?"

Norman entered the hallway, followed by Reg, looking slightly sheepish.

"Is everything okay?" she asked.

"Got a favour to ask you Jackie. Is your tumble dryer still working?" asked Norman.

"Yeah, why?"

"Reg has had a bit of a disagreement with the taps at some posh woman's house."

"Eh?" Jackie was perplexed.

"I've flooded an en suite and I've had to mop up the water with a load of towels," added Reg, "your Dad thought we might get 'em dry again in your tumbler."

"You dozy bugger," Jackie looked at him with a half smile. "Yer'd best go and get 'em hadn't yer."

"Thanks love," said Norman and shunted Reg back towards the door.

"Yeah, thanks Jackie," Reg added and followed Norman back out to the van.

Jackie shook her head as she watched them. They're like two little lads – the boys who never grew up, she thought.

The towel drying had to be done in two stages – there was too much weight for one load. While they were waiting, Jackie put a brew on and Reg took the opportunity of telling her about his phone call from the FA.

"That's marvellous Reg," Jackie enthused. She was genuinely pleased.

"I mean, obviously I'd 'ave to get more people. Can't do the full thing with just me and Norm, so I'll need to get some extra hands quick," Reg continued, enjoying himself.

"Lot to think about, eh?" said Jackie.

"That's why the silly bugger left the taps on," chuckled Norman, "too much thinking about what might be instead of what is."

"There's no 'arm in planning, Dad," said Jackie in Reg's defence.

"I never said there was," Norman said, "it's just that if

you don't keep your mind clear, you just might drop a bollock, eh Reg?"

"Get away," said Reg, "what about that time you plumbed that outside tap into the hot water pipe? That poor bugger took weeks to figure out why his dahlias were dying."

Norman laughed. "Anybody could have made the same mistake," he offered.

"Bollocks," laughed Reg, "you were too busy replaying the last five minutes of that league game where you came on and scored the winner."

"Great goal that, brilliant header," mused Norman.

"I've not seen many goals scored off the side of a bloke's head as he lay down on the six yard line," Reg laughed.

"Just goes to show you then, took skill that," Norman countered.

With five minutes to go in the game in question, Norman had dived theatrically in a vain attempt to win a penalty. In the resulting scramble, the ball had been played towards goal, cleared off the line and on to the side of the prostrate Norman's head, whereafter it rebounded meekly into the back of the net. Norman had drinks bought him for a week on the strength of it.

"Right," said Jackie, "first lot's finished." She arose from the table and opened up the tumble dryer.

Reg and Norman eventually returned to Fairfax Street at around 3.30 that afternoon. The kitchen fitters were there performing the finishing touches. They were all working in shorts with no shirts.

"All right Reg? Norm?" shouted one of the fitters. "It's bloody red hot in here. Silly cow's got her central heating on full blast."

"All right Kev? Lads?" replied Reg with an armful of towels.

"What've you got there? Laundry part of the service is it?" Kev Beckett gestured towards the towels, "could do with a few of them to mop up the sweat, eh lads?"

Kev's lads nodded and muttered in agreement. They weren't exactly happy about working in these conditions, but Kevin had promised the two of them a pint if they finished quickly.

Reg thought about telling Kev why he had the towels. Then he thought again – Kev wouldn't forget this in a hurry.

"Met a delivery man coming up the path. Surprised you didn't see him," said Reg lamely.

"Oh," said Kevin, apparently convinced, "d'you reckon you can do summat with the heating Reg? You're a plumber."

"Aye, let's just get shut of these and I'll see what I can do."

Reg and Norman went upstairs and put the towels back where they had found them originally. Reg checked the carpet in the en suite.

"What's it like?" asked Norman.

"Not bad," Reg replied, "could be better, but it could be a lot worse."

Reg rose off his haunches and nodded to Norman. "We'd better get the central heating back to normal, before the Queen gets home."

Back downstairs, they noticed Kevin had made a brew.

"Fancy a tea lads?" he asked.

"Aye, go on," Reg replied.

"Please" said Norman.

"Eh, Kev," started Reg, "I might have a bit of work

coming up in a bit. Wouldn't be anything too technical like, but I might need some strong hands. You interested?"

"Depends," said Kev. Kitchen fitters usually had to turn their hand to just about every trade – carpentry, plumbing, gas, electrics. If a qualified tradesman couldn't be found for a particular job, they would do it themselves. They were very proud of their all round skills, especially if it meant pocketing the cash they would normally have given to the tradesmen.

Kevin poured two more cups of tea.

"Milk? Sugar?

"Milk and one sugar" said Reg.

"Just milk please," said Norman.

Kevin added the finishing touches and handed the cups to Reg and Norman.

"Well it's not definite yet, but I might be getting a big heating contract. I'll be needing some help and you lads'd be perfect – you've got just the all-round skills I need," said Reg, adding a buttery note which he knew would hit the right spot.

Kevin visibly glowed. "Well if the money's right, count us in, eh lads?" His lads nodded their confirmation.

"Good," smiled Reg. "I'll let you know in the next few weeks, all right?"

Reg knew he could trust Kevin Beckett to do a job. With what he had in mind, Kevin would provide the muscle – there would be a lot of pipes to be carted about and you didn't need much brain for that. Kevin's pride had been stroked slightly and he was willing. That was good.

Reg and Norman spent the next ten minutes chatting idly with the kitchen fitters before announcing their farewells. As they sat back in their van, Reg asked Norman if he would help him prepare for the interview.

"Course I will, I've already told you that," said Norman. "Tell you what, I'll meet you in the Forest at eight and I'll ask you a load of awkward questions, all right?"

"You're on," smiled Reg, "I might even buy you a pint."

"A pint?" questioned Norman, with the emphasis on the 'a', "more like 'some' pints."

"Cheeky bugger, don't forget you're in this too."

"What do you mean?"

"I got a fax on the machine this morning. They want me to bring an assistant manager down with me, or chief coach, whichever applies."

"Chief coach?" Norman inquired.

"Yeah, couldn't work that one out myself. Maybe it's in response to my footballing cracks – you know, the sense of humour bit?" said Reg.

"Oh, that'll be it," said Norman unconvinced.

That night in the Forest Inn, Reg and Norman sat in a quiet corner of the pub, each with a pint of bitter. Reg was giving Norman all the information relating to the interview.

"According to the fax, there are two rooms booked at the Kippax Hotel for tomorrow night, and that's just around the corner from the FA place."

"Never heard of it," said Norman, who had been to London three times in a social capacity. He didn't count his footballing trips as these just involved travelling to whichever ground he was due to play at followed by a trip home.

"Doesn't matter whether you've heard of it Norman, it's probably the only hotel they could get. They're probably inundated down there with people staying for the England Germany game," said Reg.

# TUESDAY

"Eh, maybe they'll give us tickets." The idea came to Norman like a visible flash, "if we ask nicely."

"We can ask," Reg replied doubtfully.

"'Scuse me lads while I give you a wipe down." It was Carol the barmaid. Reg and Norman lifted their pint glasses off the table while she wiped it down with a damp cloth. It seemed to Reg that he was purposefully getting a right eyeful of Carol's dancing cleavage as she worked.

"I'll be back in a bit for your empties," she added. As Carol left them, Reg couldn't help watching her.

"If you fancy 'er, ask her out," said Norman.

"Shush, she'll hear you," hissed Reg. He checked – if she had heard, she didn't let on. "I'm working on it."

"Working on it? Bloody 'ell, she'll be married wi' four kids by the time you get round to it," Norman scoffed. "Good lookin' lass though, I'll give you that."

"Reckon I stand a chance?"

"Oh aye, a fat chance"

Reg pulled a face. "You gonna ask me some questions then?"

"Aye, I've been reading an article from last week's Sunday supplement."

"Oh yeah," said Reg. He sat up, interested.

"Yeah," Norman continued, "it's all about the type of questions you get asked these days during interviews. Lot different to when I was a lad."

"What? Like how many blocks did it take to build your last pyramid," smirked Reg.

"You trying to be funny?"

"No, carry on."

"Well, instead of asking you about your experience or what size of washer you'd use on a bathroom tap, they ask you things like 'if you were having a dinner party, what five people would you pick to be your guests?'"

"You what?"

"It says it's to do with assessing your imagination and how your brain works," Norman added, "although I'm not so sure how it would help pick a decent plumber."

"Bloody 'ell," sniffed Reg, "if that's how it's done these days, do you think they'll let me phone a friend or ask the audience?"

"I'm sure they must ask some proper questions, but maybe I should try some of these funny ones to get you in the right frame of mind," suggested Norman.

"Go on then," said Reg resigned to his fate already.

Norman brought a little notepad out of his jacket pocket. Reg raised his eyebrows – this should be good. Norman licked the end of the index finger of his right hand, rubbed this together with his thumb and began to flick through the notebook.

Reg was about to remark on this being somewhat akin to a military operation when Norman found what he was looking for.

"Right Mr Atkinson," he began.

"Eh?" said Reg startled.

"I'm being the interviewer," replied Norman, "I'm trying to do it proper."

"Oh right," said Reg.

"Mr Atkinson," repeated Norman, "If you were stuck on a desert island with no immediate route of escape, what five items would you consider most necessary to help you survive?"

"Bloody 'ell, Norman," cried Reg. Norman just looked at him and frowned.

"These are interview conditions Mr Atkinson," he reminded.

"Sorry," said Reg, "...errr I'd have a Swiss Army knife..."

"Good," said Norman, "that's one."

"A fridge," said Reg, "or a cool box thing to keep my food cold."

Reg took a swig of his beer. He needed inspiration.

"My toolbox," he added, "just in case the fridge conked out." Norman raised his eyebrows.

"Two to go," Reg whispered under his breath. This was difficult.

"Oh I know, Shania Twain," he said.

"Eh?" spluttered Norman.

"Shania Twain. Good looking woman that. She could sing for me and provide ent-er-tain-ment." Reg took his time with the last word, savouring every syllable.

"That don't impress me much. One more," Norman quipped.

"A toothbrush," said a relieved Reg.

"Right Mr Atkinson, that's a Swiss Army knife, a fridge, a toolbox, Shania Twain, ahem, and a toothbrush. Am I correct?" asked Norman, playing his part to the full.

"Yeah," confirmed Reg, glad to have that question out of the way.

"I would have had a short wave radio myself," said Norman smirking.

"Well, I could have said my mobile phone but I assumed that as I was deserted, I didn't know where I was. I could hardly call someone to say come and get me – I don't know where I am but it's somewhere on the right hand side of the planet." Reg retorted. He hadn't thought about his phone at all, but felt the need to get Norman's superior look off his face.

"Never assume, Reg," said Norman, launching into one of his favourite adages, "you'll make an 'ASS' out of 'U' and 'ME'."

"Give me strength," sighed Reg.

"Mr Atkinson," Norman continued. Reg began paying attention once more. "Please tell me, if you were given ten thousand pounds, to book a holiday anywhere in the world, where would you go.

Reg thought about saying a caravan park in Whitby, just to see the shock on Norman's face, the silly old sod. He put on his thinking cap and started dreaming of Vegas: he opened his mouth to speak.

Five pints down and the interview had been forgotten. Reg had taken to following Carol around the pub with a lecherous eye. Norman sat facing Reg, not saying anything. He had thought about the assistant manager business and decided it was a little odd at first. But as the bitter swilled around his belly, he became more comfortable with the idea. The FA probably wanted to see what sort of person sat at Reg's right hand. Norman considered himself trustworthy and was confident of making a favourable impression – he wouldn't let Reg down.

Carol had been over a couple of times to wipe their table and clean out the ashtray. Norman knew this was a ploy – neither of them smoked. It was as though Carol was purposely manoeuvring towards Reg. Norman was surprised that Reg couldn't see it and wondered if his friend was prepared to worship from afar. He might have to give him a nudge soon. That might be the only way he'd spring into action.

# TUESDAY

"'Another pint Norm?" Reg asked dreamily.

"Just 'alf, please Reg," replied Norman, "oh and while yer up there, ask that Carol for a dance." He roared with laughter, shaking the table. "Oops", he said noticing a bit of beer had spilled in the aftermath, "'ang on though, she might be back over in a minute with her shammy."

As Norman chuckled, Reg pulled a face. Maybe he should ask her out – what did he have to lose? If he got this contract, he'd be away for a good few months; if she said no, the embarrassment factor would have cleared by the time he returned.

As Reg weaved his way to the bar, Norman looked at him with fondness. Reg was the son he'd never had. He'd tried for a while to get Jackie to think of Reg as a suitor, but that never came off. Probably for the best, he thought, looking back at Reg's failed marriage. He remembered that Reg was absolutely devastated at the time – he had worked like a maniac building up the business so that Shirley could have a comfortable life, giving up work, joining the gym. And then what thanks did he get – she ran off with the bloody aerobics instructor.

Norman hoped that Reg would ask Carol out. He could see that she had a soft spot for him and with these sorts of things, one thing usually led to another. And a bit of the other would probably improve Reg's chances of getting this contract, he mused, tittering to himself.

Reg arrived at the bar and caught Carol's eye. She smiled and came over to him.

"Yes Reg," she beamed, "what can I get you?"

Go on, Reg said to himself, go for it. The bar's fairly empty, no one will know, just ask her, you big lemon.

"Err, C-c-carol," he stuttered, "will you, err..." come on,

get it out, "would you, I mean, is it..." God this was hard. I need a pee, he thought, "err, get us a pint and 'alf please." As Reg rushed out the last few words, he thought, "Sod it!" He was usually so sure of himself, confident, but in front of a woman – God it was different. He tried to remember back to his teenage courting days. Was it as difficult then or had he forgotten the moves?

Carol disturbed him from his reverie. "Two pound forty please," she said as she placed the drinks in front of him. "Anything else?" she inquired sweetly.

Reg was hoping the alcohol would be giving him some Dutch courage by now, but he was feeling more sober by the minute. Here goes, he thought.

"I was wondering what you were doing on Sunday night – that's your night off in't it?" he began. "I thought we might go out for something to eat."

She looked at him inquisitively but said nothing. She smiled coyly, milking the moment.

"Unless you fancied the pictures or rollerskating?" Rollerskating? thought Reg, where did that come from? Jesus this was hard – she hadn't said no yet though, so he tried a new tack.

"Or mud wrestling?" he offered, with a cheeky grin.

She laughed. Her eyes twinkled – he liked that.

"Course I will, Reg, I thought you'd never ask," she said, "but I'll give the mud part a miss. I'd spend a fortune at Boots trying to get my complexion back together."

"A meal then?" said Reg, "I've heard that new Italian's good on the High Street."

"Yeah, sure" she replied.

"Great," said Reg, enthusiastically, "I'll pick you up at your place at... eight o'clock Sunday night?"

"Okay", she replied smiling.

"Right then," said Reg, collecting up his drinks and his change. He backed away from the bar, still grinning, "I'll see you then."

"Reg," she called.

"Yeah," he replied.

"Don't you want to know where my place is?"

Reg stupidly realised that he didn't have a clue where she lived. "Good point," he said and returned to the bar. Carol took out a pen from behind the bar and jotted down her address and phone number on a bar receipt.

Reg thanked her again and looked at the paper. He made a mental note of the address before slipping the receipt into the back pocket of his jeans. He carried the beers back to the table where Norman was still waiting.

"I thought you'd drowned in your own slaver," scoffed Norman.

"Cheeky bugger," chirped Reg, "I was asking her out if you must know."

"Bet she told you to bugger off," laughed Norman, hoping she hadn't.

"Au contraire," said Reg, full of himself, "Carol recognises my vast potential and has jumped at the chance to cling to my arm as we parade around this town."

"Bloody 'ell," said Norman, "will she be allowed to bring her seeing-eye dog or will you put up with the tapping on your shins from her white stick?"

"You may mock, Norman Whaddon, but Reg Atkinson is going up in the world, oh yes," stated Reg. In his eyes, the truth was simple. Things were definitely looking up.

# THE KIPPAX HOTEL

Reg and Norman had decided to make their way down to London in Norman's old Ford Escort. For one, it wasn't worth taking the van and leaving it in a vulnerable position, especially with Reg's plumbing gear in the back of it; for another, Norman's old Escort didn't rate a second glance by would-be car thieves. Fifteen-year-old Escorts were not exactly top of anybody's 'most wanted' list.

Reg had decided to postpone all jobs in the book today in order to give them plenty of time to travel the hundred or so miles into London. As the only real appointment on the schedule was an estimate for a new washbasin and splashback in the local library, Reg felt he could easily re-arrange it.

He had decided upon his best suit for the interview itself. Luckily this had been dry cleaned after its previous airing and was still in its polythene wrapper. He didn't get to wear it much these days – the last time was at his solicitors, signing the final documents that officially made him a single man again. Maybe he could wear it again on Sunday to impress Carol. Suppose that depends whether I spill anything on it in the next few days, he thought.

The drive to London was fairly trouble-free. Norman was a careful driver – not that he had much choice in the Escort. Reg had a feeling that the top speed would not be much more than fifty miles an hour. As Norman put his foot down a little to overtake a caravan, Reg felt the vehicle judder with the strain.

"Don't get the opportunity to open her up much these days," said Norman wistfully.

"Bloody good job nearly shook all me fillings loose that did."

"Get away with yer," said an indignant Norman as he oozed back into the slow lane, "she's a grand little motor. Hundred thousand miles on the clock and still as good as new."

Reg raised his eyebrows but didn't say anything. Norman was fiercely proud of Mabel – yes, he'd even given the bag of nuts and bolts a name. The radio station began to fade. Reg attempted to tune in a new one but with the manual tuner it was difficult.

"You got any tapes, Norm?" he asked.

"Aye, in the glove compartment," Norm replied, "good selection in there."

Reg opened up the glove compartment and grabbed what he could find. He shuffled each cassette box so he could see the artist. Doris Day, Slim Whitman, Frankie Laine, the soundtrack to South Pacific and Singalongamax by Max Bygraves. What a choice, thought Reg. He tried tuning the radio into anything, anything at all, but failed dismally. He chose South Pacific and put the tape into the machine.

"Good choice," said Norman, nodding approvingly, "we can sing along to some of these."

Reg thought about removing the tape and sitting in silence, but decided a bit of background music may help the thought process. However, when Norman started to belt out 'Some Enchanted Evening' with a passion, the only thing Reg could think about was why the bloody hell he hadn't thought to bring his own tapes. What he wouldn't give now for a bit of Boxcar Willie. He turned down the volume.

"How long to get there Norman?" asked Reg despairingly. They had decided to park the car outside the centre of London and take a tube into the metropolis.

"'Bout another hour an' 'alf," Norman replied.

Reg sighed. Norman joined in with Mitzi Gaynor who was washing that man right out of her hair. Purgatory, he thought, that's what it is, purgatory.

It was nearly two hours later when they parked up near the cemetery at Golders Green. They had been caught up in traffic towards the end of the M1 and this had given Norman the opportunity to go into Doris Day heaven. Reg had found himself singing along to 'Move Over Darling' which had upset him slightly, but his thoughts were of Carol and Sunday night. Well, he thought to himself, you never know.

They had discussed the travel plan at length the previous evening. There was absolutely no point in parking in the centre of London and paying thirty quid for the privilege when it was as easy to park for free and catch the tube. Norman was reluctant at first – he had never been on the tube and the prospect sent him into a cold sweat. Reg persuaded him that it was the best option and that was that. And here they were.

Reg raised his eyebrows as Norman struggled with his antique 'Krooklok'. Absolutely no one would consider stealing Mabel, well possibly a desperate junkyard owner, but that was about it. Reg climbed out and stretched. God, he was getting old. He could not believe how much he ached. Two and a half hours in Norman's car probably had something to do with that, but Reg knew that age was finally catching up with him. That's it, he thought, nothing like a bit of optimism at a time like this...and that was nothing like a bit of optimism, boom boom.

Norman finally surfaced and turned to look at Reg, who was basking in the warm September sun. As usual around this time of year, Britain was baking a little in an Indian Summer.

"Lovely day, eh Reg?" said Norman, smiling. "Fair fills you with the joys of life."

"Aye," Reg replied, who was filled with aches and pains.

They removed their baggage and suit carriers from the boot of Norman's car. Norman locked her up, double checking every door and window before saying "Goodbye Mabel, take care."

Reg looked to the heavens. This was a regular ritual with Norman, even when he was leaving the bloody thing outside the pub. Reg said nothing, he never did.

"Ready?" asked Norman.

"As I'll ever be," replied Reg.

"Right then, which way?" asked Norman.

Reg gestured as best he could and they made their way to Golders Green tube station.

During the ride on the tube, Norman stayed silent. He was content to let Reg usher him everywhere, knowing that Reg had done this sort of thing countless times before. It was easier than he had imagined – train journeys to Norman meant interminable lengths of time waiting at stations followed by a long journey standing up in a smoke-filled carriage. Blissfully unaware of the non-smoking prevalence on public transport these days , Norman found the tube a more pleasant experience than he had expected.

"This is us," nudged Reg as the tube slowed into Marble Arch tube station. The two men stood up and manoeuvred their baggage to the doors of the carriage. When the tube train stopped and the doors opened, they jumped out. Reg ushered Norman over to a quiet wall.

"Right," he said, "let's have a look at this map they've sent us."

He removed the fax sent by the FA from the side pocket of his travel bag. He turned it around in his hand until it was the right way up and studied it closely.

"Looks like about five or ten minutes walk to the FA and then it's only about hundred yards after for the hotel," Reg announced. He looked at his watch – two-fifteen.

"Do you want to check in first and then get a sarny?" he asked.

"Aye," Norman replied, "could do with getting shut of these bags."

They made their way out of the station and Reg headed towards Lancaster Gate. The map was absolutely spot on, he thought. As they approached the FA Headquarters, Reg pointed it out to Norman.

"That's where we're going tomorrow."

"Oh," said Norman, "looks nice."

# The Kippax Hotel

It looked quite impressive, Reg thought. He had never actually seen it before – he'd seen pictures of it of course, but never in reality.

They carried on past the building and were soon in front of the Kippax Hotel.

"Is this it?" asked Norman.

"Seems to be," said Reg, "come on."

They climbed the four steps to the revolving doors and stopped. Above their heads was a sign that said 'MAINE ENTRANCE'.

"Bit odd," Reg remarked.

"Schoolboy error," announced Norman, "you'd have thought they'd have taken more care with the spelling."

Reg led the way through the revolving doors and entered the hotel. Norman followed and they both stood in the foyer gazing at their surroundings. Away from the main street, the silence was deafening.

The Kippax Hotel was at first glance a rather bizarre building. In a previous existence it had been called the Elsinore Hotel. Its current owner, Dave Bayley, was a Manchester City fanatic who had travelled from Droylsden, Manchester to London at the grand old age of seventeen for the 1981 FA Cup Final to watch his beloved City play Tottenham Hotspur. He had never returned home.

Dave had stayed in the Elsinore back then, originally for a couple of nights, but with the first game ending in a draw – thanks to the efforts of Tommy Hutchison who rewrote the history books by scoring for each team – Dave prolonged his stay to take in the replay. Unfortunately for Dave, and for City, Spurs won the replay 3-2 in one of the better Cup replays of recent times. Dave had been so heartbroken he broke down and wept in front of the old hotel owner, Max Novotny.

Max had seen this sort of behaviour many times and was used to it, but Dave seemed to strike a chord deep within him. He came to a decision – he offered Dave a job in the hotel, nothing special, just cleaning, portering, odd jobs, that sort of thing. Dave said yes believing this could be his penance: he could serve out a personal sentence in London, not leaving until City returned triumphant in a Wembley Final. In 1986, he almost achieved his dream, but City were beaten in the Full Members Cup Final by Chelsea. Dave's mother had not been too happy – he was the youngest of three and was the only one to be still living at home. She had travelled down to London in an effort to persuade him to go home, but to no avail. She had returned to Droylsden alone.

In 1992, Max Novotny died. In his last will and testament he had left the hotel to Dave. Having no family to speak of, the old man had left everything to his 'surrogate' son. Dave was astonished – obviously he had grown to love the old man and he knew Max had treated him kindly over the years, but this was completely unexpected. Dave then spent the next year trying to run the hotel as Max had, but found it difficult to meet the overheads.

In early 1994, Dave made a decision: in order to save the hotel, some changes were required. Firstly, the name changed to the Kippax Hotel – a tribute to Manchester City's main terracing. Secondly, all the rooms were given names instead of numbers – the names were of cult City players of yesteryear and gave a personal aspect to each room. Thirdly, advertising was extended from the usual tourist trade to football programmes and fanzines.

Business boomed fleetingly as the novelty value put the

newly named hotel on the map. Supporters came from all over the country to see their teams play in the capital and enjoyed the experience of staying at a speciality hotel. Not all recognised the depth of Dave's devotion, but that didn't matter at the time – it was different. But attitudes change, novelties wear off and Dave was left with a number of faithful guests and the occasional visit by the Manchester City Supporters Club. The best weekend by far in recent times had been the Second Division Play-off Final when City had prevailed against Gillingham. Dave's self-imposed exile may have ended there had he not been the owner of the Kippax Hotel.

Reg and Norman moved slowly through the foyer, taking in the atmosphere of the hotel. On each side of them, photographs of footballers in mostly white England shirts adorned the walls in glass covered frames. Some were head and shoulders shots, but most were on their haunches with the ball between their feet, one hand resting on the ball. Reg recognised a few – Trevor Francis, Mike Channon, Francis Lee for definite, a yellow-shirted Joe Corrigan – but could not put names to faces for most of them. Sunlight glinted from the pictures allowing dust motes to ride on reflected sunbeams cutting through the lobby. The footballers watched their every step until Reg and Norman reached the reception desk. Norman noticed a bell on the desk marked 'Colin'. He rang it.

Within seconds, Dave Bayley appeared.

"Afternoon gents," he said cheerily, "can I help you?"

"Party of two," said Reg, "Atkinson."

"Oh," said Dave, surprised, "and you are Mr...?"

"Atkinson," repeated Reg. He had thought his original statement had been clear enough.

"Oh," said Dave again, frowning momentarily, "I'm sorry, when the FA sent the details... oh never mind, I must have got my wires crossed."

Dave reached under the desk and pulled out two registration cards.

"Could you fill these in please?" he asked. As Reg and Norman patted their pockets ineffectually, searching for pens which they knew were not there, Dave reached below the desk again. His hand emerged with two pens.

"Thanks," said Reg, looking at the pen. Instead of the usual hotel name, it had 'LEE WON' inscribed upon it.

"Those are my Franny Lee pens," Dave Bayley said by way of explanation, "Lee Won Pen – that was his nickname, scored a lot of penalties for City."

Reg acknowledged the explanation, although he wasn't entirely clear what Dave was on about, and began to fill in the registration card. After name and address, the questions became unusual. Reg frowned, confused.

"Oh sorry," Dave said, "I forgot to tell you – this is a hotel which pays homage to football, well Manchester City anyway. The questions are designed to assess your allegiances and preferences."

"I see," said Reg, not seeing.

"I mean," Dave continued, "If you were an Arsenal fan for example, I wouldn't put you on the same floor as a Spurs fan."

"Oh," said Reg, "right."

"It also helps to determine the level of service you get off me," said Dave.

"Why?" said Norman innocently, still examining the pen.

"Well, if you're from Watford, say, and you put your favourite team as Man United, then you will probably not get good quality service because you have jumped on a bandwagon."

"Do you not like Man United then?" asked Norman.

"Bloody media circus they are. Forgotten their fan base in search of profit. Oh yes," Dave was now on his favourite subject. He continued his diatribe while Reg and Norman filled in their registration cards.

Reg filled in his place of birth and favourite team as Preston. Norman completed the necessary sections as Nottingham and Nottingham Forest, his team since childhood. Dave was still at full throttle – he had left the subject of Manchester United and was now berating Luton Town, a team that had once caused Manchester City's relegation in the 1980's.

"Oh good," he said as he examined Reg and Norman's cards, "if you'd have put Luton down, I would have chased you across reception!" He laughed. Reg and Norman returned a polite but nervous chuckle. Dave gathered the cards together and filed them away. He gave them the pens back.

"Souvenirs of your stay," he said, "right gents, I'll show you to your rooms."

The Kippax Hotel had been chosen primarily for its proximity to Lancaster Gate, but a huge benefit was that it was usually empty. It was viewed by the FA as the best possible place for the prospective new manager to be hidden until the interview and subsequent press conference.

Reg and Norman were unaware of the FA's motives. They thought they had wandered into Fawlty Towers, such was the initial impact of Dave Bayley. Dave was taking the opportunity of explaining the layout of the hotel as he escorted Reg and Norman to their rooms. He had already given them a brief history of his own – how he originated from Manchester and the reason he was the owner of the hotel.

"Everything has been named after Manchester City players or key moments in the club's history," he said grandly, "for example, did you notice the bell at reception?"

"Yes," said Reg, "Colin wasn't it?"

"That's right," said Dave pleased, "Colin Bell – and the reception or lobby is called the Maine Entrance, as in Maine Road."

"Ah, so that's why it's Maine with an 'e'," said Norman, suddenly clicking.

"Indeed," said Dave, pleased that Norman had made the connection.

"I like the footballer pictures in the lobby," said Reg, "you can sense the atmosphere as soon as you walk in."

"Oh good, do you like it?" asked Dave, "that's a collection of City players who have played for England since I started supporting them. Only trouble is that I've not had any new ones for a while."

Reg and Norman, despite their first impressions were starting to warm to Dave. His love for City was passionate and he had obviously taken every step to make sure everything within the hotel had substance, a personality. The hotel's heart beat with the same fervour as Dave's.

As Dave led them into the lift, Reg noticed that each floor had a name too, from the Alan Ball Basement, to the Mercer Floor at the top.

Norman stared at the floor names too.

"Mercer?" he enquired to no one in particular.

"Oh yes, Joe Mercer," replied Dave, "best times in the

club's history were when Joe was at the helm. We were always top when he was there, that's why I've called the top floor after him."

Norman snorted. Dave looked hurt – before he could respond, Reg interjected.

"Take no notice," he said to Dave smiling, "Norman once played football for Joe Mercer at Sheffield Utd."

"You're kidding," said Dave in awe.

"Aye," Reg continued, "three whole weeks, wasn't it Norm?"

Norman grunted and muttered something unintelligible under his breath.

"Mercer sold him...to Notts County. Norman had the cheek to ask him for a pay rise, didn't you Norm?"

"Blimey," Dave whispered. This was the first time that anybody had stayed in the hotel who had actually played under Joe Mercer. The fact that it was only for three weeks did not matter in the slightest – Norman had just achieved instant hero status.

The lift stopped at the third floor – Division One. The men heard a 'ding' before the lift doors swung open.

"I must admit that when the FA made the booking, I thought you were someone else," said Dave as he helped Reg and Norman get their bags out of the lift.

"Did you?" said Reg.

"Yeah, with all this business about the England manager vacancy, I thought you were Big Ron," Dave continued, "FA said R.Atkinson and I just assumed..."

"Never assume," barked Norman, never missing an opportunity for his favourite adage.

Reg had no idea why the FA would even consider putting an important candidate for the England job in this hotel, but saw no reason to question it. This was about the standard he would expect for someone like himself.

"Nope," he said, "I'm a plumber. I've come down to try and sort out a tender for the undersoil heating at the new Wembley. Norman's my right hand man."

"I see," said Dave in realisation, "of course, everything's happening at once isn't it?"

Reg nodded in agreement.

"Here we are." Dave stopped outside a door with 'The Royle Suite' engraved on a brass plate on the door, "I've given you two of the best rooms."

Dave opened the door and led Reg and Norman into an enormous room. 'Royle Suite' was about right, Reg thought, good enough for the Queen this. Every wall was covered with memorabilia covering Joe Royle's reign at Manchester City as manager, and even his playing days in the Seventies.

"This room has just been renovated," Dave said proudly, "it used to be the Allison Suite, after the best coach we've had, but I decided to rename it. Bit more pizzazz, eh? The Royle Suite?"

Reg and Norman nodded in agreement – it was certainly impressive.

"This is yours Mr Atkinson," said Dave, breaking the silence. "Your room is next door Mr Whaddon. Will you follow me please."

Norman followed meekly. Reg went too, he was fascinated. He wanted to see Norman's room – if it was anything like his it had to be special.

The next door had a similar brass plate engraved with the legend '10-1'.

"I thought you'd got rid of the room numbers," said Norman.

# THE KIPPAX HOTEL

"I have," said Dave, "that's not a number, that's a score – 10-1 against Huddersfield, biggest win in modern history for the Blues. The Huddersfield goal was even scored by an ex-City player."

"Was it?" said Norman.

"Yeah, Andy May," smiled Dave, "got the biggest cheer of the game it did. Made it 9-1 and brought Huddersfield back into it."

Dave laughed at his small joke, opened the door and stepped inside. Reg and Norman followed him in. In size, the room was similar, but the decoration was so much different. Memorabilia again covered the walls, but most significant were the giant inflatable bananas suspended from the ceiling.

"What do you think?" asked Dave, nervously.

"Brilliant," said Reg – he had never seen anything like it in his life.

"Well it's certainly different," said Norman.

Dave, missing the irony, carried on enthusiastically, "it's called the '10-1' but it's actually a homage to City during the period 1987 to 1989 – the Machin era."

Norman and Reg surveyed the room. There were photographs of various players from the era; team and action pictures; newspaper cuttings. One whole wall was decorated entirely in Manchester Evening News cuttings covering City games. Reg went for a closer look.

"My mum used to send me copies of the Evening News," Dave explained, "but they started piling up. So I thought, why don't I do something like this? People tell me they spend hours reading bits and pieces from it. Bit different to anaglypta, eh?"

Reg agreed. He was currently engrossed in a large section

covering City's 5-1 victory over neighbours United in 1989. Norman could not take his eyes off two large pictures: one of Imre Varadi which seemed to stare back at him, and one of John Gidman. Frightening, he thought – Varadi looked sinister, but the more he looked at Gidman, the worse he felt. As he moved to check out another wall, he looked at the Gidman picture again – he was sure the eyes were following him around the room.

"Well, I'll leave you chaps to settle in," said Dave, "call me if you need anything. There's a guide beside your bed telling you how everything works and the telly's operated by the remote on the bedside table."

"Thanks," said Reg and Norman in unison as Dave left them in the 'Ten One Suite'.

"Unusual in't it?" said Reg who was impressed. He liked hotels with a bit of character, and this was so unexpected that he was still behaving like a schoolboy, hopping from photo to article, from wall to wall.

"I'm not keen on that picture," said Norman, pointing at Varadi who looked a bit too much like Uri Geller for Norman's liking, "and that one scares me to death." He gestured towards Gidman, but couldn't bring himself to look again.

"Get away," chortled Reg, "eh listen, it's past three o'clock. Get your stuff hung up and we'll find a cafe for a sarny and a pot of tea, okay?"

"Aye okay," said Norman.

Lunchtime in Rio seemed a long time coming to Brendan. He sat in his allotted position between delegates from the football associations of Panama and South Africa listening to the various arguments over what to him was a two minute subject. What was it with people, he thought, distant wars always played a part in these things – India never agreed with Pakistan; Iran never agreed with the USA; Poland never agreed with Germany; Germany never agreed with England; Argentina never agreed with England. In fact, most countries never agreed with England as Britannia had conquered a fair few of them in her time.

There was the odd alliance – Denmark and Iceland were bed-mates, as were Finland and Russia. It was like watching the Eurovision Song Contest, Brendan thought, with mutual back-slapping and point sharing. It had been known for Norway to threaten England with the removal of the Trafalgar Square Christmas Tree gift, if England didn't back Norwegian proposals. As the clock ticked sluggishly toward the hour, the Colombian delegate objected to the shade of yellow on FIFA corner flags proposed by Uruguay as it clashed with their kit. The Colombian suggested a move to fluorescent green which was immediately pounced upon by Mexico as an infringement of their copyrighted goalkeeping jerseys.

Will this never end, he thought. The first two hours that morning had been bad enough, what with the French going overboard on fabric strength. Who cared whether silk, satin or taffeta was used as long as it flapped about in the breeze. The original flaw was that the fabric was too starched – nearly had someone's eye out, he recalled. But now...why the hell didn't someone take the bull by the horns. He could be at home supervising the installation of the new manager, instead of growing old in this place. And wasn't Rio supposed to be hot? Brendan shivered in his short sleeves. He stood up.

"Gentlemen," he called, his strident tones punctuating the

hubbub, "may I propose an early lunch?"

This was agreed by all except Argentina who dissented as a matter of course.

After traipsing around the streets surrounding the hotel, Reg and Norman found a distinct lack of suitable establishments to provide a sandwich and a pot of tea. It seemed as though most shops were closed and as the clock approached five in the afternoon, hunger had forced them into Pizza Hut. After they finished, Reg took himself back to his room at the Kippax for a late afternoon siesta, while Norman decided to see a few of the nearby sights.

Later that evening, the two men went out to sample some of the local hostelries. They found that a similar problem applied to the afternoon – not many pubs appeared to be open. After trying out the least offensive, Reg and Norman decided to return to the hotel for a night-cap at the bar before retiring for the night.

Dave Bayley welcomed them back with open arms. Reg and Norman took a seat at the bar while Dave prepared to serve them.

"What can I get you?" he asked.

"Couple of pints should do it," said Reg.

Dave poured two pints of bitter and told Reg and Norman that the drinks were being paid for by the FA so not to worry about the bar bill.

"Great!" Reg exclaimed, "you joining us Dave?"

"Don't mind if I do," said a delighted Dave, and poured a pint for himself.

"That's a nice touch," said Norman, pointing to a sign above the bar that read 'DENIS LAW BAR'.

"That came from the Kippax," said Dave, "The Kippax

was the stand where I used to go when I was a kid."

"Oh right," said Reg, "The Kippax Hotel."

"Yeah, that's where the name came from," said Dave, "the stand was demolished in ninety-four. Everybody wanted a piece of it as a souvenir. Some people got bits of concrete steps, crush barriers, you know. Me, I got this." He gestured towards the bar sign.

"I played against Denis Law in his first game," announced Norman.

"Yeah?" said Dave. Reg looked on – he had not heard this before.

"Aye," Norman continued, "Christmas 1956. Denis was playing for Huddersfield and I was at Notts County then. We had to play 'em twice over Christmas and the bugger scored in the second game."

"I cannot believe that I am in the same room as somebody who played for Joe Mercer..."

"For three weeks," whispered Reg.

"...and played against Denis Law as well," finished Dave, by now in fan heaven.

"Little sod robbed the ball off me on the halfway line and before I could get anywhere near him, he'd put it in the back of the net," Norman said wistfully, "mind you, he was about twenty years younger than I was then. You could see he was going to be a good player though."

Dave was speechless. He had a new hero.

"I retired not long after that," Norman continued, "things were getting too fast for me."

The three sat in silence for a moment, contemplating their beers.

"Tell us Dave," Reg began, "why is London shut?"

"What do you mean?" asked Dave, startled out of his

reverie. He could not take his eyes off Norman who was slowly sipping his pint.

"Well," Reg continued, "we went out this afternoon for a bite to eat but everywhere was closed. Same tonight – we went out looking for a nice pub but they're all shut. I thought the capital of England would be a bit busier than this."

"That's right," Norman confirmed, "the city that never sleeps."

"That's New York," hissed Reg.

"Same thing," Norman hissed back.

"It's funny," said Dave, "but it does look like that sometimes. It's as though all the action happens in little pockets. You probably just walked through all the quiet bits."

"Probably," said Reg, unconvinced.

"So," said Dave, rubbing his hands, "big day tomorrow then?"

"Aye," said Reg.

"Nervous?" asked Dave.

"A bit," Reg replied. He had been back to his room to retrieve his briefcase. Within the case was a potted history of Reg's work, photographs of completed projects and recommendations and references from past customers. He had placed this on the barstool next to him and now opened it. As he leafed through the documents, he came across an old photograph of a boiler-suited Tom Finney stood next to a young Reg with a ballcock in his hand. He handed this to Dave.

"There y'are," he said, "that's part of my football connection."

"Blimey," Dave gasped, "is that Tom Finney?"

# THE KIPPAX HOTEL

"Aye," Reg replied, "when I left school, my Dad insisted I take up a trade and got me in as an apprentice with Tom Finney in Preston. Not many people knew he was a fully qualified plumber."

"Blimey," said Dave again, "if that had been part of City folklore, I would have been pinching that picture and putting it on a wall somewhere." He laughed.

"Have you got any pictures Norman?" asked Dave almost reverentially, "you know, of you and Joe Mercer or you and Denis Law?"

"He wasn't near any of 'em long enough," quipped Reg.

"Oy," said Norman, feigning annoyance, "I've got some pictures at home somewhere, but I don't know if I've got any of those two with me."

"Oh," said Dave, still too excited to be disappointed.

Reg continued looking through his documents: there were photographs of bathroom suites, central heating systems, Mansfield swimming baths and many instances of Reg's work.

Norman looked at Reg – he could tell the younger man was nervous. Probably the best thing, he thought, would be to change the subject of the interview to something more comfortable.

"Do you play any football, Dave?" he asked.

"Not much now," Dave said, "although I used to play for the Under Sixteen's at school. I just don't get much opportunity these days."

"Shame that," said Norman kindly, "Reg manages our pub team – the Forest Inn. Won the league last year."

"That's great," said Dave impressed, "eh, maybe you can convince the FA to give you the England manager's job while you're there tomorrow?" They all laughed which helped relieve some of Reg's tension.

Over the course of the next hour, Reg and Norman got to know Dave a lot better and the beginnings of a friendship were established. They discussed his plans for the hotel and his certainty that the quiet times were a thing of the past. Dave was investing in an Internet site and looking at the potential for marketing the hotel in different ways. Although Reg and Norman had their doubts – especially as the hotel seemed completely empty apart from themselves – they said nothing to dampen Dave's enthusiasm: after all, this was his life. It was fairly obvious he was obsessed by City and the hotel was a monument to him. Not too many visitors would understand everything; Dave had done this for himself – it was his temple.

So, they discussed football – this was the main connecting factor in all their lives. Norman recalled his own playing days in the late forties and fifties. Reg told of his father's hero worship of Stanley Matthews and the influence he had on his life. It helped relieve any anxiety Reg had for the next day and brought the three men closer together. They also discussed memories of Manchester where Reg had spent most of his school life.

Eventually, some time past midnight and halfway down a bottle of Dave's best single malt, Reg remembered what he had come to London for and announced he was off to bed.

"Bloody 'ell," said Norman, "'s 'at time already?"

"See you in the morning Dave," said Reg, "I could keep talking all night, but like you said, big day tomorrow."

"Yeah," said Dave disappointed. He never had opportunities to talk in depth like this, with people who he considered to be the same class as himself and the same sort of background. And Norman, bloody hell, he had turned out to be someone who had rubbed shoulders with two of City's best-loved heroes. He had really enjoyed himself. He perked up again.

"Night lads," he said, "breakfast is whenever you want it. Just give us a shout okay? No time limits."

"Yeah, cheers Dave," yawned Reg. He and Norman stood up – Norman was a little unsteady on his feet. He nodded his thanks to Dave – he didn't trust himself to speak at this moment.

Reg and Norman headed for the lift. When they arrived outside their respective doors they bid each other a good night and entered their rooms. Reg was soon in bed asleep; Norman climbed under the covers of his own bed but kept looking at the picture of John Gidman which was on the wall directly facing the bed. Even in the dark, he could feel that mesmeric gaze – the eyes were boring into him.

Enough was enough – he could cope with a million bananas suspended from the ceiling, but those things on the wall…yuk! Norman clambered out of bed, switched on the light and shuffled over to the offending picture. He grabbed both sides of the frame and levered the picture around until its back was facing the room and Mr Gidman faced the wall. The back of the picture revealed an even more disturbing picture of John Bond – Norman wasn't entirely sure who it was but knew that this picture was not much of an improvement on the last. With a grunt, he took the whole picture off the wall and placed it in the wardrobe for the night.

Norman returned to bed quite happily, switched off the light and was soon asleep.

# THE INTERVIEW

Thursday morning began with the same good weather. The two other candidates for the England manager's position were awake bright and early in their separate hotels at strategic points in the capital. Both Bryan Robson and Peter Reid were a little concerned at staying so far away from Lancaster Gate, but had been assured by June Whitless that it was to put the Press off the scent.

Bryan Robson, having the earliest interview of the day, threw down a quick breakfast and made his way towards the tube. He glanced at his watch – 8.30; an hour to go.

While Reg and Norman were still sleeping off the excesses of the previous night, a collection of grumpy old men were gathering at Lancaster Gate. Not only had they been forced from their comfortable homes, but for some of them this was the second time they had come to work this week. For three of them, it would mean a late arrival at the golf club. Absolute disgrace was the general feeling, and someone was going to pay.

June Whitless sat in her office typing the anticipated rejection letters to Peter Reid and Bryan Robson. She felt sure that by the end of the day, England would have a new manager and she'd had an important part to play. Her mind had been muddled over the last few days, what with dating Sir Richard, but she was comfortable with the fact that she had done it for Brendan.

Sir Richard had been charming, of course, and although the first date had been fairly innocent, she found that the second had been anything but. Sir Richard had asked her to the theatre and she had expected some dull play. Instead, she'd had her first experience of the ballet and her adrenaline and hormone levels had reached new heights due to the passion and ferocity of the performance. Sir Richard never knew what hit him.

Although June had sat silently through the performance, her insides were in turmoil – she clenched her fists, she bit the inside of her cheeks, she cried, she smiled, she cried again. In the limousine on the way back from the theatre, her emotional sea battered her defences. She had leapt upon the surprised knight with a lust as powerful as the ballet she had just witnessed.

Her performance carried on for a couple of hours afterwards at Sir Richard's house. Waking early on the Wednesday morning in his bed, the pangs of guilt were unbearable, but as her mind awoke fully, she knew that what she had done was for a grander purpose. Sir Richard was now putty in her hands. She had looked down upon the snoring knight at that point and smiled at her choice of words.

Each committee member who had walked past the door of her office seemed to be in a foul mood. All six were now here: Charles Stannersley, FA Chief Advisor; Piers Ffytch-Bottomley, FA Secretary; Victor Podmorency, Executive Sponsor; Lord Edward Burchley, Sports Advisor to Her Majesty the Queen; John Dennison, Amateur Football Association Chief Executive; and of course Sir Richard. Apart from Dickie, who seemed fairly content with life, they were spitting feathers. The morning interviews were not going to be easy, she thought, smiling contentedly..

Her telephone rang. "Good morning, FA Headquarters. How may I help you?" she asked sweetly.

"June," it was Brendan. June's heart skipped a beat. She glanced quickly at her watch – twenty past nine. That meant it was twenty past six in the morning in Rio – Brendan was up early.

"How the hell are you?" asked Brendan from thousands of miles south.

"I'm fine," she croaked, "how's Brazil?"

"Bloody raining, interspersed with moaning Frenchies and there's some idiot playing the tom-toms outside my hotel window," he barked, "listen – how's the recruitment going? Everything okay?"

"Fine," she said, warming with confidence, "interviews today – Robson and Reid this morning and Atkinson this afternoon. I planned it that way so our man would get the easier interview."

"Good girl," shouted Brendan and June could almost feel him smiling, "now put me through to Scratcher – I want to make sure he's got his head screwed on properly."

"Okay," said June, knowing full well that Sir Richard had managed to screw a lot of things properly.

# THE INTERVIEW

Sir Richard Scratcher rocked back and forth in his plush leather chair, nursing a crystal glass containing vodka and a small dash of tonic. Another half an hour until the first interview – the Reid chap. Reid, he mulled. Doesn't matter, he thought, the name isn't Atkinson and if it isn't Atkinson, it doesn't matter one jot. He sipped his vodka and looked back over the last couple of days. Things certainly had started to look up.

The telephone on his desk rang suddenly, causing Sir Richard to jump involuntarily, drink splashing his trousers. Blasted thing, he thought. He reached out a long arm and picked up the receiver.

"Harumph," he coughed. He always answered the phone like this – he believed it unsettled the caller, "Sir Richard Scratcher speaking," he added.

"Sir Richard?" it was June.

"Ah yes, June, what can I do for you," he asked with all the charm he could muster.

"I've got Mr Fendon on the line for you," she said abruptly, and transferred the call.

"Sir Richard?" shouted Brendan Fendon from Brazil.

"How the hell are you dear boy? Good weather I hope?" asked Sir Richard.

"Never mind that," shouted Brendan, "how are those interviews going?"

"Just fine, just fine," smiled Sir Richard, "we've got two chaps this morning for show, and then we've got your man this afternoon."

"My man?" asked Brendan, "it'd better be the right man."

"Of course," said Sir Richard indignantly, "Atkinson."

"That's all right then," said Brendan, " who's on the committee?"

Sir Richard reeled off the names.

"Good," barked Brendan. "Most of that lot will have buggered off by lunch. Listen, Dickie, I feel very uncomfortable having to be down here while you're making decisions. Qualifying for the World Cup is vital so we have to make every effort to install the right man. Imagine how much revenue we stand to lose if we lose next week? Make sure this goes nice and smoothly…is that clear?"

"Of course dear boy," said Sir Richard, "as clear as crystal," he added, looking longingly at his glass.

"Just make sure you get the right man. You know what he looks like don't you?"

"Err, well…"

"Oh come on Dickie," said Brendan despairingly, "Atkinson – Mr Bojangles; permanent suntan, gold jewellery, big, bold, brash."

"Ah yes, I know the fellah," Sir Richard didn't but thought it best not to admit it.

"Right then," said Brendan, wishing he was slightly closer to the irritating Sir Richard than he was presently. "Put me back to June, would you – I need to tell her what to put in the contract. Oh and I'll be back late tomorrow evening, if the bloody Frenchies can decide on fabric thickness for these corner flags. Get June to organise a press conference for tomorrow morning, okay?"

"Consider it done," said Sir Richard.

"It'd better be," shouted Brendan. Sir Richard leapt for the button which transferred the call back to June and replaced his receiver. It'd better be, he mocked, making a face. He'd show Mister Brendan Fendon that Dick Scratcher was a man to be reckoned with. He took a large gulp of his vodka and resumed rocking.

# THE INTERVIEW

At 9.30, Reg was just about awake and looking at the ceiling of his room, wondering whether he should take a shower or have a cup of coffee first. Meanwhile, Bryan Robson was just sitting down before a half dozen of the most sullen faces he could remember being in one place.

At 9.40, Reg stepped into a hot shower and Bryan Robson realised that the interview was not exactly going his way.

Edward Burchley: "How do you feel about following your father's footsteps into the England job?"

Robson: "Pardon? Oh, do you mean Bobby? He wasn't my father…."

Burchley: "What? Of course he was your father. Are you implying we don't know anything about football?"

Robson: "No, no I'm not, but he wasn't me da'."

Piers Ffytch-Bottomley: " You seem awfully young for this job. How old was your father when he took the role?"

Robson: "Look, you've got it all wrong – Bobby Robson is not my father."

Victor Podmorency: "Is not? Don't you mean was not?"

Robson: "Eh?"

Victor Podmorency: "Passed away didn't he?"

Robson: "No, he hasn't. He's still managin'"

Podmorency: "Bobby Robson's not dead? Why isn't he here then instead of his boy?"

Burchley: "Haven't the foggiest. Must be an oversight. Fendon again."

Bryan Robson decided on his own terms that twenty-five minutes was all he could take. He excused himself and left.

At 10.00am, as Peter Reid stepped out of the doors of his hotel towards the tube, Reg knocked on Norman's room.

Norman opened the door dressed impressively in a dressing gown, which was around three sizes too big.

"Blimey Norm, you shrunk?" asked Reg in mock astonishment.

"Cheeky bugger," Norm responded, "'s just a bit on the big side. I thought I looked quite dashing, bit like Ronald Colman."

"More like Ronnie Corbett," quipped Reg, "Fancy some breakfast?"

"Not 'arf," said Norm, "let me get some civvies on and I'll be right with you."

Reg had dressed simply in sweats and joggers. There was no way he was risking a bit of cooked breakfast finding its way on to his best suit.

"You okay eating in that Reg?" asked Norm.

"What d'ya mean?" asked Reg looking down at his navy sweats.

"Well, you don't want to ruin your interview suit with your eating habits do you?" said Norm, chuckling "That is what you're wearing this aft, isn't it?"

"Get out of it you cheeky old sod," laughed Reg, "get your dress off and put some pants on."

At 10.15, as Peter Reid was making his first tube change, and Reg and Norm were announcing their presence in the restaurant, the six committee members were discussing the first interview while propping up the executive bar at Lancaster Gate. The FA Committee was an elderly group – Piers Ffytch-Bottomley was the youngest at sixty-five, with Lord Burchley the eldest at a sprightly seventy-six. Sir Richard came in third at seventy-three.

Between them, they didn't know an awful lot about

football – attaining their positions either through money, breeding, or in the case of Sir Richard, who was a director at Blackburn, being as far away from his own club as his fellow directors could put him. They relied heavily on Brendan Fendon, who not only knew about football, but had a good business brain as well. This suited Brendan – he had the power, while the committee backed him up. Although ignorant in most things football, they knew they had it relatively cushy.

"Can't understand why he wouldn't admit to being Bobby's son," said Edward Burchley, "I mean, it wouldn't have gone against him". Lord Burchley sat on various committees as a way of making sure everyone was aware of how close he was to the Queen. Sports Advisor to the Queen normally meant that his secretary would make arrangements for the Royal Box at Wembley to be made ready should Her Majesty be visiting. Normally, Burchley would embellish his involvement and have people believing that he and 'HM' – as he called her – were best of friends.

"Absolutely not," said Piers Ffytch-Bottomley, "after all, nepotism isn't an issue is it? Although sometimes, good habits do run through from father to son." Bottomley's father had been an FA advisor and Piers had automatically followed in his father's footsteps, despite his lack of interest.

"Is it too late to ask Bobby?" asked Burchley.

"Didn't apply," shouted Sir Richard, hurriedly.

"Who's next then?" said Charles Stannersley, who at the age of seventy was on twelve different committees, but if pushed could only remember eight of them. "If we can get the next bugger to pack it in after half an hour, I can be on the first green by twelve, what!" He chortled loudly.

"I really don't think that would be good for FA publicity,"

said a shocked John Dennison.

"Only a joke, old boy, only a joke," replied Stannersley, who was still chuckling and reminding himself to tell his golfing partner of the day what an absolute first class wit he was.

"Does this mean you won't be here for the afternoon interview Charles?" asked Sir Richard.

"Unfortunately not, old boy. Fund raiser at the golf club. Couldn't possibly miss it – good cause and all that."

"I won't be able to stay beyond lunch either," piped up John Dennison, "Parks Football presentation in Sheffield at three o'clock." John Dennison had represented the Amateur Football Association for the past five years, taking the position when the previous incumbent had died in a sexual liaison with oxygen starvation undertones. He had been found with a plastic bag over his head and a medium sized Jaffa in his mouth, tied to a chair in his own bedroom. Dennison unfortunately knew nothing about football and knew it was too late to try, but he was considered the safe option.

"I'll stick around, Dickie," said Victor Podmorency.

Podmorency had been a pop star in the sixties under the name Karl Krampton, with his band 'The Klub'. After four top ten hits, the hits dried up – mainly due to The Karl Krampton Klub inevitably being referred to as the KKK, which many people wrongly assumed to be a reference to the Ku Klux Klan. Political incorrectness ended their career. Victor used the money he'd made to start up a record company and had bought into a football club in 1972 as a way of dodging tax.

"I don't like to miss these interviews – you never know when you get something entertaining," Podmorency went on, "do you remember that time we had that hearing for George Graham and he arrived with a brown paper parcel? We thought that he was trying to give us a bung and it turned out to be his sandwiches. Bloody funny that."

"I remember that," said Sir Richard, "egg and cress." Sir Richard was allergic to eggs and spent the remainder of that particular interview trying to keep his stomach from lurching.

"Well, I have to finalise arrangements for HM's visit to Wembley," said Burchley, "so I'll cut a dash soon."

"Well, I'll still be here," said Piers Ffytch-Bottomley, "I'll fly the flag too."

"Just us three then," said Sir Richard, "but let's not forget the 11 o'clock man."

"How could we?" barked Burchley, "what's his name again?"


At 10.45, Reg and Norman leaned back in their chairs after a full breakfast. Their stomachs were fit to burst.

"Enjoy that?" asked Dave Bayley, who had arrived to clear the plates.

"Hit the spot, that did," said Reg,

"Aye," said Norm, disguising a belch.

The restaurant at the Kippax was a little subtler than some of the other rooms. The plaque over the doorway had announced it as the Rodney Marsh restaurant, and inside it was more sparsely decorated than the rest of the hotel.

"I like my guests to concentrate on the food," said Dave, by way of explanation, don't want people too distracted from what's on their plates."

Reg and Norm had noticed the dinner menu while waiting for their breakfast. Amongst some obvious culinary delights, it also offered bar snacks – Bobby McDonald Burgers with Keith Curle fries; Nicky Weaver's Pie; Soup of the Steve Daley; Irish 'Paul Stewart'; Perry Suckling Pig; Goalden Moulden Haddock; 'Donachie Babs', and Shaun 'Goater' Cheese. None of these sounded particularly appetising. There was even a children's menu – Fish F'Inge Haaland, and Big Mal with fries. Dave had obviously been scraping the 'pun' barrel when he came up with those, thought Reg.

The breakfast, however, had been excellent. Dave was obviously good in the kitchen.

"What time's the interview, Reg?" asked Dave.

"Two," said Reg.

"Plenty of time yet," said Norm, still rubbing his swollen stomach.

"More coffee?" asked Dave.

"Why not, said Reg, holding out his cup.

By 11.00 am, Peter Reid was sitting in the chair previously occupied by Bryan Robson. He was feeling distinctly uncomfortable. The aged faces before him all appeared to be scowling – there was not one friendly visage to be seen. Each and every one seemed to be stabbing their pens repeatedly into the A4 pads on the table in front of them. He twiddled his thumbs and concentrated on a strategically placed FA Coaching Manual in front of him. That was there for a reason, he thought. Maybe he should have swotted up first.

Edward Burchley opened the interview: "Now, Reid."

A nervous Peter Reid immediately leaned forwards and picked up the FA Coaching Manual, turning to page 1.

Burchley could not believe his eyes. "I said REID!" he shouted.

# THE INTERVIEW

"I am," squeaked Peter Reid, "give us a chance, I've only just opened it"

Podmorency: "I say, what on earth are you doing? You should have boned up on this sort of thing before you arrived."

Stannersley: "Bloody bad manners, what?"

Dennison: "Hear, hear."

Bottomley: "Outrage."

Reid: "I'm sorry, but..."

Burchley (furious): "Well dash it all, it's not good enough. I'm not sitting around here waiting for you to finish that before you deign to talk to us."

Lord Burchley rose from his chair and hurriedly gathered his things. Sir Richard smiled inwardly – this was going better than he had anticipated.

"I'll bid you good day," Burchley added as he hustled out of the room.

"Well Mr Reid," said Sir Richard loudly amongst the din of the other committee members complaining about the youth of today, "I don't see that there's any point in prolonging the agony."

"But, I don't understand," coughed the young manager, "I only..."

Sir Richard by now had risen from his chair and was making his way around the table. As he arrived at Peter Reid's chair, the younger man stood. Sir Richard put his arm around Reid's shoulders in an effort to comfort him, while gently ushering him towards the door.

"Don't feel too badly about it," said Sir Richard softly, "they're very hard to please. Miss Whitless will show you out."

A puzzled Peter Reid left the room and Sir Richard set

about calming the other committee members.

"Drink anyone?" he asked. That worked.

Ten minutes later in the bar, Peter Reid had been forgotten. Most of the committee were now taking one last drink before setting off for their afternoon's entertainment.

"This chap this afternoon," said Stannersley, "any good?"

"Can't be any worse, what?" barked Podmorency.

"It's Atkinson," said Sir Richard, "you know, United, Albion, Forest...Brendan's very keen."

"Oh well," chirped Dennison, "if Brendan's keen then I'm quite happy for Atkinson to be the man."

"Me too," added Stannersley, "Brendan knows what he's talking about."

"Indeed," added Dennison, "having looked at the first two, I don't personally feel we have any other option."

"Anybody met him?" asked Bottomley.

Six blank faces looked back in response.

"Well we know that he was a United and Albion man, oh and Forest," said Dennison, repeating what Sir Richard had said.

"I remember the fellah," cried Victor Podmorency, "he was in Madrid. I'm sure he was managing one of the Spanish teams when I was buying a villa over there in... oh God when was it... must have been '86, '87. Yeah, Atkinson... not often you hear an English name on the news when you're over there."

"European experience," blurted Stannersley, "first class. Brendan does know what he's on about."

"Pity he couldn't be here to rubber stamp it," said Bottomley, "mind you, if it goes wrong, we can always blame Brendan."

# THE INTERVIEW

"Hear hear," said Podmorency, "one last drink, Sir Richard?"

"Twist my arm, why don't you?" said a satisfied Sir Richard. Things were going very well indeed.

Reg checked his appearance in his full-length mirror. Very nice, he thought, very nice. Smart, not too dapper, but smart. His tan, though fading, was just enough to add tone to his features and not make him look too gothic in his black suit. In addition to his gold link bracelet, he wore his St Christopher medal – given to him by his Mother for his eighteenth birthday – as a lucky charm. You'll get this, he told himself, no problem. His mind kept returning to the original telephone conversation with Sir Richard, where he'd been told that he was favourite, and this encouraged him even more.

Reg turned brightly on his heels and went looking for Norman. Bloody old fool had wind and had disappeared to the toilet about 20 minutes ago. Reg checked his watch – 1.30pm. Come on Norman, what are you up to, he whispered to himself.

Outside Room 10-1, Reg waited impatiently. He couldn't take the suspense – he rapped on the door.

"Come on Norm," he shouted, "what the bloody 'ell yer playing at?"

Muffled noises came from within. After a few seconds, which seemed to Reg like minutes, the door opened and a sad looking Norman eased out.

"Do not go in there," he advised.

"Christ Norm, has summat died or what?" asked Reg, wrinkling his nose.

"I can't help it," said Norman feebly, "this always happens after a cooked breakfast. I reckon it's them beans."

"Give me strength," wheezed Reg, "'ang on, I've got a cork somewhere."

"Get out of it and leave me alone," said Norman. He was mortified.

"Let's see if we can find a Boots," said Reg, "I'm not losing this job just because you're making your trousers cough."

By 2.00pm, Reg and Norman were sitting in the committee room at Lancaster Gate. Luckily, they had found a chemist and Norman had hurriedly swallowed something to halt his wind. Unfortunately, this had not yet kicked in and Norman was squirming uncomfortably in his chair.

On the table in front of him, Reg had placed his briefcase, which contained his plumbing portfolio. All the examples of his best work, which he had been showing Dave Bayley the night before, were enclosed. He felt comfortable with it there: like an old friend with good memories.

Smiling at them from across the table were Sir Richard Scratcher, Victor Podmorency and Piers Ffytch-Bottomley. They had fed well at lunch, washing down a sublime three course Italian with a couple of bottles of Chianti. All three were distinctly mellow. Reg, unnerved slightly by the smiles, fiddled with his gold link bracelet as he waited for the questions.

Sir Richard looked Reg up and down, remembering the description Brendan had given him that morning. Suntanned? Yes. Gold jewellery? Yes. Sir Richard introduced himself, Podmorency and Bottomley before beginning. Reg introduced Norman as his right hand man.

"Now Mr Atkinson," said Sir Richard, "you know why you're here?"

# THE INTERVIEW

"Well yes," said Reg.

"Perhaps you'd like to tell us why you think you're the best man for the job," added Sir Richard.

"I'm the best there is," Reg started, "you've seen some of my work from my application – you'll find none better. Good quality, tidy, prompt – no one has ever complained about my work."

Well, thought Reg, not yet, but if Mrs Butterman goes traipsing through her en suite in her bare feet and wonders why she's getting damp, then she just might be the first.

"What did you think of Madrid?" beamed Podmorency.

"Well," Reg replied, unsure how his Spanish holiday was public knowledge, "it was lovely. Didn't stop long, but enough to see what I wanted to."

"Yes, marvellous place, marvellous place" Podmorency nodded in agreement, "I thought it was you I saw."

Reg was dumbfounded – he'd only been on a day trip. How on earth would this bloke have recognised him? He'd never set eyes on him before.

"How did you find the people? Treat you well?" Podmorency asked.

"Well yes. Like I said, I wasn't really there long enough, but they were okay."

Podmorency seemed satisfied with this and nodded. "Ever been to Budapest?" he asked.

"Err, no," said Reg.

"Oh you really should," said Podmorency, reclining dreamily, "beautiful place, just beautiful. Flower of the Danube."

"Well, let's talk about your career successes," said Ffytch-Bottomley, attempting to get back to the subject, "especially United and Albion,"

"Ah yes," said Reg now on more familiar ground. Buxton United and Burton Albion were examples of his best work.

"United wanted more power to the spray formation," he began, "the visiting teams were okay, but United just didn't have that strength for the home side – must have been something to do with the pressure."

Sir Richard nodded sagely. One thing he did know was that Manchester United teams faced a lot of pressure, both from the opposition and the media.

"So I fixed that," Reg continued, "mind you, we had to start from scratch, y' know, all new kit, didn't we Norman?"

"Yes that's right," offered Norman, surprised into releasing one cheek. Oh-ho he thought.

Sir Richard nodded again. Yes, he'd heard about the various new kits at United.

"Did you accompany Mr Atkinson to Madrid, Mr Whaddon?" asked Podmorency.

"Err, no," wheezed Norman, "I didn't."

"But you did help at the United and Albion jobs?" Podmorency continued.

"Yes, that's right," said Norman, thinking it best to be formal, "I've assisted Mr Atkinson on all his jobs for the last fifteen years."

"But not Madrid?"

"No," said Norman.

Podmorency frowned with confusion – "but you said you assisted on all jobs over the last fifteen years."

"Yes," said Norman.

"But I assumed..."

"Never ass..." Norman began.

"What Norman means to say," Reg interrupted before Norman's favourite expression hit the room, "is that he is my assistant manager, but he didn't come to Madrid as that was my holiday."

"Ah," said Podmorency, now a little clearer, "that's right, you weren't there long were you? Probably right to class it as a holiday, but still, valuable experience, what?"

"Yes, I suppose," said Reg.

"Now tell us about your recent history," said Sir Richard, "you were at Forest weren't you?"

"Yes," said Reg, confused.

"Epping Forest?" asked Podmorency, "good mushroom picking there I'm told."

"No, it's the Forest Inn, Nottingham," Reg replied. Podmorency nodded his understanding as the words Nottingham Forest appeared in his mind, "if you don't mind talking about hobbies and holidays, it was while I was doing the job at United that I got the inspiration for my 'Rambling Rose' formation I use at Forest."

"'Rambling Rose'?" inquired Victor Podmorency, thinking of Slim Whitman and a youthful time at the Bradford Alhambra.

"Yes," said Reg, now in full flow, "the 'Rambling Rose' formation. You won't find this in any textbook, which is why it's hard to defend against. It's based on a type of shower spray."

Norman shifted in his seat and unwittingly released another blockbuster.

"Now Albion was a different job entirely, but I can quite honestly say," said Reg, just picking up the first tendrils of Norman's output, "that it was a much warmer club when I left. I have some photographs here if you'd like to see them." Reg opened his folder and extracted a few relevant snapshots.

"Well done, Mr Atkinson," said a smiling Sir Richard, reaching out a hand, "absolutely splendid, now..."

Sir Richard wrinkled his nose, gauging the change in air quality. Norman looked downwards, giving nothing away.

Piers Ffytch-Bottomley had also established that something wasn't quite right. He and Sir Richard had their suspicions and looked at Reg and Norman accusingly.

"That'll be your air-conditioning," said Reg quickly, "sometimes you get the odd backdraft from the vents. Hey, I'll tell you what – I'll fix that free of charge if I get the job." Nice touch, he thought., and extracted more photographs of an air conditioning job he'd done at the council offices.

"Yes, good idea, but I think we should adjourn until the air clears," suggested Ffytch-Bottomley, ignoring the spread of photographs..

"No need for adjournment," said Sir Richard, "I think we've heard enough to be satisfied that Mr Atkinson is indeed the man for the job."

"I agree," said Podmorency, hurrying towards the door.

Sir Richard held out his hand. Reg took it and pumped it vigorously. Norman leapt from his seat in surprise, which, all things considered, was a mistake.

"Congratulations, Mr Atkinson," smiled Sir Richard, "I'll have Miss Whitless draft up a contract and we can get everything in place for you to start straight away."

"Straight away?" stammered a shocked Reg, "but..."

"You don't have anything else on do you?" asked Sir Richard.

"Well no, but..."

"...and we are on a tight schedule," continued Sir Richard satisfied. "Miss Whitless will make the arrangements. Now if we can just leave this room, I'll be an exceptionally happy man."

Sir Richard jerked open the door and all five men left the room, quickly. Reg took a few moments to gather up his unviewed portfolio of photographs and replaced them within his folder. Once outside, they all breathed deep lungfuls of clean air, relieved to be free of such an incredibly putrid smell.

"Air conditioning, you say?" asked Ffytch-Bottomley, breathlessly.

"Aye," said Reg, "happens all the time, eh Norm? Specially in these old buildings."

Sir Richard thought about this and a seed of an idea planted itself in his mind. If only he was in charge full time – he knew just the place. Maybe one day…

Five minutes later and Reg was in dreamland. The three committee members had pumped his hand vigorously in congratulation and Reg was now in charge of what would be the biggest piece of work ever to come his way.

Sir Richard had asked him about his 'backroom staff'. Obviously Norman would be his assistant, but Sir Richard had told him to appoint whoever he wanted to support him in the job. Reg couldn't wait to get in touch with Kevin and the boys to get them off the kitchen jobs.

Reg was still stunned, sitting in the reception at the FA, waiting for Norman who had found a toilet, when June Whitless arrived in front of him with papers in her hand.

"Congratulations, Mr Atkinson," she beamed.

"Thanks," he said.

"Now if you'll just sign these," she continued.

"Yes, what…?"

"It's your contract, Mr Atkinson," she smiled, "it's in three parts: five hundred thousand for completion of the job, with a five hundred thousand pound bonus for a successful result, and an immediate five hundred thousand pound bonus for signing today. You'll be on full expenses during your time with us and there'll be a review following the completion of the task in hand, where you may be asked to extend the contract."

Reg gaped.

"Here's a pen, Mr Atkinson," said June, handing him her best Parker. Reg took it. He looked blindly at the contract, not seeing a word, but the amounts were ringing through his head.

"Just here will do," said June, pointing at a place on the top sheet, "and I'm authorised to give you a cheque for the signing bonus here and now."

Reg signed.

"And here," said June, pointing again.

Reg signed that one too. Oh boy, he thought. Oh boy.

"I've organised a press conference for tomorrow afternoon at one o'clock lunchtime," June advised, "please make sure you're here about half an hour before and I'll prepare you for any questions which may arise."

"P-p-press conference?" stuttered Reg.

"Yes," said June, "perfectly normal, just make sure you're here. I've arranged for your rooms to be kept on at the hotel."

She handed him the cheque, which Reg accepted as though receiving something incredibly fragile. June made as if to turn away, and hesitated.

"I'll get this contract copied up for you and let you have your own copy tomorrow, okay?"

# THE INTERVIEW

Reg nodded, numbly and watched June as she returned to her office.

June took the signed contracts back to her desk and filed them. She'd copy them tomorrow. She sat back in her chair with a contented grin. Piece of cake, she thought. Sir Richard popped his head around her office door as she relaxed.

"Theatre tonight?" he asked.

What the hell, she thought, definite cause for celebration. "Yes please," she replied sweetly.

# SPEND, SPEND, SPEND

After waiting in the lobby at Lancaster Gate for what seemed an age, Reg eventually saw Norman making his way towards him. Reg stood and held the doors open so they could exit together. The two minute journey back to the hotel was made jauntily. Reg was feeling chipper, but still a little bemused.

"I thought you'd fell down the hole," said Reg.

"Nearly," said Norm, "but the thought of this job brought me back." Norman was as stunned as Reg. This was beyond his wildest dreams and he knew Reg would be feeling the same way.

"I can't believe it," said Reg, "I thought it'd be much harder. I mean, I didn't even have to show me photos."

"Right, then," said Norm, rubbing his hands, "celebration time?"

"Not 'arf," chuckled Reg, "I've just signed a contract for one an' 'arf million quid."

"You've what?" Norman stopped dead in his tracks.

# SPEND, SPEND, SPEND

"Woman came out of the office and said sign here," Reg said, "she said if I signed there and then I'd get a five hundred grand bonus on top of the million for doing a good job."

"'ang on, 'ang on," Norman blurted, "you've signed a contract for a million quid plus you've got a five hundred grand bonus?"

"Yup," smirked Reg, feeling happier by the minute.

"I take it you read it carefully," said Norman.

"Well, err..." said Reg uncertainly, "she said..."

"I know what she said Reg, you just told me," Norm continued, "but did you read it?"

"Well, not exactly," Reg said.

"Yer'd best give it here then," said Norman, "and see what you've let yerself in for."

"Ah," said Reg, "I haven't exactly, er..."

"You did get a copy didn't you, Reg?" Norman interrupted.

"Well, she said she'd copy it and let me have it tomorrow," Reg said quietly.

"So we can't check the finer points, then," said an incredulous Norman, whose brain had now started working.

"Well what finer points could there be apart from me earning a wad of cash?" asked Reg indignantly.

"Well, firstly, what about your staff?" asked Norman. "Are you expected to pay us out of your pocket or the FA's, 'cos either way, I'll be wanting a rise."

"Oh," said Reg.

"And secondly," Norman continued, "what about the kit? Who's going to be payin' for the machinery, parts and whatever?"

"Ah well, she said full expenses. That might mean…" said Reg.

"And," said Norman, now in full flow, "when are you going to start? Any ideas on dates..."

"Err..." said Reg.

"..'cos don't forget, you'll need somebody down here to help," Norman went on, "you can't expect Big Kev to drop everything at a minute's notice."

"But..."

"and another thing," said Norman, "what if there's some small print about money back guarantees and stuff?"

"Norm," said Reg loudly.

"What," said Norm, just as loudly.

"Shut up," said Reg. Nothing was going to dampen his mood. He'd won the lottery. He didn't care about the whys and wherefores – let Norman do the worrying. Reg was content to bask in his own limelight for the moment. Euphoria was its own medicine.

They reached the front steps of the Kippax Hotel and climbed up towards the Maine Entrance.

"After you," said Reg as he opened the doors.

Norman entered the hotel, muttering to himself, immediately followed by a grinning Reg.

Dave Bayley greeted the men as they returned through the foyer.

"Reg, Norman," he cried, "how'd it go?"

"Got it, mate," grinned Reg.

"That's fantastic," said Dave, ecstatically, "well done the pair of you."

"Aye," said Norman, "but don't ask him about any of the smaller points, will you, like, when's he start, where..."

"Eh?" said Dave.

"Oh, don't bother with him," said Reg, "Norm is good at finding problems with everything."

"Huh!" moaned Norman.

"But it's great news anyway," said Dave, "eh? Bottle of champers to celebrate?"

"Well, I..." said Reg.

"It's still on the FA's bill," Dave smiled.

"Well in that case," said Reg cheerily, "what the hell."

Dave beckoned them into the bar, where Reg and Norman took up their seats underneath the 'DENIS LAW BAR' sign again.

Reg looked at Norman – for as long as he'd known him, Norman had always had a talent for spotting the worst in every situation. He was sitting there now, thinking of the apocalypse, Reg could tell. At least his wind problem seemed to have cleared up. God, that could have spoilt everything. Reg had given himself a mental pat on the back for the spontaneity with which he had diverted the blame on to the air conditioning. That could've been the clincher.

They sat there in silence waiting for Dave Bayley to come back. Apparently he was hunting down the best bottle of Champagne he had in stock. Last time Reg had supped any quality champagne was after the Forest Inn had won the cup last year, but that was Tesco's own. He was looking forward to this bottle as it would herald a new dawn, a new Reg.

Dave returned looking dusty. He held an even dustier bottle in his hand.

"Here we go," he said, "lovely and cold and fresh from the cellar, or relegation zone as I call it."

"Looks a good 'un," said Reg, rubbing his hands on his thighs in anticipation.

"You wouldn't know a good 'un if it hit you on the 'ead," said Norman.

"Don't be cheeky,"

"Best bottle in the house," announced Dave grandly, "Bollinger '68. City won the league that year. I bought this in preparation for their next championship as it was produced during their last. Mind you, it'll have probably gone off by then."

"Bloody 'ell," Reg blurted, "how much does that go for?"

"About £200 if you were paying for it," said Dave.

Reg shook his head – some people would just shell out for this and not have a second thought. Dave placed three champagne flutes on the bar carefully. He gave the bottle a quick twist around the neck – almost like throttling a chicken, Reg thought – and the cork popped dramatically, making both Reg and Norman jump, but both cheered: it seemed the right thing to do when champagne was opened.

Dave poured the champagne into the flutes, taking care to lose as little as possible. The bubbles seemed to have a life of their own, almost leaping out of the glasses from just a small drop of liquid. Dave filled the flutes as best he could and placed the bottle on the bar. He reached for a glass – Reg and Norman did likewise.

"Here's to a successful installation of undersoil heating," Dave began, raising his glass, "and to the future successes of Reg Atkinson and Norman Whaddon."

"I'll drink to that," said Reg, and they all raised their glasses to drink a toast.

"Nice drop of bubbly that," said Norman.

"Mmm," said Reg, who couldn't distinguish it from the last bottle of Tesco's own.

# SPEND, SPEND, SPEND

"So how long do you think it'll take you?" asked Dave.

"Probably about 6 months," said Reg.

"Empty head didn't read the contract before he signed it..." said Norman.

"Oh," said Dave. Reg just shrugged and sipped some more champagne.

"...and he hasn't got a copy yet either," Norman added.

"No," said Reg, "but I've got this." Reg pulled out a cheque made out for £500,000 from his jacket pocket.

"Bloody 'ell," Dave gasped, "five hundred grand?"

"Aye," said Reg, "and that's just for starters. I wish me dad had still been alive to see this – it would have made him so proud. He always wanted me to be involved in football, and this is about as good as I'll get.

Dave poured some more champagne. He excused himself and hurried out of the bar.

"Where's he off to?" Norman wondered.

"Get some more air freshener for your room, probably," Reg quipped.

Norman made a face. It wasn't long before Dave returned carrying two small picture frames. On closer inspection, Reg saw that the frames covered what looked like betting slips.

"You know what dad's expectations of their sons are like?" said Dave.

"Yeah," said Reg wistfully.

"Well grandparents are sometimes worse," Dave continued. "My Grandad put two bets on at his local William Hill's in the mid-seventies. I was ten, and I'd just started playing for the school Under Eleven's football team."

Reg and Norman looked at the frames: they both contained William Hill betting slips. One was a ten pound bet on David Bayley to play football for England at Wembley; the other was another ten pound bet on David Bayley to score a goal for England at Wembley.

"I didn't know he'd put 'em on until after he died," Dave continued, "he used to take me to all me school games and cheer me on. 'Cos my dad left when I was a toddler and me mum didn't have time, it was always me Grandad who kept me going with football. It was him that took me to me first game at City.

"He died when I was fifteen. Part of my inheritance was these old betting slips. I just framed them – obviously there was no chance of ever winning with 'em."

"Good odds," said Reg. Playing for England was quoted at 1000/1, but scoring for England was quoted at 10,000/1.

"Yeah, not bad are they?" said Dave, "apparently, you can't get odds this good any more."

"No?" said Norman.

"Nah, the bookies caught on after a while," Dave went on, "all sorts of bets were coming in for Olympic gold medal winners, Wimbledon winners, you know. I think the year 2000 had a big part to play. The bookies got wise after a bit and offered a maximum 1000/1 – too many proud fathers putting pressure on their sons."

Reg nodded. He remembered the pressure from his Dad to play football instead of cricket. Fathers had a lot to answer for...or grandfathers in Dave's case.

Dave poured the last of the champagne.

"One more toast," said Reg, "here's to Dave Bayley. He might not have met his Grandad's expectations, but he's exceeded mine."

"I'll drink to that," Norman piped up.

Dave beamed.

# Spend, Spend, Spend

Twenty minutes later, Reg was strutting down the street, still in his best bib and tucker, looking for a branch of Barclays. The cheque for £500,000 was absolutely red hot in his pocket – Reg was sure that it would burn up if it wasn't put somewhere safe.

He checked his watch – still only half past four. The afternoon was never ending – he seemed to have done so much, but then again, the interview had only lasted about half an hour. Here we go, he thought to himself, as he spotted a Barclays' sign just down the street.

Fortunately, his bank account was held at Barclays – it was a simple matter of placing the cheque into his account and watching his balance swell. Another plus point was that the cheque – or was it a draft? Reg wasn't quite sure – was considered cash due to the FA's relationship with the bank.

Reg left Barclays a happy man. Nothing Norman could say today could dispirit him now – he felt like he'd won the lottery. Biggest thing in my life, he thought as he sauntered through the London streets.

Reg almost made it past the window of the jewellers without stopping. Almost. The sign gave the name of the jewellers as 'JH Blinkstein' – there was a pair of earrings on the model of a woman's head. The head had a look of Carol and the earrings looked dazzling. This must be that new positive advertising, he thought, or fate. Whatever, try as he might, he could not see a price tag, but the woman's head seemed to beckon him.

"In for a penny..." he whispered to himself and tried the door. Locked.

Oh well, he thought, and was about to turn away when a buzzer sounded and the door clicked open. He pushed and the door opened – an old fashioned bell heralded the imposition. Blimey, Reg thought as he walked into the jewellers and looked around, I've become Mr Benn. He waited for the shopkeeper to appear.

It was small inside, with a shop floor of no more than ten feet square. The floor was a chestnut square of highly polished wood surrounded on three sides by glass cabinets, containing dazzling pieces of gold, silver, diamond and more. Uplighters served to enhance the brilliance of the merchandise.

Reg noticed the shopkeeper, a smallish older man – JH Blinkstein? – behind one of the display cabinets around the same time as he smelt what he thought must have been jewellery cleaner. The man wore a kind of eyepiece and was polishing something carefully.

"Good afternoon sir," he said, appearing to not look up.

"Hello," said Reg in return, "I thought you were closed."

"Ach, security," said the man with the trace of an accent, "can't be too careful."

"I was looking at the earrings in the window," said Reg, wondering about the accent – German?

The man placed the object – which Reg now saw to be a gold bangle – on the top of the display cabinet in front of him and removed his eyepiece. Reg did a quick double take – the eye that appeared from behind the eyepiece looked false. A glass eye behind an eyepiece? Surely not.

"Ah yes, earrings," said the old man and moved over to the back of the window, bumping clumsily into the counter surface and the window shutter.

"Oops," said Reg, "you okay there? Want some help?"

"Ach, my depth perception is not so good," said the old man as he fiddled with a latch and swung open a small door. More evidence for the glass eye, thought Reg.

Reg watched him reach in and before he'd had chance to tell him which pair, the old man swung himself back out of the cabinet and placed the exact earrings in front of him on the counter. Reg bent down to look at them.

"Beautiful aren't they," the old man stated rather than asked.

"Aye," said Reg, amazed at the old man's guesswork.

"Eye? What eye?" asked the old man.

"Err, I meant yes," said Reg.

"For your wife?" asked the old man.

"Aye, er yes, er, no I mean..." Reg didn't know what he meant. The old man's eye was now unnerving him and not doing much for his thought processes. The old man obviously had heard this sort of spluttering before.

"A girlfriend, then. No matter. The woman who receives these earrings will love you forever," said the old man, "twenty four carat gold, diamond cluster with sapphire contrast. They are the queen of earrings," said the old man. Reg stared at him for a second longer than was comfortable. The old man caught his eye and Reg felt the need to apologise.

"I'm sorry, I can't, err...your eye."

"What eye?" asked the old man.

"Ah," said Reg, "it's just that you have a..." maybe he didn't like to admit it and he did seem touchy about it, thought Reg and changed tack. "Errm, it's an unusual colour."

"Which one?" asked the old man.

"Which one?" Reg repeated, "good question, err, the gla...I mean the...that one." Reg pointed at the old man's left eye.

"Trick of the light," said the old man, "they are both the same colour."

"Oh," said Reg, now totally uncomfortable.

"My daughter paints them," said the old man.

"Pardon," spluttered Reg.

"The eyes," the old man continued, "she paints glass eyes. It looks real, eh?"

Reg sighed with relief and part satisfaction that the conversation could now draw to an end.

"Here," said the old man. To Reg's horror he had now levered the eye out of its socket and was holding it in his hand. "See the quality, go on, you may touch it."

"Err, no thanks," stammered Reg, who didn't get to see the ins and outs of eyeballs very often, "thanks all the same, but I, err...how much for the earrings?"

"What does price matter?" asked the old man. He seemed slightly disappointed that Reg hadn't taken up his offer of a closer look — "if you want something so badly, you pay what you think they're worth."

"Hmmm," said Reg.

"And your young lady will give you what you deserve in return," the old man added. He casually slipped the eye back into its socket.

"So how much, then?" asked Reg again, more relieved than he could say.

"Three thousand, five hundred," said the old man, smiling.

"Blimey," gulped Reg, who had never spent more than fifty pounds on a pair of earrings for his wife. He mulled this over for a moment before coming to a decision.

"I'll give you three grand," he said.

The old man smiled — another one hooked.

# SPEND, SPEND, SPEND

Reg left the jewellers' shop a little heavier on his credit card debt to the tune of three thousand four hundred pounds. The old bugger had been a professional haggler and had not dropped far. Reg on the other hand had not put up much of a fight, caving in very early in the contest, for fear of the evil eye. He was sure he'd dream about that tonight.

Pangs of conscience were eating at him. He'd never spent that sort of cash before and it had given him a shiver. Carol had better appreciate it, he thought, before thinking that he was a stupid sod. He was like a kid with money. Never mind, he thought, what's money when you've won the lottery. He carried on back to the hotel whistling "Diamonds are a Girl's Best Friend."

He'd not gone too far when he noticed the Mercedes dealership across the next set of traffic lights.

"Could do with a new van," he said to himself and headed smartly over the road. It was 5.15 and he still had money to burn. He was glad Norman wasn't with him.

"Where the bloody 'ell have you been?" demanded Norman when Reg returned whistling.

Norman had been tasked with ringing Kevin the Kitchen Fitter to tell him to hand in his notice and get ready for work. He had also rung a few old contacts to discuss the same thing with them. By the time Reg returned at gone seven o'clock, Norman had managed to get four definite new employees and a tentative two more. Now he was sitting in the bar drinking a pint on his own and reading the evening newspaper.

"Here and there," said Reg, still whistling.

"I thought banks shut at five," said Norman scornfully, "'ave you been drinking?"

"No, no," said Reg.

"Well," said Norman indignantly, "where – have – you – BEEN?" Spelling it out in monosyllables usually helped Norman.

"I – have – been – OUT," said Reg and chuckled. He knew that would exasperate his old friend.

Norman grimaced.

"So," said Norman, "bought owt?"

"Might 'ave," said Reg who had just noticed the headlines in the newspaper: 'ATKINSON THE MAN FOR THE JOB'. Reg turned to Norman and said: "That about me, do you think?"

Norman rolled his eyes and laughed. Reg read the first couple of paragraphs.

"Ron Atkinson is expected to be named as England manager tomorrow. Atkinson has been the favourite to succeed Glenn Gould since Gould resigned last week, only 10 days before England's crucial World Cup Qualifier against Germany. It is thought that Atkinson has been informed already by the FA and will be meeting the squad this weekend. Mr Atkinson is making no comment and insists that he has no knowledge of the situation."

"Looks like Big Ron's the man then," said Reg, "eh, funny that – two Atkinsons getting big jobs off the FA in the same week."

"Does seem a bit odd," said Norman, "they'll probably announce it at this press conference tomorrow."

"Ah," said Reg, memory stirred, "I forgot to tell you about that."

"What?"

"There's a press conference tomorrow lunchtime at one o'clock," Reg continued, "We need to be there."

"Us?" bit Norman, "what for?"

"I dunno," said Reg, "I didn't question it."

"I'll bet you didn't with 'arf a million in your hand," Norman spluttered.

"We must have just missed Big Ron today," said Reg who was still reading the article.

"Yeah?" asked Norman.

"Sez here that 'it is believed the FA held interviews today with Bryan Robson, Peter Reid and Ron Atkinson'," Reg went on, "one of those unnamed sources says 'Atkinson was the preferred choice and will be installed as manager tomorrow. Speaking from home, Mr Atkinson denied having been anywhere near London and refused to make further comment.'"

"Probably all happened in a different bit of the FA," said Norman, "we might've only been in the working class end."

"Oy, you," laughed Reg, slapping Norman on the arm, "never mind working class, Reg Atkinson's going up in the world – definitely middle class, don't you think?"

"Yer 'ead's going up and no mistake," Norman said drily, "you'd better watch out – you'll be able to heat the pitch with all the hot air you've got in there without your heating system. FA might want a discount." Norman tittered to himself.

Reg mulled over this information before giving Norman another dig – this time in the ribs. He put the newspaper on the bar and looked longingly at Norman's pint glass, which, he noted, was now about a third full. Blimey, he thought, a third full – Mr Positive or what?

"Where's Dave?" asked Reg.

"Poor bugger's been rushed off his feet tonight," Norman replied, "seems like an army has just turned up wanting rooms for the night. Must be summat to do with that press conference tomorrow."

"Bloody 'ell," squeaked Reg, "do you reckon I'll be in all the papers then?"

"Not you, you dope," chuckled Norman, "Big Ron's the one they want to see." Norman couldn't stop laughing.

"Aw shut up," said Reg, embarrassed, "I was hoping Dave'd be round to get us a pint."

"Yer'll 'ave to get yer own," said Norman, "that's if it's not beneath a middle class fella like yerself." More laughter from Norman.

"Hardy har," Reg pulled a face. He leaned over the bar and got himself a pint glass. He then set it under the bitter tap and filled it. Reg sat down again and watched Norman down the rest of his pint.

"Aaaahhhh," said Norman sumptuously, "you not gettin' me one then?" He handed Reg his empty glass.

"You cheeky..." started Reg but the laughter came before he could finish.


Reg had decided upon an early night and had asked Norman to make sure he wasn't side-tracked into drinking into the wee small hours. Not only did he have a press conference to consider, but he also had a nice new van to sort out. He'd spent about half an hour in the Mercedes dealership with an over enthusiastic salesman who had tried to sell him every model of car that Mercedes had to offer. Unfortunately for him, there were only three models available which Reg could have more or less straight away, and they were sitting in the showroom.

Reg had made a down payment of ten thousand on a van which made his own look like the Beverly Hillbillies' jalopy. It wasn't cheap, but Reg could see the bigger picture: 'REG ATKINSON – OFFICIAL PLUMBER TO THE FA' emblazoned down the side. Nice and roomy too – he could get all his tools in there without jamming them in. As soon as he could get back to Nottingham, he'd sell the old one and farm out his remaining contracts to Geoff Taylor, one of his plumbing mates.

Norman was unaware of this – it'd be a nice surprise for him. Might take his mind off the other item – Reg had got a bit carried away and bought Norman a present. Reg's first thought was that he was not travelling back to Nottingham in Norman's old banger – he wanted luxury. There was a Mercedes Coupe in the showroom. It was silver with black leather seats, complete with air conditioning, electric windows, CD player, you name it. It was like a luxury flat on wheels. Reg had put a down payment on this as well, with a view to picking it up tomorrow.

At first, he had thought this a brilliant idea, but as the evening wore on, he had doubts. Maybe Norman would not want to lose Mabel – after all, he'd had the car years. Well, he thought, too late now. He couldn't wait to see the look on Norman's face when he rolled up in it. Tomorrow morning's plan was to go and buy some CDs, pick up the car and hand Norman the keys.

Reg was astonished at how full the Kippax had become. Norman was right; it did seem like an army had set up camp. Most of the newcomers seemed to know each other, and beside the odd courteous nod, they paid Reg and Norman no attention. Many eyes were drawn to the various pictures hanging on the walls, mouths laughing at the invariable in-joke which Reg couldn't pick up. The payphone in the lobby – Tommy 'phone' Booth: they get worse, thought Reg – had been in use constantly since Reg returned from his shopping trip.

Soon after Reg had poured his own pints, a young lad had appeared and begun serving drinks as the bar filled. Every few minutes, plates of food were carried in by another previously unseen youngster, this time a young girl of around eighteen. Reg had ordered some Donachie babs just to see what they were like. Norman had asked for rump steak and chips – Mr Safe.

"Donachie babs, eh?" said Norman, "I hope they don't come with a bit of Willie."

Reg choked on a mouthful as Norman guffawed.

"Thanks very much," said Reg, "put me right off 'em now". He looked at his meal plaintively, before nibbling carefully once more.

They had seen Dave only once during the evening. He had had a problem with one of the diners, who from what Reg overheard, seemed foreign. Dave had hold of the specials board and was painfully trying to explain one of the dishes.

"I vant two chop," insisted the diner.

"Look," said an exasperated Dave, "the dish is called 'Wanchope in Cider Sauce' – it comes with one chop."

"But I hef big happetite," said the diner rubbing his significant paunch.

"If you want two chops, I'll have to give you two 'Wanchopes' – that's two meals," said Dave.

"Nicht gut," said the diner, "I hef ze Veah Schnitzel instead."

"I'm sorry," snorted Dave, before marching away, "Weah is off."

# SPEND, SPEND, SPEND

Dave re-appeared around ten o'clock looking very harassed and tired.

"Took me best part of the afternoon to book this lot in," he moaned, "I'm gonna have to look at my guest booking system. All those questions slowed it down. Especially for the Germans. Get us a pint please Josh."

The youngster behind the bar poured Dave a pint.

"This is all to do with that press conference tomorrow," said Dave, "they're all journalists."

He thanked Josh for the beer and drank about half in one swallow. Reg's eyes opened wide.

"It means I'll be up most of the night," Dave continued, "once this crowd get their feet under the table, there's no stopping 'em. Good for business though." He winked at Reg.

"New staff," said Norman — more of an observation than a question.

"Yeah," said Dave, taking another hearty swig of ale, "Josh and Rachel. I call on 'em at short notice when I need help. They're students but they're quite happy to phone in sick at the pub where they work 'cos they know I pay twice as much. By God I needed 'em tonight."

"We've got a press conference tomorrow as well," said Norman, eyebrows raised, "apparently," he added.

"That's strange," said Dave with a frown, "you'd have thought they'd just concentrate on one thing at once."

"Maybe they just want to get both out of the way as fast as they can," suggested Reg, "after all, media's been on their back a bit lately."

Norman and Dave nodded pensively. Reg looked down at his folder of heating documents once more.

Reg had been back to his room to retrieve them so he

could just give them the once over, make himself completely familiar with the technical aspects of the undersoil heating systems of Scandinavia. He was a big fan of the Scandinavians – they definitely had their heads screwed on when it came to heating. Must be the Viking blood, thought Reg.

In one corner of the bar, two journalists were squaring up to each other – effects of the drink no doubt.

"There's some Swedish journalists in tonight," said Dave, motioning towards Reg's brochures.

"Is there?" asked Reg, "I though I heard a few foreign accents."

"Must have heard about your plans for the undersoil heating, eh Reg?" chuckled Norman.

Reg had been looking long and hard at a Swedish system of heating. He was fond of telling anyone who cared to listen that the Swedes were the world leaders when it came to beating ice and snow.

"When was the last time your Swedish train was cancelled because of the wrong type of snow on the tracks?" he'd ask, followed by a "and when was the last time a Swedish football match was ever postponed due to a frozen pitch?"

No one ever knew the answers, and Reg probably wasn't a hundred percent himself, but he had convinced many people over the years that the Swedish – although a frozen nation – basked in the heat of their admirable heating systems.

"Maine Road has a Swedish system," said Dave suddenly.

"Does it?" said Reg, interested.

"Aye," Dave continued, "late seventies I think it went in. Never any problems with it."

"No there won't be," Reg confirmed, "all good stuff as

long as you use copper tube. Some people use aluminium but that doesn't last as long as copper. Half as cheap though."

Reg was happy with this information. Now he had an example of the Swedish system already in an English ground, he felt more comfortable.

Norman hoped Reg knew what he was doing. He was worried for his friend as he never imagined that this day would have come. Norman thought Reg was out of his depth – central heating was fine; showers were a piece of cake; but complete undersoil heating systems under a football pitch? Theory would only go so far – Reg knew his brochures inside out, but how many miles of copper tube was it going to need to pull this off?

"Right," announced Reg at ten-thirty, "I'm off to bed."

"Okay, see you in the morning," Dave replied.

"Yeah, see you in the morning Reg," said Norman, "I'll be up myself in a minute."

Reg rose from his seat, gathered his belongings and left them to it. Norman thought he'd have one more brandy before he went up. He needed a bit of courage to face those pictures in his room again.

# THE PRESS CONFERENCE

There had not been many high points in the life of Reginald Stanley Atkinson thus far, but as a watery sunlight found a small gap in the curtains of the Royle Suite, Reg saw the dawn of his new life. Sleep had been short, but sweet. Rousing early to the sound of morning birdsong and the dreamlike quality of one thin shaft of sunlight as it illuminated the papers and blueprints of Swedish heating systems was enough to convince Reg that his time had come.

Speaking about fathers' (or in Dave's case, grandfathers') expectations the previous evening had reminded Reg of his perceived disappointments. He remembered the look on his father's face when, after trying all year for the school football team without success, he had been chosen to open the batting in the school cricket team. At the age of fourteen, Reg had been as proud as punch, but his overriding memory was of his father's initial scowl, before a begrudging "well done lad".

Parents were the harshest critics. Reg knew that if he ever

had the chance, he would make a good father. Maybe Carol would make a good mother. No point even considering that yet, he laughed – they'd not even had the first date yet. Anyway, he was into his forties – he didn't want any kids thinking he was an old Dad – so it would have to be fast if any offspring were to be on the agenda. Maybe his own son would turn out to be a footballer, who knows.

Shirley had never really been interested in having kids, as she was fond of telling Reg. He scowled mentally. She was too preoccupied with going to the gym and performing bedroom aerobics with her instructor. Reg was still peeved that the last he'd heard, Shirley had just given birth to twins. They could've been mine, he thought irritably.

Reg and football had always been inextricably linked. He began managing local boys' teams before moving up to pub sides and always had a flair for getting the best out of people on the pitch. He pushed his advertising the way of football clubs and managed to do quite a bit of work on local grounds – probably why he's landed this job, he mused. Then again, no job he'd taken up till now had ever potentially impacted his own football involvement. He'd have to speak to the Forest players soon as he couldn't see any way of continuing as their manager while this Wembley business was ongoing.

He glanced at his clock – 6.15am. Time to get up, he had things to do.


By 9.45, Reg was back in his hotel room, having bought five CDs from Woolworth's; spent a tidy sum on a new charcoal suit from the Next shop a couple of doors down from Woolies; and picked up a bright, shiny, silver Mercedes Coupe from the dealership down the road. What a bargain, thirty two thousand — five thousand off because of fast payment plus the fact that it was clogging up the showroom. Can't argue with that, he thought.

Reg drove the couple of hundred yards from the dealership to the hotel, managing to catch the opening two minutes of his new Shania Twain CD. He could listen to the rest later, he thought. Man, I feel like a woman...so go and get me one, he chuckled to himself.

He parked the car on some double yellow lines at the front of the hotel, placing a 'Plumber on Call' sign in the windscreen. He trotted jauntily up the steps and through the Maine Entrance, swinging the keys in his hand. He had returned to his room without seeing a single soul.

From the Royle Suite, he rang Norman's room.

"Hello," Norman answered.

"Are you ready for breakfast or what," asked Reg, "I'm starved."

"Where've you been?" Norman asked, "I've been trying your phone for the last twenty minutes."

"Just popped out for a breather," Reg answered, smiling to himself, "are you gonna keep off the cooked breakfast today or what?"

"Oh leave me alone," moaned Norman, "I'll see you outside your door in five minutes."


The breakfast room was almost full. Unlike yesterday's sitting where Reg and Norman were the only diners, there was a constant hum of voices. Dave had his hands full again, and had secured the services of Josh and Rachel once more.

Dave had kindly reserved a table for them, so they sat and looked around them. Journalists, the world's media — if it was full here, what must the other hotels look like?

Fans of the Kippax they were, but Reg and Norman knew it wouldn't be the top of everyone's ideal hotel list. Perhaps it was its proximity to Lancaster Gate.

Dave arrived at their table.

"Mornin' gents," he said, "I take it you will still be prevailing of the FA's hospitality?"

"Not 'arf," said Reg, "coffee and cooked breakfast for me please."

"I'll have coffee and muesli," said a despondent Norman.

"Muesli?" echoed Dave and Reg.

"No choice after yesterday, 'ave I?" Norman said.

"There is that," laughed Reg.

Dave left them and returned a few moments later with coffee and toast. Reg and Norman tucked in.

"I've been thinking," said Norman, as he buttered a piece of toast.

"Oh aye," said Reg.

"This press conference," said Norman, "it strikes me as a bit funny. I can imagine the England manager having to sit in at a press conference, but why us?"

"I dunno," Reg replied, "maybe they think it is a big thing, after all, when was the last time Wembley had undersoil heating installed."

"It's not even Wembley though is it," said Norman, "it's the new place."

"Well, it's the same thing," said Reg, taking a large bite of freshly buttered toast with an ample covering of marmalade.

"But why us?" Norman pressed, "look at the journalists here. There must be hundreds more in London all waiting for the same thing. Don't you think it's peculiar that they've got both press conferences on the same day? Ours'll be nowt compared to the other one."

Reg pondered this. Sure it seemed strange, but the way the FA worked was always open to ridicule, especially by the press who had marked them down as a group of old codgers who knew nothing about football.

"Maybe plumbing's the new Rock 'n' Roll in London," said Reg with a shrug, as his cooked breakfast arrived. Norman looked at it longingly, and when his muesli was set down in front of him felt pangs of envy.

"I hope that just looking at mine doesn't give you the same problems," said Reg.

"Aww leave me alone," said Norman distressed. Much as he enjoyed Dave's cooked breakfast of yesterday, he wasn't going to take any chances.

"That was good," said Reg, when he'd finished. He sat back in his chair hands patting his stomach: "enjoy your hamster food, Norm?"

"Bloody lovely," said Norman through a mouthful of cardboard.

"You right then? I've got something to show you," said Reg, standing.

"What?" asked Norman.

"Aha," said Reg, "now that'd be telling wouldn't it. Come on, it's outside."

Reg motioned Norman out of the restaurant, waving a quick farewell to Dave who was still taking orders.

"Look how that bugger's parked!" said Norman, as they headed down the front steps, "cheeky sods even put a 'Plumber on Call' sign in the window. Lucky not to get a ticket."

"Shush. Watch this," Reg tittered. He retrieved some keys

**112**

from his pocket and pointed them towards the car. He pressed a little button on the key fob and the Mercedes winked its indicators and chirped back at Reg.

"What the...?" asked a nonplussed Norman.

Reg pressed the button again... and again. The Mercedes winked and chirped happily. Norman finally understood.

"You didn't waste any time did you? Bet that money fair burnt a hole in your pocket didn't it?" he said, and wished he hadn't as Reg's face dropped slightly. Norman was aware of the various disappointments Reg had been to his father and didn't want to add to it.

"Bloody lovely car though Reg – looks quality," he added.

Reg's grin was unmissable.

"That, Norm, is your new company car."

"Mine, but..."

"Don't argue," Reg continued, "my assistant manager needs a car to show his true status. Keep Mabel in the garage and bring her out at weekends. She doesn't belong on the road any more, Norm, this is the car you should be seen in."

Norman discovered his legs and walked slowly around the coupe. It gleamed a showroom gleam. Norman allowed a hand to caress a front wing.

"Very nice, Reg," he said, "thanks very much."

"Don't mention it," said Reg still beaming, "when we go back home, you take Mabel and I'll take this."

"Okay," said Norman, "did you get yourself one?"

"Do you think it was 'buy one, get one free' or something" chuckled Reg.

"Well no, but..."

"I've got a new van on order," Reg said to save Norman discomfort, "they're painting the company name on the side of it as we speak. Should be ready in the next couple of days, and the best part is, they'll deliver it to Nottingham for me."

Reg had agreed this with the salesman. There was absolutely no way that he and Norman could take three vehicles back to Nottingham, and leaving one behind in London was not an option. In a moment of clarity, Reg had suggested this to the Mercedes salesman who, (knowing the sale and the two months' commission were riding on it) agreed on the spot.

"Want to go for a ride?" asked Reg, holding out the keys.

Norman hesitated, as though thinking deeply. "Go on then," he smiled, snatching the keys.

After thirty minutes of Norman driving his new 'babe magnet', they returned to the Kippax. Reg was unsure what to make of the change in Norman since the instant he sank lushly into the driver's seat of the Mercedes. He was like a man possessed, no longer the cautious driver who had driven to London in a battered old Escort. Norman was now forty years younger, driving with the window down, Kylie Minogue blaring from the CD player at full blast.

They found a nearby NCP car park as Norman was uncomfortable with parking illegally. Reg removed himself from the car with relief when they eventually parked up. Norman remained behind the wheel for a prolonged moment after the engine had been turned off. When he squirmed out of the sports seat, he stood by the car and patted it gently.

"So what do you think?" asked Reg.

"Very nice indeed," smiled Norman.

"Very nice? Is that it?" asked Reg.

"Mmmm," said Norman, "did they not have any Doris Day CDs then?"

"You cheeky old..." Reg aimed a pretend clip to Norman's ear as the older man fell about laughing.

"Thanks Reg," said Norman, once he had gathered himself, "you didn't have to."

"Well," said Reg, who had come over all embarrassed, "'s just a company car, you know."

"Aye, I know, but still, it's a nice touch," said Norman.

The two of them wandered slowly back to the Kippax. Reg checked his watch – they'd better get going for this press conference.

Sir Richard Scratcher was in fine form. Not only had he had his third night of passion with the lovely June, but the press conference was upcoming and this would show Mister Brendan Fendon that Dickie Scratcher was a man to be relied on.

By God but he had found the key to June Whitless' locker, and no mistake. That first time at the ballet had done it – she was uncontrollable. Subsequent nights at the opera had opened up the floodgates even more. Sir Richard felt ten years younger and ten years older at the same time. Was that possible? He sauntered around with a spring in his step but felt drained as well. A small price to pay. He'd keep this quiet from Brendan when he got back – he'd probably have something to say if he found out his secretary was dallying with a colleague.

Sir Richard rocked gently in his comfortable leather chair behind his desk. This sort of life was made for him – a couple of hours graft followed by the rest of the day off; golfing, museums, drinking, entertaining.

After the press conference, he'd have the afternoon free. A few reporter questions straight afterwards and he'd be free to do whatever he liked. Might pop down to Ascot, he thought – he felt lucky. Wonder if June likes the horses?

June sat in her office filing her nails. The main job was done – Atkinson had been offered the job and he'd signed the contract. She had the copies ready to give Reg when he arrived, as well as a contract for his little friend Norman to sign.

Everything had gone to plan. She supposed that she could now get ahead on the undersoil heating contract – after all, the pile of tenders had been sorted at the same time as the manager applications. What the hell, she thought, she needed a break. As soon as she could, she was going to nip home for the rest of the day – catch up on her sleep. That Dickie, he was charm personified. As long as she kept telling herself it was just to ensure the manager's job went exactly as Brendan had decreed, it was worth it. Not that she wasn't enjoying herself, oh no. She had readily given herself to Dickie – the ballet and opera had unleashed something primitive inside her and Dickie was available to satisfy her new found lust.

Her mind turned to Brendan's imminent arrival. He had phoned minutes earlier with arrival times at Heathrow. His flight wouldn't get in until late evening so he would be going straight home to his wife. Wonder what Dickie's up to tonight?

Brendan Fendon slept peacefully in his plush hotel room in Rio de Janeiro. The conference had taken its toll over the last couple of days, especially when the French delegates had stormed off when their fabric requirements for the new corner flag material had not been met. That had taken a while to sort out and now they were behind schedule.

At least his dreams were pleasant. He'd called June a number of times to check on progress and everything seemed to be going smoothly. Still, he wished that he was back in England supervising, but what could go wrong? Even an idiot couldn't fail to get this right.

Maybe a change in temperature made a difference, but he turned fitfully in his sleep – something was invading his dream and it looked like Dickie Scratcher clutching a football. The image faded as his body succumbed to deep sleep once more. It was replaced by an impression of Brendan in shorts holding aloft a cup of some kind. He smiled ever so slightly, dribbling a trail of saliva on his pillow.

The media room at Lancaster Gate was buzzing. Journalists from all over the country had arrived early to ensure a place. The world's media were also present and some of Reg and Norman's hotel comrades had found their way in, ensuring that European reporters just outnumbered the 'home' reporters.

In some quarters, the England job was considered vastly more important than any other country, or at least as equal in importance. The Danes, Swedes and Belgians for example, were all more interested in the events at Lancaster Gate than their own Football Associations. Of course, the English believed that Britannia still ruled the waves and that the days of Empire had never truly disappeared. Never, in the field of human conflict – to coin a phrase – had an English sports journalist ever wasted more than a few cursory paragraphs about a foreign coaching position.

Look at the history – football was invented in England wasn't it? The World Cup 'came home' in 1966. Evidence litters historical statistics that England is the birthplace of football. Remember the Norwegian commentator who, when Norway beat England 2-1 in the Seventies, was overcome with national pride. Not only had the Norwegians beaten England, they had beaten the icons of British history – Winston Churchill, Maggie Thatcher.

Domestically, Manchester United have a problem: people either love them or hate them. You will find that more people profess to hate them for various reasons, but conversely will always look for the United game on their own team's fixture list first, as this is their Cup Final. As such, every team in the country who are playing against United will "up" their performance for that game as it is perceived to mean so much. It is said that fans of Liverpool will enjoy a dour 1-0 victory over United far more than a 5-2 thriller against Merseyside neighbours Everton.

Internationally, England have the same problem. National teams playing England always seem to have that extra yard of pace; that extra ounce of aggression; that extra iota of ingenuity and skill. England invented football; therefore to beat the inventors is a great privilege. Hence the interest.

Sir Richard Scratcher surveyed the media in the crowded room and smiled to himself. It was time.

Reg and Norman had arrived ahead of schedule as per June's instructions, and had been promptly whisked away to prepare. June handed Reg a copy of his contract and also passed Norman a contract of his own.

"There's no rush to sign that one," she said, "the important thing was to get Reg's contract sorted out up front."

Norman nodded his thanks as he took the contract off her. A quick glance told him that his sole responsibility was to support Mr Atkinson in the management role and assist him in performing his duties. He noticed the money involved and his eyes widened. He found a pen in his inside pocket and signed it before anyone had a chance to change their mind. He handed the signed documents back to June. June gave him his copy back.

"Now I'm sure you've done this before," June continued, "so I won't presume on you too much."

"Well..." began Reg.

"The important thing is to stress how much you want to do the job and that you'll make every effort to ensure success," said June.

"Yes," said Reg, "but..."

"Tell them about your last job and what you're doing now in football. All you need to do now is wait right here and I'll come and get you when the time's right." June smiled sweetly and left them.

"Nervous?" asked Norman.

"Like a schoolboy on me first date," said Reg.

"She obviously thought that you do a lot of these," said Norman frowning.

"Might be the sort of thing that happens down her way," said Reg, "you know, local paper headlines: 'Plumber fixes tap'. It's like I said – plumbing is the new Rock 'n' Roll in London."

"Hmmm," said Norman unconvinced, "wonder why they keep going on about you and football though?"

Reg hopped from one foot to another nervously looking at his watch. Norman raised his eyebrows – he was used to Reg and his nerves. They tended to disappear when he was in front of a crowd – natural performer he was.

June popped her head round the door smiling again.

"It's time," she said, "would you like to follow me?"

In the media room, the buzz had intensified. Sir Richard had appeared and addressed the assembly. After a brief rundown of the criteria that had governed the selection of the new manager, Sir Richard announced the new manager of England.

"Now the man himself, Reg Atkinson."

The crowd roared with laughter and derision. Trust the FA – send out an old duffer who couldn't even get Big Ron's name right. Sir Richard couldn't understand the reaction. Why were they hooting? Had he said something stupid? Must have been a *double entendre* in there somewhere that he wasn't aware of. Oafs, he thought, bloody rough bunch the media – need birching the lot of them.

Reg and Norman came out from the wings and were immediately blinded by the flashes of hundreds of cameras. Initially, they couldn't see how full the room was – all they could hear were howls of laughter. They made their way carefully to the seats to which Sir Richard was directing them. Then they saw exactly how full the room was. Blimey, Reg thought – glad he had worn his new suit – this was a bit much.

The crowd grew quiet. They had expected to see Big Ron, appearing in a blaze of jewellery and remnants of Spanish sun. They had not expected to see this. The silence became a murmur, as reporters turned to their neighbours and whispered questions. No one recognised the new man. To a few who had stayed at the Kippax the previous evening, his face had a familiar quality, but they couldn't quite put their finger on why. It was a few moments before any of them asked a question. When the moment came, it was frenzied. Cameras clicked incessantly; flashes began like a firework display, reporters stood in groups and shouted out questions.

Sir Richard stood at the front of the auditorium and waved for calm.

"Please, gentleman, calm yourselves. Obviously this is an emotive issue, but if you can keep your questions to one at a time," he said, fixing his gaze on one group in particular who looked rowdy. Sir Richard noticed one reporter with his hand up, as though he was still in the classroom. Sir Richard liked the polite approach and gestured towards him. The reporter stood.

"Jerry Tomlinson, Evening Post," he began, "who are you?" He pointed at Reg.

"Reg Atkinson," Reg replied swiftly. Sir Richard nodded in agreement. He considered this an effective response.

"So what you doin' 'ere then? Where's Big Ron?" Jerry Tomlinson continued.

"I'm here to tell you why I'm the man for the job," said Reg, nerves forgotten, "I dunno about Big Ron. I expect you'll get to see him later."

So that's what this was all about, thought Reg. Bloody FA were killing two birds with one stone – he was the warm-up act for Big Ron and the manager's press conference. That's why there were so many journalists and reporters here. Right then, he'd warm them up all right. When he'd left here, they'd all know exactly who Reg Atkinson was.

Another journalist stood and announced himself.

"Willie Moffatt, Telegraph. Why exactly are you the man for the job? What've you done before?"

"I'd be the first to admit that I haven't done work on this scale before. In fact, I'm not sure anyone has. But I'm willing to give it a go. As for my experience, the FA have full details of all my work and qualifications. I don't think that's in question – I know that I'm not just here to do a job for myself, but the country as well." Reg answered, patriotically.

"Bernard Butler, Sun. Err, what system do you plan to use?"

"I've looked at the traditional approach and decided that current systems are outdated," Reg said to widespread murmurs, "so I've opted for a Swedish system that will give us full coverage across the pitch."

Uproar. Sir Richard stood once more and appealed for calm. Reg raised his voice to continue.

"I believe that the Swedes have got it just right. I've looked at every system currently utilised around the world and for our climate, this one is infinitely superior to all others."

"Clive Bacon, Mirror. What about away games."

"It's not a portable system you know," Reg replied, looking at this particular reporter with disdain, "it's not something you can dig up and put anywhere you like."

"Howard Davies, Times. The FA Director of Coaching himself has decreed that the English system of 4312 is the way forward at all clubs to assist England at national level. Why have you decided not to utilise this method?"

"I don't really think the Director of Coaching would have the necessary knowledge of all these systems," Reg said, wondering who made the 4312 system – it was not a product he was aware of. "If you think he does, then ask yourself why he hasn't been offered this job."

As the volume level increased again, Reg shook his head in despair. Right bunch of thickos this lot, he thought.

"David Dean, Evening Standard. Have you met the players yet?"

"Err, no," said Reg, wondering what that had to do with anything.

"So you don't know how they'd react to this news?" continued David Dean.

"They'd probably not even notice until they played in minus five centigrade," Reg replied.

"Bjorn Olsen, Norway. Who is your little friend?"

Norman ruffled his feathers.

"This is Norman Whaddon, my assistant manager and right hand man," said Reg.

"And what is your experience in football?" continued the Norwegian.

"I played professional football for Barnsley, Sheffield United and Notts County," said Norman, unsure of what this had to do with anything. He noticed lots of scribbling in notebooks in the front row.

"Bill Talbot, Daily Mail. Mr Atkinson, I don't mean to be rude but I'm sure I'm not the only one in the room who doesn't recognise you." Nods of agreement and mutterings. "Why is that?"

"Have you been to Nottingham recently?" asked Reg.

"Well, no, but..."

"Have you had need of a plumber recently?" asked Reg.

"No..." Bill Talbot was not used to having the tables turned during press conferences like this – he felt as though he was on the stand himself. Other journalists looked at him expectantly, their union code demanded he recovered.

"Well then," said Reg as though that was the end of the matter.

"This Swedish system of yours then," snapped Bill Talbot,

"tell us about it and why the whole English philosophy has been wrong for the last few years."

"Right," said Reg, about to launch into his favourite subject, "take a look back to last winter – how many trains were cancelled in Britain because of snow on the line or frozen points?" pause for effect, "hundreds. How many league games were postponed because of frozen pitches...hundreds. Now look at Sweden and ask yourself the same questions."

Reporters were looking at each other baffled. A number of Swedish reporters on the back row were fidgeting with interest. One put up his hand.

"Yes, you at the back," said Reg with authority.

"Very few," answered the Swede.

"Correct," cried Reg now in his element, "the Swedes do not have these problems. Scandinavians are accustomed to the fact that winter is sometimes cold – in England it still comes as a surprise. Which is why England stops at certain times during the winter, while the rest of Europe carries on."

The Swedes were nodding their agreement. Other journalists were making notes and shrugging – they did not have a clue where this was leading, but didn't want to be left behind.

"The Swedish system is based on coverage. Every inch of the pitch is in reach, creating a smooth, lush playing surface, even in the depth of winter..."

"Adam Sands, News of the World. Are you saying that this system will actually defrost the pitch as the game wears on?"

"I suppose you could leave it running during the game," said Reg, "but ideally, it should kick in a few hours before. It all depends on the atmosphere, but it's vital the warm-up begins a few hours before the kick-off."

More shrugs and mutterings from the journalists. This was beyond them. One of the Swedes rose.

"Peter Andersen, Sweden. It's refreshing to hear that our country is so admired. Please, who is the best footballer you have worked with?"

"Err, Baldy Charlton I suppose, but you probably won't have heard of him."

Laughter came from the auditorium. The Swede continued undaunted. "Could you tell us on what particular aspect your style of play is modelled?"

"Play?" asked Reg, "do you mean football?"

"Well of course," frowned the Swede.

"I like to call it the 'Rambling Rose' formation. It was actually based on a shower spray," Reg began but was interrupted by guffaws from the crowd. He carried on, raising his voice slightly, "it's like fine jets of effort with a central point of output, only with shower heads this remains static. In my formation, the Rose rambles, and the central jet roams all over the pitch. Confuses the opposition no end."

Norman was feeling uneasy. Although Reg was handling the questions well, it seemed as though the reporters were restless. Many were looking confused and a few were shaking their heads in disbelief. He glanced at the contract in front of him and noticed that he had Reg's copy as well as his own. He opened Reg's at page one and skimmed through it.

"Donald Parsons, Daily Sport. Reg...may I call you Reg?"

"Only if I can call you Don," said Reg.

"Okay Reg, what was your last managerial position in football?"

"The Forest Inn, Nottingham," said Reg baffled, "but what's that got to do with this?"

Norman, by now had found something interesting in Reg's contract and was desperately trying to get his friend's attention.

"What's that got to do with it?" stuttered the Sport journalist. "I'd expect someone who's just got your job to know exactly what that's got to do with it."

"All my work takes place under the pitch, not on top of it," said Reg.

Silence. The questions had dried up and the reporters were looking at Reg with stunned amazement. Norman used this opportunity to hiss in Reg's direction and tug his sleeve. As he did, a German stood up.

"Dieter Hoffmann, Germany. Herr Atkinson, what is your view of the German national team at the moment?"

"Well, they don't seem to be the force of old, but they'll probably give our lot a hard game on Wednesday. What do you think?"

"Vell, I..."

Norman was still tugging at Reg's sleeve. "Look at this," he whispered, throatily.

"What," Reg hissed back, looking at whatever Norman was trying to show him. Another reporter disturbed him.

"Stan Beagle, Express. Reg, just one question – are we good enough to beat the Germans on Wednesday. Will you have time to do the job before then?"

"Of course we're good enough, but I don't think I can lay twenty tons of copper tube before Wednesday. I might be good, but I'm not that good."

"Connor Mcleod, Echo. Reg, you've confused a good many of us today – what's this about copper tube?"

# THE PRESS CONFERENCE

Reg was looking down at the copy of his contract. Page three gave documented proof that he had agreed to become England's new manager. He looked at the words hoping that miraculously the letters would go walkabout and become something else, something he was more familiar with.

"Err," Reg said, the dreadful truth now beginning to unfold, but unable to turn off the auto-pilot, "Some people would consider aluminium tube as it's cheaper but copper has a much longer life... you pay more of course but it's worth it in the long run."

"I don't understand, Reg. By tube do you mean piping? Is it a new kit you're talking about? How will this help us on Wednesday against Germany?" asked the Echo man. Muttered remarks echoed around the room.

"It won't, but I think there's been some kind of mistake," Reg mumbled, looking forlornly at Sir Richard who seemed in a world of his own, "I'm just a plumber."

The room turned from quiet disbelief to sheer pandemonium in an instant. Reg and Norman slumped in their seats with jaws agape. Only the front row had caught Reg's final sentence, but the words were travelling fast. Sir Richard saw that all hell was about to be let loose and stood in an attempt to subdue the seething mass. The reporters were having none of it – this was big news and every one of them wanted more. Within seconds they were standing, demanding to know why a plumber was now in charge of the England football team.

Sir Richard decided that enough was enough. He hadn't really been paying attention to the later stages as it all seemed to be going very well. Atkinson had them eating out of the palm of his hand, he thought, and in about thirty minutes, he'd be setting off for his afternoon at Ascot. The time was right to end things – this media crowd was far too rowdy for his liking: gutter trash, he thought. He helped Reg and Norman to their feet and ushered them as quickly as he could from the room.

Sir Richard shuttled Reg and Norman into his office.

"Well I don't know about you two, but I thought that went rather well," said Sir Richard, totally oblivious.

"You what?" Reg was a mite concerned. "They think I'm the next manager of England."

"Yes," purred Sir Richard.

"Well I'm not," Reg added.

"That's righ...hang on dear boy, what do you mean, 'you're not'?" stuttered Sir Richard.

"He's not," said Norman, by way of clarification, "Reg is a plumber. We thought he was here because of the undersoil heating contract."

"The unders..." Sir Richard couldn't finish the sentence – his plans for the afternoon dictated that he should be leaving very soon and he'd still not spoken to June. To cap it all, this dashed fellow in front of him was hopping about.

"I've just read the contract," said Reg, "you want me to manage the England football team against Germany."

"That's right," said Sir Richard, now recovering sufficiently to recognise stage fright when he saw it, "it's right that you should be nervous – it's a big step up to international football you know."

"You're mad!" said Reg. "Come on Norman, we need to get out of here fast."

Reg headed for the door, Norman in hot pursuit. Sir Richard watched the door close behind them and headed for the gin. These managers were all the same – always panicking for some reason. He'll come round, he thought. Sir Richard took a swig of his favourite tipple. That's better.

As soon as Reg and Norman found themselves in the main corridor, reporters besieged them. All they could hear were questions, questions, questions.

"Is it true you're a plumber?"

"Why were you offered the job"

"Who appointed you?"

"Where do you go from here?"

"Have you picked the team?"

"Is this a joke?"

"Are you resigning already?"

Reg and Norman headed as best they could towards the main doors – it was difficult fighting their way through the throng of reporters. Outside was worse – it seemed like all the TV cameras had been set up purposely to capture Reg squinting into the sunlight as soon as he left the building. More questions were thrown at him.

"No comment," Reg blurted – he'd seen this sort of thing on the telly. No comment seemed a good choice at this point. They legged it back to the hotel chased by a thousand cameras.

As they sped through the foyer, Dave Bayley opened his mouth to ask how it went but snapped it shut again as he saw the stampede. Reg and Norman bolted straight past him.

"You never saw us," shouted Reg as he sprinted past.

Dave took his eyes off Reg and turned to face the mass of cameras. He smiled thinking of the publicity for the hotel.

"Yes gentlemen," he began, " how can I help you?"

Sir Richard sat at his desk with his feet up. Bloody press were like a bunch of wild dogs, he thought. They'd got Atkinson, which was apparently what they'd wanted – the people's choice, Brendan had said – and still they weren't satisfied. Some people just never knew when they had it made. Sir Richard shook his head with resignation. The telephone on his desk rang shrilly, giving him a quick jolt. Blasted thing, got him every time. Wonder if there's a button on it somewhere to make it a bit more quiet, he thought, something for Maintenance. He picked up the receiver and coughed in his usual manner.

"Harumph! Ahem," he added for good measure, "Sir Richard Scratcher,"

"Sir Richard, it's June. Mrs Fendon for you."

"Oh," wonder what she wants, he thought, "thanks June. Put her through."

"Dickie?"

"Barbara, my dear, how are you?"

"Fine thank you. Any idea when Brendan's due back?"

"Well, I'm not exactly sure, but from what I remember, it's late evening. Do you want me to get June to check?"

"No it's all right Dickie, I just wanted to get a message to him and he's probably on the plane by now."

Sir Richard checked his watch – nearly two o'clock. He tried a mental calculation of flight length and take-off times, but as he didn't know either, contented himself with a hum of agreement.

"Well I can do that for you if you like," he said gallantly.

"Oh would you? That's kind. Got a pen? You'll need one."

Sir Richard raised a casual eyebrow. Did she think his memory was going or something?

"Fire away Barbara,"

# THE PRESS CONFERENCE

"Apparently there's been a mix-up with some briefcases. Brendan's walked off with the Colombian delegate's briefcase and vice versa."

Sir Richard decided he would need a pen after all and frantically rummaged in his drawer.

"Right, Barbara, I've got that, yes," he interjected to allow him a breather. Aha, here's one – he pounced on a pen and started to make notes just as Barbara was finishing.

"Now the Colombian delegate, Mr Sanches Guimarez, is coming to London himself this weekend, so he's asked Brendan to leave the case in lost property for him. Brendan needs to tell the lost property people to be extremely careful as there's a hairline crack through the lock which makes it spring open at times, especially when something's put on top of it. Mr Sanches Guimarez will bring Brendan's case with him and leave that at lost property too. Brendan can then pick it up later. You got all that?"

"Yes Barbara, I've got it," said Sir Richard still scribbling furiously.

"Do you want me to repeat it?"

"No, no, I've got it all written down exactly as you said," he lied.

"Thanks Dickie, you're a marvel as always."

"Always a pleasure, Barbara. Goodbye."

Sir Richard replaced the receiver and set about rewriting the message. Now, how to translate this scrawl into a couple of lines that said it all. Dashed if he could remember that Colombian's name, but he'd edit it into something meaningful.

"Good afternoon, Heathrow International, this is Melanie, how may I help you?"

"Ah yes, I'd like to leave a message for Mr Brendan Fendon who's travelling back from Brazil today."

"Certainly sir, do you have the flight number?"

"Err, no I'm afraid I don't."

"That's all right, do you know the originating airport and time of arrival?"

"That will be Rio de Janeiro in Brazil and I'm not exactly sure of the time, but it should be this evening."

"Just a moment sir...the only possible flight will be British Airways flight 287 arriving 19.40 this evening."

"Sounds like the one."

"And your message is for...?"

"Mr Brendan Fendon."

"And your name, please?"

"Sir Richard Scratcher."

"And the message..?"

"The message is: 'leave the case in lost property and the Colombians will make the switch this weekend. Make sure nothing is placed on the case as the crack may cause the lock to spring open'."

"Okay, sir, I'll just repeat that to you to make sure I've written it down correctly: 'leave the case in lost property and the Colombians will make the switch this weekend. Make sure nothing is placed on the case as the crack may cause the lock to spring open'."

"That's right. Many thanks my dear."

"Sir, if I can just take a note of your number...sir? sir?"

Having hung up slightly prematurely for Melanie's liking, Sir Richard sat back and cracked open a fresh bottle of tonic. Just wait until Brendan returned, he thought, he might even get a smile out of the old dog. Now, where's that gin?

# TV STAR

Every television channel across Europe was showing the same thing. Reg was certainly having his fifteen minutes of fame...and then some.

He sat on the corner of his bed in the Royle Suite with the TV remote control in his hand, switching from channel to channel. Every single station was saying the same thing – Reg Atkinson is the new England manager.

Norman sat with him – both looked totally nonplussed. They sat there in silence as the story unfolded until well into the afternoon. Live reports were being shown throughout the afternoon; programmes were being cancelled; reporters were camped outside Lancaster Gate and his hotel, hoping to get some footage. Essentially the story was the same:

"...plumber, Reginald Atkinson. Mr Atkinson from Nottingham issued a clear no comment..."

Flick! went the remote.

"nothing more than a plumber..."

Flick!

"Mr Atkinson has been holed up in his hotel since the..."

Flick!

"...another seemingly disastrous decision by the FA..."

Flick!

"...the latest in a series of decisions which have been in question..."

Flick!

"...a number of personalities have already lamented the state of the English game, but..."

Flick!

"Will you stop flickin'," shouted Norman, "leave it on one channel so I can tell what's goin' on."

"You what?" barked Reg, "you want to know what's goin' on? Where've you been for the last hour?"

"I want to see what's bein' said," said Norman, "now shush and listen."

The channel hopping landed on Sky Sports. An interviewer was putting questions to a number of ex-England mangers, including Terry Venables, Glenn Hoddle and Graham Taylor. Graham Taylor was currently facing the camera from his training ground at Watford.

Sky: "Have the FA lost the plot?"

Taylor: "Who are they? What do they know? In the last decade, England have had five managers, so why haven't they got us all together to ask us what we think? I think that's important, do you see? I know better than the people on the FA what it's like to be England manager. All they've done is appoint a plumber!"

Sky: "How do you see the future of English football now?"

Taylor: "If this appointment doesn't work out then everyone involved in choosing Atkinson should resign, every man jack of them. Do you see? Brendan Fendon is supposed to be changing things around at the FA, but I'm amazed at the way they went about appointing a new manager. It's ludicrous, Machiavellian."

The coverage returned to the studio, where the presenters were having a high old time discussing the appointment of Reg Atkinson as England's new manager.

"Well obviously, there's been a mistake. There is absolutely no reason why a man of Atkinson's inexperience should be given the top job in English football. That is the belief expressed by everyone we've spoken to. As the afternoon wears on, we hope to bring you more details about the man who is supposed to take us through to the next World Cup Finals. Join us again after the break."

Reg and Norman looked blankly at the adverts, which were now showing on screen. Was it a coincidence or did IKEA, Volvo and Scotland's forthcoming friendly against Sweden figure more prominently than normal.

The two men sat in silence for a few moments before Reg decided to speak.

"What do I do now?" he asked.

"Well you can't manage England, can you?" said Norman.

"I'll just have to phone up and tell them it's a big mistake," said Reg.

"Aye, maybe they'll let you off with the money you've already spent 'an all," said Norman.

"Oh Christ!" said Reg, "I'd forgot about that. I'll have to take 'em back."

"'Em? What do you mean, them?" asked Norman.

"Oh," said Reg – he'd not told Norman yet about his other purchase – "err, nothing, I mean the car and van."

"Don't forget Kev and the lads have jacked in their jobs,"

said Norman, "what are we going to do about them?"

"God knows," said Reg and sat on the edge of his bed rocking gently as more reports and interviews appeared on screen.

"I've nothing against him – he looks like a gentleman, but I find it difficult to see why he's been appointed. A plumber will not know the mentality or culture of the national game. It's for a special breed of people."

"The FA are telling us they're not a bunch of old farts any more. They're showing you how clever they are because they're designer people now. By choosing a plumber, they're saying we, the FA, will show you the way forward. Next thing you know they'll be installing a foreign coach."

"Is he a tactical genius? What has he done? Who is he? It makes me angry that the future of the game is in the hands of a bunch of old men and a plumber. God rest the soul of English football."

Reg held his head in his hands as the Sky Sports studio returned and the presenter introduced details of the press conference again. Cameras were thrust into the face of Sir Richard Scratcher as he left the building. His mood was temporarily blackened as June had apparently already left, so he had no company for the races. Maybe next week, he thought, she'd enjoy the races.

Sky: "Sir Richard, why Reg Atkinson?"

Sir Richard: "Reg Atkinson proved himself to be the best candidate for the position. His experience is without question and he was the unanimous choice of the FA to succeed as England manager."

"Sir Richard, should this decision have been made in the absence of Brendan Fendon. Could you tell us if it's true that he's out of the country?"

# TV Star

"Yes, he's in Brazil at a very important conference representing his country. The decision to appoint Mr Atkinson was made with Brendan's full knowledge and satisfaction. In fact, he called me this morning to rubber-stamp the deal. Now if you'll excuse me, I have other engagements."

Sir Richard left hurriedly. The Sky reporter turned to the camera.

"There you have it. The FA clearly believe that Reg Atkinson is the man to lead England to the World Cup Finals. Back to the studio."

"What do we know about Reg Atkinson?" asked the presenter. "We have our investigators on the hunt for the clues and this is what we've found."

"Bloody 'ell," said Reg, as the screen showed a familiar sight, "that's my house."

Voice-over: "Reg Atkinson is by trade a plumber and lives here in Nottingham. Nothing is yet known about his football knowledge, but we have located some of his friends here to give us some background."

"It's Lance!" cried Norman as Lance Lovejoy's face appeared on screen, smiling the Lovejoy smile.

Lance: "He's a good bloke. Best manager we've ever had. We won the league last year."

Reporter: "And your team is?"

Lance: "Forest Inn."

Reporter: "The Forest Inn? And in which league do you play?"

Lance: "East Midlands Sunday League. It's a pub league."

Reporter: "A pub league? And this is where Reg currently works?"

Lance: "Yep."

Reporter: "Do you know if he's ever been in charge of any other clubs?"

Lance: "I think he's done a few under sixteen types, but he's concentrated mainly on us for the past few years. Made us tick, you know."

Reporter: "But has he ever been in charge of a league side?"

Lance: "Don't think so. He did do the showers at Burton Albion once – he likes to bring that up."

Reporter: "Thank you Lance Lovejoy. Back to the studio."

Studio: "Well, what can we make of this latest news? It appears that Reg Atkinson, the new England manager is, in actual fact, a plumber, working in and around Nottingham. He does have experience of managing football sides, but this experience seems to be confined to pub leagues and schoolboys. Is this the sort of experience which the FA considers when appointing a new England coach? We have Ron Atkinson on the phone from his home in the Midlands. Ron, hello and many thanks for talking to us."

Ron: "Hello there Richard, my pleasure."

Studio: "Ron, you've been reported as being the favourite for the position since the resignation of Glenn Gould last weekend. How do you feel about this decision by the FA?"

Ron: "Well obviously it's a strange one. I dunno, my first impression was that they meant to offer me the job, but got mixed up with this plumber." (He laughs).

Studio: "Very good, Ron, but what do you really think happened? What sort of criteria were the FA looking for?"

Ron: "I dunno. Nothing surprises me any more. Early doors I would have said get somebody experienced in to act as a caretaker for the one game and then see how it went from there. Now it looks like they've decided a specialist plumber is better than a caretaker. Bit ironic if you ask me."

Studio: "But this seems to be a total departure from that Ron. Were you expecting the call from the FA?"

Ron: "I suppose I was in a way. I'd been named in every newspaper all week and yet no one from the FA approached me or even responded to my application."

Studio: "You applied?"

Ron: "Oh yes. As soon as I knew what was happening, my application went in."

Studio: "Ron, thanks very much for talking to us."

Ron: "My pleasure. If you talk to Reg at all, see if he'll bob round to fix my bath taps."

Studio: "Ron Atkinson. What must be going through his mind at the moment – the people's choice – ignored by the decision-makers in favour of a plumber. Join us again after the break. We'll be bringing you more reaction and hopefully some more insights into the cloudy background of the new England manager."

A knock at the door made both Reg and Norman jump. Reg crept warily to the door and looked through the eyepiece. It was Dave. Alone. Reg opened the door.

"All right, Reg?" asked Dave.

"In a fashion," said Reg, "where's all them reporters?"

"Gone," said Dave. "I managed to convince them that you had come in, but had sneaked out of a window at the back."

"Good man," said Reg, "I'm not quite sure what I'd say to them at the minute."

"I've been watching telly," Dave continued, "and it seems like you're the new England boss."

"So it seems," said Reg.

"Well you pulled the wool over my eyes with all that undersoil heating stuff," said Dave. Reg looked at him hurt, until he recognised the glint of a joke in Dave's eyes. He laughed despite himself.

"What am I going to do, Dave?" Reg asked, plaintively, "I've already spent a sackload of their cash on cars and vans."

Norman shifted uncomfortably in his seat.

"It's the contract," he stated, "you signed a contract. You'd better see if it can be unsigned."

"But that won't solve the problem of me getting refunds for what I've shelled out for," said Reg.

"Or Kev," said Norman, "I'll try calling him now before he does 'owt daft."

"Okay," said Dave, "let's break down the problem. You've signed a contract to become the next England manager. Correct?"

Reg nodded.

"You've already spent some cash based on your new higher earnings. Correct?"

Reg nodded again.

"Is the money easily refundable?" asked Dave.

Reg shrugged. "I doubt it," he said. "I could sell the car at a loss probably, but the signwriters will have finished with the van now, and the earrings are non-returnable."

"Earrings? What earrings?" said Norman absently, only half listening with the phone to his ear.

"Never mind that," said Dave, "you also have somebody who's jacked in their job so they can start work for you down here. Correct?"

"Yes," Reg nodded again, "but there's a couple of other lads too."

"Hmmm," said Dave, "you're shafted. If you can stand the loss, all well and good, cancel the contract. However, if you can't stand the loss, then you'll have to stick it out and wait for the FA to make their move."

"But why? I might as well call them now and tell them it's all a big mistake," said Reg.

"Don't you see," said Norman, giving up with the phonecall which remained unanswered at the other end, "Dave's right. Wait for them. If they cancel, they might write off your losses."

"A friend of mine's a bit of a lawyer," said Dave, "if you like, I'll get him to run through the contract and see if there's anything that you can use."

"Great, Dave, that'd be good," Reg felt slightly better. Doing nothing was an excellent option. Let the FA make the mistakes – they were good at that.

The news spread like wildfire that night. Every evening paper devoted their paper to one story: Reg.

Reg was also the sole topic of conversation on radio and television. Reg was big news and the media were getting frantic trying to talk to him. He had disappeared and no one, with the exception of Norman and Dave Bayley knew where he was. The media had decided to turn their attentions to the FA, and had begun a campaign to oust the current members of the committee and have them replaced by younger men.

By eight o'clock that evening, a tired Brendan Fendon landed at Heathrow slightly behind schedule after a long flight from Brazil. Brendan had not slept due to fears of deep vein thrombosis which he had read about affecting long haul passengers and wanted to stretch his legs at every opportunity. He hadn't gone as far as impromptu aerobics in the aisle like some passengers, but he had made a seated effort while watching film after film.

Despite numerous attempts to get hold of Sir Richard and June, he'd failed. Oh well, if anything had gone wrong – not that it could – he'd have heard by now. He was looking forward to a quiet night at home followed by a good night's sleep in a comfortable bed, without Pablo the tom-tom player launching into *La Vida Loca* at five-thirty each morning. Brendan made a mental note to try Sir Richard from home as he ambled along to join the small queue at passport control. It had been a little chilly on the plane and he was glad that he'd decided to wear his overcoat.

Passport control officers generally do not speak. They usually cast a perfunctory hand and expect your passport to be open at the appropriate page. As Brendan strolled past with his passport picture in full view, he was taken aback when the fellow took the passport in his hand and opened his mouth to speak.

"Mr Fendon, we've been waiting for you." The officer waved and two security guards appeared from nowhere.

"Could I ask what this is about?" asked Brendan with a hint of fear in his voice.

"If you'd just like to come with us sir, we'll explain everything," said one of the uniforms. As Brendan was led away, he noticed the remainder of the queue at passport control watch him with a mixture of sympathy and relief.

He was taken to a small office out of the view of the public gaze and asked to remain there until a customs officer came to see him.

# TV Star

Behind a two-way mirror in an adjacent room, two customs officials watched Brendan Fendon for forty-five minutes. They knew he couldn't see them, but had been hoping he'd do something to prove his guilt. So far, Brendan had just sat there; crossed his legs; uncrossed his legs; checked his watch at five minute intervals, but nothing to arouse suspicion.

"He looks too relaxed. He's done this sort of thing before."

"Yeah, he's got balls, I'll give him that. Not tried to hide it or anything has he?"

"Thought he might be trying to flush it down the lavvy by now but it looks like he's going to brave it out."

"Probably knows about the mirror and knows we'll see it. Wanna go in yet?"

"I'll give him another ten minutes. See if he'll sweat a bit."

Eventually, Brendan heard the door behind him click open. He swivelled round to face his captor.

"At last," he said annoyed, "do you know who I am? You'd better have a good reason for keeping me here."

"Mr Fendon, my name is Andrew Hull. My colleague here is Frank Copeland. We work for the Customs and Excise here at Heathrow." He gestured towards the non-speaking partner who nodded. "Mr Fendon, the answer is yes, I know who you are. I know where you've been and what you've come back with."

"Pardon?" said Brendan, bemused.

"It's my understanding that you have returned to the country carrying a large quantity of narcotics, with the intention to make a deal with the Colombians this weekend."

"What?" Brendan croaked, "but that's absurd."

"Mr Fendon, I'm not going to beat about the bush here." Andrew Hull moved threateningly closer to Brendan who gulped involuntarily. "The information we have suggests that your case is so packed with cocaine that it could burst open if treated without due care."

Brendan gasped. His mouth opened to speak but nothing came out. He had to content himself with making his eyes bulge in the hope that this proved how mistaken the man was.

"We have investigators currently going through the luggage looking for your case. Any objections if we look through it?"

Brendan shook his head. He was now wishing he hadn't worn his overcoat – he was starting to sweat.

"And there's the question of your hand luggage. We'll need to go through that as well. Could I see your case please?"

Brendan nodded and lifted the briefcase wearily to the table-top.

"Keys?" asked Hull.

Brendan patted his pockets before realising he hadn't locked it. He opened the catches himself and caught his breath in surprise when the contents revealed themselves. This was not his case.

"This isn't my case!" he exclaimed.

The two customs officials moved closer. Hull took careful notice of the various magazines and papers, in particular the fact that they all seemed to be in Spanish or Portugese. He wasn't quite certain which, but he knew they definitely weren't English.

"So these are not yours then?" he asked, waving this

month's Bogota Boobies in Brendan's face.

"Err, no," said Brendan.

"Looks like he could have already made the switch on the plane or in the airport," Hull said to his colleague, still holding the magazine, "check out all arrivals on that flight and have the sniffer dogs in the Arrivals Hall just to be on the safe side. Get names of the people he sat next to and especially the ones who will be leaving London within twenty four hours."

The other official nodded and left.

"Now Brendan, may I call you Brendan?" Brendan nodded. "Tell me where the cocaine went and I'll be easy on you." Hull dropped Bogota Boobies on the table in front of the sweating Brendan.

"I do not honestly have the first idea what you are taking about," said Brendan, unable to take his eyes off Conchita and her 'magnifico 42DD' chest. "Who gave you this information anyway?"

"I'm not in a position to name names, Brendan, just that some people eventually get fed up of people like you using their position of power to abuse the system. You think you're above the law, don't you?"

"Not at all," said Brendan, "there seems to have been a dreadful mistake."

"You're right there, and it seems to me like you're the one who's made it. Now if you're not going to be co-operative, Brendan, I'll have to do this the hard way," Hull added as he snapped on a tight rubber glove with a resounding thwack.

Dave Bayley's friend Patrick Levine had been sitting in Reg's suite reading the contract for about an hour. Patrick was in his final year of law school – like Josh and Rachel who helped out in the hotel when Dave was busy. Patrick had manned the Denis Law bar for a couple of years until his studies became too concentrated to give up the time. Gave up one bar for another, he was fond of saying. Dave had briefed him on the background and to his credit, Patrick had not laughed once.

"It looks fairly watertight," he said to Reg, "can't see any loopholes or anything that will give you a get out clause. Bit of small print here indicates that if you renege, then you lose all rights to money. You could probably count on not receiving any compensation or fulfilment of the salary terms and certainly have to pay back what you have spent so far."

Reg looked glum as Patrick continued to pore over the contract. Norman, as usual, sat at his side quietly.

"Off the record, I'd advise you to do nothing until they contact you. It wouldn't surprise me if they had their legal team doing exactly what I'm doing now, looking for a way out. Unfortunately for them, it's pretty much cut and dried. Their next step will be to try and get you to admit culpability and ask you to voluntarily renege. If you do that, then they may seek compensation or some kind of redress for you impersonating a football manager..."

"But I.."

"...which could mean a law suit or a custodial sentence, for what they might try and say is fraud. If you don't want to lose out," Patrick continued, "then admit nothing. If they cancel, they'll be required to fulfil the terms of the contract. So just sit it out and see what they say."

Patrick looked at Reg, who just sat there looking small and lost. Patrick smiled fatherly, which was ironic as Reg was around twenty years older.

# TV Star

"Look Reg, you can't lose out if you stick to your guns. Do they know where you are?"

Reg shrugged.

"Well I can't imagine it'll be too long before they figure it out. Until then, bask in the limelight – you're the next England manager, if only for a few hours. Make the most of it."

Reg managed a watery smile and mouthed a thanks. Patrick stood and made for the door, but hesitated and turned round.

"Listen," he said, "I've got a friend who works on a production team for the BBC. It'll probably do you some good if you appear on something saying how excited you are about the challenge."

"But..." Reg was horrified.

"You don't have to mean it," Patrick continued, "it would show that you're intent on keeping your side of the bargain and you don't think a mistake has been made. You say how much it means to you and that you'll do everything to ensure a success."

"If it works, then..." mumbled Reg.

"Then it'll show the FA that you won't be taking the blame for something that is entirely their fault. It should force them into offering you some compensation to step down. Do you see?" Patrick said.

Reg saw. Norman touched his hand to acknowledge support.

"It sounds like a good idea, Reg," Norman said.

"Aye," said Reg, "well if you think it makes sense."

"I do," said Patrick, "I'll get it set up."

Patrick left the two men alone in the Royle Suite. Upon leaving, he had a quick word with Dave to let him know how they had fared. Patrick also used the telephone in

Dave's office to ring his friend Sean, who immediately saw the opportunity to progress his career. Within an hour, a reporter was on his way to the Kippax for an exclusive interview for the ten o'clock news.

Barbara Fendon switched the television to the ten o'clock news just in time to see the interview with Reg. She slipped in a video tape – Brendan would want to see how his new man performs in front of the cameras. Wonder where he is, she thought. He should be home by now. She turned her mind to the television, where Reg's interview was beginning.

Voice: "I'm in the company of Reg Atkinson, who was today announced as the new England manager. Reg, thank you for joining us at short notice."

Reg: "My pleasure."

Voice: "Now, the events of today appear shrouded in mystery (Reg nods emphatically). Unfortunately we've not been able to get hold of the FA for their version of events, but can you shed any light on what's happened."

Reg: "Well, I have accepted the position of England manager and have every intention in doing justice to the role. I appreciate that my experience is probably not what most people would expect, but I'm excited by the challenge and am determined to see it through."

Voice: "This is the one thing that we're unsure of Reg – why do you think you've been chosen above the likes of the other candidates, Bryan Robson, Peter Reid, Ron Atkinson, for example."

Reg: "To be honest, I don't know. All I know is that I've been offered the job and I've accepted."

Voice: "From what I can see – and I don't mean to belittle

you in any way – you have not really had much experience in top flight management."

Reg: "No I haven't, you're quite right. When I look at this in context, my belief is that I can bring a refreshing change to the game. I'm not constrained by the standard way of doing things. Granted, my main experience lies in the Sunday leagues, and I am by trade a plumber, but I'm determined to give this job my best shot. I'm meeting the players tomorrow morning for the first time, so we'll take it from there."

The camera crew was packing up at the Kippax. Dave had arranged for the interview to take place in the Book Room – after Tony, he explained, the only realistic name he could give the library. It had been the perfect setting for the incumbent England manager to hold court. Books on football lined the shelves, books on Manchester City mostly, but Reg noticed a few others dotted about. Gave a natural backdrop, he thought.

Patrick had insisted on knowing all the interviewer's questions up front and had stayed to school Reg in the replies. Half an hour well spent as Reg came through the experience very well. As the news team left, Patrick congratulated Reg on his effort.

"You did well," he said, "you gave just the right performance."

"I was scared to death," said Reg. He had recognised the interviewer from somewhere but couldn't put a name to the face.

"Looked okay," Dave confirmed, "came across well. Good advert for the Kippax too."

"I hope this works," said Norman, who as usual had

convinced himself that the world would come crashing around their ears very soon.

"It will," said Patrick, "everyone will know now that Reg is up for the job and it's down to the FA to make the first move. I'll tell you what – there's a good book in this."

"Thanks for all you've done Patrick," said Reg and shook the younger man's hand.

"Hey, my pleasure," said Patrick beaming, "let me know if you need anything else and good luck. Don't let the bastards grind you down."

Patrick made his farewells and left.

Reg, Norman and Dave headed for the bar. A handful of journalists had congregated there and Reg answered questions for half an hour based on his previous replies before Dave invited them to leave. The hotel was now a closed shop.

Andrew Hull could not find what he wanted. Despite a thorough search of Brendan's luggage, his clothes and his internal workings, there was absolutely nothing except Bogota Boobies which could be considered against regulations. Reluctantly, he allowed Brendan to leave without charge.

"You'd be surprised what people try and smuggle in. I once found a live parrot inserted up someone's rectum. He'd taped a tube down its throat to help it breathe and had the end dangling out of his arse. Poor thing would have suffocated if he'd sat down for too long."

Brendan wasn't interested. "You'll be hearing from my solicitor," he said menacingly.

"I wouldn't waste your money," said Hull, "if we get any sort of message about people carrying crack, we have the power to search without prejudice. Your solicitor will know that."

Brendan scowled. Crack? he thought. Wait till he found out who left that message. It was just before midnight when Brendan hobbled out of the Arrivals Hall looking extremely dishevelled and angry. His suitcase dragged behind him with items of clothing hanging out of the joints. Someone somewhere was going to pay for this. By God, his solicitor would be speaking to the Head of Customs at Heathrow, despite what that fellow in there had said about the law being on his side. Nothing gave him the right to examine him internally with such vigour. Brendan winced at the recent memory – he wouldn't be able to sit down for a week.

He flagged down a black cab outside the airport and clambered in. He lay down in the back seat to avoid any undue pressure on his nether regions and laid his suitcase down on the floor of the cab. The briefcase had been kept for evidence until the Colombian magazines had been investigated further.

"Where to guv?" asked the driver.

"Wimbledon, 23 Orchard Gardens, very carefully please. Try to avoid any potholes." wheezed Brendan.

"Right you are. 'Ere, funny do today wasn't it? I mean..." began the driver. Brendan lay in the back in obvious discomfort not listening. All he could hear was the sound of the road under the wheels and the shrieks from his rear end as the taxi surged over the tarmac. The last thing he wanted was to be engaged in conversation with a taxi driver. He occasionally caught snippets of the driver's monologue, but most of it sounded like insane rambling.

"I mean," said the driver, "it's not every day you get a qualified plumber to manage the national team. That's if he is a plumber. Could be just newspaper talk. Never trust the newspapers – they'd have you believing all sorts if you let 'em. That BSE thing. Nobody had ever heard of BSE before the papers got hold of it. Now they're trying to have us believe that we've got a plumber leading us to the World Cup Finals. Nah, don't believe it meself. FA couldn't drop a bollock like that could they, I mean, if it was Ron Atkinson they wanted, why pick this bloke. I suppose his name's similar. Eh, do you think they're related – Ron and Reg? Bit like the Krays. Bit spooky that, maybe it's some gangland thing, eh guv?"

Receiving no reply, the driver looked in his mirrors and noticed Brendan almost supine on the back seat with his eyes closed. He tutted to himself and drove on in silence. He considered driving up and down for a while before getting to Wimbledon but this bloke looked the sort who knew the fare to the penny. Ah well, he could continue with his gangland theory – that should keep the journey interesting.

Brendan left the taxi feeling very unsteady. He had eventually resorted to telling the driver to shut up – in between the drone of the engine and the hum of the road, the constant drivel about plumbers, gangland killings and JFK finally broke him. He handed the driver his money and minced to his front door as best he could dragging his untidy looking case behind him.

Barbara Fendon opened the front door for him.

"Brendan Fendon, what time do you call this? Dickie said you'd be landing this evening."

"Spot of trouble at the airport, dear," said Brendan, helping himself into the house using the door frames. "Would you mind just getting my case, Barbara?"

"Oh, did you get your message about the Colombians?" Brendan's face was a mask of steel as he looked upon Judas.

"You..." he said, beginning an accusation but not having the strength to follow it up.

"Yes dear," said Barbara, not realising Brendan's mood, "they rang to tell me about the mix up in the briefcases and Dickie very kindly offered to leave the message at the airport. You got it then?"

"Scratcher, the buffoon!" Brendan raged. "God help me I'll swing for him. What the bloody hell did he tell them?"

Barbara shrugged. She only knew her side of the story.

"What's this?" asked Brendan as he was passing the table in the hallway. Next to the telephone, an evening newspaper lay with the headline 'ATKINSON IN – FOOTBALL DOWN PAN'.

"That phone's not stopped ringing all night," said his wife.

Brendan held the paper in his hand and read the big news about Reg. Reg, he thought, surely they mean Ron...oh God, Scratcher, what have you done. The awful truth did not take long to sink in once Brendan started to concentrate.

"I taped the news for you. Do you want to see your new man?" she asked. Brendan nodded dumbly and they headed for the lounge. He picked up the remote and hit the play button.

"It'll need rewinding," said Barbara. Brendan tutted noisily and rewound the tape. When it had finished, he pressed play. Brendan's jaw dropped when Reg appeared on screen. Barbara thought she heard it hit the carpet. He moved closer to the television, brow furrowed. As the unseen reporter asked Reg about his thoughts on the game, and the squad available, Brendan was screaming in disbelief.

"What the hell have they done?" he shouted to no one. Barbara knew to keep quiet. "I've been away for four days. I leave instructions that Ron Atkinson is to be the new manager and what happens? The bloody fools have brought in a plumber to run the national team. A bloody PLUMBER!"

Brendan carried on watching the interview with mounting fury.

"He's meeting the players," Brendan gasped, "he's meeting the bloody PLAYERS! Who the hell does he think he is?"

Brendan was tearing about the house looking for his car keys. Ah, top drawer in the hall stand – just where he didn't leave them – thank you Barbara. Bloody woman was always tidying up.

"Off out dear?" she asked from the comfort of her chair.

"Yes I bloody well am," Brendan shouted from the hall, "someone has to sort this mess out."

Brendan slammed the front door shut on his way out.

"Seems nice, your new manager," Barbara shouted, but fortunately, Brendan didn't hear her. Two minutes later, Brendan had returned.

"That was quick, dear," Barbara said as Brendan hobbled past her and into the lounge. He didn't say a word in response, just grabbed a cushion off the sofa and headed back outside to the car.


Brendan dashed to the house of Piers Ffytch-Bottomley who lived nearby. It wasn't easy driving whilst sat on a cushion, but the feeling of his rear on the hard leather of the seat was unbearable. Ffytch-Bottomley proved useless – after five minutes of screaming at a man stood in his hallway in his pyjamas he realised he was getting absolutely nowhere. So he made an equally rapid journey to the home of Quentin Ridgeley, legal adviser to all manner of institutions, including the FA.

Unlike Ffytch-Bottomley, Quentin had not already retired to bed and seemed to be expecting Brendan. He had a copy of the contract already there – June had seen to it that it had been assessed by Quentin as a matter of course. Brendan fidgeted around in Quentin's study waiting for the verdict.

"Well it's absolutely watertight old boy," said Quentin, "wouldn't have it any other way, would you?"

"No way around it then?" asked Brendan.

"You've got two choices," Quentin continued, "you get this fellow to renege, in which case contract cancelled and you save your brass, or..."

"Or what?"

"Or you cancel the contract and you pay him off."

"No chance," said Brendan – more than his pride had been hurt tonight.

"Look, old boy, I saw the news tonight and your man has pledged his troth to the nation. He's looking forward to it," said Quentin, "if you cancelled now, you'll be preventing him from carrying out his job which essentially is breach of contract. You'd be liable for the full value."

Brendan looked deflated.

"However," Quentin went on, "if there was some way to deflect your man from carrying out his duties, someone laying obstacles in his path, leaning on him, you know..."

"Go on," said Brendan looking interested.

"Well if he had to resign because he couldn't cut it, it could be classed as dereliction of duty, then you'd probably have a good case for compensation. At the very least you'd walk away without having to pay him anything more. Get yourself a decent solicitor and you might even convince the court that he acted fraudulently."

Brendan considered this for a moment. This is where his inherent devious streak would come to the fore. He needed to mull this over for a while.

"Thank you, Quentin, Thank you very much," he said, rising squeakily from his high backed leather chair and pumping Quentin's right hand rigorously with his own.

"My pleasure old boy," Quentin smiled and led Brendan to the front door.

Brendan sat outside Sir Richard Scratcher's house waiting for the old duffer to return home. From Quentin Ridgeley's house, Brendan had decided to approach Sir Richard first to give him a good grilling. Unfortunately, he hadn't been home, which had given Brendan time to formulate a plan of attack.

At just after two a.m., Brendan had pieced together the foundations of his strategy, when he noticed a pair of headlamps coming his way. His car stood on the opposite side of the road to Sir Richard's front gates, under the cover of a large tree about two doors down. At this hour he was relatively invisible. This was good as he intended to give the old fool the shock of his life when he got home.

The headlamps soon became recognisable as Sir Richard's Daimler. Brendan clenched his teeth and prepared to launch himself out of his Jaguar. The Daimler rolled to a halt outside Sir Richard's gates. As usual, Sir Richard's chauffeur drove the Daimler so Sir Richard could enjoy himself. The chauffeur stopped the car and opened the back passenger door. Brendan waited for the sleek grey hair to appear but to his surprise and horror, observed the blonde ringlets of his mistress.

"What the...?" he hissed through gritted teeth.

By now, Sir Richard had also left the car and was publicly showing his intentions towards June Whitless, who was making no attempt to ward him off. In fact, she seemed to be enjoying the whole experience as the older man kneaded the dough of her buttocks and lifted her skirt up slightly.

In a rage, Brendan threw open the door of his Jaguar, and marched toward the giggling monstrosities before him. To his shock, somebody else had the same idea. Two figures in black launched themselves from the bushes either side of Sir Richard's driveway and filled the night with explosions of light. It took Brendan a moment to figure out that they were camera flashes. This decided his next course of action – he returned quietly and sheepishly to his car, watching the scene unfold. Once the photographers had been chased away by the chauffeur, Brendan started the car and drove thoughtfully home.

# SATURDAY

It took about an hour for Reg and Norman to get to the England squad's training ground at Bisham Abbey, and then around the same length of time for them to gain access to the training ground as no one was prepared to let them in. Fortunately, one security guard recognised Reg from his television appearance the night before and allowed them through. Security didn't seem to have the same rules for members of the press who appeared to be let through quite freely.

It was like a dream come true for Reg. The top footballers in the country were going through their individual training routines in front of him, led by one of the national coaches. As the players saw him, they stopped what they were doing and approached.

"All right lads," said Reg, glad that his voice didn't break, "you may or may not know, but I'm the new England manager."

There were a few puzzled shrugs amongst the players.

The coach nodded confirmation. All the while, Reg could hear the clicks and whirrs of many cameras from the huddled media near the edge of the training ground.

Unperturbed Reg began. "My name is Reg Atkinson and I'll be taking over until we get through the Germany game. This is Norman Whaddon, and he'll be my assistant coach through all this." He waited for dissension in the ranks, but there was none.

"Now," he continued, "I'll do my best to make this work but you have to work with me. I have a new system I want to try out and I'm sure that you'll be able to carry this out perfectly."

Reg briefly explained the theory of the 'Rambling Rose'. It didn't take long before the twenty-two players before him were itching to try this out. Reg split them into two teams, insisting that one team play the English way as described in the FA coaching manuals, and the other play the 'Rambling Rose'. Reg appointed Michael Owen as the focal point of the 'Rambling Rose' as this required an all-round athlete with an eye for goal.

Reg started the game. He and Norman took much the same involvement as they normally would during one of the Forest Inn training sessions – moving around with the players, coaching, advising and watching for any danger signs. For an hour, Reg and Norman were the happiest they'd been in a few days – oblivious to the crowd of photographers – helping and cajoling the best players in the country in what was going to be the most important few days of recent footballing history.

After two half-hours of play, Reg signalled the end and took the players through a warming down session before they headed for the changing rooms for a much needed bath.

# SATURDAY

"Mr Atkinson," said a voice. Reg looked round – it was Michael Owen.

"Yes Michael," he said.

"I enjoyed that," said the Liverpool forward. He had scored three goals. "Are we playing that way against Germany?"

"I should think so," Reg replied, "it'll confuse the hell out of them. Well played by the way."

"Well that went well," said Norman as he watched Michael Owen join the rest of the players.

"Yeah, it did, didn't it?" said Reg in wonderment. Could it possibly be this easy?

Brendan had spent a night tossing and turning in an effort to find a position of minimum discomfort. Unfortunately, this had been beyond him, so he was prowling the house with a snarl. Barbara knew to keep well clear of him in this kind of mood and Brendan had to be content with scowling at the odd inanimate object.

His lack of sleep had, however, given him time to think and he was now ransacking his study trying to pick the fruits of his thoughts. A few years previously, he had heard of a man who would put the frighteners on people for a small fee. Somewhere in this mass of paperwork, there was a business card. Brendan smiled grimly as he recalled the name: 'Tugwell', and that the man referred to himself as a 'facilitator'. Brendan had this image of facilitation as thumbscrews and drills through kneecaps. Just the job, he thought, there's a few people in this world he'd like to see hobbling about after what he'd just been through.

Where had he put that bloody card? The last time he'd seen it was had been when he forced an England manager to resign. After a run of poor results, the press had been manipulated into giving him a hard time but there was no shifting the fellow. Tugwell had posed as a rotten journalist who had put the fear of God into the manager's wife and that had been that. Brendan opened the filing cabinet and looked under 'T'. Success! There it was attached to the front of the first file in the drawer – 'Barry Tugwell: Situation Facilitator – Discretion Guaranteed'.

Brendan cursed himself for not looking in the obvious place sooner, but took the card to his desk. Pausing momentarily to place his cushion on his chair, he sat down carefully.

Brendan dialled and waited. "Tugwell," came the answer.

"Ah yes, Mr Tugwell," said Brendan, "this is Doctor Proctor. You did some work for me a few years ago."

"Doctor Proctor, of course. How can I help? Are you having trouble with a patient?"

"Actually yes. Dashed fellow's got himself into a bit of a pickle and needs helping out."

"No problem. Meet me at the Carter's Arms on Longdale Road at twelve noon." The phone clicked. Tugwell had hung up. Brendan checked his watch – he had ninety minutes. He nodded with satisfaction at the irony.

His telephone rang and he picked it up quickly.

"Brendan Fendon speaking... yes... yes... that will be fine. Yes, two o'clock. Is that the docklands one? Oh good. Yes I'll see you there."

Brendan hung up the telephone. A good morning so far, he thought to himself, Tugwell on board and a live television interview this afternoon. I'll get this sorted out if it's the last thing I do, he said to himself with a steely determination. Quick five minutes with the papers and then he'd better get moving. Oh Sir Richard, what a mess you've got yourself into...

Sir Richard was not happy: June even less so. Sir Richard had sent his chauffeur to buy a copy of every tabloid so he could assess the damage. It was worse than he thought. The photographers last night had managed to hit the late editions everywhere and made front page headlines.

'IS THIS WHY THE FA GOT IT WRONG?'
'MORE FA BLOOMERS'
'UP TO SCRATCHER'
'JUNE IS BUSTING OUT ALL OVER'

June was mortified. Every front page had a picture of her with her blouse gaping and Sir Richard with one hand on her bottom, the other on her chest, giving her a fierce open mouthed kiss. It was fairly obvious she was willing and it was fairly obvious – especially from one angle – that Sir Richard was enjoying himself immensely.

The general feeling from the press was that the FA were too busy canoodling their secretaries to make major decisions such as appointing the next England manager. This was why the country was relying on a plumber to take the national team through to the World Cup Finals. The press did not hold back and some of the comments were downright rude.

The witch-hunt was starting in earnest, and June and Sir Richard were on the stake. What would she say to Brendan – what could she say? Was there a believable excuse? It suddenly hit her how stupid she'd been – she thought she'd been doing it for the right reasons, to keep Dickie under control, when all along it was him playing with her. She'd lost the plot and no mistake. She started to cry – small sobs at first that travelled gently downstream before gaining force. Before long June was aflood with tears.

"It'll soon blow over June," said Sir Richard, soothingly, "it'll be all right, you'll see."

June sniffed, he didn't know the half of it, she thought and wondered what Brendan would say.

As he pulled into the pub car park, Brendan was wondering exactly the same thing. The newspapers had not shocked him at all – obviously a scapegoat was required and this would serve Dickie Scratcher right. After all, it was his fault in the first place – he couldn't be trusted to carry out the most simple of instructions. If his brain was where it belonged, in his head instead of his trousers, then he might have had half a chance.

This should play to my advantage, thought Brendan. I can get rid of two millstones in one go – June was getting to be a nuisance with all her incessant gabbling about Brendan leaving his wife for her. She just didn't get it – he would never leave his wife: the divorce settlement would crucify him. And Sir Richard? About time he hung up his boots anyway, stupid old sod.

Brendan smiled to himself and played out the drama in his head: Sir Richard resigns; Sir Richard blamed for appointment; Brendan does his best to remedy the situation; Brendan comes out smelling of roses. So what if the game is sacrificed – Brendan would be sure of his position for a few years to come. Oh yes, this was going to work out just fine. Just fine.

He parked the car, getting out with some difficulty, he grabbed his cushion and headed into the pub. Brendan made his way to the bar, spotting Tugwell immediately sitting on a high bar stool, nursing an orange juice.

"Mr Tugwell, how nice to see you again," smarmed Brendan, holding out a hand. Tugwell took it and squeezed.

"Doctor Proctor, the feeling's mutual. Drink?"

Brendan nodded – "Perrier water, if I may," he said, breathing a sigh of relief when the pressure on his hand decreased.

"Good man," said Tugwell, "alcohol dulls the senses." He clicked his fingers and a member of the bar staff came scurrying over. Brendan's concern was not for his senses but for the effect on his rear end should anything untoward be consumed.

Brendan recalled his original impressions of Barry Tugwell. The man had been recommended to him by a solicitor friend, as someone who could help get the best situation all round. Brendan had expected a thug, but had been surprised to find that Barry Tugwell was articulate, intelligent and had a presence about him which commanded submission. Although just over six feet tall, Tugwell's authority made him appear larger. Brendan knew he had used violence in certain situations, but usually relied on the power of his personality. On this occasion, Brendan couldn't care less, as long as he got what he wanted.

"Shall we find a quiet corner?" Tugwell said as Brendan's water arrived. Brendan nodded.

Within fifteen minutes, Brendan had told Barry Tugwell all he needed to know. A cash price was agreed with a bonus on delivery. Brendan wished all his meetings were so productive – usually, as in the case of the corner flags, one decision was made in the space of three days. As he whistled merrily on his way back to the car, Brendan realised that it had been a while since he felt so cheery – what other people's misfortune could do for you, eh? He settled his cushion down again on the driver's seat and set off to the studios.

Reg and Norman called at a pub in Banbury on their way back north to Nottingham. Norman had left Mabel in London and had insisted on driving his new Mercedes down all the A roads rather than the motorway. Fortunately, no one seemed to be following them.

As they nibbled through their lunch, the television news came on. Reg recognised Brendan Fendon from the previous week's television interview after the resignation of the previous manager. He asked the barman to turn up the sound.

TV: "...Glenn Gould has voiced his disapproval over the new manager and suggests that you have got your way. Is it true that he resigned because he was fed up with you enforcing tactics and the selection of players?"

Brendan: "Absolutely not. Mr Gould had *carte blanche* to select his own squad, name his own team, and to use whichever strategy he deemed fit for each game. After all, he is... sorry was, the manager and the buck stopped there. I think it a little unfortunate that he's trying to apportion the blame for his resignation to someone else. Maybe he now regrets his actions and is looking for me to assuage his guilt. Don't forget, Mr Gould was not forced to resign ten days before the most crucial game in the country's recent history – it was his choice."

TV: "Mr Fendon, if we can speak about Glenn Gould's replacement; you've returned from Brazil to learn that a manager has been appointed in your absence. Why were you in Brazil?"

# SATURDAY

Brendan: "Unfortunately, my commitments to the country mean that on occasion I have to provide a presence at FIFA and UEFA conferences. If I failed to attend, decisions could be made in my absence which could affect the very foundations of the English game. Unfortunately, this conference – important as it was – happened just at the wrong time. While I was away, the FA Committee members decided it was prudent to appoint a new manager. However, you have to look at this in context – if nothing had happened, the press would be asking why the national team have no manager. Instead they're now asking why we have one."

TV: "Mr Fendon, what can you tell us about this morning's newspapers and the allegations that the FA are too busy in the bedroom to care about the nation's chances of progression to the World Cup Finals."

Brendan: "As I previously stated, I have been in Brazil, representing my country at a FIFA conference, so I'm not totally up to date with the allegations reported today. What I can say is that I'm sure the pictures I've seen this morning are an isolated incident and do not reflect on the FA as a whole. The allegations certainly do not hold credence when it's stated that the FA have any other priorities other than that of ensuring that England qualify for the next World Cup Finals and win the competition. In fact, it's ridiculous to suggest such a thing."

TV: "What do you know about the new manager, Reg Atkinson? Is he someone you have been watching?"

Brendan: "The FA has long believed that the manger of England does not have to be one of the recognised English coaches. Until now, tradition has decreed that it has and we have had some good results because of this, but also some poor ones. We have failed on occasion to reach World Cup Finals where the likes of Belgium and Switzerland have qualified. It's time for a fresh approach and the appointment of Mr Atkinson is testament to this belief. Rest assured, that Mr Atkinson has my full backing and the full backing of the FA."

TV: "Following the allegations in the press today, where does this leave Sir Richard Scratcher, Mr Fendon?"

Brendan: "I have not had the opportunity to discuss the events with Sir Richard as of yet. When I do, be sure that the we'll takes the best step forward for the good of football in this country."

The interview ended. Norman wiped a stray piece of egg from the corner of his mouth.

"You have the FA's full backing Reg. Does that make you feel comfortable?" he asked.

"Looks a bit devious that Fendon, doesn't he? Wonder what he's playing at," said Reg, more to himself than in answer to Norman's question. He returned to his lunch.

Brendan returned to his car satisfied. The interview had gone rather well, he thought, and he'd also got the germ of another idea. This business of traditional English coaches being a thing of the past was something to work on. He would give this some thought. Meanwhile, let's see how Atkinson is shaping up. He used his mobile to call one of his coaches who would have attended that morning's training session.

After a terse five minute call, Brendan fumed. He could not believe that the players had enjoyed playing this new tactic and how successful it had been at first glance. Even his trusted coaches were saying it could work. This was not good. Any amendments to the FA Coaching Manual would mean massive cost, as well as Brendan having to oversee changes. No, not good at all. 'Rambling Rose'? If it got out that the FA had endorsed a system of play named after a shower head, the they'd be a laughing stock. No, check that, Brendan Fendon would be a laughing stock. He'd never be able to hold his head up again in FIFA, or UEFA, or anywhere else for that matter. The pantomime ended here, he said to himself and headed home.

Reg and Norman returned home that afternoon and were amazed to see bunting and banners on Reg's street, glorifying the new England manager.

'ATKINSON FOR ENGLAND' was prominent.

"Probably left over from last week's prints when they thought Big Ron was going to get it," chuckled Norman.

"Get out of it," said Reg, gazing around in wonderment. People were now coming out of their front doors and waving. Norman drove especially slowly so Reg could milk the moment. Reg was so proud; there was a tear in his eye.

"I don't think I can do this," he said.

"Pub?" asked Norman.

"Pub," confirmed Reg. Norman did a quick U-turn and headed for the Forest Inn.

Brendan sat on his cushion in his study in front of the computer, treading the Internet path. He had written to every chairman and every manager of every club in the land advising them of the position with the new England manager. Unfortunately, he had said, the new man – although chosen on merit – had decided to go his own way as far as tactics and strategy were concerned. This was against the express wishes of FA sanctioned coaching standards as set out in the official handbook.

"This new system represents a serious danger to the future of English football," he continued. I should at this point remind all clubs of their commitment to the FA's doctrines that make up the bedrock of our game from the grassroots up. It is therefore with regret that we are forced to announce that any player selected to represent his country will remain uninsured for the duration of his stay with the national squad. If injury occurs while representing England, the player will not receive compensation, nor will his club. The player's pension rights will also be revoked as the dangers of this system are as yet unknown. As footballers' careers are short and very highly paid, the pension companies will not tolerate any member further jeopardising their career in this manner.

Brendan spent around two hours getting the wording exactly right – he phoned Quentin Ridgeley for a spot of advice and in the end was happy with the result. He added a short paragraph on cancellation of appearance fees and copied the letter to the players' union, before hitting the send button, taking the letter to every footballing inbox in the country.

Some years previously, the FA had decided to nominate certain weekends during the year to be free for certain clubs who were due to lose players to international commitments. This weekend was one such weekend, and the Saturday fixture list was so sparse that non-league clubs found their names on the pools coupon.

However, just because the top clubs had no games, it did not mean that the grounds were empty. Stadia were populated by the remaining playing staff, managers, board members, chairmen and executives. All in all, plenty of people around to discuss the latest missive from the FA which had just arrived at inboxes throughout English football.

The view was unanimous. In light of the dangers inherent in any unauthorised system played by the national team, there could be no alternative. Every board in the country could not – would not – allow any one of their prized assets to risk injury without the possibility of compensation. The Players' Union stood by the advice of the FA and began instructing their members to withdraw their services due to potential legal wrangles over pension entitlements.

By early evening, every player in the England squad had been recalled by his club while each potential replacement had been refused permission to be called up, and every other Englishman in the league had been warned of the risks in jeopardising their short careers. A few had objected at first, but the Union made them see the wisdom of their eventual choice.

Brendan Fendon sat at home with his PC turned on, watching his inbox swell with return mails. He smiled contentedly. A good plan, he thought – simple yet very, very effective. Each mail he opened contained the thanks of various high-profile Premiership figures – thanks for alerting them to the possibility of risk to their players, their assets and their clubs.

He sat back, pleased with his day's work, steepling his fingers towards his lips and chin in a temple of thought. Now for the sacrificial lamb, he thought to himself, and picked up the phone to call Sir Richard.

Early evening. Reg is sitting at home alone. He and Norman had slipped into the Forest Inn at usually one of the quietest times and discovered it was packed to the rafters with people who wanted to catch a glimpse of him.

He'd been back-slapped and handshook till he could take no more. Ken Mercer, the landlord, told Reg he was on free drinks for the rest of the week, as a thank you for increasing profits by a thousand percent since the announcement.

Reg had eventually made his way to the bar to see Carol. He asked her if she was still on for tomorrow and she responded positively.

"Not every day I go out with a celebrity," she said in good humour.

Reg had then made his excuses and left. He needed time to think, which was why he was sitting alone in his front room, with the TV pictures dancing around on screen, but the mute button pressed on the remote.

Why me, was his one question. Why not some other bloke? He knew it was all a mistake now, how on earth had he ever thought otherwise? At least it hadn't gone totally pear-shaped. Thanks to Dave's lawyer friend Patrick, he even had the basis of a plan. Hopefully this should allow him to avoid making a loss, which he knew he could not afford. But there were always the dark thoughts lingering, especially after seeing that greasy Brendan Fendon this afternoon giving him his full backing. How many managers had had the Board's backing before feeling the cool sharpness of the blade on their necks?

Don't worry about it, he kept saying to himself. It's the FA's fault, not yours. You accepted the contract in good faith. It's not your fault they got the wrong bloke, but still...

# SATURDAY

Reg sat up in his chair. Brendan Fendon was on the telly and he knew that he had to hear what he had to say. He fumbled for the remote that had somehow slipped down between the cushion and side of the chair.

"Come on, come on," he hissed before grabbing on to the offending object. He pointed it at the TV and the sound resumed.

TV: "...have any bearing on the decision to resign?"

Reg was sorry he'd missed the first bit – if Brendan was resigning, then his worries might be unfounded.

Brendan: "I'm not at liberty to say. What I can say is that after a conversation with Sir Richard this afternoon, when I asked after his welfare, he told me that his position had become untenable and he felt he had no choice to resign from the FA Executive Committee and to pursue other interests."

TV: "His other interest being, of course, your charming secretary June Whitless?"

Brendan: "I'm a great believer in peoples' private lives remaining private and I do not see why this has to be aired in public. Sir Richard obviously thinks that his judgement may have been clouded by his ongoing affairs and has taken the gentleman's course of action."

TV: "Brendan, would you say there was any connection with the resignation and the fact that a plumber has now been offered the England manager's position? A decision that was taken while you were out of the country.

Brendan: "Obviously, representing one's country is a great honour and one should feel satisfaction when doing it, but I must admit to being disappointed that I wasn't in the country when the decision was made. I'm not saying I would have made a different decision, but I believe I could have offered a different perspective on each candidate. I do feel that in that regard I have possibly let the FA down at a very important time. Unfortunately I cannot be in two places at once. In my absence, Sir Richard was the deciding factor in the appointment of Mr Atkinson. I'm confident that this appointment was made in the best interests of everyone, in Sir Richard's view."

TV: "Many people are blaming you Brendan. Previous managers have been very negative about the appointment and are suggesting that no decision would have been made without your approval. One view is that you wanted a caretaker but got a plumber. What's your view on that?"

Brendan: "The people to which you refer should ask themselves why they no longer hold the position of England manager. It's fine to be flippant about this appointment, but is there a fear that the new man Atkinson – a plumber – could prove more successful than they themselves? We have to give him the chance to prove himself. If it turns out to be the wrong appointment then you need look no further than the door of the FA when apportioning blame. All I can say is that although I wasn't here to confirm the appointment, the committee knows I support their decision."

TV: "So are you saying that you didn't make that decision?"

Brendan: "What I'm saying is that I did not become aware of the appointment of Reg Atkinson until late Friday evening following my return to Brazil. The decision to appoint was made in my absence as a result of a committee meeting."

TV: "Brendan, there's a rumour that certain players have withdrawn from the England squad today. Is this true?"

Brendan: "I believe that is true, yes."

TV: "Could you tell us why? Is it a protest against the new management team?"

Brendan: "As far as I can tell, no, but I'm sorry, I don't have the full details to hand at the moment. There are normally a few dropouts due to injuries received in training, but I don't think that is any reflection of the squad's lack of faith in the new manager. As I said earlier, the new man has the full backing of the FA and will remain in the job as long as he is able."

TV: "Brendan Fendon, thank you."

Brendan: "Thank you, and may I wish the country well and the team good luck against Germany."

Reg sat back in his chair. Certain phrases spewed out by Brendan Fendon just didn't add up. He was increasingly worried about the penultimate sentence – "will remain in the job as long as he is able." Sounded like he expected Reg to conclude he wasn't up to the job.

Reg mulled this over – if Brendan Fendon was expecting him to quit then he was mistaken. Reg was concerned about the question about the squad players dropping out. He'd not heard about that.

He picked up the phone and called Norman. Norman answered fairly quickly.

"Thought it might be you Reg,"

"Did you see Fendon on the telly just now?" Reg asked.

"Certainly did. Slimy little bugger in't he?"

"Have you heard about these players dropping out?"

"Well I hadn't," said Norman, "but I can't say it surprises me. That weasel's probably got at 'em."

"But it'll come out won't it, if he has?"

"Depends. If he's as crafty as he looks, it'll look like somebody else's bright idea," said Norman.

"What do you reckon I should do, Norm?"

"You could either sit there and wait for the morning papers or ring the players."

"The players?" asked Reg shocked.

"Reg, you're the England manager, you're allowed to talk to your players."

"Oh yeah," said Reg stunned, " Cheers Norm. See you tomorrow."

"Bye,"

They both hung up.

Reg wondered where he'd get the players' numbers from. Dave would know, he thought, and picked up the phone again.

Sir Richard Scratcher sat at home in a leather armchair, nursing the latest in a long line of triple vodkas. He hadn't spoken to June since she burst into tears. The only person he had spoken to since was Brendan Fendon.

Brendan had been diplomacy itself, allowing Sir Richard to believe he was on his side. The conversation took the format of Sir Richard apologising for everything that had happened since the year dot and Brendan consoling him and telling him that it wasn't all his fault. The more Brendan spoke, the more soothing his voice had become and consequently more persuasive. It hadn't taken long for Sir Richard to come to the conclusion that his resignation from the FA was the only way out of this problem.

In the lingering shadows of his home, Sir Richard was now wondering whether he'd made the right choice. It wasn't all his fault – Brendan himself had told him who to appoint, he couldn't blame himself for getting mixed up. Had Atkinson ever said outright that he was a plumber?

# SATURDAY

Had he given any indication? No...and who would have ever thought that a plumber could have sneaked into the manager's pile. Brendan had told him who had filtered the applications – June. His dear June had set the wheels in motion and now Sir Richard's career was plummeting downhill at an alarming rate.

June. He who lives by the sword, dies by the sword, he thought as he took another swig of the vodka. It was obviously his dalliance with June that had affected his judgement. June Whitless. It was because of June that his picture was on the front page of every newspaper as the man who had wrecked England's chances of making the World Cup Finals. He was a pariah, a leper. Brendan had mentioned that Atkinson would also pay. It wouldn't be too long before he resigned, and if he resigned, then Brendan would sue him for something or other. What had he said? Something like misrepresentation with a view to defraud?

He needed inspiration; something to keep him going and his mind active now that working was no longer an option. He thought as long and hard as he could about what he should do. Staring deeply into the ice nestling at the bottom of his glass, he came to a decision: it was time for another bottle.

June Whitless sat at home alone, nursing a teddy bear, curled up on her sofa. She too was in turmoil. It was obvious Brendan would not want her now, after the in-depth coverage of her in all the papers, skirt aloft. It was also obvious that Sir Richard had been scared off as he'd not called her all day. So where did that leave her?

She looked at the phone. It had rung three times today: two from journalists who had uncovered her phone number and one from a magazine wanting to know if she'd be interested in showing a bit more for their adult male readers. She hadn't heard a peep out of either Brendan or Sir Richard. Surely Brendan would know, especially after all the front page headlines. She had expected him to be around in a flash demanding to know what she'd been up to while he was away. She could have handled that but this was worse – she had no idea what he was thinking.

Should she call him, she thought. What if his wife answered? That would probably make it worse. Oh God, what a mess. She sat there in silence, rocking gently until the room went dark around her.

Reg had spoken to Dave Bayley who, in turn, had spoken to Patrick Levine, who in turn, had spoken to his friend at the BBC. Patrick had then relayed the news to Dave who, in turn, was now on the phone to Reg.

"The best we can find out is that most of the squad has been recalled by their clubs, but we're not sure why."

"But they all seemed fine this morning...I wonder if bloody Brendan Fendon has got something to do with this," Reg seethed.

"Dunno Reg. It's usually only injuries that force the players to leave the squad, but it wouldn't surprise me if the FA are after you quitting. Patrick reckons that the only chance they've got of getting their cash back is if you resign. Sounds like they're trying to put a bit of pressure on you," said Dave.

Reg thought about this. So that was what Brendan was on about – he had the job as long as he was able to do it.

"The way it looks is player revolt. Nobody's got anything definite to say but it seems to have come from all the clubs recalling their players. At the end of the day, the clubs pay their wages so they have the final word."

"Thanks Dave, you've been a great help."

"No problem Reg. Sorry it couldn't have been better news. Patrick says hang on in there – you can always pick a new squad."

"Aye, I suppose so. Bye Dave." Reg hung up. This needed some thought. A noise from the back of the house disturbed him. What the...he thought and trotted through to the kitchen. He looked out of the window to see someone stealing his rubbish. As his jaw gaped, the figure outside looked up, smiled and flashed a press badge. Unbelievable, thought Reg, and was about to charge out of the house in a rage when he noticed some photographers lurking in his garden, behind the man going through his rubbish. Bastards, he thought and left them to it.


Brendan Fendon had had a very busy day – even at midnight he was still beavering away at his computer. His plans were well underway and seemed to be succeeding nicely. Not only had he convinced most chairmen that their players' involvement was a non-starter, he'd even found himself a couple of very tame journalists who were willing to write a couple of complimentary articles.

Such were the benefits of his position. People were allowed to talk to him but at a price. This Atkinson would cave in soon – he'd never be able to survive the pressure of the situation. Biggest match in England's recent history and Atkinson wouldn't even be able to field a team. What sort of manager let his countey down?

Brendan smiled again. The forthcoming game was expendable. So what if England had to forfeit the three points and lose out on the World Cup Finals. Brendan saw himself coming out of this mess smelling of roses. Decisions had been made in his absence which he was trying manfully to resolve for the good of the nation. That is what the people would believe. He was prepared to back the new man to the hilt: that was also what the people would believe. It would be Atkinson's fault if the game were forfeited, no one else's. The people of England would crucify him.

As long as there was that belief in Brendan, he could carry on in his position at the FA for another four years, by which time, he'd be ready for retirement.

Back to work, he thought, no point mulling over the success of his plan before it had had a chance to succeed. He had questions to provide his tame reporters. Better make them good ones, he thought.


Reg was awakened from a light sleep by a familiar squeak from downstairs. He couldn't be sure if it was the usual noise made by opening the fridge door or whether he'd dreamt it. He lay in bed looking at the ceiling in the gloom wondering if it was his imagination playing tricks. After a short while, he checked his digital clock, which said it was just after two o'clock. Then he heard the television. Hadn't he turned that off? He thought he had, but his mind was all shot to pieces. He could have left the thing on, the front door open, the oven on and he wouldn't remember.

He swung his legs out of bed, found his joggers and sweatshirt and made his way downstairs in his bare feet. Stopping at the kitchen first, he saw the fridge door was closed. He opened it, then closed it, hearing the squeal of the hinges. Hmm, was it that I heard, he thought. He padded into the lounge to see that he had indeed left the television on. He crossed over through the gloom to turn it off.

"Oy! I was watching that." The voice from behind him almost sent him through the roof with shock, but Reg managed to swivel around to face the intruder.

"What...who...what the...?" Reg couldn't get the right words in order at first, "how did you get in? Is nothing sacred? First you go through my bin, now you break in to my house and watch my telly. I've had just about enough of this – you've got ten seconds to get out before I call the police." Reg's voice had raised in anger.

"Touch the phone and you lose the use of your fingers," said Barry Tugwell. There was something about his voice which made Reg check; something hypnotic behind the London accent.

"Sit down, Reggie. We need to talk."

"Don't you tell me to sit down in my own house..." snarled Reg recovering some of his composure.

"Reggie, sit," countered Barry Tugwell. Reg sat.

"Now, I have an employer who is not best pleased with you. My employer..."

"What do you mean employer? You're not with the press?"

"Reggie, if you interrupt me again, I will hurt you. Do you want me to hurt you?" Reg shook his head. "Okay then. My employer would like you to resign immediately and return the cheque which you took on Thursday. If you do that, my employer is prepared to forget this unfortunate situation and leave you alone. However, should you choose not to take this advice, then I cannot promise either your safety or your loved ones."

"Loved ones?"

"Let's just say that after you were dripping all over that

lovely young lady behind the bar tonight, I became interested. Even asked her out, but she said that she already had plans...with you."

"You were in the pub? You talked to Carol?" Reg stammered.

"Oh yes, I was in the pub looking for you Reggie. Amazing what you can pick up in a pub. Your little friend Norman, he's a card isn't he?"

"You leave Norman alone! And Carol for that matter. Whatever I've done, you can deal with me, just don't bring them into it." Reg stood and moved threateningly closer to Tugwell in the dark. Tugwell also rose to counter Reg's threat.

"But they're involved, Reggie. You can't forget about them. Just by meaning something to you, they're involved. Now about that cheque."

"I haven't got it. I cashed it. It's in my bank." Reg was now standing in the centre of the lounge after recognising that a tussle with the intruder was probably a mistake. He sounded too confident – probably one of these gangland heavies who could break an arm with one finger.

"Tsk, tsk, tsk. Cashed it, eh? Oh dear Reggie. My employer is not going to be pleased. I promised I wouldn't leave you tonight without that cheque. So where does that leave me?"

"Dunno," said Reg, "but it's not exactly an ideal time to go down to the bank is it? They won't be open until Monday."

"No you're right there."

"As far as I can tell, you're a reasonable man," said Reg, "by now you know that you have no chance of getting that cheque tonight. So why don't I go to the bank on Monday morning and get it all sorted out."

# SATURDAY

Tugwell pondered this. "Why should I trust you Reggie?" he asked.

"You don't have to. Just realise that you have at least a chance of getting the money back on Monday, whereas tonight you have no chance."

Tugwell laughed. "You've got some balls Reggie. Tell you what, if you don't come up with the goods by ten o'clock...no I'm feeling generous, twelve o'clock noon here on Monday, I'll pay your ladyfriend and your boyfriend a visit. Okay?"

"You'll get your money, just stay away from my friends."

"I will, providing you come up with the goods. Don't forget that resignation letter – I want that too."

"Your employer?" asked Reg, "it's Brendan Fendon isn't it?"

Tugwell mimicked a thinking pose: "name doesn't ring a bell," he said.

Reg watched the dim figure leave the lounge. There was the sound of the front door opening and then closing. Reg breathed a huge sigh of relief – at one point there he thought he was in trouble and would be spending the rest of the night in hospital. But what could he do about Carol and Norman – he'd have to get the cash. The problem was, how to make up the difference from what he'd already spent. Reg fumed. Besides, he hated being called Reggie.

# SUNDAY

Reg was awoken early by the telephone. "Hello," he mumbled, still half asleep.

"Reg, it's Dave,"

"Hiya Dave. What time is it?"

"Just before nine. Listen, two things. One – turn on Sky Sports for the latest news, and two – Patrick has booked you on to Richard and Judy tomorrow morning."

"Eh?" said Reg, startled.

"It makes sense. Patrick says the FA have started getting aggressive. It must be this Fendon bloke. The media is giving him a hard time and he's biting back. Doesn't look like he's going to back down and he's trying to make things as difficult as possible for you..."

Reg flicked on the television and turned on Sky Sports. Dave continued in his right ear.

"...without actually coming out and saying it was all a mistake. Fendon is giving you full backing but he's definitely up to something."

"Hang on, did you say Richard and Judy?"

"Oh yes, Patrick's idea."

"But..."

"He thinks it will give you a bit of street cred. You know, appeal to the daytime brigade. If we can get the country behind you, then it will show the FA that you have got the people's backing."

"Oh, I see," said Reg, not seeing.

"There'll be someone giving you a call this morning to arrange times and venue. Good luck Reg."

"Right...cheers Dave. Thanks again," Reg finished. He turned his attention to the television – the 9 o'clock session was just beginning.

TV: "Today's Headlines...is this the face of the man who will take England on to the World Cup Finals (big full screen picture of Reg in one of his shiftier poses) or is it the face of the man who has instigated the biggest players' revolt in modern times?"

Reg gaped.

TV: "Good morning. The entire England squad has pulled out of the World Cup clash with Germany, apparently due to differences of opinion over the tactics the new manager is employing. Our man, Stan Miller has been speaking to some of the players."

The news coverage then went outdoors as Stan Miller asked the same question of a few famous footballers, all of whom Reg had met for the first time yesterday. In response to the question: 'Why have you decided to pull out of the squad?' players basically gave the same answer: 'for personal reasons'.

Reg was staggered. There had been no mention of this yesterday when he'd been with the players. They had all seemed to enjoy the change in tactics, Michael Owen had even told him so. Michael Owen's face appeared on screen.

Stan: "Michael, tell us why you've had to pull out of the squad."

Reg sat bolt upright.

Michael: "It was a club before country decision. My manager told me to come home as there was some dispute going on."

Stan: "What sort of dispute?"

Michael: "I don't know. All I do know is that my club pays my wages and at the end of the day, if they tell me to do something, I do it."

Reg's phone rang. It was Dave.

"Reg, take a note of this number." Dave read out a telephone number.

"What's this for?" asked Reg.

"It's a direct line to the Sky Sports production team. Patrick got it for you. Get in there and put your point of view across. Best form of defence is attack."

Dave hung up and left Reg with the telephone number scrawled in pencil on the back of yesterday's Daily Mirror.

As Reg picked up the telephone and began to dial, Brendan Fendon appeared on the television screen.

Brendan was comfortable under the warm lights of the studio. He had always had a talent for this sort of thing, coming across as confident, well-educated and a man of principle. When he knew the questions beforehand (especially when he'd written them himself), he felt even more comfortable and could concentrate on his facial expressions. After all, he wanted the British public to see a man who was hopelessly patriotic trying to do his best for the country.

Face and words, Brendan, he told himself, face and words.

Brendan: "Well obviously, it's unfortunate, but these things happen. Players are always pulling out through injury, but a mass revolt is a new thing for us all. I'm not sure I remember such a thing happening before under any England manager."

TV: "Do you blame Reg Atkinson for this then?"

Brendan: "Not at all, please don't misunderstand, but Mr Atkinson is relatively inexperienced in the role and has a lot to learn. Unfortunately, with the game on Wednesday, this situation has to be resolved as soon as possible. We don't want to have to forfeit do we?"

TV: "Is a forfeit possible?"

Brendan: "If we cannot field a team on Wednesday night, then a forfeit of the game is the only solution. We cannot possibly expect FIFA to postpone the game because the England manager is inexperienced and unable to field a team. Goodness me, no. The Germans would go on to the World Cup Finals by default."

TV: "So what do you see as the next steps? Reg Atkinson is going to have his work cut out in the light of having no players available to train in the short term. Will it be possible for him to select a new squad in the time involved?"

Brendan: "Mr Atkinson must do what he can in the face of adversity. He has my full backing and the backing of the FA as a whole. If he wants assistance, then he can always come to us for help."

TV: "Has he done that yet?"

Brendan: "Unfortunately not, otherwise I'm sure we'd have resolved the problem by now. As I have stated, Mr Atkinson has our full support while he continues to perform his duties to the best of his ability. He will need to take

**187**

stock over the next few days and do what is right for the country."

TV: "But if that means resigning, where will that leave the national team?"

Brendan: "Let's not discuss resignations at this stage. Mr Atkinson has signed a contract of employment and we expect him to perform his duties. He is not under any pressure from the FA at this stage as we believe he deserves the chance. Mr Atkinson, however, may have a different view in the face of public opinion."

TV: "You've received some criticism in the morning papers Brendan. The headlines 'HANNIBAL SPECTRE' and 'IT'S GOT SWEET FA TO DO WITH ME' in particular refer to the period you spent out of the country while the Reg Atkinson appointment was going through."

Brendan: "The media will always look for a sacrificial lamb and it's disappointing of course. However, if you take a less insular approach, you'll find that some newspapers actually back my position on this, in particular..."

TV: "Brendan, I'm sorry but we must interrupt. Apparently we have Reg Atkinson on the telephone now. Reg, good morning."

Reg: "Good morning."

If Brendan looked momentarily flustered, he recovered well. His smile returned almost before it left his face. The interview had been going very smoothly up until now, but you could never trust live television.

TV: "Reg, what's your view over this supposed 'player revolt'?"

Reg: "I'm not sure how I see it. I trained with the players yesterday morning and we worked through a few new things. The session went very well and comments from the players themselves gave the suggestion they'd enjoyed it."

TV: "But things must have changed since. The entire squad has pulled out and returned home."

Reg: "I believe so, perhaps Mr Fendon can shed some light as to the reasons why."

Brendan: "I'm sorry, why on earth..."

Reg: "Regardless of having your full support Mr Fendon, I didn't see one player on the interviews this morning who gave the exact reasons why they pulled out. Neither did I hear any player blame my tactics, strategies, styles of play or otherwise. The one common factor seemed to be that they came home because their clubs insisted upon it. In addition, my home was broken into last night and I was physically threatened to resign."

TV: "Brendan, can you answer this?"

Brendan: "I'm sure Mr Atkinson is looking for someone to blame for the player revolt, but I don't really think he can throw that back at me. As far as threats go, I have no idea what he is talking about. All I can say is what I have said on numerous occasions – that he still has our full backing."

Reg: "That particular record seems to be stuck Mr Fendon. Can you tell me why – if I have your full backing – that I couldn't contact any of the squad players last night to ask why they'd left? Could you tell me why, when I rang your offices that I was denied access to the list of players and their telephone numbers? Could you tell me why the clubs involved recalled their players after a particularly successful training session yesterday? And could you tell me why you're sitting there so smugly endorsing the credentials of a man, who, up until Friday morning, was a plumber and Sunday league football manager?"

Brendan's face had coloured. This was not going well.

TV: "Brendan, is it true that your offices denied Reg access to the players?"

Brendan: "It most certainly isn't (it was – those were Brendan's explicit instructions to the evening receptionists) and Mr Atkinson should be ashamed of himself for suggesting it. We want nothing more than to enjoy a successful reign under the new manager and this is all the thanks we get..."

Reg: "Thanks? You think you deserve thanks? I know what you do deserve..."

TV: "Okay, let's just try and get to the bottom of this now. Brendan, does Reg have a point?"

Brendan: "I don't think he does. I..."

TV: (leaving Brendan floundering in mid answer) "Reg, these threats. Tell us more."

Reg: "I have been told to resign on Monday or I am in danger of adding to the National Health bed crisis. I can't prove anything but I'm pretty sure I know where the origin of the threat lies."

TV: "And you think it's the FA?"

Reg: "I couldn't possibly comment on that. As I said, I have no proof. I would not want to name names on television and risk legal action."

TV: "Reg, what are your plans between now and Wednesday?"

Reg: "My plans are to get a football team together for Wednesday night. If the players that have pulled out don't want the honour of playing for their country, I'm sure there are thousands more who would cut off their right arm to be on that pitch and do their country proud. This afternoon, I'm going to say goodbye to my players in Nottingham and following that I'm going to call up more players. Mr Fendon there is going to give me unlimited access to all qualified English players so I can set about doing what he's paying me to do."

Brendan: "Of course. There's obviously been a little misunderstanding that I'd be only too glad to resolve. Call my offices this afternoon and I'll arrange for everything you need."

Not on your Nelly, thought Brendan, and smiled again. His composure had returned – all right, so Atkinson had interrupted his moment; so he'd come over as a man of passion. If he couldn't get a team on to that pitch on Wednesday and get a result, he'd be forced out. Brendan's smile was almost feline. He'd let Reg have access to the club directories – let him deal with the managers rather than the players.

TV: "Reg – sounds like Brendan Fendon is giving you his full support after all. You say you're saying goodbye to your players this afternoon?"

Reg: "That's right. Forest Inn versus the Golden Pheasant from Newark. A win today will keep us clear at the top of the league."

TV: "Good luck with that Reg. Thanks for coming on and participating in what's been a fascinating debate. Brendan, thank you too. It's been very interesting."

Brendan: "Always a pleasure."

As Brendan took off his microphone, the production team was already on the phone to the Golden Pheasant public house, Newark. Brendan left the building without a second glance.

Reg turned up at the Forest Inn at the usual eleven o'clock to sort out the arrangements for the game against The

Golden Pheasant. Norman was already there with the players.

Sundays like this were Reg's escape from the real world of work. It was his chance to become a child again almost as much as it was for the players. It surprised him sometimes how willing they were to get changed from their car boots, on touchlines, pub car parks and really dingy outhouses. It was all the same for them, just somewhere to get rid of their joggers and reveal the kit.

Today was a home game. Ken Mercer usually opened the pub early to allow the players to get changed inside and then walk the two hundred yards to the pitch. Like most Sunday leagues across the country, the Forest Inn team played on something that resembled a park. One massive square of land divided up into around twenty separate pitches, every single one of them in use at the same time. As a result, footballs were sometimes in play on two pitches at once as defensive clearances and wayward shots encroached into other areas. It had been known for referees on one pitch to book players from another, as sliding tackles were prone to continue over touchlines and end up taking out someone's legs on the pitch next door.

The pitches were prone to waterlogging and mud was something which had become part of the game. For this reason, Ken Mercer did not allow the players to return to the pub once they'd left it, unless they had washed and showered first. Except his son Malcolm, of course, who lived there.

"Hi lads," said Reg as he entered the pub lounge.

Various responses greeted Reg and he couldn't help laughing as the entire team began bowing with arms aloft shouting "We're not worthy, we're not worthy."

# SUNDAY

"Get out of it, you lot," he laughed, "are you up for this game today or what?"

"Course we are," shouted Lance Lovejoy.

"Right then," said Reg, "shut up and listen. This will probably be my last game in charge of you buggers..."

"Not if you get sacked after Wednesday, man," shouted Geordie Best.

"...so I want a special performance," Reg continued, pretending to ignore Best, "get out there and win it – I don't want my last match to be a defeat. Send me off on a good 'un."

"Yes boss," growled the baritone of Baldy Charlton, amidst a chorus of positive cries.

"Right, well get out there and enjoy yourselves," Reg clapped his hands together and rubbed them animatedly.

As the team roared out of the pub lounge in the direction of the pitch, Reg turned to Norman.

"Did you hear about 'This Morning'?" said Reg.

"I saw it. That Brendan Fendon's so twisted, he'll meet himself coming backwards. And what's this about threats?" said Norman.

"Eh?" said Reg, not wanting to worry Norman, "no I don't mean that, I mean the programme 'This Morning', you know – Richard and Judy."

"Bloody 'ell, you're not going on that are yer?" said Norman.

"No, *I'm* not – we are!" said Reg.

"What d'yer mean, we?" Norman's jaw dropped.

"Well you're my assistant aren't you? There's a car coming to pick us up at eight in the morning – wear your posh frock," Reg chuckled.

Norman stood motionless as Reg followed the players

outside. Reg looked back to see how shocked Norman looked. He tittered to himself: you had to laugh, he thought, otherwise it might all seem so bloody tragic. Reg's humour faded – it had just dawned on him that an appearance on This Morning would mean that he wouldn't be able to sort out that cash from the bank. Oh bugger.

As the players were walking to the pitch, they noticed for the first time the crowd that had built up. Sunday games like this usually attracted a handful of people – mostly family and friends and the odd bloke walking his dog. Today, there were people all over the place.

A referee peeled away from the crowd to talk to Baldy Charlton.

"Y'all right, Baldy" said the referee.

"Aye Joe," growled Baldy, "what's going on?"

"They've all come to see your boss. I've had to swap pitches for your game – you're on the outside corner," said Joe, pointing towards a corner slot with trees lining one side and a large section of grass and a car park on another.

Baldy looked and nodded. "Thanks Joe," he said. He could see the logic – a large crowd could not be accommodated around any of the enclosed pitches, they'd just spill over on to the pitch next door. At least this way, they'd have two open ends.

Joe raced back to the pitch, he knew most of the teams who played on Sundays and most of the players by name. More benefits of the Sunday league.

Reg eventually caught the team up.

"Bloody 'ell," he said, nodding at the crowds. "Where've this lot come from?"

"You're famous now boss, don't forget," said little Johnny

Mullen, wizard of the wing.

"Definitely your fault boss," said midfielder Michael Quarry.

"Joe's swapped pitches," said the unmistakable growl of the hairiest man in Nottingham, "gives the crowd more of a chance to see us in action."

"Right," said Reg, "go on then, get out there and win."

The players trotted on to the pitch and started to stroke a few footballs around. Fat Jennings took up his usual position in goal and allowed Johnny Mullen and Lance Lovejoy to give him some catching practice. The other players warmed up as best they could – the morning was overcast and slightly chilly. The team from the Golden Pheasant arrived on the pitch and before long the game was underway.

Reg looked on with pride – this was the culmination of all his efforts. It seemed that the team were trying their best to send him off in style, with a commitment that he'd not seen at this level before. Reg's hands were warm with applause, as the Forest raced into a four goal lead after twenty minutes.

Around this time, Norman nudged Reg and nodded towards the nearby car park. Reg spotted a large truck with satellite dish on top, 'Sky Outdoor Team' on the side, unloading equipment hurriedly.

"Oh-ho," breathed Reg, more to himself than Norman.

The Sky team set up the cameras just before the end of the first half. The commentator – who Reg recognised but couldn't name – came over to him.

"Reg Atkinson?" asked the commentator.

"Yes," said Reg.

"Alan Parry, Sky TV." So that's who it was, thought Reg.

"We've come to cover the second half of the game today so that the British public know what you've achieved."

"Oh," said Reg.

"Is that all right with you, Reg?" said Alan Parry.

"Yeah, I suppose so," said Reg.

"How are they doing so far... playing well?" asked Alan Parry.

"Five nil up at half time," Norman interrupted – he wasn't sure if Reg had seen the fifth so didn't want his young friend to drop a clanger.

"Doing me proud," said Reg.

"Great. Well we'll get everything set up for the second half and if it's okay, we'll ask you a few questions before it starts and then again afterwards."

"Yeah, okay," said Reg.

Alan Parry positioned himself in front of the nearest camera and began to speak. It was the usual introduction – Sky giving exclusive coverage of Reg Atkinson's final game in charge of the Forest Inn Sunday League side. Then he turned to Reg, asked him more or less the same questions as before, wished him luck and advised of a quick break while the adverts came on.

As the film crew disappeared Reg noticed the lack of room around the pitch. The entire pitch was circled; people had resorted to climbing the trees parallel to the touchline in the hope of a better view; others were stood on roofs of cars in the car park. Unbelievable, he thought to himself, how things could run away from you. What was the word he was looking for... juggernaut, that was it – running away like a juggernaut. He was still mulling that one over when the referee blew the whistle to start the second half.

# SUNDAY

The second half was around ten minutes old when Reg knew he had a problem. His players had obviously spotted the Sky cameras and were attempting a spot of showboating. This would be all well and good for professionals, but the amateurs of the Forest Inn should really have been aware of their own limitations. Little Johnny Mullen was no longer content with providing pinpoint crosses, he now wanted to beat every player on the pitch before releasing the ball to someone else.

Other players were behaving the same way – a long hopeful ball into the Forest box should have been food and drink to Fat Jennings, but Fat gave his interpretation of Columbia's Rene Higuita's flying scorpion. Unfortunately this involved him landing flat on his face, having knocked the ball into the back of his own net for the Golden Pheasant's opening goal – 5-1.

Minutes later, Andy Tate tried an ambitious overhead back pass from near the corner flag which had Fat Jennings scurrying across his six yard line. The fluffed clearance went straight to a Pheasant forward – 5-2.

Malcolm Mercer, the least skilful of the players, managed a winding run from inside his own half, all the way to the opponents' touchline, before doubling back to his own penalty box. Having beaten fifteen players, including some of his own who wanted the ball themselves, Malcolm decided he should score and planted the ball in the back of his own net – 5-3.

Centre half Roy 'Cropper' Brooks had decided on his own little game of keepy-uppy, and to the roars of the crowd had amassed 26 before being robbed by the opposing centre forward, who again, finished well – 5-4.

Reg had had enough of this. He had sat through most of

it with his jaw around his ankles, totally dumbstruck. By way of contrast, Alan Parry was very animated as he shouted down his microphone. Fifteen minutes left and his team had nearly thrown away a five goal lead and were in danger of losing the game.

"BALDY," he shouted, "sort the buggers out."

Baldy nodded and growled at everyone individually – he was the only player who had so far not succumbed to limelight poisoning. Meanwhile Reg continued to lambast his side for the remaining quarter of an hour. Fortunately, the score remained the same.

As soon as the final whistle blew, Alan Parry's microphone was stuffed into Reg's face.

"Reg, what are your views on that performance? Three points in the bag, but almost threw it away in the end didn't they?"

"Bloody show-offs. They were trying to perform for the cameras. If they'd have thrown that game away because they'd acted like schoolkids I would have bloody throttled them," seethed Reg.

"Is that the type of performance we can expect to see against the Germans?"

"I would hope not. Hopefully professional footballers will be used to the cameras and not try any of the things you saw out there today."

"Do you think the result would have been any different under different circumstances?"

"If you lot hadn't 'ave turned up, we would have won by about twelve-nil," said Reg and decided that was about enough. He wanted to catch up with his prima donnas before they escaped into their cars and buggered off home.

"Well, probably not the performance Reg Atkinson

wanted in his final game," concluded Alan Parry to a shell-shocked home viewing audience, "but hopefully Wednesday will be a different game." As he wound up his microphone lead, he spotted a familiar figure in a sheepskin coat at the far touchline. The figure had been scribbling frantically in a notebook and was now walking quickly to a car parked away from the rest. John Motson had obviously decided to add to his wealth of knowledge by noting down information on the Forest Inn side. Now that's what you call commitment, thought Alan Parry.

As the Sky coverage concluded, many watching Germans sat rubbing their hands with glee. The events of the last week had brought nothing but confidence to a nation who had been fearing the worst. Following live coverage of the worst team performance any of them had ever seen, they were supremely confident that the Germans could book their tickets for the World Cup.

Reg caught up to Norman.

"Norman, 'Spanner of the Day' award?" Reg asked.

"We haven't got enough bog seats, Reg,"

Now Reg's whereabouts were common knowledge, he could not escape the reporters and TV crews which seemed to dog his every move. Questions were constantly being thrown at him, and he thought his tolerance levels would not last much longer.

He had called the FA offices and been given a list of e-mail addresses – apparently, this was the preferred method of the FA and the League and Premiership clubs for official call-ups to national squads. Reg cursed – he didn't have the internet at home and preferred to use the telephone. However, Norman came to the rescue – his daughter Jackie again. Reg and Norman had installed themselves at her PC, mailing clubs with details of call-ups. Jackie had left instructions on how to set up an e-mail address and left them to it while she and her family went off to B&Q.

"Did you understand any of that?" Norman asked, after she'd left.

"Not really, but it can't be that hard can it?" said Reg, looking down at his list of club addresses, "let's give it a whirl and see how it goes."

Norman typed in the first mail. They were both happy with the content and sent it.

"Why's Bournemouth first on the list?" asked Reg, "it looks alphabetical except that one."

"That's cos it's AFC Bournemouth," said Norman.

"Oh," Reg replied, "not 'cos Fendon's got a holiday home there?"

"Wouldn't have thought so. Be too warm for the old devil there. He needs to be in the Arctic somewhere, bloody frosty bugger."

"Try putting more than one address in on the next one," Reg laughed, "it's gonna take ages doing ninety two of these."

Between them, they managed to figure out the helpful address box and by the time Jackie had returned clutching wallpaper, they were trying their hands at 'surfing'.

"You two okay?" she asked, bobbing her head around the door.

"Aye, done and dusted," said Norman.

"Just waiting for responses," added Reg.

"What e-mail address did you choose?" Jackie asked.

"All of them," said Reg waving his list.

"No dopey, I meant your personal one," she laughed.

"Eh?" said Reg.

"You did choose one like I said?" Jackie said.

"Well we didn't understand that bit," said Norman.

"We just typed 'em and sent 'em," Reg added.

Jackie laughed and barged her way through them to the PC. She moved the mouse to a set of menus and then checked what they'd done. She screamed with laughter and startled the two men.

"What's up?" asked Norman.

"You're a right pair, you two," she said, "wait till I tell our Dave. You've sent all these very official looking mails to these very professional football clubs under my sign-on."

"And...?" said Reg, wondering where she was heading.

"Have you had any responses yet?" she asked.

"Dunno. We've not checked yet," said Norman.

"Well check this response and see who it's addressed to," she suggested, pointing to a return mail from Coventry. She clicked on the mail and Reg read it.

"Dear MrsFunnyBunny... what do they mean Mrs Funny Bunny?"

"That's my personal e-mail name. You think of something personal to you, and see if it's taken. If it's not, then you can use it under one of the e-mail providers."

"So we've sent all these mails out signed by MrsFunnyBunny?"

"Aye," she said, still laughing.

"Oh brother," said Reg.

"That's your fault," said Norman.

"What d'ya mean, my fault? You typed 'em."

"I'm too old to know about the internet. You just fall into the 'should know' section," groaned Norman.

"You cheeky bugger!"

"Come on, I'll show you how to do it," said Jackie, and within five minutes, Reg had a new e-mail name – 'atkinsonforengland'.

He and Norman typed a hasty apology to each club and resent the mails.

"Look," said Norman, "I'll stay here and look for the responses. If we get nothing, I'll keep trying and I'll ask for details of players who are available and then we'll take it from there. You go and get yourself tarted up for your date. Take the Merc if you want"

His date! Reg had almost forgotten. He thanked Norman, reminded him about the next morning – to which Norman scowled – and shot out of Jackie's house with a rushed goodbye. He raced home followed by his entourage.

Reg arrived at Carol's in his best going out gear. He had showered, shaved, been to the toilet three times, dappled himself with Calvin Klein's Obsession and generally felt very nervous.

"Hiya," said Carol as she opened the door. She looked over Reg's shoulder at his fan club of reporters.

"Nervous?" she asked.

"A bit, why?"

"Well you seem to have brought your friends," she smiled.

"Oh, no, er...they're not..." Reg fumbled. He looked at Carol who had tipped her head slightly and had that enigmatic smile on her face. She was having a little fun, he decided. He shut up before he blushed. She looked great – long red dress and a black choker around her neck. Her hair, usually tied back in a chestnut ponytail was now allowed to flow freely over her shoulders. Hubba hubba, he thought.

"Come on in," she said, "I'll just be a minute."

# SUNDAY

Reg sat down in her front room. Music was playing as background, but he couldn't make it out. Probably All Saints or something, he thought. He might get it for the Merc — see if Norman liked it.

"So, you're a rich fella then?" shouted Carol from upstairs.

"Pardon?" said Reg, who had heard the question, but wasn't expecting it.

"I said you're rich then," Carol was now in the room with him, her voice smooth and languid. Reg, who hadn't sat down, noticed that they were about the same height — he'd never noticed before. Probably due to her heels, he thought, taking in the full picture. He liked it.

"Well, depends how you look at it."

Carol, looked out of her front window, moving the lace curtain to one side with her right hand.

"I'm looking at a rich man's car," she said, "wanna take a poor girl out in it?"

"Yeah," said Reg, "you look fantastic by the way."

"Thank you Mr Rothschild," she said.

As they reached the front door, Reg paused.

"On the count of three then," he said.

Carol laughed. It was music to his ears. He opened the door and sprinted to the car, doing his best to avoid the questions and camera shutters. Carol on the other hand, took her time. She ignored the reporters but didn't rush.

Reg had opened the passenger door for her and she climbed in. She's done this before, thought Reg, as he watched her, legs swinging in together, not showing anything which might embarrass her later. Reg closed the door behind her and raced around to the driver's side.

"You took your time," he chuckled, "I'd have thought you'd have run."

"In these heels?" she replied. Reg chuckled, and drove away.

Pino's Italian Restaurant on the High Street was not somewhere Reg had been before. He knew it hadn't been open long but from reading reviews in local papers, he thought it might be somewhere to try should he need to.

Tonight, he needed to. He was glad he'd suggested it, as taking Carol to a pub would have been a bit too much of a busman's holiday. The fact that she'd dressed for the occasion as well showed she wouldn't have enjoyed anything less.

Reg had tipped the head waiter to keep the reporters outside. A few of them wanted to come in and keep closer tabs on the new England manager and his new girlfriend, but an autographed menu and the promise of a photograph to put on the new restaurant's wall was sufficient to keep the wolves at bay.

The inside of the restaurant was in keeping with what Reg held as an archtypal Italian bistro. The tablecloths were in green, orange and white, and some of the tables around the edges of the room had been structured into little alcoves. Red tile roofs sloped down towards the tables giving the appearance of a piazza; vines were interwoven through the alcoves and trailed down the walls. They were obviously fake, Reg mused, but added to the atmosphere.

"Nice place," said Reg as he peered over the top of his menu. He took a sip of his glass of lager. Carol hadn't touched hers yet

"Hmmm, very nice," Carol replied, "you decided yet?"

Reg glanced back down at his menu. They didn't do stuffed crust pizza, so he was narrowing down a choice of the least offensive.

"I was looking at the Pollo and pasta in Arriabiatta sauce, but I wasn't sure about mints and pasta going too well together," said Reg.

"Fool," Carol giggled, "I'll have the Parma ham salad to start and this tuna steak one." She pointed out a tasty sounding dish in a tomato and garlic sauce.

"Better get some garlic bread as well – if we both smell of garlic it won't be too bad," said Reg.

"Watch it you," said Carol, smiling her Mona Lisa smile.

"What sort of wine do you like," asked Reg.

"Red," said Carol, "and full bodied – nothing wishy washy."

Reg gulped at the wine prices. What the hell he thought, I've got money now. The waiter arrived and Reg ordered Mozzarella and tomato salad for him, followed by the chicken in arrabiatta sauce. Carol's selections were also noted. Reg ordered a Barolo from the wine list.

The waiter bowed slightly and left, leaving Reg and Carol to themselves. There was a slight pause, which Reg broke.

"Should have brought that polar bear,"

"Sorry, why?" asked Carol bemused.

"To break the ice," grinned Reg.

Carol laughed. "Do you think you need to. I thought we got on quite well."

And so they did. The wine arrived and they chatted for a while before the starters arrived. Carol's salad looked good; Reg was a little concerned about his mozzarella cheese – it looked like three giant golf balls sitting on large slices of beef tomato. The cheese itself looked wet, as though it had been submerged for a while before being dumped on his plate. Reg prodded one ball gingerly with his fork, making it roll a little.

"What's up?" asked Carol, a mouthful of ham on its way to her mouth.

"Not what I was expecting," said Reg, "I thought it would be like pizza cheese."

Carol nearly choked laughing.

"No, I mean I thought it would be melted over the tomatoes," Reg added, "it looks like..."

Reg was almost about to add bollocks, but thought better of it. He cut a slice off one ball. It looked more like chicken, the way it parted. He tasted it, carefully.

"Hmmm," he said, "not totally horrible, but I don't reckon I'll eat it all." He continued to pick at pieces of cheese and tomato. When Carol finished hers, Reg still had most of his left, and when the waiter reappeared, he knew he had to ask.

"Was everything a all right a signori?" asked the waiter, in his best Italian accent, looking at Reg's plate.

"A bit different," said Reg, "What exactly is mozzarella then? I thought it would be melted cheese."

"Zis is ze purest mozzarella," said the waiter, "ees kept in a water until a ready to eat. Ees made only in Italia from buffalo..."

Bollocks, thought Reg and shuddered.

"...milk," finished the waiter.

"Ah," said Reg with relief. Carol was now holding her napkin to her face in a futile attempt to disguise her amusement. As the waiter left with their plates, she looked at Reg.

"I don't believe you," she said, "your face when he mentioned buffalo."

"Well, I thought he was going to say..." Reg paused. Carol guffawed again.

"Not quite one of life's sophisticates, but at least you know how to show a girl some fun," she said, still laughing.

The rest of the meal went well for both of them. Reg was surprised how easy it was to talk to Carol and felt very comfortable with her. The troubles of the last few days were forgotten. Carol for her part felt very much the same: Reg was still like a little boy at heart and that's what she liked about him. When they both realised that they were the last ones in the restaurant, they were a little surprised.

Reg paid the bill and when Carol offered half towards it, wouldn't dream of taking it.

"Absolutely no way," he said, "this is my treat. Oh and I nearly forgot..." Reg put his hand into his jacket pocket and it came out holding a small box.

"I should have given you these earlier, but what with all the fuss..."

He handed the box to Carol. She frowned slightly before she opened it. When she did, the diamonds sparkled temptingly.

"Oh, Reg, they're beautiful, but I can't..."

"Course you can. Consider it a thank you for tonight."

"So you wouldn't have given them to me if I had been a bit of a witch, then?" Carol feigned indignance.

"Probably not," said Reg, "I would have worn 'em myself. Now put 'em on and let's see how they look."

Carol took off her current set and replaced them with the new ones.

"Well?" she asked.

"Not bad," said Reg non-committally, laughing when he

saw the tightness creep into her lips, "they look great, but I think it's you that makes 'em look that way."

"Reg, you old smoothie, what are you after?" Carol leaned across the table, hand positioned underneath her chin as a rest. Her lips parted slightly and Reg could see the whiteness of her teeth.

"A back door would be good," he said, nodding towards the reporters who were still camped outside, "come on, let's go."

The media were becoming impossible. Reg was not inclined to drive too fast on half a bottle of red wine – he didn't know how close to the limit he was. The back door exit had seemed like a good idea at first, but he reckoned without the tenacity of his new friends. The fact that they knew his car didn't help matters.

As he pulled up outside Carol's house, the car was surrounded once again by cameras.

"Next time we do this, can we do it all a little more privately?" asked Carol.

"Next time? Yes of course, I hope." Reg answered – next time, he thought, great.

"I'd invite you in, but we'd probably end up on the Adult Channel," Carol smiled, showing milk-white teeth. Wow, he thought, I am besotted.

Carol kissed him lightly on the cheek.

"Thanks, Reg. I really enjoyed tonight," she said, opening the car door, "and thanks for these." She tickled her ear lobes creating little starlight explosions in the interior light.

"My pleasure," said Reg, "I'll call you...when I've got this game out of the way. Give you my undivided attention, then okay?"

# SUNDAY

"Okay, Reg. Good luck." Carol smiled once more – was it tinged with a little sadness – and was lost in a sea of reporters. He could just spot her flow silkily to her front door. One last wave and she was gone.

Reg drove off. He was feeling good and ready for anything. Bring on Richard and Judy; bring on Germany, bring on the press and the bloody FA and all the thugs they could throw at him.

# GOOD MORNING BRITAIN

Reg made sure he was up early, showered shaved and was in his best suit for the trip down to London. He was fairly apprehensive but was now becoming used to the fact that he was in the spotlight. My fifteen minutes of fame, he thought.

He had spent another mainly sleepless night, working out the best plan of attack with Brendan's thug. Next time they met, he was determined to find out the bloke's name. Might as well be on first name terms with the man who'd break his kneecaps, he thought. The best solution he could come up with was to leave a short note of apology and promise to be there the next day at the same time in an envelope on his coffee table. As he wouldn't be there to greet Mr Thug, it was fairly obvious the bloke would find his own way in again. If he found no Reg, but a letter inside the house, then he just might leave Norman and Carol alone.

He stood at the window of his house looking down the street. It was empty apart from Lou Thompson jogging down to the paper shop for his daily read. The joys of modern suburbia, he thought. Even the press had homes to go to, unless they were in his back garden sleeping under the trees. Where were they when he needed them last night? He'd bet good money on not one of them getting a shot of the intruder. All he had to do was pick his nose and it'd be in the next edition, but someone breaking into his house – not a chance.

A large black vehicle cruised down his street, breaking his train of thought. This must be them, he thought to himself, as it stopped outside his house. Reg scampered out of his front door and down his path. A chauffeur was ready to open the rear doors for him. Big car, thought Reg – a limo, very nice. He slid into the rear of the vehicle when the door was opened for him.

Inside the limousine, Reg made himself comfortable on leather seats. He noticed he had a mini-bar and television, complete with remote control. Blimey, he thought, so this is how the other half live. He thought of asking the chauffeur to drive round to Carol's, but decided against it. He gave him Norman's address instead and they headed there.

"This is posh," said Norman when he was safely installed in the limousine. The driver pulled away from Norman's house and began the journey down to London.

"'S all right, in't it," said Reg.

"Here," said Norman, "thought you might want to have a look at this." He handed Reg a Daily Mirror.

"Bloody 'ell!" Reg shouted. A full page headline read: 'TREASON!' and, in smaller but still fairly large type: 'New England Manager snubs British Motor Industry'.

The main point of the story was that Reg had driven in a German car to meet his secret ladyfriend. Carol was described as a mystery woman in her early thirties who was unavailable for comment.

"No doubt I'll get asked about that today," said Reg.

"I'll bet you will," said Norman chuckling, "daytime telly likes a bit of gossip to chew over."

Reg continued with the story: his entire date had been reported, even down to their goodnight kiss in the car. Bloody media, he thought – if this is what being a celebrity was all about then they could forget it. He liked his privacy. He'd call Carol and see how she's taking it as soon as he could. Last thing he needed was for her to take the hump, and he could do with giving her advance warning of the... God, how do you tell someone that a nutcase may be after her?

"I think you're mentioned on about thirteen pages out of the forty," said Norman, in a matter of fact way.

Reg turned to the back and was treated to another banner: 'NO TURNIPS, BUT MAYBE A SWEDE!' This one bore reference to Reg's comments about the Swedish heating system being the best in Europe, and how he might compare to Graham Taylor who some newspapers viciously reported as a turnip during his unfortunate reign as England manager. The Editor's comment advised that although Reg was seen as a joke in this country, in Sweden he was seen as a God.

It was strange reading about himself like this. Reg had never liked taking home school reports because of the fear of somebody else thinking badly of him, but this...This was like being on trial across the length and breadth of the country. And not just England, he thought, the rest of Europe was having its say. Bloody Germans were falling all over themselves trying to have digs at him. Cheeky sods – some German politician was suggesting they make Sir Richard Scratcher an honorary Chancellor for appointing a plumber to take charge of the biggest game in years.

"On page seven they've got one of those ten things you didn't know about you," said Norman.

Without thinking, Reg flicked to page seven. What am I doing, he thought. I should be chucking this out of the window. He started reading instead: aloud.

"Ten Things you didn't know about the new manager of the England football team. One: Reg Atkinson's middle name is Stanley, after the comedian Stan Laurel. Bloody cheek! They've made that up!" Reg spluttered. Norman held back a laugh.

"Number two," Reg continued, "Reg Atkinson is divorced and lives in Nottingham where he has a plumbing business. That's better. Number three – Reg's first wife Shirley left him because he would never amount to anything. Ha! Serves the daft cow right."

Reg read quickly through the others, which were fairly dull: mainly a potted history of his upbringing, until he got to number ten.

"Look at this one," he shouted, almost falling off the seat, "Randy Reg's 'Rambling Rose' formation was invented after he spent a night in a Swedish massage parlour."

"Was it? I thought it was based on a shower spray," said Norman, struggling to contain his mirth.

"Course it bloody was," Reg cried, "Bloody Swedish massage parlour – people will be thinking all sorts of things. I know what's coming next. I'll get asked if it's Golden

Showers or something. Oh God. And… what are you laughing at?"

Norman couldn't help himself. His giggles had evolved into a full chortle and now he was laughing like a drain.

"Sorry Reg," he gasped through tears, "just don't believe everything you read in the papers."

Reg curled the paper into a cylinder and gave Norman a clout on the head.

"Cheeky old git," he said and then collapsed into a fit of giggles himself.


The journey to London was incredibly comfortable. Reg and Norman helped themselves to a touch of Dutch courage from the mini-bar and turned on the TV to see the build-up to 'This Morning'. Reg wasn't too well up on daytime television, and found the choice of early morning programme strangely fascinating. He flicked between 'My partner gave me a sexually transmitted disease' and 'How can I tell my husband I want to be a man?' During some adverts, Reg discovered that he was down to appear on the show at around eleven and experience a live phone-in. He shuddered with the prospect.

They arrived at the studios at just after ten o'clock. Reg and Norman were escorted to a dressing room where a make-up girl was assigned to powder their faces.

"It's just to reduce the glare of the studio lights," she said, "are you nervous?"

"A bit," said Reg. Norman nodded meekly.

"You'll be fine. Richard and Judy are lovely – they'll make you feel right at home," said the girl, "make sure they like you and make sure that you like them."

"Eh?" said Reg mystified.

"They're very popular. If the viewers see that you like them and they like you, then the viewers will like you. All makes for good TV. Get the viewers on your side and you're laughing. People's careers have suffered if Richard and Judy take a dislike."

"Oh, I see," said Reg, who had a tenuous understanding of what she was trying to say.

"Right, I'm done," she said, "Good luck."

"Thanks," said Reg, "and thanks for the advice too."

"'S all right. Enjoy yourselves." She smiled and left.

"Nice girl," said Reg.

"Yeah, maybe she can go on with you," said Norman, "do I 'ave to?"

"Yes you do Norman Whaddon," said Reg sternly, "you're my right hand man don't forget."

"Oh God," said Norman plaintively. He looked at the clock: fifteen minutes to go.

As the clock ticked slowly towards eleven, there was a knock at the door. Reg looked at Norman quizzically before ambling over to open it. Television's most famous couple, Richard and Judy, stood on the other side.

"Come in," said Reg, heart a flutter.

"Great to meet you," said Richard, grabbing hold of Reg's hand and pumping it enthusiastically.

"Yes, it's really good of you to come along today," said Judy smiling, "we're really looking forward to it."

Reg introduced Norman, who fell victim to Richard's handshake.

"Our producer thinks it would be a cracking idea if you could demonstrate how to resolve simple plumbing problems. You know the sort of thing – what to do if you've got a leaky tap, or my ballcock keeps getting stuck and flooding the bathroom when I least expect it," said Richard.

"Oh so, it's not just about the football then?" said Reg.

"Normally it would be," replied Richard, "but we've never had a plumber as the England manager before and we have to cater for our viewing audience so we thought it'd be brilliant if we could link the two on the phone-in."

"Yes," Judy jumped in excitedly, "we could try and find plumbing problems related to football..."

"Like the team bath being too cold..." said Richard.

"...or funny stories about people losing their kit in the washing machine..." said Judy.

"...ooh yes, and we could ask people to ring in with what's the most bizarre piece of sportswear they've ever lost in their washing machine. We might even get a few jockstraps." Said Richard.

Richard and Judy threw a few more suggestions on the same theme as Reg wondered why he'd allowed himself to be led into this. He could understand the reasons why he had to, and could understand why Richard and Judy needed to please their usual daytime audience, but he felt an element of concern that he might look stupid if he wasn't careful.

"We're running about five minutes late at the minute," said Judy, "there was a bit of an incident with some curling tongs in this morning's makeover. Took a while to get the extinguisher foam out of that girl's hair. We'll get back to the set and when you see this light come on..." Judy pointed to a green light over the door — "that means you have two minutes to go. Someone will come and get you. Good luck."

"Yep, good luck," said Richard and they let themselves out.

Reg looked and Norman and raised his eyebrows. Norman said nothing.

The studio used by Richard and Judy is probably the most recognisable set on television. Watched by millions on a daily basis, Richard and Judy are the epitome of teamwork, working for and covering each other. Both had started quite innocently on regional television, but had bridged the gap to national TV with apparent ease. They were comfortable in front of the cameras and the viewers loved them for it.

Richard: "Now on 'This Morning', we have a treat. Not only does the country have a new football manager, but he is also a plumber."

Judy: "What a combination. And we're delighted to have him on 'This Morning'. Please welcome Reg Atkinson and his assistant Norman Whaddon."

The cameras turned to the chairs containing a nervous looking Reg and even more petrified Norman.

"Hello," said Reg, trying out his voice – it didn't break.

"Morello," said Norman, who had been running through 'morning' and ' hello' in his mind in an effort to choose the best option. Richard and Judy continued without missing a beat, ever the professionals.

Richard: "Reg, Norman, many thanks for coming on the show. Now you've got an important game on Wednesday night against Germany. How are things going?"

Reg: "The pressure is obviously on to get a result. Obviously, I would have liked a bit longer in the job so I could work with the players, but that hasn't been possible. I'm not trying to make excuses and I'll give it everything I've got."

Judy: "Norman, you're Reg's right hand man aren't you,

on both the footballing level and a plumbing level. How has this changed your life, being in the public eye?"

Norman: "Err...it hasn't really. Reg is the one who's gettin' the attention."

Richard: "I've seen some of the attention you've been getting in today's papers Reg. Does it hurt sometimes, reading what they're saying about you?"

Reg: "Yes it does and I don't think it'll be something I'd ever get used to. Mind you, half the stuff is made up. They should check their facts before printing it and maybe people would see that I'm just an ordinary bloke trying to do a job. Until Friday morning, I was convinced I'd landed a plumbing contract. Now it looks like I'm leading my country's team out in the most important game for years. It's definitely been a strange few days."

Judy (to the camera): "Now Reg and Norman have very kindly agreed to participate in today's live phone-in and the lines are open now. Just call the number on the bottom of your screen if you have a question for Reg or Norman on any topic involving football or plumbing."

Richard: "Yes do call in, and we've also got a special make-over planned for Reg by Nicky Clarke towards the end of the programme and Norman will be assisting Andrew Nutter in creating a culinary extravaganza based on football favourites. We'll be back in a few moments after this break."

As the cameras blinked off-line, Reg leaned over to Richard and whispered.

"What special make-over?"

"Oh it's nothing, you get dressed up in a posh suit. You'll look good, honestly. The viewers will love it, which is the main thing. They'll see you as a man of the people."

"Right," said Reg unconvinced.

"What about me? Am I cooking?" asked Norman looking at his shoes in dismay.

"Don't worry," said Judy, "Andrew does the cooking. He might ask you to chop some carrots or something, but apart from that you just stand next to him and get to taste every now and again."

A man with headphones appeared with a clipboard and began to countdown from ten using his fingers. They were back on air.

Richard: "Welcome back everyone. We appear to have our first caller, Betty from Stockport. Good morning Betty, are you well?"

Betty: "Yes. I'm eighty-two you know."

Judy: "Are you really? That's wonderful."

Richard: "Bless you Betty, what's your question?"

Betty: "My husband was a plumber."

Judy: "Well that's a coincidence, isn't it Richard?"

Richard: "It certainly is. What's your question, Betty?"

Betty: " My husband Arnold was a plumber..."

Judy: "Yes..."

Betty: "...but he never became the manager of England..."

Judy: "Oh dear..."

Betty: "...and I'd just like to know why."

Richard: "Good question, Betty, tell me, did Arnold apply for the vacant manager's job."

Betty: "No, he died five years ago."

Judy: "I'm sorry to hear that Betty..."

Richard: "And I would have thought that there would have been some regulation or other preventing dead people from taking up that particular post."

Betty: "He was a plumber though."

Judy: "Did he ever apply to become a football manager while he was alive?"

Betty: "No. Plumbers don't apply for things – people ring them up. He had his number in the Yellow Pages. It was as clear as anything. I'd like to know why that plumber has got this job and my husband didn't."

Richard: "Reg, do you have an answer to that?"

Reg: "Well I don't think my plumbing experience had anything to do with the fact that I'm now the England manager. I like to think that my management experience and fresh views were instrumental."

Richard: "Actually, that reminds me of a story, Betty. A few years ago, a friend of mine told me about a time when his Mum had gone shopping in Manchester, when she bumped into Francis Lee in Sainsbury's. She dropped her shopping and Francis Lee offered to help. 'Can you manage,' he asked. 'Not for you I couldn't' she replied, picked up her shopping and walked off."

Judy: "Wasn't that a joke, Richard?"

Richard: "No, no, it was a serious offer. In the end Francis Lee brought in Alan Ball so it proves that he missed out with my friend's Mum. Any of us could get the call any minute."

Judy: "Okay, thanks for your call Betty. Are we ready for the next call? Kath in Doncaster. Kath, are you there? Welcome to 'This Morning'."

The phone-in continued in the same vein for the next ten minutes. Reg and Norman both warmed to Richard and Judy and it was easy to like them. They seemed genuinely interested in what the callers had to say and were never patronising to anyone, even though Reg was sure *he* would have been. The questions, which came Reg's way, were a mixed bag of football and plumbing, but all were fairly simple to answer. Even Norman grew in confidence and jumped in for one question on water features and how they can enhance the average garden.

All in all, it seemed to go rather well, Reg thought. He just had the makeover to worry about.

The show progressed. Nicky Clarke had actually done a good job with Reg's hair, which was a minor miracle in itself. Nicky had also dressed Reg in the traditional English gentleman's outfit complete with top hat and umbrella. Reg felt like a toff, and after his initial displeasure thought he looked quite smart. Nicky even supplied a red rose as a buttonhole to complete the effect.

Norman's cookery section was also much simpler than he had anticipated. Andrew Nutter had set out the football fan's ideal lunch – meat pie and chips washed down with a cup of Bovril. Norman added a Wagon Wheel, which he'd brought down for his lunch, but convinced himself that it would complete the dish.

As everyone gathered around the food table – which by now contained luke-warm food, and therefore had become more authentic – Judy thanked her special guests. Reg and Norman both blushed as they realised she meant them. She then announced it was time to go over to Fred Talbot on his weather map at the Albert Dock Liverpool.

Alongside Fred, stood a figure in airman goggles that seemed to be German Luftwaffe style. It was Stan Boardman, who seemed intent on reminding everyone how his Grandad's chippy in Liverpool was bombed during the war, and that Reg and Norman would revenge his family's honour once and for all. Fred attempted to perform his normal weather broadcast while Stan hopped about from city to city on the map advising which parts of the country – bombed during the war – could also expect revenge at last.

As Fred became more irritated by the constant interruptions and fake droning of Spitfires, his fans – the legions of Talbotites, who worshipped his every move – decided enough was enough and jumped on to his floating map to help him remove the offensive Scouser. As pandemonium ensued, with a number of people falling into the dock from a now unsafe floating map of the United Kingdom, the transmission ended.

Richard and Judy, professional as ever, made light of the situation and closed the show.

Reg and Norman were thanked again before they returned to the safety of their dressing rooms.

"Reg," said Norman. He was sitting in a corner of the dressing room while Reg clambered out of his Savile Row suit.

"Yes, Norm,"

"I didn't tell you this morning 'cos I didn't want you in a bad mood on the show," Norman said.

Reg stopped what he was doing. The bloody trousers had that many buttons on them that they were difficult to figure out anyway.

"What yer on about?"

"When you left our Jackie's last night, I went through all the clubs in the league...and I mean all of them. Have a guess how many players we've got for the squad," said Norman.

"I dunno – twenty?" said Reg.

"None," said Norman.

"None?" said Reg, "did you say 'none'?"

"None," Norman repeated, "absolutely bugger all. There seems to be a conspiracy – nobody wants to release players to play for England."

"Bloody 'ell," said a forlorn Reg, "what we gonna do?"

"Dunno," said Norman, "you're gonna 'ave to ring that Fendon bloke and see what's goin' on."

"Great," said Reg.

Reg's first call was to Carol. He dug the phone number out of his pocket and called her.

"Hi," she said.

"Hiya, it's Reg. Did you watch 'This Morning'?"

"Oh yes," she said, "I thought you looked like John Steed in your posh suit. I hope you've got that one on next time you take me out. I'll get my Purdey wig out."

"Har har," snorted Reg, "Listen, I've got a few things to sort out for this game on Wednesday so I'll give you a ring nearer weekend."

"I suppose that means you're not asking me to the game, then."

"Eh? Oh, I never thought..."

"It's okay Reg, I'm messing with you. Thanks for last night. There's some good pictures of me in today's paper."

"Ah, sorry."

"Hey, no need to be...I look great," she laughed.

"Aye, you do that."

"Smoothie. I'll talk to you soon then. Good luck Reg," she said.

"Hang on before you go. I need to tell you something."

"Sounds ominous," she said.

"Did you speak to a bloke in the bar on Saturday night?"

"Only about a thousand. Why?"

"It would have been one in particular. I didn't want to say anything last night in case it spoiled things, but someone broke into my house on Saturday night and threatened me. Said if I didn't resign as England manager, he'd sort me out," blurted Reg.

"Oh my God. Are you all right?" Carol sounded concerned, Reg noted with a pang of pleasure.

"I'm all right, but he said if that didn't work, he'd come and see you."

"Me? Why me?"

"Said he spoke to you in the Forest and asked you out. You'd said no as you were seeing me."

"Now that rings a bell. Big fella, swarthy, confident?"

"Aye, that's the one," Reg confirmed.

"Don't worry about me Reg. I'm due a couple of days off. I'll go visit me Mum in Sheffield. You keep at it and don't let 'em get to you. You take care of yourself mind, I don't want to be visiting you in Nottingham General every night for a month. Good luck for Wednesday."

"Thanks," said Reg and they both hung up.

Reg's next port of call was the FA. Again, his pocket contained the necessary, a piece of paper appeared in his hand.

June Whitless had bitten the bullet and arrived at work as normal at nine o'clock. If she behaved as normal, she thought, maybe Brendan would say something. His silence had terrified her more than anything had over the last few days. Maybe he was building up to a rant; she just didn't have a clue.

She kept her head down all morning – Brendan remained in his office and didn't say a word. She concentrated on the undersoil heating contracts and managed to respond to most of them by lunchtime. Strange, she thought as she went through them, how that one of Atkinson's had slipped into the wrong pile. She was sure that she'd cleared them all with Brendan. Ah well, the plumbing stuff was easy – if it didn't contain the word plumbing at some point, it was rejected. This Peter Taylor for example – all he goes on about is football. Do they have no idea what to put in a tender? The strident ringing of the telephone interrupted her. It was Reg.

"Doctor Proctor?"

"Yes."

"Your patient has not turned up for the allotted appointment."

"Oh?"

"He has however left a sick note, excusing him from duty until tomorrow."

"I see."

"Would you like me to accelerate the treatment?"

"Do you think it necessary?"

"He seems genuine. There are other parties he has to consider. I think another twenty-four hours may prove remedial."

"I agree with your prognosis. Keep me informed."

"Yes Doctor. By the way, you should check out the ITN news at the moment."

Brendan turned off his mobile phone and turned his private television to ITV. A brief report was almost at an end, praising Reg for his performance on 'This Morning'.

# GOOD MORNING BRITAIN

Brendan sat behind his desk fuming. Not only was Reg Atkinson becoming a favourite with the public, June had arrived in for work and the bloody Sun had launched an 'Out with Hannibal' campaign. Bloody Sun and bloody woman, he thought. He wished she'd give him an excuse to sack her, especially after what she'd done. The pictures hadn't bothered him too much, nor had her dalliance with Sir Richard, the old coot. No, it was more the fact that she was instrumental in delivering this burden of Atkinson upon him. Christ almighty, he'd practically spelt it out before he left; he'd checked up from Brazil and she'd told him everything was going to plan, and now look.

A few seconds deliberation and he came to a decision. He rang a temping agency he knew and gave his requirements, he followed up with a call to a tame journalist from one of the rags and gave him an exclusive he'd just thought of. Then he contacted Lord Burchill to advise him of what he'd be reading in tomorrow's papers. Lord Burchill, who was finalising the seating arrangements for Her Majesty's entourage, said he would attend to the matter immediately.

Brendan sat back in his chair. There, he thought, a couple of phone calls is all it takes. He smiled felinely and was about to further his strategy when the phone rang. He pushed a button for loudspeaker:

"Yes," he said.

"Mr Fendon, I have Reg Atkinson for you." June's voice was strangely tinny through the speaker. Should make it easier to do what he had to do, thought Brendan.

"Thank you June," said Brendan as Reg came on, "Reg, how are you?"

"I'd be fine if I knew what was going on," said Reg, "I

can't get any clubs to release players for the game on Wednesday."

"Oh, that's not very good is it?" smiled Brendan.

"Well, no," said Reg, "I was thinking that maybe you could tell me why."

"From what I hear, there's some sort of Players' Union situation. Apparently, the Union are unhappy about the experimental tactics and are concerned that their members may not be covered in case of injury," said Brendan.

"But that's rubbish!" shouted Reg.

"I know," Brendan smiled, "but the Union is a law unto itself. Could be weeks before the matter is sorted out."

"So what do you intend to do about it?" asked Reg.

"Me? I don't think there is anything I can do," said Brendan, "obviously I'll speak to the Union spokesperson, but the FA has no stranglehold over the Players' Union. My hands are pretty much tied. I suppose this casts a cloud over Wednesday's game?"

"I suppose it does. Tell me, if we don't get a team on the pitch, what will happen? Can we postpone until the Union get this sorted out?" asked Reg in desperation.

"Not at this late stage. FIFA take a dim view of last minute postponements. I would think they'd want us to forfeit the game. The Germans would get all three points and they'd be going to the World Cup Finals instead of us," said Brendan, now struggling to keep the levity from his voice.

"But that's not fair," shouted Reg, struggling to keep his cool, "I can't get a team on the pitch if no one wants to play. What the hell do I do?"

"As I said earlier, the FA will give you full backing while you are the manager of England, Mr Atkinson," Brendan smiled, "but should you fail to fulfil your side of the bargain, then I'm afraid that the English public just won't like it at all, no matter how much we're on your side."

"So have you got any advice for me at all?" asked Reg, the heat rising in his voice. He wanted Brendan to just come out and say the word 'resign'.

"Yes, something came in earlier," said Brendan, "Her Majesty won't be attending the game."

"And..?"

"Mr Atkinson, this is an international match. If it is to take place, the FA must be represented by a figure of authority. Unfortunately, I've had to advise the Royal Liaison this morning that there may not be a game to attend."

"Well call them back," said Reg desperately.

"I'm sorry, Mr Atkinson, these things cannot be easily rearranged," said Brendan, "I believe Her Majesty has now been rescheduled. It's your responsibility to find a replacement."

"Eh?" blurted Reg.

"Yes, if you check the terms of your contract, you'll find it in there, " Brendan added.

Brendan heard a click as the line terminated. Atkinson had obviously had enough. Well, nothing to do now but wait. Oh there was just one thing. He pressed a button on his telephone to activate the intercom.

"Miss Whitless, come in here for a moment will you."

He sat back in his chair and waited.

Reg sat in the dressing room with the phone cradled in his hand. He had thought about a five-minute rant, but decided against it. Brendan was much too smarmy for his liking. He had wanted to ask whether his lackey had reported in with details of his absence but had thought better of it.

"I take it that didn't go too well?" Norman asked.

"I have the FA's full backing as usual," said Reg forlornly, "but Mr Brendan Fendon doesn't seem to want to do anything to help me. Well, he says he can't anyway, but I get the feeling he's enjoying this."

"So what next?"

"I don't know Norm, I just don't know," said Reg, "I've got to find a replacement for the Queen as well."

"I didn't know she was down to play," said Norman. Reg narrowed his eyes.

"Fool. She was supposed to be in the Royal Box, but now Fendon's told 'em that there might be no game on, she's gone off doing something else," said Reg.

"Well don't the FA sort that side of things out?" asked Norman.

"Apparently not," said Reg, "according to Mr Bloody High and Mighty, it's in my contract somewhere."

A knock at the door interrupted them. Reg looked at Norman.

"Don't look at me, it's your show," said Norman.

Reg puffed as he got out of his chair and went to the door. He opened it slightly and looked out. Richard and Judy were on the opposite side. Reg swung the door open and gestured for them to come in.

"We just wanted to thank you for coming in today," said Judy.

"Yes, it was very good of you at short notice and we appreciate how busy you must be," added Richard.

"It was no problem," said Reg.

"We just really wanted to wish you luck for the game on Wednesday," said Richard.

"And to say thanks for a very entertaining show. We've had hundreds of phone calls at the switchboard wishing you well," said Judy.

Reg slumped into his chair, the magnitude of the moment finally hitting him.

"Are you all right Reg?" asked Judy with concern. She rushed to his side.

Reg told them what had happened. For the next five minutes, it was like a dam had broken and all his troubles were free to flood the dressing room. Richard and Judy listened to it all, nodding occasionally.

"Looks like you're in a spot of bother," said Richard when Reg eventually dried up.

"Aye," said Reg who had been hoping for something a bit more profound.

"Never mind, Reg. At least you've got the plumbing to fall back on. That's more than a lot of people in your position," said Judy with a warm smile. Reg nodded dolefully – again, he had been hoping for a bit more.

"I'll tell you what Reg," said Norman, "if you're looking for a replacement for the Queen then you've got two likely candidates here."

"Pardon?" said Richard. Judy tittered.

"'Ey, that's not a bad idea Norm," said a rejuvenated Reg, "how about it, Richard, Judy? Would you like to sit in the Royal Box as guests of the FA? We need someone who's well known and important and you two definitely fit the bill."

"I'd love to..." began Richard.

"...but we have a fondue party at the Greaves' darling," Judy interrupted.

"Oh, couldn't we...?" begged Richard.

"I don't think so, we couldn't possibly cancel now. I'll tell you what Reg, we'll ask our guests between now and Wednesday morning whether they'd like to take part. Leave it to us and I'm sure we'll find the right sort of person for you," said Judy.

"Okay, thanks," said Reg. He supposed it was as much as he could hope for.

June Whitless slowly packed her belongings from her desk and waved a tearful goodbye to her office. It hadn't taken Brendan long to tell her that her services were no longer required. Not only had she taken the rap for appointing the wrong man in the position of England manager but she had also been photographed in public *in flagrante* and generally bringing the FA into disrepute.

June had not argued. She had a feeling that this would happen. She also knew that if she decided to take it further, it wouldn't do her any good. Brendan seemed to have a knack for coming out on top in these situations.

He had not mentioned her relationship with Sir Richard. This had somehow made it worse – it was as if he didn't care. If he had shown the slightest sign of jealousy, she would have been happier, but there was absolutely nothing to be given away in his cold eyes.

She closed the door of her office behind her for the last time and headed for the exit, quietly sobbing.

Reg and Norman finally arrived home in mid-afternoon. They had spent the first half of the return journey in the limousine trying out ideas and suggestions, but as they both realised the futility of it all had spent the second half of the trip in relative silence.

As they pulled up outside Reg's house, Reg noticed a brand new white Mercedes van parked outside his house. 'REG ATKINSON – OFFICIAL PLUMBER TO THE FA' was painted boldly in patriotic blue and red on each side.

"Oh bugger," said Reg, "I'd forgotten about that."

"Nice van though," said Norman, straining to look out of Reg's side of the limousine.

"Aye, and a nice price too," said Reg, mentally calculating how much he'd get for it if he sold it straight away. "You know, Norm, I think there's only one way out of this mess."

"What's that then?"

"I'm going to have to resign aren't I?" said Reg.

"But you can't. Think about the money," Norman said anxiously.

"I'll have to get a loan, won't I?" Reg added.

"Do you honestly think that'd work. Think about the lost business."

"We'd soon get it back," said Reg.

"Don't be so sure – everybody's going to see you as the plumber that deserted your country in its time of need. Nobody'd want you," said Norman.

"Ah," said Reg who hadn't considered the negative publicity and the effect on his business. He told Norman about the threats and the possibility that it wasn't just himself in danger.

"Bloody 'ell," said Norman, turning pale.

"I told him to leave you alone and that you're too old to be threatened."

"Too old, you cheeky sod!" said Norman indignantly, "I could still show you a few moves." He bobbed and weaved in the confines of the back seat, which at least brought a faint smile to Reg's lips.

"Just keep thinking and sleep on it," Norman continued as he calmed down, "I'll ask around and see if anyone has any ideas."

"Be careful, okay? I don't want to hear about another pensioner being beaten up and it's you."

Norman muttered something under his breath about pensioners, but Reg didn't catch it as he was climbing out of the limousine. As it slowly made its way down his street to drop off Norman, Reg waved pathetically. As he did so, he noticed a few photographers snapping away – he was definitely flavour of the month with the paparazzi.

He trudged to his front door and noticed with dismay that it was open. As Reg stepped into his hall, he knew immediately something was wrong. He moved slowly into his lounge – the place was trashed. Moving from room to room in a daze, he saw that nothing had escaped. Someone had been through the entire house ransacking every room.

In his front bedroom, he righted a wicker chair, sat down in it and wept. Obviously the note of apology had not been enough. After twenty minutes or more of self-pity, he called the police.

# THE PERFECT PLAN?

As Reg wept amongst the ruin of his home, Norman was making an effort to get things moving. Reg's suggestion of resignation had hit Norman hard, even with the hint of possible injury. There was no way he'd allow him to do it – he'd lose too much. And in this particular case, Norman was thinking about himself too – if Reg's business went west, then Norman would be looking for a new job as well, and at his time of life there would be slim pickings available. He'd be forced into retreat – he might as well just curl up and die, he thought. The prospect of a beating was positively soothing in comparison.

Fortunately, Norman had eventually got hold of kitchen fitter and potential undersoil heating helper Kev Beckett, and told him that things hadn't exactly gone to plan. Kev had realised this as he was downing a pint in his local and watching television. He'd been shocked to see Reg's face looking back at him, but thought it might have been the drink. However, he hadn't at that point handed his notice in so breathed a sigh of relief – promising himself a good shout at Norman and Reg next time he saw them.

Norman had also spoken to Dave Bayley. Dave had listened to Norman's tale of Reg's woe and offered the suggestion of a number of ex-internationals that may just jump at the chance to play again.

"Think of it Norman," he'd said, "Franny Lee, Colin Bell, Joe Corrigan... you could ask the likes of Mick Mills and Kenny Sansom. What about Lineker up front – he'd have a chance to break Jimmy Greaves' goalscoring record."

Norman had thought about it, but the logistics of contacting a team of football veterans in less than forty-eight hours would be even more difficult than getting them to last a full ninety minutes.

Norman then tried contacting clubs in the Nationwide League lower divisions. On most counts he was refused permission to even speak to the players, the ones that didn't respond would probably come back tomorrow with a nil return. He then tried the Conference with the same result – nothing. He was beginning to think that Reg was right when the phone rang.

"Norman," it was Dave, "The evening papers are out down here and they're dishing the dirt on Reg."

"Eh?" said a startled Norman.

"Well not dirt as in scandal, but they're saying that he can't get a team together for Wednesday night because he refuses to play to a tried and trusted method. They're saying that because he wants to use experimental tactics in a crucial game like this, the whole country should turn against him and force him to resign."

"Oh 'eck," said Norman.

"I've spoken to Patrick and he says that it's probably a

story leaked out by our good friend Brendan Fendon. He thinks that if the pressure is on Reg to resign it'll play right into Fendon's hands. What we have to do is make sure that Reg gets a team out on to the pitch on Wednesday night at all costs. If he can do that then he's sorted."

"Easier said than done," said Norman sadly. He told Dave about the threats to Reg, himself and Carol.

"Leave it with me for a bit," said a concerned Dave, "Patrick might have an idea. I'll get back soon."

"Okay, Dave. See you soon," said Norman as Dave bade his own farewells.

Norman went to his fridge and got himself a nice cold can of Guinness, which he poured slowly into a glass. Brain food, he told himself.

Sir Richard Scratcher sat in his study pondering another empty bottle of vodka. They empty so very quickly he thought. Every bottle must have a leak so that you have to go and buy them more often. It was only nine o'clock, he said to himself; Thresher's will still be open if I get my skates on.

He jumped as the telephone on the table next to him exploded into life, then recovered to take the receiver off the handset.

"Ahem," he coughed into the mouthpiece, "Scratcher speaking."

"Sir Richard?"

"Yes," said Sir Richard – he didn't recognise the voice.

"My name is Patrick Levine and I represent Reg Atkinson."

"Who...ah yes, Atkinson, I remember the fellow. What can I do for you Mr..?" asked Sir Richard amiably; despite the fact that he thought that Reg's lawyer might just want to sue him. Seemed to be a lot of it in the air at the moment.

"Levine. Patrick Levine. I have a proposition for you Sir Richard. A proposition which will get you back in public favour and may just find you reinstated at the FA."

"Oh really," said Sir Richard, now sitting forward in his seat and becoming more interested by the second.

Patrick spelt out the details of the plan as Sir Richard listened intently. Sir Richard mentioned that Brendan had threatened Reg with some sort of court case following his resignation, but Patrick told him not to worry – it wouldn't come to that. When Patrick had finished and hung up, Sir Richard felt better than he had in days. He looked again at his empty vodka bottle before tossing it into the waste paper basket. No need for that now, got to stay sober for the next couple of days, he thought. It was the drink that had allowed Fendon to get the better of him that's for sure. How could he have believed the man when he had said it was June that started off the chain of events that led to this?

He picked up the telephone and called her.

June looked at the phone in despair. If it was that magazine editor again asking about the possibility of a nude photo session, she'd probably say yes, just to stop the ringing. She thought about not answering but relented.

"Hello," she said.

"June, it's Dickie."

"Dickie, I..."

"I didn't want to call you in case you needed your space," said Sir Richard. He was aware that younger people needed their space but wasn't too sure what it meant.

# THE PERFECT PLAN?

"I've felt so alone," sobbed June, "I thought you'd forgotten me."

"Good heavens, no," said Sir Richard aghast, "it's just that what with Fendon forcing me to resign and those pictures, I thought the best thing would be to leave you..."

"Leave me?" sobbed June again. At Sir Richard's end of the phone, his eyes rolled – women, he thought.

"Let me finish, June," he said, "I was going to say leave you to get on with your job so that Fendon wouldn't get on your case."

"Oh," said June.

"Anyway, I've had this marvellous idea," he bragged.

"Oh," said June, her conversation starting to stick in a rut.

"And I'd also like to take you out to dinner and discuss it," he said, "I'll pick you up in half an hour."

"But..."

"No buts. You deserve better June." He hung up.

June stared into space momentarily before dashing to the bathroom. She hadn't mentioned she'd been sacked. That could wait till later, she thought. She had perked up slightly – this impulsiveness was just what she needed.

Reg had taken the phone off its hook while he endured constables Timmons and Rodgers for a good hour. How did he know if anything was missing? Look at the place – things he'd forgotten he had were now on full view. No, he'd not touched anything, well he didn't think he had. Yes he had spotted suspicious people… about a million of them over the last few days. No he hadn't reported last night's break-in as nothing was stolen and nothing happened. No he probably wouldn't be around over the next few days…

The constables left having taken copious notes and an autograph each. Reg had a fair idea who was responsible for this and even the thought of Brendan Fendon made him angry. He also knew that he was at the end of his tether – if someone could do this in broad daylight, then God help Norman and Carol. Tomorrow morning he'd send in his resignation and pay back the cash. It'd probably bankrupt him; he'd have to remortgage the house, but what was the alternative? As long as his friends were safe and well, then bollocks to it. Tomorrow morning then, he said to himself, and took himself to bed.


Over dinner, Sir Richard told June that he was immensely fond of her, something he'd not said to any woman in years. He was mortified to discover that she had been sacked, but wasn't totally surprised. It appeared as though Brendan Fendon saw them both as sacrifices required to appease the gathering press hordes.

June was in too much of a lather to listen to most of the plan. Sir Richard's revelations of his feelings had immediately sent her into fantasies of Lady June at Ascot, Lady June at the garden party at Buckingham Palace. She caught a few titbits of it but wasn't really listening. Dickie seemed to have it all worked out – she'd happily go along with it.

"Are you all right June," he asked at last, "you don't appear to be listening to a word I've said."

"Oh I have Dickie," she simpered, "just tell me what you'd like me to do and I'll do it."

"All we have to do is to help that Atkinson chap out and show that we're supporting him to the hilt. We're showing we've realised our mistake and we're doing our very best to put it right. When the press realise its Fendon that's putting the boot in, it'll be curtains for him." Sir Richard was reluctant to elaborate, as he wasn't entirely sure that he'd got every aspect absolutely spot on. That Patrick seemed to know what he was talking about – as long as he gave clear instructions, everything should be all right.

Patrick Levine had been a busy boy. When Dave Bayley had originally asked him for a bit of advice with Reg's contract just a couple of days ago, he had been glad to help out his old employer and friend. He hadn't realised then what a complicated web of intrigue would emerge, but was now determined to prove his true worth.

Fortunately, he hadn't yet begun his final year of law – that didn't begin for another week yet and he'd already prepared his first term's work. This was the type of machination that he could really get his teeth into and he was revelling in it: SuperPat versus Hannibal Fendon.

In Patrick's mind, Brendan Fendon was doing exactly as he had predicted earlier: he was attempting to force Reg into a resignation. Sir Richard had mentioned the fact that Hannibal intended to sue Reg as soon as his resignation arrived on his desk. Patrick was well aware that with a decent brief, Brendan could probably get Reg sent down, however innocent he was. With the latest newspaper articles already on show in the Monday evening papers, and ready to hit the Tuesday morning papers early tomorrow, Brendan must now think he had the upper hand. Reg could not be allowed to cave in – it would be the end of him.

Patrick was convinced that Brendan had now reached the extent of his capabilities and it was Reg's time to fight back. Brendan's game plan relied on Reg's resignation – as long as this didn't happen, then Reg had the upper hand...but these threats worried him. He had to get everyone safe and out of harm's way, but how? Further information from Norman had revealed that Carol was out of the equation, so that left Reg and Norman in the firing line.

Patrick soon found an answer. Phone calls to FIFA, UEFA and the European Court of Human Rights had confirmed his plan was viable and it was the obvious way forward. Firstly, he had to get Reg out of the glare of the media. Reg could issue a short statement and then disappear until the night of the game. Second, Sir Richard and June would have to get the paperwork moving. Finally, the team would have to get out on to that Wembley pitch and...well, you can't ask for everything. Reg deserved a happy ending, but Patrick couldn't really plan that with any degree of confidence.

Brendan Fendon sat at home with his trusty cushion, his feet up and copies of the evening papers scattered around him. Very nice piece of journalism, he thought, couldn't have done anything better myself. He laughed to himself.

"You look like the cat that got the cream," said his wife Barbara. She was working on some embroidery.

"I have a certain level of satisfaction," said Brendan, "oh and you'll be happy to know I had to replace June Whitless today."

"Oh?" Barbara had always had her suspicions that Brendan had more than a business interest in Miss Whitless, but had never dared to investigate.

"Yes," Brendan continued, "the FA has to act when a prominent member of staff is caught with their pants down."

"I noticed that – Dickie Scratcher wasn't it?" asked Barbara.

# THE PERFECT PLAN?

"Indeed," said Brendan, shuddering at the thought of Sir Richard's prominent member, "a girl from the temping agency starts tomorrow. Hopefully, she'll be a bit more tactful than Miss Whitless."

Barbara said nothing. She kept her head down and continued with her embroidery. Brendan sat there, an insidious smile on his face. If Barbara hadn't been married to him, she would have loved for someone to come and wipe it off his smug face.

"How's your erm…?" she asked.

"Same," said Brendan wincing with the memory. That did the trick, she thought.

Reg was up fairly early the next morning. He shaved, showered and dressed before heading downstairs for a spot of breakfast. A quick peek out of the windows showed him that the invading hordes of the media had not subsided – in fact, they seemed to have multiplied during the night. Make a good 'Wildlife on One' programme for David Attenborough, he thought; they breed faster than any life form on the planet. He chuckled to himself and made a mental note to try that one out on Norman.

On his way to the kitchen, he retrieved his morning paper from the letterbox. His face was all over the front and back pages. As he grilled some bacon, he scanned over the articles. Somehow or other, the press had found out about the lack of players and had now assumed that there would be no game. His reputation as a manager and as a plumber was at stake. This sort of behaviour in refusing to conform and trying experimental tactics was treason to outweigh his driving of a German car and van. They'd even gone so far as to name the van as Exhibit C in the case for bringing back beheading for traitors to the realm.

**243**

"Oh Gawd," muttered Reg as he realised the bacon was blackening. He hurriedly rescued what he could to make a bacon muffin with lashings of brown sauce.

Reg flung the paper on the kitchen table and set down his plate and a mug of tea. As he opened his mouth to take a mouthful of burnt bacon, a loud rap came from the front door. Bollocks to that, thought Reg, and completed his bite. The knocking continued and a voice came through the letterbox.

"Reg, Reg. It's Patrick Levine. Are you there?"

Patrick? Thought Reg. What's he doing here? He dropped his buttie back on to the plate and headed for the door.

Once Patrick was safely inside – which was tricky given the amount of cameras which tried to get in with him – he heaved a sigh of relief.

"How long has it been like this? It's like you're under siege…good grief!" said Patrick, noticing the mess around him.

"Tell me about it," said Reg, "it wasn't too bad at first but then they started gathering last night. This is courtesy of our dear friend Mr Fendon. As you can see, I have the full backing of the FA."

"You sure it's Fendon?" asked Patrick.

"Who else could it be?" Reg replied.

"I heard about your Sunday night business. Sounds a little too coincidental."

"Aye," said Reg, "and then as if it couldn't get any worse…" he gestured towards the crowds outside.

"Probably about the same time as the stories hit last night's papers. I see you've got the morning edition here." Patrick gestured towards the paper on the table.

"Yeah, got it in for me now haven't they?" said Reg

plaintively, "I've been thinking the best way forward is to resign and just get out of the way. It'll probably skin me, put me out of business and make me a laughing stock but at least nobody gets hurt."

"Oh, don't be silly," smiled Patrick, "this is the worst it can get. It's all plain sailing from here. Didn't Norman speak to you last night?"

"No," said Reg, "ah, but I had the phone off the hook. He wouldn't have been able to get through."

"Well, Reg, we have a plan," said Patrick, "Hannibal Fendon has set his stall out and now it's our turn."

"A plan? Oh Patrick, it's good of you but I've had enough. I'm giving up. There's too much at stake."

"Oh come on," Patrick continued, "what have you got to lose? Pack yourself an overnight bag – I'm going to hide you somewhere. Carol's safe, Norman will be later, no one can touch us."

"Eh?"

"We need to hide you away from the public eye. You need to be with your team, uninterrupted. You've got a game to prepare for."

"Eh?" said Reg again. Patrick laughed and shoved him towards the stairs.

"Come on Reg, we've only got until tomorrow night," he laughed.

Reg headed upstairs, still totally confused. It was too early in the morning for this.

Reg had hurriedly packed and was now installed in the front of Patrick's ageing Astra. At least I'm in a British car, he thought and allowed himself a grin.

Patrick had refused to tell him anything about the plan inside the house except that all would soon be revealed.

Reg didn't mind the mystery and had soon given up asking Patrick what he had in mind. Reg was happy that there seemed to be a glimmer of hope.

Patrick had good reasons for keeping his mouth shut. In Reg's best interests, he didn't want to reveal too much too soon just in case Reg got the jitters. Similarly, Reg may have been tempted to say something to the press outside his house. That was too risky – this had to be kept quiet until the last possible minute. There had to be no chance of Brendan Fendon finding out while he still had time to do something about it.

Norman knew what was going on and was all for it. The main thing was to get a team out on the pitch and this was the best way of doing it. Reg had one task to perform upon leaving the house that morning and that was to read a prepared statement provided by Patrick.

"Gentlemen," Reg had announced after opening his front door, "I can confirm that I have had some difficulties in selecting a squad for the game against Germany, but I am happy to say that reports about tomorrow night's match being postponed are totally incorrect. England will play Germany as scheduled."

That was that. After a bit of shoving and plenty of "no comments", Reg was whisked south in Patrick's car. Patrick answered one of Reg's questions – they were going to his place.

Norman spent all morning making the arrangements for the players. Every one of them said 'yes' without a moment's pause. This was a chance in a lifetime for them.

"Bloody unbelievable," said Michael Quarry, "absolutely bloody unbelievable."

# THE PERFECT PLAN?

"We travel down this afternoon," said Norman, "can you get off work?"

"Too bloody right," said the 'Rock', "I feel my glands swelling up something rotten. Probably contagious."

The story was the same for the rest of the Forest Inn players. Although totally bewildered, none of them could pass up the chance to play at Wembley and against Germany for their country. The giant defender Roy 'Cropper' Brooks cried for a full half-hour as emotion got the better of him. Lance Lovejoy, for once, was stuck for something to say and contented himself with nodding his approval down the phone. Baldy Charlton growled his thanks to Norman and grunted something that Norman couldn't quite catch.

Little Johnny Mullen was the most difficult to convince – he worked in a bank and was in charge of the office balance. It took Norman ten minutes to convince him that he could use this as a training exercise for someone else, despite its obvious importance to the daily routine.

Norman told them to meet at the Forest Inn at two o'clock. He'd pick them up in Reg's new van and they'd travel down to London from there.

The drive down to London for Reg went quite quickly. Now Patrick was happy that Reg could be hidden from public view for a while, he let him in on the secret.

"My players?" Reg said incredulously, "My Forest Inn players?"

"Yes," said Patrick.

"But they're pub players," said Reg.

"Ah yes, but technically they're also part-timers," said Patrick, "and I can't find any rule which states that part-timers are not allowed to represent their country at football."

"But…" said Reg, who couldn't think of anything to ask, yet knew he had to say 'but'.

"Here's where the fun starts," Patrick continued, "Sir Richard Scratcher has very kindly offered to act as patron for the Forest Inn public house team, which will be now known as Forest Inn FC. Your first team squad have been registered as part-time professionals, despite the fact that they have never earned anything from football. Forest Inn FC has applied for membership to the Unibond League, an application which has been accepted by Sir Richard."

"L-l-league?" stammered Reg.

"Don't worry about that, you can resign from the league with no penalty. In fact, when the committee finds out about it they'll probably kick you out anyway," said Patrick with a chuckle.

Reg silently took this in.

"So what you're left with is a non-league team with a squad of part-time professionals who are eligible for national duty. You also have a squad of players who know your system and will be happy to play for you. There's just one thing which needs clarifying and I'm not sure confirmation will come in time." Patrick paused.

"What?" Reg asked on cue.

"The number of substitutes you're obliged to have. You only have eleven regular players – as far as I'm aware, you may not formally need any more, but for argument sake, I've listed Norman, Dave Bayley, Josh Reynolds – Dave's student barman, myself…and Sir Richard volunteered to be the fifth. At least now, you'll have a squad list to put forward."

# The Perfect Plan?

"Sir Richard?" spluttered Reg.

"Sir Richard feels very badly about the whole thing – thinks he's let you down personally and has offered to help in any way. Of course, it helps that he's basically been sacked by Brendan Fendon and would like any opportunity to get his own back."

"Will it work?" asked Reg.

"Well, you'll get a team on the pitch. After that, it's down to your lads," said Patrick.

Reg thought long and hard about this. Every plan has its downside, he thought.

"Now," said Patrick, "I've told you my side. Tell me about this heavy that came round."

Brendan Fendon sat in his office at Lancaster Gate surrounded by the morning papers. He was pleased with the results of his labours – every single newspaper had picked up on the possibility that Reg Atkinson may be handing the game to the Germans by not being able to field a team. Brendan sniggered – Atkinson would have no choice now. That quick shot he'd seen on the news that morning of Atkinson leaving his house had confirmed that. Bravado thought Brendan, pure bravado. There was no way on earth Atkinson could get a team on that pitch, absolutely no way on earth.

He shifted position on his cushion and pushed the papers to one side for a moment before pressing the intercom button.

"Tanya," he said.

"Yes Mr Fendon,"

"Come in for a moment would you. Bring your pad." His finger left the intercom. Tanya had arrived this morning straight from the agency. Brendan had given her a quick once over through hooded eyes as she entered the building that morning. Brunette, twentyish, very easy on the eye – just what he was looking for.

Now that the Atkinson saga had reached its conclusion, he'd better start looking for a replacement. He'd had an idea about a foreign coach – save face a little by not crawling back to the English coaches they'd insulted by appointing Reg. A good opportunity to test out Tanya's dictation skills as well. He smiled contentedly to himself as Tanya walked into his office.

"Tanya, how are you enjoying your first morning?" Brendan said, more reptilian than human.

As Brendan was easing into smug self-satisfaction, Reg was unloading his travel bags from Patrick's car and gazing up at Patrick's one bedroom apartment in Shepherd's Bush.

Patrick had been through the plan with him in great detail on the way down and although Reg wasn't entirely certain of the full picture, he knew his role. Patrick had made a quick pit stop at Watford Gap to make a phone call to Nottingham police. He told Reg later in the car that there would be a surprise waiting for his large friend should he decide to make a repeat appearance at either his house or Norman's. He had thanked Patrick many times on the journey to London and made the younger man blush. All Patrick had wanted in return was a quiet night in while Reg told him the whole story from the beginning. Not much to ask, Reg had thought.

Patrick showed Reg into the building and escorted him up a couple of flights of stairs to his flat.

# THE PERFECT PLAN?

"It's basic, but liveable," said Patrick as he opened his door.

"Looks all right to me," said Reg as he glanced inside at what looked like a typical student room.

"There's just the one bedroom, but I've got a camp bed and sleeping bag," Patrick added, "I'll take that and you can have the bedroom."

"Wouldn't dream of it," said Reg, "camp bed's good enough for me. You've done enough work already."

Patrick offered again but was thwarted by Reg's insistence. Reg put his bag down and stepped towards the window to view the outside world. Not much to see and the street was fairly empty – a bit different to the last couple of days outside my house, thought Reg with relief.

"Norman should arrive in London about four o'clock," said Patrick, "the team are staying at the Kippax tonight."

"Okay," said Reg.

"And you'll be allowed to train on the Wembley pitch tomorrow morning," Patrick continued.

"Blimey," said Reg.

"I'll leave you to get yourself sorted out then," said Patrick and left Reg to himself.

Training on the Wembley pitch: it's a dream come true, thought Reg. Just think, a nice flat pitch instead of the local park with its mud heaps and holes and dog turds. He made a mental note to make sure every one of his lads enjoyed themselves. Wednesday would be the only chance for any of them to set foot on the hallowed turf, and if all went well, they'd be going back in the evening.

He set about unpacking.

Barry Tugwell let himself in through the back door of Reg's house. He tutted to himself – he would have had chains on each door by now. He opened the fridge and extracted a bottle of water. Opening the nearest cupboard door, he found himself a glass and poured a cold half-pint of water, drinking it in one swift motion. He left the glass on the draining board and made his way into the lounge. Wonder what excuse Reggie boy had today, he thought, and smiled about yesterday's experience. He'd never had a sick note before.

Tugwell made his way to the lounge, realising that someone had done a number on the house and knowing through experience that Reg would not be in – the air was too still. His army training told him that human presence caused a different atmosphere to the one he was experiencing now. He looked around for another note, but where could it be in this mess? Who the hell had done this? Every step took him on to a piece of Reg's life – a saucer, a coaster, a paper…he felt vulnerable and decided to leave. At that point all hell broke loose – the front door was kicked down; figures in black ran from the back and ordered him to put his hands up. Well, he thought, this is unexpected.

Norman arrived at the Forest Inn at a quarter to two that afternoon. All the players were there except one – Lance Lovejoy.

"Where's Lance?" asked Norman.

"Dunno," said Andy Tate. Everyone else shrugged and pleaded ignorance. Lance worked at a printing house, working on anything from business cards to signs as big as a house.

# THE PERFECT PLAN?

"Probably printing himself off some new cards – 'Lance Lovejoy, International Footballer and Playboy'," said Fat Jennings to roars of laughter.

"Right, come on then. Get your sorry bodies into the back of the van," said Norman, and watched as they outside. As Norman followed them, he came to a halt before the van.

"What the bloody 'ell's up wi' you lot?" he shouted as he careered into the back of Alain Boule.

The players were pointing towards the van and sniggering.

"Lance has turned up," said someone. Norman craned his neck around to see what was so funny.

Lance stood as innocently as he could at the back of the van with his holdall in his hand. Norman noticed the message on the sign of the van no longer read 'REG ATKINSON – OFFICIAL PLUMBER TO THE FA'. On the evidence at hand, it appeared that Lance Lovejoy had made himself a new sign to stick over the top of the existing one – 'REG ATKINSON – BALLCOCKS TO THE FA'.

"There you are Pops," Lance shouted to Norman, "thought you were gonna be late. Come on and get this van open."

"You cheeky bugger," chuckled Norman, "wait till Reg sees his nice new van. He'll string you up."

Lance made a face of mock horror as Norman fumbled with the keys. As soon as the doors were open, Lance jumped in.

"Brains before brawn," he shouted, and was soon pounced upon by the rest of the team. Norman shut the doors behind them.

"Norman," came a plaintive voice from inside, "it's a bit dark in 'ere. Norm? Norman?"

Norman chuckled to himself. If team spirit was anything to go by, they'd beat the Germans hands down, he thought.

At five o'clock that afternoon, Reg and Patrick met Norman and the players at the Kippax Hotel. Patrick had gathered everyone there who was involved in the squad, which included Sir Richard and June and young Josh who had been named as a substitute. After a great deal of backslapping and mutual appreciation, Reg got down to business.

"Firstly," he said, "I have seen my van." Splutters from the audience. "And although I approve of the sentiment, it needs to come off before tomorrow. I can't be seen to be at war with the FA. Okay Lance?"

Lance attempted to feign astonishment but then just nodded lamely.

"Secondly, this little outing is extremely hush hush. Nobody says a word to anyone except the people in this room," said Reg with a good deal of authority, "is that clear?"

More nods.

"If I find out any leak to the press has come from this room, the player concerned will not be playing in tomorrow's game. If the press do come sniffing around tonight, just tell them you've come to see the game. They'll believe that."

"Are we really going to play against the Germans, Reg?" asked Malcolm Mercer.

"Yeah, Reg. It all seems like summat off 'You've been Framed'," said Geordie Best.

"Well I promise you it's for real. Tomorrow night, you are all playing for England. It isn't just the Forest Inn any

more, you're representing your country. Not only that but it's against Germany – a chance to nick the bloody deckchairs from them."

Reg paused while the titters died down.

"There's a couple of thank yous to be said and I want you to know the scale of my appreciation for the amount of work and sacrifice people have put in for me, for us. Patrick Levine," said Reg, gesturing towards a furiously blushing Patrick, "has devoted himself tirelessly to helping me out over the last few days and keeping me off the scrapheap; Sir Richard Scratcher and June over there have lost their jobs at the FA because of me but are still here helping us out getting you registered to play for England; Dave Bayley is putting you all up at the FA's expense in his hotel, despite your lack of house-training; and I'd like to thank you Norman, and the rest of you lot for agreeing to play."

Reg was silenced by applause and cheering. The lads were certainly in good form.

"Tomorrow morning, we're going to Wembley for a quick training session and a look around. I don't want you lot being played off the park during the game because you're looking at the architecture of the place," said Reg, "I can't help thinking about that last game when the cameras arrived at half time."

Reg noticed a few sheepish looks and decided that was enough to be said about that.

"So I'll see you there at eleven o'clock. Norman will get you down there," Reg said, "I need to get away from here before anyone sees me so enjoy yourselves tonight. Dave will make sure you toe the line so no misbehaving."

"Yes boss," they all muttered. Dave Bayley had promised

to limit the alcohol consumption and serve up a high protein evening meal. The players didn't know this yet, but they'd soon find out when they tried ordering beer.

Reg and Patrick made their escape. Sir Richard introduced himself to each player in turn. He'd decided to stay the night himself so he could bond with his new team-mates. He'd invited June to stay too and Dave had very kindly offered them the bridal suite, although being the Kippax Hotel this was called the "Honeymoon Period". Sir Richard couldn't wait for bedtime.

Brendan Fendon was readjusting his cushion when his mobile rang.

"Yes?" he said.

"Who's that?"

"Pardon?"

"Who's that?"

"What do you mean?"

"What is your name?"

"But you rang me."

"Yes, to find out who you are. Sir, this is DI Lang from Nottingham CID. We've apprehended a man breaking into the home of a resident here and he seems to have your telephone number programmed in on a fast redial. I can check the telephone records but it seems a little foolish as I have you here on the phone now."

Brendan gulped. This was not going how he'd expected.

"Sir?"

"Yes?"

"Could I have your name, please?"

"Doctor Proctor."

"Doctor Proctor?" the emphasis was on the Doctor.

"Yes, the man is a patient."

"A patient?"

"Yes."

"How do you know?"

"I'm sorry," said Brendan flustered.

"How do you know he's a patient? I've not told you who he is."

"Ah, he err...I assumed..."

"Doctor Proctor, I'm afraid I'm going to have to ask you to..."

Brendan didn't wait to find out what he was going to be asked to do. Curse that Tugwell, he thought. Once he'd finished with Atkinson he'd intended Tugwell to deal with a smart little customs and excise chap at the airport. See how he liked having something the size of a forearm shoved up his jacksy. Better ditch this phone and report it stolen on the way home, he thought.


Patrick and Reg shared a pizza for their supper. Patrick had opened a bottle of red wine and ordered the pizza from a local take-away.

"'S good," said Reg through a mouthful of dough.

"Mmm, you can't go wrong with pizza when you're a student," said Patrick.

"Sorry, I keep forgetting," said Reg, "I keep thinking you're a lawyer."

"Don't apologise," laughed Patrick, "it's just something that I felt I had to do. My father was a solicitor in Halifax, his father was a solicitor in Halifax – I just wanted to take it one step further and become a barrister. You know, small town boy makes good? Seemed to fit the way my mind worked but I'm not so sure now."

# THE PERFECT PLAN?

"Why? You'd be top of my list any day," said Reg.

"I'm just coming up to my final year now," Patrick continued, "and I'm pretty sure I'll make it after the end of this year. I've enjoyed this last few days though, it's given me something to think about other than the Crown versus Purvis in September eighty-three. I'd really like to try my hand at writing, but up until now, I haven't really had any ideas for a book which hadn't been done before. Which is where you come in."

"Huh?" said Reg astonished.

"Your story would make a great book – it's original, it's funny, well maybe not to you, but just imagine the comedy of errors which has taken place to get you this far. The whole thing is so bizarre, it can't be real and yet it is. I'd like your blessing to write the book."

Reg was stunned. He'd never thought of him being the main character in any story, well maybe certain films he'd seen where he wished it was him in the lead role, but...

"A story about me?"

"Yes Reg. I reckon it'd sell really well if I kept to the truth. I might have to change some names to protect the innocent, but I think it's something I need to do. I'd take a year out and if it didn't go well, I'd go back to my final year of law and hit the bar, so to speak. What do you say?"

"Well, yes, I mean, yes," said Reg, who was still stunned.

"Thanks, Reg, that's fantastic," said Patrick grinning from ear to ear, "I was hoping that tonight, you'd be able to tell me how the whole thing started and we could work things out from there."

"Yeah, I suppose it'll help me get a few things straight myself," said Reg.

"Just a minute then," said Patrick and bolted towards his

bedroom. He returned with a tape recorder, "Do you mind?" he said.

"No," said Reg.

"It's easier than taking notes. Something we're advised to do for witness statements," said Patrick.

Patrick found himself a supply of blank tapes and inserted one into the machine. He pressed the 'record' button and placed the recorder on the table next to the empty pizza box.

"Right Reg, where does it begin?" he asked. The phone rang and Patrick turned the tape recorder back off.

"Sorry, do you mind?" he said. Reg shook his head and motioned with one hand that he was okay with it. Patrick picked up the phone.

"Hello. Yes. Oh yes. You did? That's great. Doctor Proctor? No. Does he? No, he's lying. Hmm, I see. Right, yes, well thanks very much. Yes please do. Thanks. Goodbye."

Patrick returned to the settee. Reg looked inquisitively.

"That was DI Lang from your local police force. It seems as though they've arrested some fellow for breaking into your house. Ex-army type. Not actually said anything yet other than he's a friend of yours and called round to see you to wish you well for tomorrow. They confiscated his mobile phone and called the first number on there. You heard of a Doctor Proctor?"

Reg shook his head.

"Well they're keeping him on suspicion of burglary. Says he had nowt to do with trashing your house and they believe him."

"Do they?"

"Apparently they've got hold of some journalist bloke

who was bragging about it in his local. Seems like he walked in through an open door yesterday and took advantage. This bloke they've arrested today left the door open when he left yesterday. Probably still laughing about the sick note you left him."

"There's a turn up," said Reg.

"This DI Lang wants to help us out keeping Tugwell in the cells. Likes the idea of a Nottingham lad managing England."

"Better not tell him I'm from Preston had I?" Reg quipped.

"Want to carry on?" said Patrick, laughing. Reg nodded and Patrick restarted the tape recorder.

"Well," said Reg, "I suppose it was when I decided to apply for the undersoil heating tender for the new stadium. I was stood at this post box for ages..."

# THREE SPANNERS

Reg had tossed and turned for most of Tuesday night, thinking about the day ahead. He had enjoyed the previous evening with Patrick – it had given him the opportunity to get everything off his chest and he was surprised as to how much he actually remembered. The fact that his potential attacker was now safely installed in Nottingham nick made him much more comfortable. The knowledge that Norman and Carol were safe added to that comfort and he knew he owed Patrick big time. Twenty-four hours previously he had been at the end of the road, facing remortgage, massive loans or bankruptcy. Not to mention the fact that his closest friends would probably end up in hospital, but now… he had a hope.

At some points he found himself embellishing slightly but Patrick seemed to recognise this and brought him back on track with a couple of calculated questions. You could tell he was a lawyer in the making, thought Reg. Reg could tell, however, that Patrick was really interested in the tale. If this was the only payment he wanted for all his help and advice over the last few days then Reg was happy to do it. After all, he thought, must be saving him about fifty grand in returned contract fees not to mention the potential legal action if he'd resigned.

The morning light limped in through Patrick's cheap curtains, creating a pale line down Reg's camp bed. Reg yawned and stretched, moving his legs fluidly over the side. He had a thought. Strips! Kits! Who was going to provide the kit? Oh my Gawd, he thought. He couldn't remember whether he was supposed to organise his own back room staff or whether the existing people would do all this.

He jumped out of bed and hurried to the bathroom. After a quick swill and toilet duty, he emerged to find Patrick standing cheerily in the front room near the window.

"Big day then Reg," he said smiling.

"Patrick," Reg spluttered, "Kit? Do we have kit?"

"Oh yes," said Patrick, "couldn't possibly forget about kit could I? Every time I walk into Dave's hotel I'm surrounded by pictures of people in their England kit."

"Phew!" Reg breathed a sigh of relief.

"Fendon's old secretary, June, got hold of the right person and you'll have brand new kits waiting in the changing rooms with boots if you need them. She's even arranged for the lads to have the names on the back."

"Thank God for that," said Reg, "I thought we'd be playing in our normal kit for a minute."

Patrick laughed, "Don't worry Reg, it's all under control. I'm just off to get a paper. You take your time getting ready and I'll be back in about ten minutes."

Reg watched as the younger man stepped jauntily out of the flat and went whistling down the stairs.

# ATKINSON FOR ENGLAND

As Reg stood outside Wembley stadium awaiting the arrival of his England team, he hoped that he could find the words to tell them how proud he was. Reg Atkinson, manager of the England football team and his lads from Nottingham who had done him proud for the past three years. All he needed was a bit of luck and the right decisions and maybe they could keep the score below ten. Some hope, eh, he thought. Who was he kidding? The boys might be the best in the East Midlands pub league, but bloody hell, this was Germany they were playing. He'd definitely have to work on his motivation speech.

He noticed his new white van heave into view. As it stopped beside him, the rear doors flew open and the team spilled out.

"Thank Christ for that," shouted Lance Lovejoy as he landed on the tarmac, "it's like a bloody oven in there."

"Sorry we're a bit late Reg," said Norman moving from behind larger bodies, "we got a bit lost."

"My fault," said Sir Richard who had been up front with Norman, "not too good with maps, old boy."

Reg looked at his watch – ten minutes past eleven.

"Doesn't matter," he said, "it's only ten minutes. Come on, I'll show you in." With a spring in his step, Reg led them all into the stadium.

Reg had no intention of working them too hard. He smiled to himself as he watched them look around the pitch – training was more or less impossible anyway and he didn't want anyone injured before the game itself. He had them do stretching exercises and allowed them to act like tourists.

"It's smaller than I imagined," said Johnny Mullen.

"Bit like what your wife said on your honeymoon, John,"

came back Lance Lovejoy to roars of laughter.

"Yours didn't object when I showed it her," said Johnny.

"Probably wondered where you'd put the cocktail stick," said Lance.

Reg laughed with them. It was good to see that despite the obvious awe and respect for the place, they were still enjoying themselves. He noticed Sir Richard and Dave Bayley joining in and giving it their all. That was good – team spirit was important in games like this. Dunkirk, he thought; Michael Caine at Rorke's Drift in *Zulu*. He imagined Lance shouting 'and don't throw those bloody spears at me' in his best Caine impression and tittered to himself.

Reg allowed them to take it easy for their allotted hour – the Germans had their own session for that afternoon. Once they'd done sauntering around the pitch, Reg called them in for showers. Eight hours to go until kick off – best get them fed, he thought. What he'd do with them for the rest of the afternoon, he didn't know. Best bet was to get their mind off the game.

Patrick arrived as the lads were in the showers with an offer Reg couldn't refuse.

"I've managed to get a dozen free tickets for all the tourist attractions with a tour bus thrown in," he said, "all courtesy of the FA, which Brendan Fendon doesn't know about yet," he finished in a whisper.

"Blimey," said Reg, "that'll be great to take our minds off things,"

"Them, Reg, not you unfortunately," smiled Patrick, "the tickets are for the players and Norman. You have a couple of interviews to give before the game."

"Oh Gawd," said Reg.

"Oh and Richard and Judy have found someone to sit in

the Royal Box tonight. And someone to sing the national anthem. They won't say who, just that it'll be a nice surprise and the people are really looking forward to it."

"Oh Gawd," said Reg again.

After a meal of fresh pasta and chicken, the players revelled in the sights of London. Most had been down before but had never managed to see everything from an open-topped bus before. Unlike the usual tours, they were allowed to spend some time on the ground too, visiting Harrods, Madame Tussauds and the Tower of London. Norman was under specific instructions not to let them walk too far or get tired. A simple instruction that proved difficult, but the trip did have the effect of taking everyone's mind off the game.

Reg meanwhile was treating the media to his presence, wit and repartee... he wished. Over the past couple of days, he had gone from Mister Popular to 'the man who let England down', and all this before the game had taken place. Most of the questions he was forced to answer were based on the initial premise that the game would not take place as there were no players. How would Reg cope with an angry Wembley crowd who had paid good money to see a game where only one side had turned up?

Reg hadn't thought about this, but interpreted it into his own question for himself: how would the crowd react when they discovered they had paid international match attendance fees to watch a pub side? He gulped.

Patrick stuck by him for the whole afternoon, helping out when the questions got tough. The basic principle of Reg answering the media questions was to let them know that the game would definitely go ahead and he would be announcing his team as late as possible.

# THREE SPANNERS

Reg's favourite part of the afternoon was a Radio Five Live interview with Stuart Hall. Reg loved the great man from 'It's a Knockout' where he had achieved hero status with the nation. Stuart had lost none of his colourful expressions or descriptive language and could be relied upon to make the most banal item sound the most interesting thing he'd ever seen.

"Ladies and Gentlemen, we have with us a charming man from Nottingham," Stuart began, "who rejoices in the name of Reginald Stanley Atkinson. Mr Atkinson will be leading out our gallant heroes against mighty Germany this evening. Reg, if I may be so bold, we can compare these footballing battles with historic events: the World Wars, Cleopatra versus Mark Anthony, Coronation Street versus Eastenders, Potsie versus Fonzie...Reg, how important is this game to you?"

"Well," said Reg, just avoiding a chuckle, "it's definitely the biggest game I've ever been involved with. We've had a few problems in the run in to the game, what with the players' strike and what have you, but I think we've got that sorted now."

"Ah, so you have a team in mind, then, little Michael Owen racing to the fore like a Thomson's Gazelle, swerving gracefully on slender limbs to avoid certain death in the face of a sleek lioness?"

"Err, no, Owen is unavailable."

"But Beckham, with dainty feet, quick and nimble, right foot like a conjurer's wand, reaching out to stroke the ball and mesmerising the sphere with its magnificence, using the contours of the ball to create a vacuum within the opponents' defences allowing attackers time to caress the ball into the back of the net, which bulges like a porpoise trapped in a fisherman's catch."

"Err, no, Beckham's not playing either."

"Then Tony Adams, the mainstay of our defences, holding off the foe like Henry the Fifth at Agincourt. Once more unto the breach, dear Tony, proudly bearing the three lions as his standard, marching on to war, like Boadicea triumphantly standing tall against the Romans?"

"Like Michael Caine in *Zulu*," mused Reg remembering his earlier thoughts, "but no, Adams won't be playing either."

"So, do I dare to ask, Reg, for the listeners will now be rapt, agog with fear that we will face the foe without our heroes...do I dare to ask which proud boys will be heroes tonight?"

"I'd love to tell you Stuart, honestly I would, but I have to keep my cards close to my chest. I'll be naming the team as close to kick-off as I can. Don't want the Germans to know what's going on do we?"

"That is perfectly reasonable, Reg. Lord Haw Haw may provide the Germans with intelligence that we obviously want to keep to ourselves. Strike late and strike hard, treat the Germans to a brave display and force them from our shores in misery, reeling from the glorious failure of defeat."

The interview continued for about ten more minutes, by which time Reg had managed to speak one word to every twenty of Stuart's. Overall, Reg thought it went rather well and he left the BBC studios happier than when he first entered.

Brendan Fendon listened to the interview at home. He was not in the best of moods as the police had been round to ask him about his mobile phone. Yes he had lost it; no he'd not reported it yet but he intended to do so; no he wasn't aware of people masquerading as doctors. It had taken a long half hour to get rid of them and on top of all that, his cushion had developed lumps. That bloody woman! She bought enough of the bloody things, why couldn't she buy good quality ones that lasted. He was now in possession of a vivid orange one that he knew would be much more noticeable than the chintz original.

He had hoped to take the afternoon off to prepare his address to the nation in the aftermath of the latest resignation by an England manager. From what he had just heard, Atkinson was still under the illusion that he could get a team together, but Brendan knew better. How many times had he checked now? Dozens? No one would play. It wasn't worth the risk to their careers. Atkinson was just playing the game.

He continued with his statement...

"It is with regret that I have to announce the resignation of Reg Atkinson from the position of England manager following the debacle yesterday evening..."

Before Reg had realised, it was five o'clock and time to head towards Wembley. He looked once more at the team sheet in his hand, which he had to call in to June Whitless fairly sharpish. Nobody knew whether it was an hour before the game or sooner that the teamsheet had to be handed in. He thought it best to be sooner – just to be on the safe side.

# ATKINSON FOR ENGLAND
## ENGLAND

| 1 | Jennings (gk) |
|---|---|
| 2 | Tate |
| 3 | Allison |
| 4 | Brooks |
| 5 | Boule |
| 6 | Mullen |
| 7 | Lovejoy |
| 8 | Charlton (c) |
| 9 | Quarry |
| 10 | Best |
| 11 | Mercer |

**Substitutes**

| 12 | Bayley |
|---|---|
| 14 | Levine |
| 15 | Scratcher (gk) |
| 16 | Whaddon |
| 17 | Reynolds |

He had avoided the number thirteen as he thought it quite obvious that he needed all the luck he could get.

Patrick had given him June's telephone number to ring through the details: "Ring June and she'll type it up for you and hand it in on time," he'd said before dashing to the toilet for the third time in half an hour. Even Patrick was beginning to feel the nerves.

Reg looked again at his list: he really hoped he wouldn't have to use any of his substitutes. He'd selected Sir Richard as reserve keeper, purely for the fact that he was the tallest and would probably fit the strip better. As for the rest, he knew Norman was good for no more than ten minutes and that Dave had played at school, but Patrick and Josh were complete unknowns.

He sighed and picked up the phone. Time to call June.

Reg met up with the others at the Kippax. Sir Richard had requested to be driven down to the stadium by his chauffeur and had been joined by Patrick and Josh. Reg, Norman and the first team were in Reg's van again, having avoided a gaggle of journalists vainly trying to find the England manager.

"Look what I got us," shouted Lance Lovejoy. Everyone watched as he unfolded a couple of white tee-shirts with a badge printed upon a white background. The badge depicted three rows of spanners surrounded by nuts. Reg looked closer at the motto below the badge that said 'nil leakum'.

"Three spanners on me shirt, Jules Rimet still gleamin'," Lance sang. To a man, they all laughed before joining in.

"We can wear these during the game. Then if any bugger scores, we'll show 'em off to the crowd. The new national crest seein' as we've been disowned."

"Who said we're a nation of shopkeepers? Should have been plumbers," said Dave Bayley, grabbing a shirt for himself.

"Just don't start showin' 'em off if Germany score. Crowd might get fed up of 'em" laughed Norman, as the rest of the team helped themselves to shirts.

"'Ere... and I've got this too." Lance pulled out yet another of his signs – 'OFFICIAL ENGLAND TEAM BUS' and Reg nodded his approval. The sign was stuck in the front of the van on the windscreen and a couple of

England scarves placed in the windows.

On the way to the stadium, they received a few second glances from onlookers but were probably assumed to be a group of fans on their way to see the game, thought Reg. The whole thing seemed surreal but he was determined to enjoy the moment – after all, he'd never experience anything like this again.

They arrived at a fairly quiet Wembley. Sky had arrived and set up their cameras; the BBC was doing likewise, and Reg noticed an ITV truck doing exactly the same. A few fans were making their way down the concourse, but two hours before the game was a bit early for most.

Reg was allowed by security to drive the van into the main arena towards the official team areas. He was surprised by how easy it was to get in, but imagined that Patrick had already worked his oracle. They met up with Sir Richard's car inside and made their way to the changing rooms.

It took Reg about ten minutes to calm Roy Brooks down. As usual the giant defender had burst into tears of joy as he had entered the dressing rooms and found an England shirt with the number 4 and the name Brooks above the number. The rest of the players were delighted with their own shirts and took time to twirl around in front of a massive mirror to examine their new look.

Reg beamed with pride. Even the substitutes had their own kits with surnames printed upon the shirts – obviously, June had not only faxed the details through to the match officials, but also someone who could perform this small but effective task at short notice, as no one knew the formation until he'd called it through. International standards or not, it was a nice touch.

# THREE SPANNERS

They'd struck lucky on the shirt sizes, Reg thought, until he noticed that one of each size had been done for each player. Nothing left to chance, Reg thought – probably Patrick's idea again.

"Okay lads, listen up," he began, "you all look absolutely brilliant."

"Thanks boss," sniffed Roy Brooks, still reining in the tears.

"Now, I'd like you all to go out on to the pitch in a minute. It's still an hour before kick-off but I want you to get used to the atmosphere as soon as possible. I don't want to see you looking around at the crowd after the referee blows his whistle because you'll be three goals down before you know it."

"Only three?" asked Andy Tate.

"You do yourself an injustice Andy," Reg continued, "you lads have played together now for upwards of three years. You know each other inside out and if you play like you do week in week out with the team spirit you've showed us all over the last couple of days, then you're going to have a chance." Reg paused – he had them interested.

"Don't forget, they might be professional footballers, they might be German, but they all come from separate clubs and are thrown together for international games. You know each other, you work for each other and above all, you fight for each other. The Germans are men, that's all, men. You go out on to that pitch and everything is equal. Eleven against eleven." Reg paused again, he had them now.

"Do you doubt me?" he asked. "What do you think went through the minds of the Liverpool players when Wimbledon beat them in the Cup Final. What about Yeovil the giant-killers, Walsall beating mighty Arsenal?"

"Halifax beating Manchester City," offered Patrick, inducing a scowl from Dave Bayley. This had been a private joke over the years they had known each other.

"Yes," Reg continued, "teamwork can beat skill, teamwork can defy the greatest of teams. It's all about ninety minutes of football and who is the hungrier. Be hungry and you can beat this lot. They think it'll be a walkover – they think it's cut and dried. Their manager has probably looked at the team sheet for England tonight and thought 'What the bloody hell is this?'

"Was ist das? More like," said Lance Lovejoy to a few muffled titters, but Reg noticed their collective determination now.

"Go out on to that pitch and know that you are playing for your country tonight. This is the biggest night of your lives so far and tomorrow it'll all be over. Make the most of it, play your best, enjoy yourselves. Keep it simple, work hard, remember everything I've told you over the years and keep your shape. If we can rattle 'em, we'll beat 'em and if we beat 'em you'll be on a free meal ticket for the rest of your lives."

Reg closed to mutters of grim determination. They were of one mind – win. Reg hustled them out of their seated positions and told them to go and warm up on the pitch. He gave them a few balls to pass around and get a feel for the place, becoming accustomed to the atmosphere and hopefully settling their nerves. He wished his nerves would settle – even after his Winston Churchill impression he felt shaky.

Out on the pitch, the lads soon got into a nice rhythm, just hitting a few long passes to each other and generally having a look at the rapidly filling seats. Reg saw the Germans were also out on the pitch, running in unison, stretching in unison. They looked like a team, he thought, unlike his ragbag of players. Dear God, it'll be a massacre.

Norman had a funny feeling about the game when he saw whom Richard and Judy had lined up for the national anthem. He'd not seen Don Estelle since the early eighties when 'It Ain't 'Alf Hot Mum' was still on the telly, but there was no mistaking the little fellow now, still wearing his pith helmet and army surplus.

"Is that who I think it is?" Reg asked as he came to stand by Norman's side.

"Don Estelle," said Norman.

"Thought so," said Reg, "wonder who else was a guest on today's show. I forgot to watch in all the excitement."

"Dread to think," said Norman, as the band began to play the opening strains of God Save the Queen. Little Don jumped into life sounding like an angry wasp in the arena.

"If that doesn't put the willies up the Germans, I don't know what will," said Norman.

"And they don't like it up 'em do they Norm?" chuckled Reg.

Reg was pleased to hear the crowd in full support, singing at the top of their voices. Mind you, prior to Don Estelle's appearance, they had been in full voice with Baddiel and Skinner's 'Three Lions' and the 'Great Escape' theme.

"Makes you proud to be English, doesn't it Norm?"

"Ask yourself that question when you've got seventy thousand fans chasing you down Wembley way wanting their money back," said Norman.

Hmmm, there is that, thought Reg.

Don Estelle finished his performance on an excruciatingly high note, which the crowd struggled manfully to get somewhere near. Don left the podium to rapturous applause – he waved to his public and left centre stage.

The teams lined up for introductions to what is traditionally an important figure in either a royal sense or a leading figure in FIFA or something similar. Richard and Judy had certainly had some interesting guests on today's show, thought Norman as the Chuckle Brothers came out to meet the teams followed by some minor FIFA dignitaries. They went to shake the hand of every England player, individually introduced by a gruff but inwardly proud Baldy Charlton.

"To me, to you," shouted a delighted Lance Lovejoy over the din of the crowd, as both Brothers shook his hand at the same time. Lance was a big fan.

When the brothers were introduced to the German team, they began their usual antics of pretending to drop something, bending together, banging heads. Lance was in stitches on the opposing line-up. Reg and Norman shook their heads in despair – this was turning to farce. Come on, ref, thought Reg, get 'em kicked off.

Brendan Fendon smouldered in the Royal Box. Usually he'd be down on the pitch rubbing shoulders with royalty and the top dogs of FIFA. This time, he'd considered the trip down to the pitch a waste of time as there wouldn't be anyone there. How wrong he'd been. He cursed himself – what part of his strategy had misfired? Down on that pitch he could see people wearing the England strip and he was livid. The minute he found out who they were, he'd have their pensions cancelled in a minute; he'd have their match

fees rescinded; he'd have them up for treason; he'd...

He felt himself at boiling point. All his ministrations had proved fruitless. Bother! He continued to smoulder, arms folded all the way through Don Estelle's national anthem. Dear God! Don Estelle: they could have had Dame Kiri, Luciano, Michael Ball, but no, Don Estelle. He shook his head sadly – this all came of him leaving a fairly simple matter in the hands of a lunatic alcoholic who knew nothing at all about football. To make things excruciatingly worse, he'd left his cushion in the car, convinced he'd have no game to watch.

The tannoy announcer began reading the names of the England team: Jennings, Tate, Allison...each one received a muffled cheer from the crowd who were still trying to work out who the hell they were watching. Word was getting round – but Brendan couldn't care less. His mind was with his cushion, his only friend – alone, in the driver's seat of his car. The crowd was muttering – a pub team? At Wembley? How could this have happened? They were beginning to get behind them. At least there was a match on and that was all they cared about.

The Chuckle Brothers were almost the last straw. He was forced to watch their routine in front of a seething Wembley crowd, but then he noticed something that resembled Sir Richard Scratcher in a goalkeeper's jersey. Seconds later, the announcer confirmed it. Brendan wept.

Reg had a quick two minutes before the kick off to rally round his troops.

"I just want to say I'm proud of you," he began, "no matter what happens, I'll still be proud. But I know you can beat this lot. You're more relaxed, Lance has met the

# THREE SPANNERS

Chuckle Brothers (smiles all round, clenched fist of joy from Lance) they're over-confident and think all they need to do is to turn up. They're wrong – you can be their worst nightmare. Just get stuck in, kick 'em up in the air if you need to, but most of all keep hold of the ball. If they don't have it, they won't score. Now get on out there and do what you have to do."

The players as one, turned without a second glance and headed off on to the pitch.

Reg looked at Norman and shrugged. It was up to the lads now: Reg hoped they wouldn't be humiliated. They took their place in the area allocated to the England management team and got ready for the game.

Brendan was still weeping silent tears when a nudge in his ribs made him look up.

"Shove up Grandad," said Barry Chuckle, "we're the Royal Chuckles."

Brendan's face was a picture as the brothers took their seats, nattering to each other incessantly. As they sat, they saw the referee put the whistle to his mouth. Game on.

# A Tense Opening

"Ladies and gentlemen, settle down and join the largest viewing audience of the year. Don't break away for a minute; don't make a pot of tea till half-time and don't turn off your sets. Your match commentators are John Motson and Ron Atkinson."

John Motson thanked his lucky stars that he'd attended the Sunday performance by the Forest Inn. He was an absolute stickler for data and information and considered anything less than a hundred and ten percent commitment to detail as letting the viewers down. His notes on players taken during the game on Sunday were now standing him in good stead. He read out the team sheet and gave a little pen portrait of each player, before beginning a pre-match discussion with Big Ron.

Motson: "Well, Ron. In all my years as a commentator I don't think I've ever witnessed anything quite like this. The England team is made up entirely of part-timers. For the viewers at home, please bear with us on this as it could be difficult to identify the English players. Fortunately I have done my homework and have a bit of information on each player."

Ron: "Motty, if you know anything about any of this lot, it'll be a miracle. Have you seen the bench? Looks like they've just come off an old folks' trip."

Motson: "Yes Ron. You'll be referring to Norman Whaddon, the player-coach and Sir Richard Scratcher. Definitely the two oldest players ever to don the England shirt. It's nice to see the England players have their names on their shirts today – should make life a little easier. The team news is that Reg Atkinson has named his Forest Inn pub side to take on Germany. An incredibly bold decision which some might say foolish."

Ron: "Foolish? Lunatic."

Motson: "Ron, before the referee starts the game, have you any predictions?"

Ron: "Fifteen-nil to Germany! I'd like to see England come up with a result, but let's face it, I might as well pull on a shirt myself!"

Motson: "And here we go. England against Germany. Germany have kicked off and are stroking the ball around their back four, just getting a feel for the ball."

The opening minutes proved difficult. The Germans kicked off and passed the ball backward initially to take stock of their opponents. When they saw that the white shirts of England were not pressing them, they moved the ball forwards through midfield. The Germans pressed for an early goal and attacked in waves sensing the game could be finished early. England could not control them at all, and after the first few exchanges, the Germans began laughing at their lack of basic ball skills.

# ATKINSON FOR ENGLAND

Reg watched helplessly as the Germans nutmegged their opponents, dribbled around them as if they didn't exist and generally outclassed them. Apart from a rather pathetic throw-in taken by Joe Allison, none of England's outfield players had touched the ball in the first five minutes. The busiest England player had been goalkeeper Fat Jennings. His goal had been peppered with ambitious efforts from the Germans as each one sought to open his account. Fortunately, only one shot had actually been on target, a rather weak effort from German striker Karl Dichter. Jennings had made a fairly nervous save, but the feel of the ball in his gloves gave him more confidence.

Reg was worried. He knew his players were nervous, but also knew how important it was for them not to concede a goal for as long as possible. The longer his lads held out, the more frustrated the Germans would get and the more confident his lads would grow.

He looked at his companions in the Manager's area: Norman as usual, sat at his right hand side. He looked smaller in his England tracksuit and worry was etched all over his face. Dave Bayley sat to Reg's left: he was beaming, so proud to have the chance to even sit with the players. Sir Richard, Patrick and Josh sat with a mixture of fear and nailbiting, hoping they wouldn't be called into action.

"It's not happening is it?" Reg said, to no one in particular.

"What Reg?" asked Norman.

"The 'Rambling Rose'," Reg replied, "we've not even got out of our own half yet."

"We've only been playing for ten minutes, Reg," said Norman comfortingly, "Give it chance."

Reg considered rising off his seat and barking instructions to Baldy Charlton. Norman was right, the Germans were too strong for this tactic to work positively. The opening ten minutes had been played entirely in England's half and the defence needed all the support they could get.

"Cloughie used to do this all the time," said Dave Bayley.

"What?" asked Reg, as another German effort whistled past Fat Jennings' post.

"Brian Clough used to play people out of position all over the park – used to confuse the opposition no end. It's style of play and formation that counts. Once you get into the 'Rambling Rose', the Germans might have forced themselves out of position, you never know," said Dave.

Reg wasn't so sure. It was definitely one way traffic at the moment, but at least some of the players had now touched the ball; and the game was still goalless. Reg looked at his watch – thirteen minutes. Bloody hell, he thought, this was going to be a long game.

Brendan Fendon had witnessed probably the most one-sided opening ten minutes in his footballing memory. How the Germans had failed to score was beyond him. Oh well, just a matter of time now before the floodgates open, he thought. His mind was already working furiously – this situation had to be turned to his advantage or he'd be out on his ear. If only these blasted Chuckle Brothers would shut up, he'd have a chance.

He shifted uncomfortably in his chair. How he was going to last till half-time without his cushion, he'd never know.

While the Germans applied the pressure, the England supporters were subdued. They had opened with a great deal of noise and excitement, but once the match had started they quickly realised that their side really was full of amateurs.

The fans, unaccustomed to seeing such poor play, should have poured abuse on the players. Much to Reg's relief they simply sat back in their seats and remained silent. Had they started booing then his side really would have crumbled.

On the pitch, ginger-haired defender Alain Boule had somehow managed to prise the ball away from a German midfielder. In a state of shock Boule immediately kicked the ball to get rid of it. Miraculously it arrived at the feet of full back Andy Tate, who ran upfield. The England fans, surprised at this sudden burst of energy, started to cheer. Tate, inspired by the crowd raced forward.

A German defender moved towards him but before he could manage a tackle Tate sent the ball to Michael Quarry. There was a little too much pace on the ball and the 'Rock' struggled to control it. He realised it would be quickly taken off him as two defenders were close at hand, so he decided to hump the ball towards goal. Hans Nurdling in the German goal was unable to catch the ball, so he punched it clear. Fortunately for England the punch was not a good one and tricky John Mullen, who had moved infield, managed to bring the ball down, control it, and then shoot, about a foot wide of goal. The crowd paused for a second while they checked the name of the player, and then they burst into song: "One Johnny Mullen, there's only one Johnny Mullen."

Mullen was immensely proud, as was Reg who, along with the rest of his substitutes had leapt from their seats with the sheer drama of the moment. For a few moments Reg felt hope, but this faded quickly. The shot seemed to give the Germans more motivation and they started to attack straight from the goal kick. They charged towards the England goal, leaving every member of Reg's side struggling, and within no time at all Fat Jennings was all that stood between Germany and a one goal lead. Jennings knew this would be his make or break moment. He had to stop whatever the Germans threw at him. He considered his options. He could either stay on his line and hope the Germans commit themselves before he does, or he could try to narrow the angle and race towards the German centre forward. It was a tough call, especially as there were at least four German players within striking distance of the goal.

Jennings chose to narrow the angle. He raced towards Karl Dichter, only to see the wily German pass to Bernhard Glaspfand. With a more or less empty net, Glaspfand's job should have been easy, but he blew it. He fired a rather poor effort across the goal and out of play. The German fans were horrified. This had been the best chance and Glaspfand had blown it. The England fans cheered and began singing "England's Fattest One!" to Fat Jennings. The keeper acknowledged the fans' support and, in much the same way as Bruce Grobbelaar had entertained his fans when called a clown, Jennings lifted up his shirts to show everybody his rather full stomach. The crowd responded with "He's fat, he's round, he bounces on the ground, Fat Jennings, Fat Jennings!"

In the commentary box John Motson enjoyed the moment. He turned to Ron Atkinson and asked: "Didn't they used to sing that about you Ron?"

"They sang a lot of things about me, Motty, but I never played in goal," Ron countered, "and I'll tell you what, I don't think I've seen a belly on a keeper like that since Neville Southall turned out for Bradford."

John: "I remarked earlier that he's the heaviest keeper since Willie 'Fatty' Foulkes, and you can see why. According to his mother, his favourite food is Chicken Tikka Masala between two naan breads, a bit like a sandwich."

As John spoke the crowd started 'Land Of Hope and Glory'. John turned to Ron: "This may seem a little strange Ron, but I believe the England fans recognise this side has no chance of beating Germany and seem to have decided to enjoy themselves anyway. What do you think?"

Ron: "I'll tell you what I think…I think they were so shocked with the team selection when they heard it this evening that they spent the last hour getting totally bladdered! That's what I think! Like the rest of us they know this Reg character is a joke, but they have a situation where they grin and bear it or tell him to stick his 'Rambling Rose' formation up his…"

John interrupted: "Thanks Ron, err, good tackle from Quarry there – a rock in midfield…I suppose that's why they call him the 'Rock'."

Ron: "He's not having a bad game you know. He's left that German player in a right old heap. Referee's stopped the game."

Motson: "Ron, while there's a lull in the action, let me ask you…many people believe the FA picked the wrong Atkinson when they gave Reg the job, what do you think?"

Ron: "I think my answer is pretty predictable. It makes me fume – Reg Atkinson should not have happened. I'm not saying I should have got the job, but I've done a bit. This bloke hasn't. He's a plumber not a manager and unfortunately the FA have seen fit to give him the job just before this game. And you know what really rattles me… The fact that I can't get anybody out to mend my faulty boiler!"

Back on the pitch, England were struggling again.

# A TENSE OPENING

Glaspfand seemed determined to make amends for his rather poor shot, as he charged forward at every opportunity. It seemed only a matter of time before Reg's men conceded their first goal, but with a combination of luck and appalling German shooting they managed to keep the score level.

Reg was beginning to relax a little. He realised that his side were being outclassed, and that they stood little chance against Germany, however they had managed to keep a clean sheet for the first twenty minutes. This was probably twenty minutes longer than most had anticipated. He turned to Norman:

"You know, I'm beginning to feel that we might just keep a clean sheet until half-time."

"Shut up you daft sod," barked Norman, "we've been bloody lucky so far – are you trying to break it?"

Much of football is about superstition and luck, and Norman felt that by suggesting there would be a clean sheet until the interval, Reg was tempting fate.

As Norman and Reg debated superstitions and their impact on the game, Germany went close once more. This time star striker Baldy Charlton came to the rescue as the effervescent Uwe Thalfang darted into the area. Baldy, realising this could be the crucial moment in the game, threw himself onto the floor a yard or so in front of the German. Thalfang could easily have gone around the prostrate Charlton but was so surprised at the actions of the hairy England player that he stopped dead in his tracks. It was as though someone had thrown a large bearskin rug in front of him. His hesitation gave Fat Jennings the perfect opportunity to take the ball straight from the German's feet.

"Phew!" said Reg, "close call."

Naturally, Germany complained, but the referee waved them away. In a universal language known by all referees, he pointed out that the yellow card would be coming out soon if the Germans did not stop their protests.

Jennings threw the ball out to Lance Lovejoy, who sauntered forward in an extremely casual manner. So casual in fact, that the Germans were still uncertain whether the referee had stopped play following the Charlton incident. As Lovejoy moved forward at a strolling pace Baldy Charlton started to fulfil his role as the 'Rambling Rose'. He swapped places two or three times before suddenly arriving in the centre-forward position. Lovejoy sauntered on. Then, when he realised Charlton was ready, he tossed the ball forwards to the hairy rambler.

Charlton only had the German keeper, Hans Nurdling, to beat but caught hold of the ball all wrong, sending the ball some way down the players tunnel. The German fans laughed, while the English supporters retaliated with: "We've got a werewolf, we've got a werewolf, you've not, you've not!"

In the commentary box, John Motson was checking his statistical information: "Interestingly enough, that's the first time that chant has been sung at Wembley, although in April 1893 there was a friendly between Ardwick and Gorton Villa in which a player was believed to have been a werewolf. The local newspaper reporter filed a match report which stated 'all was fine until the Villa custodian started howling. Within minutes a pack of wild dogs appeared and the custodian vanished over a wall'."

Ron: "Are you sure you're not thinking of Gary Bailey? When he was in nets for me at United we used to call him

# A TENSE OPENING

Dracula because he was afraid of crosses!"

Despite the Charlton effort, the Germans kept control of the match and with only ten minutes of the first half remaining disaster struck. A large punt from Hans Nurdling found Karl Dichter who charged forward like a man possessed. Once in the England half he passed to Bernhard Glaspfand on the left. Glaspfand was challenged briefly by Roy Brooks, but the England man stood no chance, and the German moved into the centre. He only had Fat Jennings to beat.

Jennings advanced off his line, certain he would be able to stop the German from scoring by narrowing the angles. Glaspfand feigned a shot and then dropped his shoulder as the keeper threw himself at the feet of the German. Glaspfand expected the amateur goalkeeper to take this approach and deftly swerved with the ball, calmly stroking the ball into the open goal. The Germans were ecstatic, and their fans chanted: "Hier wir geh, hier wir geh, hier wir geh!"

The goal was certainly deserved, but it was still a depressing blow for the English fans. Reg realised that the game was probably up – he had every confidence that the Germans would take great heart from this and win easily.

"I know what you're thinking," said Norman, "but don't. We've been behind at half-time before and won. You've just got to have a bit o' faith."

Reg could not understand Norman's supreme optimism and shook his head in disbelief.

"Norman," he said, "this is Germany, not the Dog and Duck."

"Just let them know that there's not long to half-time. Tell them to kick the ball out of the ground to waste time," said Norman.

# Atkinson for England

Reg considered this: it was actually not a bad idea – one-nil at half-time was certainly better than he had ever imagined. Maybe the lads will muster up some confidence for the second half. Reg rose from his seat and walked nearer to the playing surface.

"Baldy!" he shouted to Baldy Charlton, "BALDY!"

Even with the din that was going on within the stadium, Baldy heard his manager's voice.

"Kick it up in the air for five minutes," Reg bellowed.

Baldy acknowledged him to confirm he understood and turned to growl instructions at the players. As Reg returned to his comrades on the bench, he saw Brendan Fendon for the first time in the Royal Box, smiling with contentment.

Bastard, he thought. It angered him that this buffoon could be so delighted with England losing at home in such a crucial match.

The final minutes of the half were extremely tense. England were as poor as in the opening minute, with the Germans tearing into England at every opportunity. It was not a pleasant experience for any of the players or management. Fortunately, one England player, 'Randy Andy' Tate was playing extremely well. He had been improving throughout the half, but as soon as Germany took the lead Tate impressed further... Every time Germany attacked from then on Tate seemed to block them. With the rest of the players hoofing the ball as far as they could to waste a bit of time, the Germans once again became frustrated.

With one goal behind them, the Germans were attempting to kill the game off before half time. With the ball sailing around the stadium, this was proving difficult and they introduced a cynical side to their game. The first victim of this was the unfortunate Tate. Having displayed a modicum of talent during the last few minutes, the decision was taken to limit Tate's opportunities. With only two minutes left in the first half Tate went to block an attack by Kohler. Rather suspiciously, the German player collided with Tate. The two men fell to the ground, with Kohler landing on top. The referee stopped the match.

After rolling around clutching his back, Kohler recovered dramatically and seemed fine as soon as he realised that a yellow card was not coming his way, but Tate was still down clutching his leg. Reg came on to the pitch in his alternative role as Physio. It did not help matters that he did not have a physio's bag or magic sponge. He only had his trusty old toolbox: but there was only so much you could do with a selection of plumbing tools and a tub of flux.

"Where does it hurt?" asked Reg concerned.

"Everywhere," Tate shrieked, "bastard put his elbow in me ribs and his foot in me knee. God it hurts."

"Where? Here?" asked Reg, prodding Tate's side.

"OW!" screamed Andy Tate, "what did you do that for?"

Reg did not dare touch the full back's knee – it looked swollen and it still had the souvenirs of a size twelve boot indelibly marked upon it.

As Reg examined Tate's leg, he realised the full back could not continue. If he hadn't been given a busted rib, he must definitely have knee trouble. Could be one of those cruciate jobs. Reg hoped not and wondered who he could send on. He looked back at his substitutes. Norman was keen, but Reg couldn't risk him, not with over half the game left. Dave Bayley was the only option. Although he had never seen Bayley play a competitive match he was convinced the mad Mancunian did possess some skill somewhere, and so he motioned to him.

Dave was nonplussed – he pointed to himself and mouthed "me?". Reg nodded.

"You'd best get your self warmed up Dave," said Norman, "looks like we're in trouble."

Dave Bayley sat motionless for a moment. Then he suddenly jumped upright as though an electrical charge had just passed through him.

"Right," he said, "right..."

His tracksuit was off in seconds and he stood there in his England kit. Reg approached him, toolbox in hand.

"Dave, I want you on there," he said, "Andy's had it – I reckon that bastard German has stamped on his knee – he's got studmarks all over the place."

"Oh, right," said Dave, momentarily a man of few words. He was mechanically hopping from foot to foot in an effort to warm up the muscles and tendons in his legs.

"Calm our players down and wind the Germans up. Can you do it?" asked Reg.

"Course Reg. Count on me," said Dave, delighted to be able to tread the hallowed turf. "Where do you want me?"

"On the pitch of course, you..." replied a dismayed Reg, who as soon as he said it, regretted it. "Take up the right full back role and kick that sod up in the air." He pointed to Kohler who was looking innocent.

In the commentary box Motson and Atkinson were concerned. John: "With Tate injured England really will struggle. Ron, who do you think Reg will bring on?"

"How should I know? I haven't a clue who he's got on that bench!" replied Ron.

John: "Actually it looks as if Dave Bayley is to make an appearance. For those of you that don't know – and I guess that's the entire population – Dave is the owner of the Kippax Hotel in London. He is a Manchester City supporter, and his idol was Tommy Hutchison. Tommy, if you remember netted both goals in the 100th Cup Final – one for City, and an own goal for Spurs! Let's see what Dave can do."

Ron: "God help us! Look at the way he's warming up! He'll be lucky to last the few minutes till half-time. Looks like a demented rabbit."

Dave made his way onto the pitch while Tate was stretchered off. The hotelier immediately took the free kick and sent the ball to John Mullen. The winger should have gone on a mazy run through the German defence, but instead he was hacked down within seconds and left to consider what might have been.

Reg was off his feet in a flash, lambasting the Germans for the foul. In addition to being incensed by the tackle, he was also concerned about the fitness of John Mullen who had been well and truly scythed down. The referee allowed Reg on to the pitch to provide first aid. Again, the toolbox contained nothing that could help. Reg contented himself by calling the offending German – Beenhakker – every name he could think of, while the referee brandished a yellow card. A small consolation, Reg thought, pity the bugger couldn't have been sent off.

Mullen brushed himself down, spat a few blades of grass from his mouth and gingerly got back to his feet. The referee insisted he left the pitch for treatment and Reg escorted him to the touchline. Bloody stupid rule, Reg thought.

"You okay?" he asked the winger.

"Yeah boss, just a bit winded," replied Mullen, "I'll be all right. I'll sort that bugger out when I can."

"All right," said Reg, "just be careful okay? This ain't your average pub team."

"They've still got ankles though, 'aven't they?" said Mullen, "ankles can get quite painful, you know."

"I suppose they can," said Reg, thinking he understood what Mullen had in mind.

The referee motioned for Mullen to rejoin the fray. The winger returned to his position. Beenhakker faced him, smiling. Mullen returned the smile and brought his concentration back to the game.

The Germans continued to attack in force and it wasn't long before Dichter sent the ball flying past Jennings and into the net. The away fans celebrated, but only for a moment. The linesman was flagging for off-side. It looked to be a close decision, but the English were not going to complain.

Further German pressure followed throughout the final few minutes but with the help of the aerial tactics, England managed to muddle through to half-time. To everyone's relief, the Spanish referee put his whistle in his mouth and blew up, just as Dave Bayley piled clumsily into Kohler. Kohler writhed around for a moment before realising that everyone was heading towards the dressing rooms. He hobbled off with the rest of them.

The players left the field a little down, but in a fairly positive frame of mind. 1-0 was still respectable. Reg and Norman followed them down the tunnel – all was not yet lost. Reg could see a little ray of hope at just one goal down. Maybe he'd have the opportunity of bringing the 'Rambling Rose' to its ultimate conclusion: if Norman had been practising, he hoped.

# A TENSE OPENING

Brendan was surprised at the scoreline. One-nil did not do the Germans justice, not one bit of it. Maybe Atkinson did know what he was doing, thought Brendan and wondered what it would have been like with the proper players out there, but no, get that thought right out of your head, he said to himself. He levered himself off his chair. Must get that cushion or I'll die, he thought.

"Are you off Grandad?" asked Barry Chuckle, "see if the pies are on sale yet, will you."

The Chuckle Brothers had opened a holdall and were tucking into some sandwiches and what looked like a flask of tea. Brendan looked at them disconsolately: he was used to rubbing shoulders with royalty – it should have been the Queen here tonight. Instead, he had to put up with some idiotic children's entertainers for two hours. God in Heaven!

Brendan closed off his mind to the crowd and the Chuckles and headed back to his car.

# NORM WUN-PEN

As the players made their way back to the dressing room for the half-time interval, Reg led his bench personnel in pursuit. He had mixed emotions: pleasure in only being one goal down, but fear in that the game could rapidly turn against them if they weren't careful.

The crowd seemed quiet. Seventy-odd thousand people in tonight and you could hear a pin drop. Reg decided to get out of their way as soon as he could in case they started hurling abuse. He was used to a few insults from the Sunday League crowds but that was from crowds numbering dozens not tens of thousands.

There was a mixed atmosphere in the dressing room too: half the team were disappointed because they'd conceded a goal just before half-time, but the other half were buoyant because they had not been steamrollered by the German machine. Reg now had to choose the words to bring the team back to harmony – he wanted them to remain positive.

# NORM WUN-PEN

"Lads, I'm proud of you. You stood up to everything they had to offer and you matched them. So what if they sneaked a goal; so what if they had more of the play; so what? Look at the way they play – they haven't got the skill of the Brazilians and they haven't got the winner's mentality like France. This is a German team which is probably as low as it can get. They're pedestrian, they're predictable and they're a shadow of the teams that won the World Cups in the seventies and eighties."

Reg looked at his players. The steel was beginning to return to their expressions.

"Now Andy can't continue because of his knee but Dave Bayley's played some football and he should slot right in. Help him out if he needs it and remember, stick together as a team. You've done it so far, so don't let them work you over. They only have the one tactic and that is to attack slowly and deliberately and they all move together. The 'Rambling Rose' should sort that out. Baldy, make sure you make some early moves as they won't know what to do about it. Because they all move as a unit, they'll be too busy looking at you and it should free up someone else."

"Right boss," growled Baldy.

"Johnny Mullen, keep at that full back. He's been yellow carded and if he tries anything funny, he'll be off. Just be careful if you're looking for a bit of afters, okay?"

"Yes boss," said a smiling Mullen.

"Above all, keep your shape. It's important to know your position when we haven't got the ball and I know you've done that so far, just keep your mind on the job. If they score again because we're going forward, don't get worked up over it. Don't let your heads drop – work hard and we'll get our rewards."

# ATKINSON FOR ENGLAND

Reg didn't want to mention what had happened the previous game, where showboating almost cost them the game. There had been no sign of that so far and he didn't want to push it. He reached into his holdall and pulled out a bottle of Jamesons Irish Whiskey. The players' eyes opened wide.

"My Dad used to tell me about this," said Reg, pouring a shot of drink into a selection of plastic tumblers, "they did it during the cup finals in the fifties. One shot of Whiskey for each player used to get the warmth in the bellies that fired their hunger. It worked for Blackpool against Bolton in fifty-three, so I can't see any harm in us trying it."

Reg passed out a cup to each player who accepted it gratefully. They all downed the shot in one, grunting their approval immediately afterwards.

"Now don't forget, the main thing is spoiling their only tactic. Do that and we'll get a result. Me and Norman have worked out that we're averaging four goals a game this season, so there's no reason why we can't score today. Keep at it and lads... (they waited expectantly) ...go kick some German arse."

Fists clenched, the players cheered as one. The referee appeared at the door to warn that the second half was about to start and Reg led them back to the pitch, faces masks of sheer determination.

Over in the BBC commentary box John Motson and Ron Atkinson were enjoying their half-time break. The coverage had moved across Wembley and into the match day studio occupied by Gary Lineker, Mark Lawrenson and Trevor Brooking, leaving Motty and Atko free to discuss the important issues.

"Fancy a Bourbon, Ron?" asked John.

"I'm not a big fan of French biscuits. No chocolate Hobnobs?" asked Ron.

"We've got Bourbons and Rich Tea, and that's about it."

John was rummaging around in a biscuit tin marked 'Match Of the Day – Keep your hands off Sky!' Suddenly he spotted a rather chunky biscuit in a wrapper: "I think we've got a Club biscuit here, Ron." As he pulled it out he noticed the wrapper: "Oh dear! It's not a Club, Ron. It's a United biscuit. Do you fancy it?"

Ron was not impressed: "I've not touched United biscuits since 1986 when I was kicked out of Old Trafford, and I'm not starting now. I knew I should have brought my own. What drink have we got?"

"You've got a choice – Tea or Coffee. I prefer the tea but Alan Hansen is more of a coffee man. He reckons tea is a weak English drink, whereas coffee is drunk by Brazilians and other skilful footballers like himself."

John poured Ron a coffee while the two men chatted merrily about their favourite beverages. After a few minutes John asked Ron his prediction for the second half: "England haven't a chance! When we're on air I'll try to be a little more positive, but these guys are complete jokers. You do realise that I should have been managing England today don't you? Instead we get this lunatic. 'Rambling Rose'! What the hell's that all about? Wilting Pansy more like!"

As they talked, Sky TV's Jimmy Hill appeared at the BBC's commentary position. Jimmy started chanting: "We all agree, Sky is better than Auntie!"

John turned to Ron and said: "Ignore him. We've been getting this every game since he defected to Sky. He's just trying to goad us into an argument. If you ignore him long enough he'll go away!"

As John spoke, Jimmy Hill started pulling faces. Then he started quoting various made up statistics in a pretend Motson voice, "These are the best Bourbon biscuits we've had since Jimmy Hill bought a new packet on 23rd September 1989. At that time they cost twelve pence a packet from Tesco."

John and Ron covered up their ears and started humming to block out the noise from the Big Chin. Eventually Hill moved on. John Motson seemed relieved: "I hope that's the end of it. Sometimes he plays knock and run just as you start commentating. I just hope we don't get Des Lynam next gloating about his ITV salary, and how much the ladies love him!"

Ron Atkinson was surprised by all of this pettiness. During his time at ITV he only ever remembered one prank, and that was when Everton fanatic Elton Welsby was forced to present in the nude following Everton's embarrassing appointment of Howard Kendall for a third time.

The production team indicated to them that there were thirty seconds to go before the second half and they got readied themselves.

"Should have had a pee," said Ron.

"Funnily enough Ron, Reg's late father had a saying about that – 'a wise man pees when he can, a fool pees when he has to'."

"Motty?"

"Yes Ron?"

"Pee off."

Brendan reached his car and unlocked it. He reached inside and pulled out his cushion, smiling with relief. He caught himself in a rare moment of emotion and mentally cursed.

"You're becoming quite attached to the cushion, Doctor," said a voice from behind him. Brendan turned quickly – Tugwell.

"Mr Tugwell, what a surprise," said Brendan coolly.

"I've been trying to call you, but your phone seems…disconnected," said Tugwell.

"Yes, it seems that the line was no longer safe, so I'm afraid the phone was lost. Tell me, what happened? I thought you had control of this situation," hissed Brendan.

"Unforeseen circumstances. I revisited the patient as we discussed and found the police waiting for me. Looked like the house had been trashed and they wanted to fit me up for it. That wouldn't have been anything to do with you would it?" Tugwell looked menacing in the gloom.

"Don't be stupid," said Brendan, "what would I gain by that?"

"Seemed ever so…convenient that I was in the house when the whole of Nottingham constabulary burst through the doors. Had you got a bit impatient and decided to do the job yourself. You turned the house over looking for that cheque didn't yer?"

"No I didn't," said Brendan, now tiring of this conversation, "why on earth would I do that when the blasted thing was cashed last week. I checked myself this afternoon. Atkinson must have cashed it the day he got it in his grubby little hands."

"Ah," said Tugwell, somewhat mollified, "so now what? I had to hire an expensive brief to get me out of a hole today."

"Mr Tugwell, let me remind you that you have been paid to do a job – half up front and half on delivery. You have had the up front payment but you have not delivered. If things go as expected, Atkinson will get his comeuppance in around…(he checked his watch)…forty minutes. Now if you'll excuse me, I must get back to the second half."

Brendan turned on his heel and escorted his cushion back to the Royal Box. Barry Tugwell stood disconsolately in the car park, thinking back on the last twenty-four hours. Ah well, he thought, you win some, you lose some. He looked up at the twin towers as a crowd murmur gathered momentum. Might as well cheer Reggie boy on now – go on son!

Germany started the second half as they started the first. Obviously their manager had given them some badly needed confidence after they went in a goal up. Glaspfand and Dichter in particular dominated play and made it difficult for Reg's men. Dave Bayley found it hard to adjust to the speed of the game and appreciated the help of Johnny Mullen who kept retreating to help out.

The atmosphere continued to be dulled by the apathetic crowd. The odd sporadic chant worked its way down from the terraces but not much more. It seemed like they had given in a long time ago, but this didn't affect the players, who were used to playing in front of dozens of people, not thousands.

Norman whispered to Reg: "Reg, I think it may be approaching the time when we force the 'Rambling Rose' to its ultimate conclusion."

"Not yet, Norman, let's give it a chance," Reg replied. The ultimate conclusion was something they'd discussed a number of times and tried only twice. It had worked, but at a cost.

"Don't leave it too late, will yer?" said Norman.

"Shush Norm, we can still win this."

Suddenly Dichter found himself alone in front of goal forcing Jennings into a point-blank one-handed save, sending the ball for a corner. An audible sigh of relief came from the terraces, followed by a lively rendition of "England's fattest goalie!" several times.

Ron Atkinson: "I'm a firm believer in things like that changing the course of a game, John."

John Motson: "How's that, Ron?"

Ron Atkinson: "Well, it's moments during the game – a good save, a great tackle, just something that causes players to think that maybe things could go their way. Changes the emphasis of the game, you know."

John Motson: "Well let's see what happens from this corner."

The ball swung into the England penalty area and was half-cleared by the towering figure of Roy Brooks but only as far as Kruntz who tried a speculative effort from about thirty yards out which troubled only the ballboys behind the goal.

Dave Bayley began to grow in confidence, and he tried to break down the Germans on several occasions but they were still too good for him. That is, until the sixtieth minute when a fast moving Dichter approached the England area. Bayley, amazed by his own success, somehow managed to hook the ball away from the determined German. The Kippax Hotel owner then took the ball to the halfway line with ease – the Germans seemed shocked that England had managed to get the ball and were retreating slowly – and then passed to the tricky little winger, John Mullen. Mullen dodged two German defenders – well, they actually allowed him far too much room and he easily avoided being stopped – and then looked to see if there was an England player to cross to.

By this time, Baldy Charlton had started his ramble around the pitch, while Bayley ran into a central position. Mullen had two choices: either send the ball to the hotelier, or wait for the rather more reliable Charlton. He was uncertain what to do. He was not an instinctive player and as he pondered, the Germans made their move.

Defender Gerd Trautmann charged towards Mullen, took the ball off him, and then raced up the wing. He passed to Dichter who realised that with both Dave Bayley and Baldy Charlton forward there were enormous gaps in the England defence. England's number ten, florist Geordie Best, was supposed to swap places with Charlton whenever the 'Rambling Rose' kicked in. Unfortunately Geordie was as stunned as the rest of the players when England got their chance and he had not moved back. Bayley, on the other hand, felt a little responsible for the German break – though it was nothing really to do with him – and so the hotelier raced back to cover.

As Bayley charged back, the Germans casually passed the ball between themselves. They gave the impression of cats playing with a mouse before going in for the kill, and they certainly seemed to be enjoying themselves. Dichter passed to Glaspfand. Glaspfand passed to Thalfang. Thalfang to Dichter. Each second's delay gave Bayley hope. Like a mad man he raced towards his own goal.

As Dichter paused a little outside the penalty area, Bayley

raced in. The Kippax Hotel owner took the ball from the German and then...

In the commentary box John Motson and Ron Atkinson were shocked. John turned to Ron: "I'm stunned! Ron can you talk us through the action replay?"

A thoroughly depressed Ron replied: "Only if I have to!"

John: "My producer has asked me to point out that we are only paying you on performance."

Ron: "Reg Atkinson should be paid in the same way! Okay then, it's like this... He charged backward like some kind of great lumbering rhino, while the Germans had total control. Bayley managed to get the ball off Dichter, as we can see here, and then took a couple of steps forward. He passed the ball to his keeper Fatso Jennings, or whatever he's called, and we can clearly see here Fatso had no choice but to pass it back to the silly City fan. Remember that the keeper couldn't pick it up for two reasons: one the pass back rule, and two, he's too fat to lift it up! ... And then, (and only he knows why he did this!) the big plonker shot past his own keeper to give Germany their second goal, and not only that, but he also celebrated for a second before realising his cock-up! What kind of a player is that?"

John Motson was equally bemused: "Quite! To be fair to the player, I do think it was an instinctive shot, and I must say it was actually the best shot of the match. It may even be a contender for Goal of the Month!"

Ron: "It's bound to be. Let's face it, the BBC only have access to a couple of games these days so this goal is bound to be one of the best scored unless, of course, you allow goals from the Eastenders five-a-side team to be included!"

While Ron talked, John sought out his 'Big Book of

Football Statistics'. He was searching to see which records the own goal had broken: "Well, there's a few interesting points to note about this goal. Firstly, Dave Bayley has emulated his hero, Tommy Hutchison, by scoring an own goal at Wembley. Secondly, that was the first own goal scored by an English part-timer in an international match since Walter Wensleydale netted for Scotland in the 1870s. And even then Wensleydale thought he'd give Scotland a helping hand as they were losing 4-0 at the time."

"Does all this matter?" asked Ron.

"No, but I like to keep the viewers informed."

On the pitch Bayley was distraught. As Motson had predicted, it was instinct that had made him score, and again instinct that made him celebrate. Scoring a goal at Wembley was a dream come true for any man, but scoring an own goal shouldn't have been. When he realised his error he was inconsolable. The tears flowed, causing Motson to compare the hotelier with Paul Gascoigne. Fat Jennings tried to console Bayley but it was no good. The Manchester man seemed certain he had cost them the game and England their place in the World Cup Finals.

Brendan heard the goal as he made his way back to the Royal Box. Cursing Tugwell for keeping him in the car park, he accelerated up the steps. As he emerged into the open air, he could tell immediately that it wasn't England that had scored.

"Blimey Gramps," said a Chuckle, pointing at Brendan's orange cushion, "that's the biggest pasty I've ever seen. Give us a bite."

Brendan gave him a stare that warranted no comeback. After Tugwell, Hannibal Fendon was afraid of no man.

He settled down on to his cushion and prepared for the inevitable goal feast. At least tomorrow he'd have the benefit of Reg Atkinson being crucified in the papers.

On the touchline, Reg and Norman looked at each other. Should they substitute Bayley? Norman wanted to bring him off: "Let's face it Reg, he's not a true Forest Inn player anyway! If there was one man destined to cock it up for us it was him. I say we take him off straight away, and instigate the ultimate 'Rambling Rose' solution."

Reg was still not convinced: "If I take him off now he'll never recover. Let's leave him on for a few minutes and see how he goes. In the mean time I don't want any more talk about the ultimate solution. If we're still losing with ten minutes to go, I'll do it, but not before."

Reg's 'if' seemed a little hopeful. There seemed no doubt England would be losing.

Reg shouted to Dave Bayley on the pitch and gestured to him to keep trying and keep his head up.

When play restarted England were a disaster to watch. Simple, basic mistakes were made time and time again. It was bad enough that the England side was made up of amateurs, but now these first time internationals were struggling to do anything right. They needed direction. Normally, Reg'd be right on the touchline barking orders at anybody and everybody, but at Wembley he was forced to sit some distance away from the action. There was also the noise from the crowd to contend with. Reg felt his players were on their own. Could he make a difference by making a substitution? He looked at the faces on the bench and thought not.

As he contemplated making changes, the Germans

seemed to ease off. 2-0 was enough to see them through to the Finals. Nobody expected England to come back, and it seemed ridiculous to even consider that Reg's men could find the net once never mind twice.

With the Germans becoming more complacent, the England players were given more opportunity to get back into the game. They still made mistakes – lots of them! – but they started to feel more at ease. Dave Bayley was determined to make amends and was perhaps putting in too much effort, just as he had earlier when he scored the own goal. Fortunately, he managed to avoid making any major errors.

Lance Lovejoy, who had been anonymous for most of the match due to his defensive duties, started to find a role for himself as the German pressure eased. He successfully managed to mark Uwe Thalfang, and even started to beat the German to the ball on occasions. Reg recognised this sudden change and shouted to Baldy Charlton to make use of Lance more; also to get the ball out to the wing for Johnny Mullen.

Norman still wanted to change the approach but he realised there was no point arguing at this stage. There were twenty minutes remaining in the match. Still time, thought Norman, to instigate the ultimate 'Rambling Rose' solution.

In the commentary box John Motson and Ron Atkinson were arguing. John believed the England players were starting to look a little more composed. Ron thought otherwise "No matter which way you look at this Motty, these players are rubbish! They stand no chance of scoring. In fact I'd go as far to say there isn't a single member of this side capable of running ten yards without getting out of breath."

"Metres!" interrupted John. "The Beeb's gone metric now."

"ITV never had any complaints with my use of yards," replied Ron.

John explained: "ITV appeal to a different audience to the Beeb. We're a worldwide player. So instead of yards we have to use metres... inches and feet become centimetres... and so on."

Ron: "So if I want to say that the England players need to keep it at their feet I should say centimetres?"

"Ron, you're just being silly now!"

While they debated European measurements Charlton, Lovejoy, and the determined Bayley started to work well together. True, Germany were relaxing and possibly complacency was setting in, but even so, England were starting to dominate play a little. Not much, but enough to give Reg hope. Then with only fifteen minutes left to play a miracle happened.

Lovejoy took the ball from the feet of Thalfang and immediately passed it to Bayley. On seeing this Charlton started to ramble. Kruntz, the nearest German at the time, tried to follow Charlton. Gruber, who appeared half-asleep, panicked and headed towards Charlton and Kruntz. Central defender Gerd Trautmann saw the gap left by Gruber and warned Hans Nurdling in the goal that Charlton had started his ramble. The two Germans agreed that Charlton had to be stopped. Trautmann moved forward in a bid to cut off the hairy Englishman. This now meant that three of Germany's better players were attempting to stop a player who didn't even have the ball.

While the Germans focussed on Charlton, Bayley and Lovejoy were able to move forward with ease. Malcolm

Mercer, by far the worst player on the pitch, was also free. Originally he had been marked by Trautmann, but with the German preoccupied with stopping Charlton, Mercer managed to walk in a casual sort of manner goalwards.

Bayley passed to Lovejoy, then as Bayley and Mercer reached the box, the Germans started to panic. Charlton had not rambled into the centre-forward position as expected, instead he had held back, forcing the three Germans interested in him to find themselves badly out of position. Lovejoy decided it was time to put the Germans under real pressure and sent the ball into the area a fraction in front of Mercer. The no-hope England man should have easily scored but being the most uncoordinated player on the pitch, probably in the stadium, he somehow managed to hook the ball behind himself.

Nurdling had already dived, believing that Mercer would shoot, when the ball landed at the feet of Dave Bayley, who struck it without thinking about it (for if he had he would surely have mis-kicked) and the ball rocketed into the top right-hand corner of the German net. 2-1!

The England fans celebrated wildly. Reg threw Norman into the air, Bayley did a somersault a la Peter Beagrie, the Germans sank to the floor, the Chuckle Brothers chuckled, and even Brendan Fendon raised a smile. Oh, and Ron Atkinson kissed John Motson. Lance was the first to reach Dave.

"Your shirt Dave, your shirt!" he cried.

Dave had forgotten about the shirt business, but now ran around the pitch with his England shirtfront over his head, exposing his three spanners tee-shirt. The crowd strained their eyes to see what it was but got the full picture when the rest of the team did likewise near the touchline.

# ATKINSON FOR ENGLAND

The BBC showed replay after replay of the incident with both Big Ron and Motty enjoying every minute of it. Ron: "As I said before, these players are rubbish, but I tell you… they've got guts. Bayley got himself into the box early doors to create the situation and what a finish!"

John: "You know, Ron. I've just realised that Bayley, the City fanatic who owns the Kippax Hotel, has now emulated his hero Tommy Hutchison. I mentioned before about the own goal, well if you remember Tommy scored both an own goal and a City goal in the 1981 Cup Final, and Bayley has just done the same. Could this be an omen?"

Ron: "I hope not! City lost the replay, and we don't want England to lose, do we!"

John: "I really think the England players wanted to score today – did you see the tee-shirt? Three spanners – must be a reference to Reg Atkinson's plumbing business."

England now seemed the positive side. They had scored and who would have given odds on that at the start of the game. Reg could see the change in attitude – it was the Germans who had their heads bowed, their shoulders drooping. Their coach had leapt from his position in the manager's area to berate them mercilessly. They were ripe for England to cash in now and Reg prayed that they could do it.

Fifteen minutes were left on the clock when England scored and for the next five, they seemed to have the upper hand, without actually threatening the German goal. Then Johnny Mullen got the ball and made a charge down the right wing. He noticed his nemesis – Beenhakker – racing towards him in an attempt to stifle the move. Mullen slowed fractionally and thought of revenge. As Beenhakker slid in,

# NORM WUN-PEN

Mullen knew what was coming and in a sleight of foot known only to the nimblest of men, he kicked Beenhakker on the inside of the ankle, while sending himself sprawling. To the untrained eye, it looked as though Mullen had been scythed down again.

The referee blew his whistle. Beenhakker was writhing around clutching his ankle, while Johnny Mullen clambered gingerly to his feet and rubbed the grass off his shirt. Eyes popping, the referee brandished another yellow card, followed by a red one – Beenhakker was off. The ref then tenderly asked Mullen in broken English whether he needed treatment, but Johnny waved his satisfaction and hobbled away.

From the resulting free kick England managed to get a corner. The nervous Germans shouted at each other while Malcolm Mercer swung the ball in, left-footed. He curled the ball into the middle of the box where Geordie Best managed to get a clear header. The crowd held their breath but the ball looped straight into the hands of Hans Nurdling. A poor effort really, but one which demonstrated that England could find a way of getting level. Best held his head momentarily before retreating into position.

The final ten minutes were tense, but at the same time enjoyable for Reg and the England party. For the first time in the match the Germans were panicking. Their coach made a couple of quick substitutions to fortify the defence. As the minutes ticked inexorably away, England were unable to capitalise on their chances. The Germans, meanwhile, remained a formidable force, even though nerves plagued them, and apart from corners and dead ball situations, they still managed to keep England at bay.

On the bench Norman started to pester Reg about taking

the 'Rambling Rose' to its ultimate conclusion. Reg was still not convinced, but he also realised that he owed it to Norman to give it a chance. Reg looked at his watch – six minutes plus injury time. Eventually he gave the elderly plumber the news he'd been waiting for: "Go on then – you're going on!"

In the commentary box John Motson was merrily describing play when Ron Atkinson tapped his arm: "Motty, look! Look at the bench! Some old geezer is taking his tracksuit off! Do you think he's senile? Surely the police or security men will stop him. We can't have pensioners wandering on to the pitch during international matches can we? This is Wembley, not Lord's!"

John recognised the man: "Actually Ron, that's one of England's substitutes. That's Old Norman Whaddon, Reg's right-hand man. He bears an uncanny resemblance to Norman Wisdom, I might add. It looks like he's coming on. I think that's a rather bold move."

"Bold!" exclaimed Ron, "it's bloody foolish! For the first time in the match we're beginning to look at ease, and then we scupper it all by sending a pensioner on. What next?"

John: "I tend to agree, but do you think this might be Reg's way of saying the game's over, the battle's lost? Maybe he promised Norman that he would play and, with about six minutes left, Reg recognises that time's running out?"

"Well, it's certainly running out for that old guy! Look at him! He makes Peter Reid look youthful!" added Ron.

"Yes indeed, Norman Whaddon is now officially the oldest player ever to pull on the England shirt in a full international," Motson added.

On the touchline Norman winked at Reg and told him that England would win. Reg was nervous, but he realised it was now or never for his side. To accommodate Norman, Reg took off Malcolm Mercer, but he also reshuffled the side. Baldy Charlton moved on to the wing, while Norman took up Charlton's 'Rambling Rose' position. This fooled everyone in the stadium, apart from Norman and Reg of course. No one could understand why the oldest player, possibly the oldest man at Wembley, apart from Jimmy Hill, was in a position that required a great deal of movement. Nevertheless the fans, who were still in high spirits following the goal, started chanting to Norman: "Oldie, Oldie, give us a wave, Oldie, give us a wave."

Norman obliged, and then concentrated on his game. There were barely five minutes remaining.

The Germans had control when play resumed, but it wasn't long before a mistake by Dichter gave Charlton the ball. As soon as Norman saw this he raced – or at least went as quickly as it was possible for a man of his age to travel – forward. He didn't bother worrying about doing the sort of ramble Charlton had made, instead he charged, like a demented Corporal Jones from Dad's Army, towards the German goal. Charlton held up play long enough for Norman to arrive heavily marked, in the German box.

The fact that he was closely guarded should have made Charlton think twice about sending the ball to him, but it actually seemed to encourage him. As the ball floated towards Norman, the Germans jostled for position. Somehow, and only Norman knew exactly how, the elderly England man was sent crashing to the ground. The Norman Wisdom lookalike lay on the floor holding his left leg, while the referee spoke with Gerd Trautmann. The England fans started to chant: "Off! Off! Off!"

# ATKINSON FOR ENGLAND

John Motson and Ron Atkinson became rather excited by it all. John, in particular recognised that this could give England a chance to equalise. The ref had not yet signalled for a penalty, but John felt certain it would come "It looks like he's going to consult his linesman, sorry referee's assistant."

"Is that another metric term, Motty?" asked Ron.

"No, that's a FIFA directive. Anyway, it does look as if a penalty will be awarded here, Ron. Who do you think should take it?"

Ron was indignant: "You keep asking me questions like that, and I don't even know who the England players are. When are you gonna learn? I may as well say Shirley Poppins will take it?"

John: "Don't you mean Mary Poppins?"

Ron: "Is she on the team sheet?"

"No."

"Well, why would I mean her then? Whoever takes it needs to think carefully. For years now I've been saying the perfect way to take penalties is to blast it at the keeper and you'll be all right. They always dive, so you're bound to score."

John noticed that a decision seemed imminent: "The referee's assistant has given the referee his views and now let's wait and…. he's signalled for a penalty! Yes! Eng-er-land, Eng-er-land, Eng-er-land!" A rather excited John added: "And look, he's getting the red card out and sending off Gerd Trautmann, the key German defender. This is amazing. This is incredible. This is like 'Roy of the Rovers'. But who will take the spot kick? My money's on Baldy Charlton."

As John talked, Norman finished receiving treatment. He

stood up, limped a little, and then made an attempt at running. He looked in agony, but that didn't stop him from taking the matchball off the referee and placing it on the penalty spot. "I don't believe it! Old Norman is going to take it!" exclaimed John.

"When are we going to learn? That man is an OAP with a dodgy leg. Why is this clown of a manager allowing him to take it?" Ron added.

On the pitch everyone prepared for the penalty. The English and German players crowded around the box; Hans Nurdling stood nervously on his line; and old Norman calmly stepped back from the penalty spot. He walked about ten paces away and then waited for the referee.

As soon as the referee signalled, Norman started his run up. But as he got to within three paces of the ball he clutched his chest. Hans Nurdling was the first to see Norman's agony and the German keeper, still on his line, pointed at him. Norman continued to move, somewhat slower it must be said, and then in one dramatic moment, fell to the ground and also kicked the ball into the bottom left corner of the net. Nurdling ran to him before realising the ball nestled in the net behind him. The keeper saw the huge smile on the elderly Englishman's face and realised he had been conned.

The referee signalled for a goal, and Norman leapt up from the ground, exposing his tee-shirt. The Germans crowded around the referee but to no avail. The goal was awarded and England were level at 2-2. The celebrations really began with the England fans chanting "England's oldest one!" to Norman. Before long, the crowd had engaged in a version of 'Three Lions', substituting 'Spanners' for 'Lions'. Reg listened with pride.

"Three Spanners on the shirt,
Reg's nuts still gleaming,
Norman's scored a goal
To send the home crowd screaming…"

The game still had about three minutes left and so the England players tried to remain composed, but it was difficult. For everyone this was a major once-in-a-lifetime achievement, and they wanted to party. Baldy Charlton tried to calm them while Norman tried to avoid the attention of the angry Germans who were still protesting.

In the commentary box John Motson was speechless, leaving Ron Atkinson to do all the talking "Well, I think this changes my view of how to take penalties. I think from now on I'm gonna encourage everyone to fake a heart attack. If it works for Norman then I'm sure it'll work for Michael Owen. I don't think it's legal, but the goal's been given so who am I to argue."

In the stands the fans were partying. No one could have predicted that a team of no-hopers could fight back against one of the World's best sides from 2-0 down. They started chanting in support of Reg's players, focusing mainly on old Norman: "We all agree, Norman is better than Beckham."

They then called to Reg: "Plumber, plumber, give us a wave", and followed this with:

"He's fat,
He's a ballcock,
It was a f\*\*king shock,
Atkinson, Atkinson"

And:

"Reg Atko's a football genius"

And:

"I'd walk a million miles for one of your boilers, oh Atko!"

And:

"We've got a plumber, we've got a plumber, you've not, you've not!"

Reg felt satisfied, and as the game entered its final seconds the England players defended like crazy. They were not going to concede another goal, especially now the Germans were down to nine men. Or were they... Reg was checking his watch again – ninety minutes were up and they were about three minutes into the allotted four minutes of injury time when Glaspfand and Dichter played a one-two just outside the England box. This dissected Brooks and Boule and allowed Glaspfand to break through.

Jennings, spotting the break, raced off his line and threw his considerable bulk at the fast approaching Glaspfand, who touched the ball past the keeper but collided meatily with Fat's body. The crowd gasped as the ball crept a matter of inches (centimetres? thought Big Ron) past the right hand post. Goal kick, thought Reg with relief.

But wait, the referee was pointing to the spot. Jennings was still on the ground clutching his shoulder and the referee was pointing to the spot. Penalty to Germany! Glaspfand – having performed a roll which would rival Amanda Barrie as Cleopatra in 'Carry on Cleo', emerging from a rolled up carpet – happily received the plaudits of his teammates and gestured to the referee that a card should be produced. The referee was having none of it and waved for play to continue with the spot kick.

Reg was panicking. Fat Jennings was still on the floor. He grabbed his toolbox once more and raced on to the pitch where the players were calling for a stretcher.

"Sub goalie," he shouted to the bench as he ran away from it, "sub goalie."

It was worse than he had feared when he arrived at the scene. Fat had dislocated his shoulder and was in no shape to continue. The stretcher came on and Fat went off. As Reg trudged back to the side of the pitch, he grunted a quick 'hello' to Sir Richard who was wandering past him on to the pitch. It took Reg a few seconds before he realised what was going on.

He swivelled around to survey the pitch – the players were looking at him incredulously as Sir Richard made his way valiantly towards the goal.

"Change it! Can we change it?" shouted Reg to the fourth official. Oh God what had he done – he'd sent on a man who knew nothing about football; a man who had appointed a plumber to take charge of the England football team; a man who was older than Norman and if that wasn't enough, just about to face a penalty in a World Cup Qualifier.

As much as he pleaded with the fourth official, nothing could be done. His three substitutes had been used and officially recorded. Reg raced to the touchline and told Baldy to go in goal, but it was too late. Sir Richard was already installed and looking confident but uncomfortable. There was no way back.

# DREAMLAND

Brendan Fendon had watched the game with amazement. The events of the last fifteen minutes had even brought a muted silence from the Chuckle Brothers. He had flirted between wishes of a German victory and the unlikely event of the draw remaining valid. Whatever happened, he had the right plan in his head. If England lost – he'd blame Atkinson for the players' revolt, turning the press against him. If they got the point they required, he'd take credit for appointing Atkinson and backing him to the hilt.

But as he watched Sir Richard Scratcher take his place in the England goal, he scratched his head. What was Atkinson playing at? Why didn't he send one of his proper players to do the job? Well, he thought, I suppose it's a foregone conclusion anyway. The Germans are too professional to let this chance slip.

"Surprisingly enough Ron, Norman's Whaddon's record as the oldest man ever to pull on an England shirt has now been broken by Sir Richard Scratcher of all people," said John Motson, "I'll have to check my record books, but I do believe him to be the oldest player ever to play at Wembley in all competitions too."

"I can't believe what I'm seeing here, Motty," countered Big Ron, "getting back to two each was a miracle, but now Atkinson...the plumber that is, has lost the plot completely."

"Do you think it makes a difference who they put in goal, Ron?"

"I suppose not. You know what I say about penalty taking, don't you?"

"I believe I do, Ron. You treated us to that one just five minutes ago."

"It's Kruntz," said Big Ron who had spotted the German midfielder holding the ball.

"That's correct, Ron. Kruntz has taken Germany's last five penalties and scored them all," Motson confirmed.

Down on the pitch, Baldy Charlton had managed to snatch a quick word with Sir Richard.

"Just do your best. Pick right or left and dive. Try and spread yourself as much as you can." Even as he said it, he realised that there wasn't much hope. Sir Richard did not look the most athletic of people and if he did dive, they'd probably spend about an hour putting his bones back in the right order.

"Right you are," said Sir Richard dramatically, "for England and Saint George, heeh? I say, when do I lift my shirt up?" Baldy was already making his way out of the penalty area and didn't answer.

Kruntz laid the ball carefully on the penalty spot. The referee checked his watch – they were now eight minutes into injury time, but with the keeper's injury this would have been about right. It was fairly obvious to everyone that the penalty would be the last kick of the game, so the match was down to the courage of two people – Frederick Kruntz and Sir Richard Scratcher.

Sir Richard stood on his line and tried to look as menacing as possible. Kruntz took his time placing the ball before backing away. He did not take his eyes off the ball. The crowd jeered, but with the tension of the moment, the jeers faded and yet again, you could hear a pin drop. As Kruntz reached the limit of his run up, he had still not decided which way to place it.

The referee blew his whistle and Kruntz paused fractionally before starting his run up. As the whistle went, Sir Richard dived in a fashion to his right. The old man's collapse put Kruntz off and he stopped in mid run up, gesturing to the referee. The referee blew his whistle and brandished a yellow card in Sir Richard's direction.

John Motson: "What do you make of that Ron?"

Ron: "I thought he'd had a heart attack Motty, but apparently that trick only works once a game."

Motson: "Could he have been trying to anticipate the spot kick, do you think?"

Ron: "If he was, he was about three weeks early. He needs to stand up tall – this German's going to blast it"

Sir Richard didn't understand what had happened. He thought he had to dive one way or the other and he had done just that. Baldy Charlton ran to him and advised him to wait until the German's foot was about to touch the ball before committing himself. Sir Richard nodded in eventual understanding.

"Right you are," he said, as Baldy made his way back to his position, snarling at Kruntz on the way past. Sir Richard attempted a snarl too and remembered a goalkeeping pose he'd seen during the war – slight crouch with arms bent at the elbow, but outstretched.

Kruntz backed away once more. He replaced the ball on the spot and slowly backed away glancing quickly at the old man in goal who now resembled Max Schreck in Nosferatu. The old man was obviously trying to psyche him out. The tension for everyone in the stadium was immense. The referee blew his whistle once more and a deadly hush descended. In a moment of clarity, Kruntz decided that the best way of dealing with the pressure was to belt the ball as hard as he could down the middle of the goal. The frail old man would surely dive in vain again.

Sir Richard watched Kruntz amble towards the ball and wondered which way to dive. Not right again, he thought, that would be too obvious. But left would give him a problem because of his tricky hip. Right again might bluff the German, who may think he couldn't possibly go the same way again. He was still deciding when Kruntz put his foot through the ball, hitting it so cleanly there was barely a sound as leather struck leather.

Sir Richard stood like a ramrod on the goal line. He did not move one iota. The dilemma of right versus left remained unresolved. In the perfect silence of the moment, the one thought that rang as loudly as a bell as he saw the ball rocketing towards him was "Ah." He didn't even have the chance to move his hands as the ball rebounded from his jaw at about eighty miles an hour.

Kruntz followed through majestically but came to rest in disbelief. He took time to react as the ball squirted past him to an alert Johnny Mullen who hoofed the offending article way into the crowd.

# DREAMLAND

The referee put the whistle to his mouth and blew for full time. The England players rushed to Sir Richard to congratulate him and Reg wasn't far behind them. The poor old knight was out for the count when they got there, but it didn't stop them hugging him on the floor.

Motson: "Ron, I can't believe it. England have done it!"

Ron: "Absolutely unbelievable Motty. The old bloke must have been reading my mind. I've told every goalie I've ever had to stand up straight at penalties but none have ever listened. This bloke Scratcher is brilliant. Look at that replay – he doesn't move a muscle. Fantastic keeping that."

In a style not dissimilar to David Pleat after his Luton side had relegated Manchester City in 1983, Reg skipped across the pitch to his right hand man, Norman. The two embraced.

"We did it, we did it," shouted Norman as he danced around the pitch "I told you it would work, the ultimate conclusion worked. They're all convinced I got fouled, and that penalty trick worked a treat."

"Risky, very risky, but it worked like a charm. Makes a change you not getting sent off for diving," said Reg, "but what about Sir Richard. How did he know that the ball was going straight down the middle?"

"Dunno Reg, but he did...he just bloody well did!"

Motson: "Well Ron, have you ever seen anything like that to conclude a game of football?"

Ron: "Motty, that was without doubt the tensest final minute of any game. It makes a nice change for any player to do exactly what I tell him as well. The way Scratcher dealt with that penalty was all about guts, well face anyway. Brilliant situation for the lad."

The stretcher-bearers came on for Sir Richard and carried

him off the pitch to a hero's farewell. Within seconds the rest of the team had surrounded Norman and Reg. Half the team lifted Reg, the other half Norman as plumber and his assistant were chaired around the stadium to the strains of "Football's Coming Home."

Brendan couldn't believe his eyes. Scratcher? A hero? My God what was the world coming to. This added a new aspect to his mental calculations. The Chuckles were singing and dancing in the Royal Box. As Brendan stood to applaud the heroes on the pitch, Barry Chuckle grabbed Brendan's cushion and flung it skywards towards the pitch.

"My cushion!" shouted Brendan, reaching forlornly after it. Too late – he saw it arc down towards the hallowed turf, spinning violently through great wads of ticker tape. It bounced twice, finally coming to rest just over the touchline.

"My cushion," he whispered and sat down sadly, "ow!" he added, standing up again quickly. He looked daggers at Barry Chuckle who couldn't have cared less.

"Chill out Grandad, we did it!" he cried through the din, and Brendan had to accept that England – Reg Atkinson's England actually had done it.

The next few hours went by in a blur for Reg. He didn't actually digest much of the experience at the time: shell shock had set in. Everyone journalist wanted to talk to him and ask how he'd drawn against the Germans with a team of part-timers, but that was as far as his memory would allow.

Certain memories prevailed: microphones, cameras and being shown endless replays of the penalties at both ends.

Norman's fall had been very dramatic and to the naked eye had also looked genuine. Replays showed that the German had been nowhere near him and the referee had been conned. However, the arguments were balanced by the fact that the final German penalty also had an element of over-acting.

But there was one question that he did recall clearly. One question out of a multitude of words which rang out like Big Ben in his mind:

"Will you be staying on to lead England to the World Cup finals?"

His mouth had opened but no words had come from it. He had not even considered it. His only thought before the game was keeping the score below ten, how on earth could he think about leading England on to the World Cup? Norman had been asked a similar one and taken the sting out of Reg's.

"Only if I can get a good deal from SAGA holidays," he'd said.

The players had milked the moment for as long as they could, lapping up the applause and cheers as they ran circuits of the pitch. Rocky Quarry contented himself by shouting "there ain't gonna be no rematch" at every opportunity and the crowd loved it. Their euphoria was total, and no Englishman could bring himself to feel sorry for the disconsolate Germans who had trudged weary and dejected from the turf. After what seemed an age, Reg's England team made its way triumphantly back to the dressing room. The crowd caroused them every step of the way, singing the Three Spanners version of the football anthem.

Street parties began outside; television cancelled normal schedules to bring extended news bulletins; celebrities and veteran footballers were rolled out to give their expert opinions; and England had a new set of heroes.

The partying carried on long into the night. As free beers were available for England's new heroes and they'd not had a pint in at least forty-eight hours, London was the scene of some loud rejoicing. Car horns were blowing, banners were flying – it's as though we've won the war, thought Reg. Mind you, football is almost as important, he reminded himself.

The fountain in Trafalgar Square was the traditional conclusion on a night like this. New Year came at the beginning of October as thousands of joyous supporters, plus a handful of players who were still conscious, immersed themselves in the icy water. Reg had drunk himself sober by the time he found himself propped up against a lamp-post, with his trousers rolled up and shoes and socks missing. Patrick and Norman were hailing a taxi.

"Seen me socks?" asked Reg, but he went unheard in the continuing hubbub. At last a cab arrived and Reg was bundled into the back of it.

The following morning was definitely a hangover day. This went for the majority of the country and not just Reg, who had spent the night back in the Royle Suite at the Kippax. He arrived at the breakfast table in a fairly bedraggled state, feeling the sound of a bass drum between his ears and a thousand hornets over his eyes. Norman joined him, grinning wildly.

"You look happy," Reg mumbled through a mouth coated in fur.

"Reg, we just qualified for the World Cup," Norman

beamed, "you should be jumpin' about."

"If I jump, I die," said Reg closing his eyes dramatically.

"Mornin' boss," said Dave Bayley arriving at the table.

"Sit down, Dave, I can't look up there yet," said Reg, "ceiling's still going round a bit."

"Here," said Dave, thrusting an armful of newspapers on the table, "get a load of these."

Reg was front-page headlines wherever he looked. The triumphant team were pictured everywhere and were celebrated national heroes.

"You'll be picking up your winnings then Dave?" asked Norman.

"What win...oh aye, bloody 'ell Norm, I'd forgot all about that bet," said Dave and shot from his chair.

"Oy," shouted Reg, "too fast, you're moving too fast."

"Best thing you can do is get some breakfast down yer neck," said Norman, chuckling.

"Aye, gimme some of that muesli," said Reg, "you seen the rest of the lads?"

"Still in bed," said Norman, "some of 'em didn't roll in until an hour ago."

"Blimey," said Reg, still looking through the papers, "did I dream all this Norm?"

"Nope."

The pair of them sat there silently for a while, reading articles and looking at pictures of the game. Josh took their order and returned with a plate of cooked breakfast each.

"You sure you should be eating that?" asked Reg.

"Don't see why not," Norman replied, "not planning on any interviews are we?"

"Well don't forget your cork, eh?" said Reg.

Norman looked pained for a moment and then began

to laugh – a full wholehearted laugh that typified the general mood of the country. Reg joined in until his brain hurt.

Reg and Norman arrived at the hospital at around lunchtime. After leaving the hotel, they'd given a few interviews and talked freely about the game. Reg realised that he now felt no fear – the ordeal was over and he'd come out of it smiling.

Andy Tate, Fat Jennings and Sir Richard Scratcher lay in three adjacent beds in a quiet ward. All had been given painkillers and were feeling mellow: Sir Richard was still drowsy, as he'd been unconscious for an hour after the penalty.

'Randy Andy' Tate had been told that the doctors would check his knee the next day once the swelling had reduced, but didn't have anything to worry about. He'd already fixed himself up with a student nurse who had been fluffing his pillow that morning and was quite pleased with himself. Fat Jennings shoulder had been manhandled back into place and had been told he would be out the next day in a sling. Sir Richard's nose was broken and he was missing four of his front teeth.

Reg handed him a little Tupperware carton.

"Washiss?" Sir Richard asked, still feeling groggy.

"Your teeth," said Reg, "the ref picked 'em up. Thought they could stick 'em back in or something." Sir Richard shook the container and put it down gingerly on his bedside table.

"Fanksh," he said, closing his eyes again.

Brendan was delighted with the way things had gone. Never in a million years had he expected this: Reg Atkinson certainly was a man full of surprises. Brendan was determined to make the most of this opportunity and had already spoken to a number of reporters himself, claiming the credit for Atkinson's appointment.

The following morning he received a call from the Vice President of UEFA to congratulate him on a spirited performance and to discuss this revolutionary 'Rambling Rose' tactic. By the end of the conversation, Brendan had been offered a new job on twice his salary, representing the future of European football and not just the English game. He had accepted without a second thought. Subsequently he asked Tanya to fix up a meeting with Reg for as soon as possible.

Over the next few days, as Sir Richard recovered his senses, he realised that his own fame and fortune had turned full circle. No longer was he the butt of the press jokes about his liaisons with the lovely June; no longer was he being blamed for the appointment of Reg Atkinson. He was now a national hero – not only was he primarily responsible for bringing Reg into the England job, despite what Brendan was saying, but he'd also played for his country and stood up to be counted in its hour of need.

June's visits made him realise what a lucky fellow he was. There was one obvious natural step to discuss with her. Three days after the game, June visited Sir Richard as Miss Whitless and left as the future Lady Scratcher. She walked for an hour around London in a state of shock. At last she unscrambled her thoughts and headed for Selfridges where she could check out the bridal department. While heading up the escalators, she made a mental note to ask him to fix his teeth before the wedding.

Dave Bayley held both framed betting slips in his hands and cried at the memory of his grandfather's faith in him. He was torn between keeping the slips framed as a lasting memory or cashing in what amounted to over a hundred thousand pounds. It didn't take too long to come to a decision – he headed to his local branch of William Hill to see what he had to do to.

After a satisfactory half hour with a cashier who gave him the details of payouts in these cases, Dave returned to the Kippax and wondered if life would ever be the same again. He walked slowly through his lobby, looking at the pictures of his old heroes. At last he could add to his collection which had remained stagnant for some time. Not totally within the original rules, but what the hell, he thought.

That afternoon, he picked up two packages from his local photographers. He had asked them for suitable photographs to be made up into full size walnut-framed portraits and blow the expense. As he unwrapped them back at the hotel, he was amazed by how real it looked – himself in an England shirt. But why shouldn't it look real, he thought – it happened. The other photograph was of the team – the England team with which he'd played and scored. The team that had drawn against Germany against all the odds and proved that spirit can overcome anything. He looked carefully and fondly at each face, memorising every detail.

Reg sat in Brendan's office looking at his nemesis. Reg had not yet recovered from the Wednesday night performance despite the days speeding by.

"Reg," said Brendan, "I'm sure you know that you weren't my choice for the job. If it wasn't for Sir Richard Scratcher,

you'd still be plying your trade in the plumbing business."
Reg kept quiet.

"Now," Brendan continued, "if I'd have had my way... if
I hadn't have left the country, then Ron Atkinson would
have been in charge. We'd have played Germany with a
full-strength team and I might have been sitting here now
talking to Ron about the forthcoming World Cup.
Conversely, of course, I could have been talking to him
about failure to qualify, who knows what cards the hand
of fate would have dealt us."

Reg bided his time. Once and for all he'd got to meet
Hannibal face to face. He thought he'd be scared to death
– this was the man who could chew up and spit out any
manager he wanted to, but over the last few days, Reg had
been lodged in his teeth. Now all Reg felt was relief – he'd
done something to be proud of and nothing this jumped
up little upstart could say could rob him of that.

"I've asked you here to discuss your contract," Brendan
added. Ah, thought Reg, here we go.

"As you know, there is a clause in the contract to review
your position following the game against Germany. With
qualification for the World Cup, you are now entitled to
the full settlement of one million pounds outlined in section
twelve. This will be transferred to your account in the next
few days."

Reg gulped but remained silent.

"What we have to consider now is whether you are the
man to lead this country on to the World Cup Finals and
win it," said Brendan, "and I must say that prior to the
game I had my doubts. However, I must appreciate public
opinion and it's clear that the country is behind you and
think you are the man for the job. What I'm proposing

Reg, is a three-year contract, which will take us past the World Cup and through the next batch of European Championship Qualifiers."

Reg was numb. He had expected the sack; he had expected a slanging match; he had expected to punch Fendon on the nose...but this? This was totally out of the blue.

"If you'd like some time to think about it, then please do. There's plenty of time," said Brendan smiling.

"Err, yes," said Reg, "err, yes I'd like to think about it, I mean. What about Norman?"

"Ah yes, the little fellow. He will be paid according to the terms of his contract and a similar role awaits him should you accept."

Reg excused himself and left, while Brendan congratulated himself on a job well done. It made no difference to him whether Reg accepted or not. The money was immaterial – England would make ten times that or more from the World Cup, what with promotions and merchandise. If Reg did accept, then Brendan would leave his post knowing that he had made the popular choice and would be remembered always as the man that signed Reg Atkinson. If not, then he had a certain Swedish manager in mind, and Sweden was at the foremost of everyone's mind with Reg's blathering about undersoil heating. Couldn't possibly go wrong, he thought.

Reg lurched out of the exit and into the cool October sunshine, his mind in turmoil. Norman was waiting for him in the Merc.

"Sort the bugger out then Reg?" Norman asked as Reg fell into the passenger seat.

"Huh? Oh err..." Reg didn't quite know how to put the words in order.

"Aww, you didn't let him just sack you did you? I was hopin' you'd belt the little Hitler."

"He wants me to stay on – take England on to the World Cup," said Reg breathlessly.

"Yer what? He's dafter than you are! What've yer said?"

"I said I'd think about it," said Reg.

"Should've told him you'd chew it over," Norman laughed at his own joke, "chew it over…Hannibal…d'yer get it?"

Reg raised his eyebrows and couldn't help release a quick titter. Norman was in stitches as he gunned the accelerator and took off.

"He paid me the balance of the contract, Norm," Reg said.

"Yer what?" screeched Norman as he slammed on the brakes. Fortunately nothing was coming fast enough to hit him but the sound of horns blaring could be heard.

"Said I'd fulfilled the contract and he's transferred the rest of the cash. Suppose I'm a millionaire now."

"Well you can give me half of that. I'm due me wages," said Norman.

"No chance mate," said Reg with a half smile, "you're getting' nowt of mine."

"Oh," said Norman. He'd only been joking but now he sounded hurt. Reg laughed.

"Get out of it you silly old sod," he chuckled, "you signed your own contract. You're getting' paid an' all. And the job offer extends to you too. You should be paying me!"

Norman looked at Reg in total shock and then a wide smile appeared on his face.

"Result," he said, gunning the accelerator again.

Reg watched Norman as he drove down the street. It

was good to see the little man so happy.

"Oh look," said Norman, pointing at a shop window.

"Isn't that our tee-shirt?" said Reg.

"Aye, some cheeky bugger's cashing in on you Reg. You want to get a piece of that action as well."

They didn't see Lance Lovejoy parading around the foyer of the shop smoking a large cigar. In a rush of opportunity, Lance had run off two thousand tee shirts bearing the 'Three Spanners' design. These had sold within hours and Lance was now branching out with shops across London.

The weeks passed, and life began to return to normal. The players remained popular and accepted countless advertising jobs and television appearances – Lance's favourite being when they appeared on the 'Feel the Sportsman' slot on 'They Think It's All Over'. Lance of course had become an overnight success anyway. As well as the tee shirt business which had boomed, Lance owned the copyright to all things bearing the 'Three Spanners' logo. All over the country, shops were selling the shirts, mugs, flags, and pens. All manner of clothes were now being mass-produced, and talk soon turned to a chat show, hosted by Lance. The team even hit the charts with a rendition of the Three Spanners song. Their record company ensured it hit number one in its first week of release.

After long and thoughtful consideration, Reg decided that he preferred life before his rise to stardom – amateur football and plumbing were the things he did best. He couldn't compete with the likes of Brazil, Argentina and France. He tendered his resignation to the FA and reminded them that he'd still like to be considered for the undersoil heating contract. Norman showed initial disappointment as this automatically negated his contract offer, but he knew it was for the best.

Reg moved in with Carol and returned to the plumbing business to find that business was booming for an ex-England manager and national hero. The interviews tapered off as he thought they would – reporters were no longer camped at his front door and his television appearances decreased. He still checked the newspapers for articles about himself in a natural desire to feed his ego. On one such occasion, he read that Brendan Fendon had accepted a cushy number with UEFA, and smiled to himself. Bugger's landed on his feet there, he thought. He also read that Sir Richard had been tempted out of retirement to take up Brendan's old position at the FA. Good old Sir Richard, he thought, and reached for the phone.

Sir Richard was as pleased as punch about his appointment and hero status within the game and country as a whole. He'd had word from the palace that the Queen intended him to receive the George Cross medal for service and valour above and beyond the call of duty.

Reg had called him to wish him well and offer any help during his reign. Sir Richard had decided that his lack of knowledge of football might prove a barrier to success following the events of September and October. He appointed a task force on a consultancy basis to confirm his decisions and ensure that no major mistakes were made. The task force included, Reg, Norman and Patrick Levine. He asked Dave Bayley, but by this time, Dave had set his mind on another project – opening a Kippax Hotel Mark Two in his home city of Manchester. This was to be opened in time for the Commonwealth Games of 2002 and the subsequent move of his beloved City from Maine Road to the new stadium in East Manchester.

Brendan had given Sir Richard one piece of advice before he left: Sven Goran Eriksson, the Swede. This is the man to take England onwards – forget the English coaches, not that any of them would want to follow Atkinson – any slip-ups would be too embarrassing. Eriksson is the one and Sir Richard should move heaven and earth to make sure he accepts.

Sir Richard took this advice on board. If nothing else, Brendan had knowledge and knew the ins and outs of the politics of the game, so in this respect he could be trusted. There was one more thing that he'd set his heart on: remembering the foul stench that originated from the air conditioning ducts during the interviews, he arranged for FA headquarters to move. In a piece of English football history, the HQ moved from Lancaster Gate to Soho Square. The vote was carried unanimously by all members of the committee, some of whom were delighted as their afternoon's entertainment was now on their doorstep.

So that just about wraps it up...oh, except for...

# EPILOGUE

Heathrow: a tall middle-aged man approaches passport control. The man is a construction engineer and has been out of the country for some time working away. In his jacket pocket, he has a surprise mail from the FA who would like to offer him a lucrative contract subject to a satisfactory interview. Probably something to do with the new stadium, he has surmised.

"Purpose of your visit," he is asked.

"Business," he says. The passport control officer checks the passport and sees the name Steven Gordon Eriksson, dual nationality – English/Swedish. He is waved through. Outside the airport, he hails a cab and heads for Soho Square.

Nottingham: Reg and Carol lie in bed. It's Carol's birthday and Reg has made her breakfast in bed and delivered the morning post. He opens one letter addressed to him while

Carol devours a slice of toast. Reg reads 'You are cordially invited to accept the position of manager of the Bermudan national football team.' He smiles, and after similar offers from Lithuania, Albania, Everton and The Faroe Islands, decides that this one just might have potential. Their previous manager had led them through qualification for the World Cup but died recently following a fishing accident. He shows it to Carol who nods in agreement.

"Quite fancy that one," she says with a twinkle in her eye, "but you could hold out for the Maldives."

"I thought Sweden – I'm a God over there," he laughs.

"Well it doesn't look like you'll be hearing about the undersoil heating contract does it? I thought your mate Sir Richard would have put a word in for you," says Carol, "did you ever hear what was happening with that?"

Reg shakes his head – he's heard nothing.


London: at the new Wembley, work is finally under way and the undersoil heating is being installed. We see a large man in white overalls, followed by a smaller figure also in white, carrying a length of pipe between them. The overalls both indicate they belong to Atkinson Plumbers.

"Where does this one go?" asks the smaller figure.

The larger figure stops, takes the pipe off his shoulder and turns round.

"Just about here I reckon," says Big Ron.

# THE END